NOV - - 2019

Biblioasis International Translation Series
General Editor: Stephen Henighan

P9-ELO-062

1. *I Wrote Stone: The Selected Poetry of Ryszard Kapuściński* (Poland)
   Translated by Diana Kuprel and Marek Kusiba

2. *Good Morning Comrades* by Ondjaki (Angola)
   Translated by Stephen Henighan

3. *Kahn & Engelmann* by Hans Eichner (Austria-Canada)
   Translated by Jean M. Snook

4. *Dance with Snakes* by Horacio Castellanos Moya (El Salvador)
   Translated by Lee Paula Springer

5. *Black Alley* by Mauricio Segura (Quebec)
   Translated by Dawn M. Cornelio

6. *The Accident* by Mihail Sebastian (Romania)
   Translated by Stephen Henighan

7. *Love Poems* by Jaime Sabines (Mexico)
   Translated by Colin Carberry

8. *The End of the Story* by Liliana Heker (Argentina)
   Translated by Andrea G. Labinger

9. *The Tuner of Silences* by Mia Couto (Mozambique)
   Translated by David Brookshaw

10. *For As Far as the Eye Can See* by Robert Melançon (Quebec)
    Translated by Judith Cowan

11. *Eucalyptus* by Mauricio Segura (Quebec)
    Translated by Donald Winkler

12. *Granma Nineteen and the Soviet's Secret* by Ondjaki (Angola)
    Translated by Stephen Henighan

13. *Montreal Before Spring* by Robert Melançon (Quebec)
    Translated by Donald McGrath

14. *Pensativities: Essays and Provocations* by Mia Couto (Mozambique)
    Translated by David Brookshaw

15. *Arvida* by Samuel Archibald (Quebec)
    Translated by Donald Winkler

eros - - NOV 2019

16. *The Orange Grove* by Larry Tremblay (Quebec)
    Translated by Sheila Fischman

17. *The Party Wall* by Catherine Leroux (Quebec)
    Translated by Lazer Lederhendler

18. *Black Bread* by Emili Teixidor (Catalonia)
    Translated by Peter Bush

19. *Boundary* by Andrée A. Michaud (Quebec)
    Translated by Donald Winkler

20. *Red, Yellow, Green* by Alejandro Saravia (Bolivia-Canada)
    Translated by María José Giménez

21. *Bookshops: A Reader's History* by Jorge Carrión (Spain)
    Translated by Peter Bush

22. *Transparent City* by Ondjaki (Angola)
    Translated by Stephen Henighan

23. *Oscar* by Mauricio Segura (Quebec)
    Translated by Donald Winkler

24. *Madame Victoria* by Catherine Leroux (Quebec)
    Translated by Lazer Lederhendler

25. *Rain and Other Stories* by Mia Couto (Mozambique)
    Translated by Eric M. B. Becker

26. *The Dishwasher* by Stéphane Larue (Quebec)
    Translated by Pablo Strauss

WITHDRAWN

THE DISHWASHER

THE
DISHWASHER

STÉPHANE LARUE

Translated from the French
by Pablo Strauss

Mount Laurel Library
100 Walt Whitman Avenue
Mount Laurel, NJ 08054-9539
856-234-7319
www.mountlaurellibrary.org

BIBLIOASIS
Windsor, ON

Original French copyright © Le Quartanier and Stéphane Larue, 2016
Translation Copyright © Pablo Strauss, 2019
Originally published as *Le plongeur* by Le Quartanier, 2016

All rights reserved. No part of this publication may be reproduced or transmitted in any form or by any means, electronic or mechanical, including photocopying, recording, or any information storage and retrieval system, without permission in writing from the publisher or a license from The Canadian Copyright Licensing Agency (Access Copyright). For an Access Copyright license visit www.accesscopyright.ca or call toll free to 1-800-893-5777.

FIRST EDITION

Library and Archives Canada Cataloguing in Publication

Larue, Stéphane, 1983-
[Plongeur. English]
The dishwasher / Stéphane Larue ; translated from the French by Pablo Strauss.

(Biblioasis international translation series ; no. 26)
Translation of: Le plongeur.
Issued in print and electronic formats.
ISBN 978-1-77196-269-8 (softcover).—ISBN 978-1-77196-270-4 (ebook)

I. Strauss, Pablo, translator II. Title. III.Title: Plongeur. English.
IV. Series: Biblioasis international translation series ; no. 26

PS8623.A77383P5613 2019   C843'.6   C2018-904442-X
C2018-904443-8

Edited by Stephen Henighan
Copy-edited by Allana Amlin
Cover designed by Natalie Olsen

Published with the generous assistance of the Canada Council for the Arts, which last year invested $153 million to bring the arts to Canadians throughout the country. Biblioasis also acknowledges the support of the Ontario Arts Council (OAC), an agency of the Government of Ontario, which last year funded 1,709 individual artists and 1,078 organizations in 204 communities across Ontario, for a total of $52.1 million, and the contribution of the Government of Ontario through the Ontario Book Publishing Tax Credit and Ontario Creates. Biblioasis also acknowledges the financial support of the Government of Canada through the National Translation Program for Book Publishing, an initiative of the *Roadmap for Canada's Official Languages 2013–2018: Education, Immigration, Communities,* for our translation activities.

PRINTED AND BOUND IN CANADA

For Marlène

To Bébert and to Bob

PROLOGUE

THE SNOWPLOW'S rotator beacons light up the buildings' white-coated facades as it slogs up Hochelaga pushing snow. We finally manage to pass it and turn onto a small, dimly lit street. Low-hanging cottony clouds fill the dark sky. The comfortable warmth of the car interior is almost enough to put me to sleep. You can just hear the dispatcher's voice on the CB. Mohammed turns down his music the moment you get into his black Sonata. He keeps his car immaculately clean. No crumpled-up newspaper floor mats, no old coffee cups or leftover food in the compartment under the radio. Just a small Koran with an illuminated cover and a receipt book. The leather seats are good as new. A fresh, minty aroma suffuses the car.

We pull onto Rue Ontario. Tall snowbanks line either side of the street.

Mohammed ignores a call on his cell. He never answers when he's with a customer. In the extra rear-view mirrors he has mounted on each side of the windshield, I can see his serene face and wrinkled, baggy eyes under bushy eyebrows. We keep driving to Sicard, then turn right. I don't have to give him directions. Mohammed knows the route by heart, has for some time. Mohammed, Car 287, is senior driver at the cab stand on the corner of Beaubien and des Érables. Mohammed is the cabbie who nightly takes home half the bar and restaurant workers who ply their trade in Rosemont. Mohammed is a fifty-four-year-old Algerian. He's owed favours by every taxi driver working the area between Saint-Laurent and l'Assomption from west to east, Jean-Talon and Sherbrooke north to south. Even the old guard, the holdouts still driving for Taxi Coop, respect him to a man. Half the time I catch a taxi at the stand, I don't have to say where I'm going; every third time I don't even give my address. It doesn't matter who's driving. They know me because I'm a customer of #287. Mohammed is as generous as they come. The kind of guy who'd pull over to help two people moving, stuck under a fridge on their outdoor staircase.

I remember one time two or three years ago. We were driving down D'Iberville, getting close to my house, must have been 1:30 in the morning. The moment we turned onto Hochelaga I had a nagging doubt. This was back when I was closing by myself. At the end of a busy night I'd be so spent I'd sometimes forget some of the closing jobs, like making sure the heat lamps were turned off, or that the cooks hadn't left the convection oven on. That night I just couldn't remember if I'd locked the back door of the restaurant after taking out the dining room garbage. Mohammed stopped in front of my place. He looked at me in one of his mirrors. I still wasn't certain, but I convinced myself I must have done it automatically. I got out of the cab. I stood there next to the car, hesitating, with my hand on the open door. Mohammed turned around and said:

"Get back in, my friend. We're going back."

He didn't turn the meter back on. It turned out I hadn't locked the back door, and the meat order hadn't been put away in the cooler. When we got back to Aird and La Fontaine, where we'd started, I held out sixty dollars.

"No no, my friend. The usual fare."

He wouldn't take more than twenty.

"It was my pleasure. You'll sleep better tonight."

Sometimes, in the depths of the night, you come across people like Mohammed. After years of night shifts, years of going to bed at four in the morning, I've gotten to know all kinds of characters, from young kids so jacked up on coke they chatter uncontrollably to hard cases content to ride their downward spiral all the way to rock bottom. The night sadly doesn't belong to the Mohammeds of this world. But they're out there, making it a more hospitable place for its denizens.

So we're heading down La Fontaine. It must be midnight, maybe quarter past. The taxi stops on the corner of Aird. The tires squeal in the snow tamped down by the plow. I pay. Mohammed says bye, bids me goodnight. He has the powerful voice of a Russian lumberjack. I get out of the taxi with a final glance at the back seat. The streetlights gleam orange. The vehicles parked on either side of the road have disappeared under snow. I close the door. The cab drives off, turns onto William-David and disappears. The night is hazy and mild. I leave my leather jacket unbuttoned. I'm the only living thing for miles around. You can tell the snowplow did a pass an hour or two ago. In the distance I hear metal scraping on sidewalk. I look up at the dark windows of my apartment, as I pull out my keys. The steps up to my house are covered in snow. It looks like icing sugar.

I steady myself to throw a leg over the snowbank and clamber onto the sidewalk. That's when I get a feeling: something disturbing the calm of this night. It's coming from the other side of the street, probably the apartment directly across from mine. I don't turn around. Someone is hurtling down the staircase on the second floor, really stomping. There's another grunt, clearly intended to get my attention. It's not the first time I've been accosted in the middle of the night. It must have happened a hundred times since I moved to Hochelaga. An addict trying to sell me a TV picked off the sidewalk; some girl far too young to be out, barefoot, asking if I have a smoke, five bucks, a place to crash. So as I'm getting ready to go up the stairs I hear a "Hey!" that sounds like a challenge. I stop. I recognize that voice. It hasn't changed. I heard it for the first time maybe twelve or thirteen years ago. I turn around. It's him. I feel a big smile forming on my face.

Now he's coming toward me, this big stocky guy with a shaved head walking right out of his building, right out of my past, bundled up in a Canada Goose parka. He blows out a puff of smoke and flicks the butt. I zip up my jacket and greet him.

"Bébert. Jesus, man . . ."

He chuckles. His laugh is deep and contagious and he holds out a massive hand. I let a few seconds go by, as it sinks in that it's really him. Then I shake his hand. He almost unjoints my shoulder, seems he's just that happy to see me. His palm is callused. I start laughing too.

He's a little fatter, and though it's a touch rounder he still has the same face of a cartoon alcoholic punk. If he'd been born in another era Bébert wouldn't have lived long, carrying on and partying the way he does, never stopping to catch his breath. His cheeks are puffed up and red from the cold and the booze. It's hard to believe that a whole slab of my past is standing there, more or less intact in the lamplight, solid as a stone stela or barrel of rum.

"What are you doing here?"

"I've lived across from you for weeks, man. I've seen you walk by a bunch of times, but never caught you."

"Where are you going like that?"

I still can't believe it. Bébert has been living across the street from me for weeks. His sugary breath condenses into little curls of cold air. He passes me a bottle of St-Leger whisky. It's two-thirds empty. His smile takes on its full bloom. The guy hasn't changed a bit. He hasn't been to the dentist. He's still missing the same eye tooth he lost, after the worst ass-kicking of his life, somewhere in the middle of a three-day bender.

Bébert lifts the bottle up toward me. Its green neck gleams. So do his eyes.

"You've got time for one drink with me."

"I was on my way to bed, man."

He shakes the bottle in my face. I laugh loudly.

"And I don't drink hard liquor anymore."

"Get lost!"

I pick up the bottle and take a healthy swig, then wipe my mouth on my cuff. I'm expecting it to go down like bleach—but it feels nice, lights a little fire in my throat. I take another sip and give the bottle back to Bébert before I start hiccupping.

"Give me a minute."

I climb the stairs to my apartment. Push the key into the lock and carefully turn. Go in and gently close the door behind me. Even the hallway is warm. Pale yellow light trickles in from the living room. The whole apartment smells like cumin and coriander. I go into my office to put down my bag and my cat comes up to rub its face on my snow-covered ankles. I cross the living room and pick up a cup of tea left out on the coffee table, take it to the kitchen sink. A pot of dahl is cooling on the counter. I'm hungry, a bowl would be nice. I go down to the bedroom. It's pitch dark, but I can still see Isabelle sleeping. She's pushed the covers away and is lying on her side with a pillow under her thigh. I take a long look at her, then remember Bébert waiting for me outside. The endless nights we spent together all come flooding back. Twenty-four-hour benders, party-hopping across the city. For a moment I contemplate leaving him out there. I feel like taking off my boots and crawling into bed with my girlfriend. I turn the bedroom thermostat down a notch. Look at her for another few seconds. Then I retrace my steps back through the apartment, careful not to make the floor creak. I head out and lock the door behind me.

I go down the stairs to meet Bébert on the sidewalk. The storm has blown over, leaving only the odd flake drifting between snow-covered branches. The cold is getting sharper.

"All right. Where we going?"

Bébert polishes off what's left in the bottle and tosses it into the distance. It lands soundlessly in a snowbank. He turns back toward me, expressionless. For a second his face seems to tighten up, as if shot through by a sharp pain. His smile soon returns.

"You okay?"

"Let's go. Plenty of time till last call."

Bébert gets walking, weaving slightly. He's got Etnies on his feet, an unzipped jacket, and nothing on his head. A halo of condensation rises from him, like when you pour water on a hot rock in a sauna.

This was around the time when all the old bars in Villeray and Petite-Patrie were being bought up by younger people, fixed up and modernized. But the wave of renewal that had crashed and washed up all the way to Boulevard Masson hadn't yet reached Hochelaga. We're talking back when Brassette Letourneux was on its last legs, the Crazy was boarded up, and the Davidson still had no competition on Ontario—the exact moment when the face of this street begins to change, abandoned factories start turning into condos, greengrocers move into former pawnshops, and young families move in.

We grab a table. The lights are bright as a dentist's waiting room, the furniture looks like it got auctioned off when the factory cafeteria shut down. Six or seven old timers are shooting pool in the back. Sleeves rolled up, forearms a jumble of faded tattoos, knuckles ringed with skulls and crossbones. They all kind of remind me of my ex-girlfriend Jess's dad: a party guy who never really made it out of the seventies. He worked as a welder when he managed to sober up long enough. Kind of guy who's a little too sketchy to really go straight, but too lazy to make it as a real criminal. He may have had a biker gang after him, but the person he feared most was his landlord. He'd go in and out of his apartment through a window to avoid running into him. You know, the type who just keeps trying to fend off bad luck by stuffing it away in the back of his closet or under his sink. The bartender here is the same age as his customers: late-fifties, early sixties. Everyone is on a first-name basis with Réjean, who wears a white shirt and a black leather change-purse around his waist. There are salt-shakers on the yellowed linoleum tables and the walls are like a basement recroom, covered in wood panelling and decorated with neon signs for beers that were already off the market when I drank my first Bull Max. Two TVs hang from the ceiling. One shows a hockey game, the other a baseball documentary. I sit down in front of the baseball. Catch a segment with the Yankees up to bat. That was my dad's favourite team in the American League—the only team besides the Expos I paid attention to when I was a kid. Yankee Stadium is sold out, and the packed stands make me think of the nearly empty ones at my very last Expos game at the Big O. For once, it was me who brought my dad. A customer at my restaurant had given the owner two free tickets. I'd just done two double shifts in row, and he wanted me to do two more. I almost told him where to go, but he won me over with the tickets. The Padres slaughtered the Expos. But it was worth it to sit in those stands one last time, with my dad who had taken me so many times as a kid. We used to see ten games or so a summer, sometimes more. It was one of those summers when he gave me his softball mitt. We'd while away hours playing catch after dinner, talking away, until it got dark.

I pour my big Tremblay into a small glass, like the other patrons. Bébert drinks his straight from the bottle. He's taken up a position with a view of the whole room. His eyes dart from the bar to the TV to the front door to the pool players. Suddenly he looks nervous. I take out the book I've been carrying around in the back pocket of my jeans and put it down on the table next to my beer.

"So this is your spot?" I ask.

"No. Second time I've been here."

"Like the neighbourhood?"

"It's all right, I guess. If you're into hookers and shooting galleries."

He scratches his stomach. The Yankees hit a homer, which captures his attention for a while. It cuts to an interview with Derek Jeter.

"C'mon, it's not all that bad anymore. It's getting cleaned up a bit."

You hear stories about landlords setting shitty old buildings on fire and building condos in the ashes. Not a week goes by without some gang of crack dealers getting busted up. The other day they took down a doorway on Aylmer: battering ram, SWAT team, the whole shebang. Bébert tells me not to worry, there's still plenty of drughouses left in the neighbourhood. Says he found himself in a lovely crack house a couple days ago, just a few blocks from us. People who don't know Bébert well think he's full of shit. His girlfriends call him a good-for-nothing liar. But over time I've learned that the more improbable whatever comes out of his mouth is, the more likely it is to be true.

"What were you doing in a crack house?"

Bébert flicks his pack of smokes around in circles on the glossy tabletop.

"Nothing, man. Just hanging out."

A peal of laughter breaks out in the back of the room. You can hear the sharp loud clack of two billiard balls colliding over the music. The players swear in appreciation. I turn around. The guy who clearly just shot is already leaning over the table, concentrating like a sniper calculating wind speed.

"Last time I saw you, you were working in the Old Port, right?"

Bébert stares off into the distance. I say it again. He takes another look at the door.

"When was that again?"

"I ran into you at the bar. You were with your staff."

"Hold on a sec."

He puts his elbows down on the table. A crease appears on his forehead.

"The time we ended up on the roof, with Johnny's absinthe?"

"No, that was at least two years earlier. You were going out with a tattoo artist."

"I don't remember that at all. I must have been really fucked up. Was it winter?"

"It was summer. It was hot as hell. At the Zinc."

His eyes light up, and he chuckles.

"Yeah, now I remember! I woke up at the McGill Hospital. Emergency Room."

Six years ago, just a few months before I stopped working on the Plateau, I'd run into Bébert in a bar on Mont-Royal Avenue. He was out with his work crew. It must have been the entire kitchen staff, plus some busgirls, and half of them were riding the white horse. I went over and sat with them. Bébert was completely out of control, stealing beers from other tables in between rounds, dropping out of the conversation after a few comments, doing big keys of coke in front of everyone and walking around barefoot as if he was in his living room. The bartenders just let him run wild, they'd long lost control of the bar. The tables were overflowing with empty glasses and half-drunk pitchers, beer was dribbling onto our thighs. The kind of night when everything is bathed in a dirty pool of beer. The sous-chef was ordering rounds of shots, twenty at a time. I tried to keep up. I knew one of the busgirls, we'd worked together at Pistou, and she came and sat between me and Bébert. She told me about a time, on the day of the sidewalk sale, when they were still taking new tables two hours after closing. Two of the cooks said fuck it and slept in the restaurant, right in the booths, so they'd be there to open the next day. For the entire hour she spent beside me her hand never left my forearm, and she gave me a squeeze every time she wanted to emphasize a point. She was practically talking right in my ear. We'd always been kind of into each other, but that night I met my Waterloo. I'd gotten too drunk too fast. When she said she had a little weed and asked if I wanted to go out and smoke, the Jameson came up in my throat. I jumped up, bumping the table on my way, and made it out of the bar just in time. The nausea subsided a moment but I ended up a few streets away puking my guts out in front of a McDonald's, holding myself up against the window, in front of an old couple peacefully sipping coffee. Bébert never saw me leave.

"You were at Portico, right?"

"If I was at Portico we're talking more like five years ago. Maybe six. Yeah, six."

Bébert is tearing the label off his bottle, one strip at a time.

"How'd you end up here?"

He leans back on his chair and gave me a quick look.

"That's a long fucking story, man."

His shoulders are a little broader than back in the day. His big cheeks are just as red. Alcohol and rosacea. Bébert was never one to look after himself. But he might have laid off the pills and stuff.

"I tried to open a restaurant in Sainte-Agathe," he said, rubbing his skull. "It failed. Bad. One of our partners fucked us over. But on paper he was in the right. There was nothing I could do. Couldn't even get back the money I'd put in."

"How much?"

"That was like a year and a half ago. Anyway, I came back here, broke as fuck and kind of pissed off. Took me a while to find a decent job. I worked for a Portuguese bastard who never paid me my full hours. There's someone waiting to rip you off around every corner, man. Then my roommate took off with three months' rent, my TV, my DVD player, and an ounce of hash I had stashed. Motherfucker, when I moved in he looked me in the eye with his pretty-boy suburban face and was all like, 'I always pay on time, you better not make me chase after your half of the rent.' Two-faced bitch. Hadn't paid the rent in months. If I ever see him again he'll be leaving in a coffin. In the end I had to sneak out of that apartment too."

He runs a meaty hand over his bald head. In a way he looks like Frank Black playing Kurtz in *Apocalypse Now*. In another way he looks like Buddha. On speed.

"I've sorta been couch surfing since then. That's how I ended up across from you. At my buddy Doug's place."

I remembered Doug. No dad, looked after his younger brothers, and his mum too, for ten years, until she was confined to her hospital bed. Huntingdon's disease. That made him kind of angry. Guy wouldn't say a word until he started drinking. But once he was drunk he had a real big mouth, and he was drunk most of the time. He'd order liquor by the bottle, at the bar, whichever ones hadn't banned him yet. Then he'd go on a GHB binge. Got arrested a couple times—possession, assault. At the Living he managed to permanently disfigure some dude with the cast on his arm, a souvenir from his fight with a doorman a couple weeks earlier.

"Where you working now?"

"I'm not working. Got laid off in the fall. Saw it coming though. I've got two months of unemployment insurance left."

If he could talk about it so calmly, this must have been one of his smoother exits. Either that or he'd pulled something dirty on his way out the door. That was Bébert's style: the man just enjoyed getting even. On his last night at Tasso he'd unplugged the seafood fridges when he was closing. At Saisons, where he got me a job seven or eight years ago, he'd taken all the knives, tongs, and ladles and frozen them in buckets of water just to make sure the team got to start the next day empty-handed.

I take a sip of my Tremblay. The taste of moist grain fills my mouth. Bébert's keeping one eye on the hockey game, and one hand on his big bottle of beer. He has tattoos all the way down to his fingers now, and his hands have grown fatter, hands inscribed with the scars of twenty years in the kitchen, burned daily and gouged by wayward oyster shuckers and subjected to malevolent blades severing tiny chunks of fingertip; thousands of shifts spent shelling, peeling, dicing, stirring, gutting, deboning, and chopping; the never-ending repetitive handling of foods raw and cooking and cooked; the infinite cycle of frying pans and scouring stainless counters with steel wool and industrial-strength degreasers.

"You looking for a job?"

"No, I've got plans. Might have a job in a hotel, in Belize."

"Belize."

He nods and then takes a long swig of beer, with his head turned at an angle so he can keep watching the game.

"You could go sailing. Still go once in a while?"

Two guys came in right as he was going to answer. Bébert followed them with his eyes. He tensed up. They look like a couple back-alley wannabe gangstas in their mid-thirties, kind of dudes who finished high school in prison. The first is wearing a Celtics jersey under his X-large Ecko parka. Tattooed temple, unlaced Timberlands. The other one's rocking an unzipped puffy coat with an Ed Hardy panther t-shirt and red Pumas. The guys at the back of the bar lift their heads from the pool table a moment, then look back at each other, and the table. The two guys head toward the bar, in no rush. Bébert take his eyes off them. I figure he knows them.

"What about you. Where are you now?"

"I work with Fred."

"Therrien?"

"No, Kazemian."

"Freddy-E. He took you in the kitchen?"

"No, I'm on the floor now. Been out of the kitchen for a while."

It took a while, but eventually I got fed up with the shitty pay and unrelenting rushes, the hours cooped up in microscopic kitchens in suffocating heat, your face dripping sweat and grease, parked in front of your station while new orders just keep pouring in by the thousands without an extra minute to put them out, until you end up slapping the finished plates down with venom. Yeah, when I got the chance to move to the floor I jumped.

"So that's why you're clean-cut now. Clean-shaven, cleaned up."

"Yeah, I have to shave now. I guess I'm cleaning up my act a bit too."

"Cleaning up your act, c'mon. You were always chill. Never made waves. Always had your shit together."

"Yeah, I guess compared to you we're all pretty chill."

This cranks up Bébert's laugh, like a powerful croaking. But it doesn't last long, and he's back in serious mode pretty quick. Sort of. He lifts his bottle at an angle. It's empty. I keep talking.

"Yeah, I do some managing, and some serving."

He smiles in the corner of his mouth. Waves the bartender over. One of the two guys, in the Timberlands, is playing with his phone. Mr. Puma is playing the VLTs. From my seat I can see the combinations scrolling down on the coloured screen. He's playing *Crazy Bells*. The results come up. Nothing playable on the horizontals, just one 7, no bells, not even a cherry.

"It's going pretty well," I said.

"No surprise there."

There was not a trace of friendly mockery in his voice.

"Hey, did you hear that La Trattoria shut down last week. I heard it from Fred."

The bartender comes over, still watching the hockey game. He asks Bébert:

"Same again?"

"Yeah, but also," he says, lowering his voice, "I also want you to take two 7Ups to those two clowns over there."

Without changing his expression the barman looks over at the two guys, then turns back to Bébert.

"You sure?"

"Yeah, yeah. Look at those faces. Kind of guys that just love a good 7Up."

The bartender looks at Bébert for a few seconds without saying a word. His hands are panning through the change in his pouch. He's sixty, easy. Skinny chin, close-shaved, a long laugh line on either side of his mouth, hair slicked back. David Carradine in *Kill Bill*.

"Funny," he says. "They don't strike me as the kinds of guys who like 7Up."

"Well we'll never find out if you don't take them one!" Bébert has a big grin as the words come out. His teeth are a shit-show.

At the back of the bar one of the pool players breaks explosively. There's more swearing. Bébert and the barman turned around. Four balls in succession drop into their pockets with a muffled sound. Two of the players high-five.

"Come to think of it, I'm out of 7Up," said the bartender. "I'll be back with your beers."

He walks away from us, toward the pool table.

"You haven't changed, eh?"

"Why would I? Got millions of friends, no faults to speak of. It's all good."

"Speaking of friends, heard anything from Greg?"

"It'd surprise me if I did."

"Why? Where's he at? What's he up to?"

Bébert looked me square in the eyes.

"Remember what I told you back in the day. About Greg. And asking questions?"

"Okay, okay."

I sure did remember. I had to laugh, a little ruefully, and take a last sip of beer to chase the bitter memory.

"What about Bonnie, any news?" I eventually asked.

The bartender comes back with our beers and puts the two big bottles on the table. Bébert hands him a twenty. The bartender gives him his change without a word.

"Bonnie, man—haven't thought about that chick in ages. Haven't heard that name in five years. She went back to Ontario. Got married to some hippie grows organic vegetables. Somewhere in southern Ontario. She's through with cooking and shit."

"Married. Damn."

"I'm sure she's just as confused as ever. What about you, you hear anything from Renaud?"

"Uh, yeah. I did."

"You ever run into him?"

"I must have seen him a couple times since La Trattoria."

"Well if you see him tell him to fuck off, from me."

I fill my glass with beer. Take a look at the bartender, then at Timberland and Puma sitting at the machines. Timberland catches my eye and gives me a cocky wink. I turn back to Bébert.

"That'd be tough. Renaud's dead."

I take a sip and push back my hiccups. Bébert doesn't react. Then he leans back and takes a big swig, as if he hadn't had a drink in weeks. I go on:

"Died last year."

"Well tell him to fuck off anyway. Asshole."

He makes a move to get up. The legs of his chair scrape on the floor tiles, but he sits back down. He looks over his shoulder. The two guys are coming toward our table. They're walking slow and nonchalant, as if to let us know that they own this joint. I can see from the expression on Bébert's face that this night is about to take a sharp right turn. Or maybe it's headed exactly where it was going all along and he'd merely neglected to inform me. From a distance these guys may have looked like a part of two-bit clowns, but now that their hard-luck faces are right up in our grills, the joke isn't so funny. Bébert leans back in his chair again, as if he was the one who'd decided to stay put, and calls out to the bartender:

"Same again. Just me and him though."

I don't say a word, though I've barely touched my bottle. Suddenly I realize I can't hear the pool game any more. The guys are almost frozen in place, staring at us. For a few seconds no one moves. No one says a word. An entire verse of "Living on a Prayer" rings out into the emptiness before one of the players leans over the table again. The shot rings out throughout the bar.

Timberland puts down his gin-and-tonic and sits at one of the little tables, sprawls right out. The other guy backs up a bit, arms crossed, between us and the front door. He looks like he just bit into a lemon. I should have stayed home, warmed up with a bowl of dhal. I should have come up with an excuse for Bébert, to put it off until another time. It was late, I would have drifted off to sleep, next to my girlfriend.

Bébert gives Timberland a cocky grin. It looks forced. He stretches, forming a V with his arms, and moans like a moose. Clearly I'm the odd man out in this new grouping. I decide to stay seated and bide my time.

"You didn't choke. Smart move," says Timberland.

"Tell him we don't have all night. I've got wet fucking feet."

Timberland's hands are red and chapped, like beer deliverymen during the holidays.

"You should try wearing boots like everyone else," he says, turning slightly toward the guy wearing Pumas.

Bébert is tucking into his third big beer. I can feel him coming to a boil. Timberland acts like he's suddenly noticing me. He stares me down. I lower my eyes. Fucking Bébert.

"Who are you? We don't know you."

He looks at Bébert, who's grinning like an idiot. He stinks like an ashtray.

"So you brought a little bodyguard?"

Bébert lifts up his hand, with his palm toward the guys—like Magneto stopping a hail of bullets. I've never seen him tense like that, caught without a comeback.

"I'll catch up with you boys in a minute. We're not done here. You guys are kind of in the way, eh?"

Puma uncrosses his arms with a sniffle. My armpits are wet and I can feel sweat running down my back. I can see the bartender staring at us, oblivious to everything else. Timberland slaps his thighs and gets up heavily.

"Sure. We'll go for a little walk while you guys catch up. And you better be here when we get back. You've been jerking us around long enough."

Timberland claps Bébert on the shoulder and heads out. Puma's already outside, lighting a smoke. I let out a sigh of relief and take a big sip of beer.

"Jesus, Bébert, you could have warned me."

"Don't worry about that. That's nothing."

"Who are those guys?"

Bébert's got his big crooked smile on again. He looks at me.

"Man, it's good to see you again."

CHAPTER 1

WET SNOWFLAKES drifted onto the windshield. You could hear the back-and-forth of the wipers and the dampened whirring of cars driving by in front of us. Malik was parked in the street, behind a Tercel that had seen better days. He had turned down the music and was staring straight ahead. The sky was growing dark. It was barely four p.m. People hurried up Saint-Hubert, necks tucked into their shoulders. Some carried armfuls of packages. Apartment windows gave off yellow or orange light. The fake-happy holiday vibe was in full swing on Mont-Royal Avenue in front of us, and I felt nothing. Barely audible, idiotic Christmas tunes came sputtering from loudspeakers on lampposts. Malik kept his hands on the wheel. I brought my coffee cup to my lips. He sighed, as if preparing to undertake an onerous task that could no longer be postponed. He still wasn't looking at me. I broke the silence he'd maintained since we'd crossed back to Montreal.

"Grandpa was born on this street. Did you know that?"

My cousin gave me an icy stare. He'd been chewing the same gum since we left Trois-Rivières. The tension in his facial muscles was visible even in the fleshy part of his cheek. It was as if he'd gotten mad all over again. Like he was replaying the scene from the week before as a prelude to dragging me home by the scruff of my neck. He was getting ready to say his piece. I had a pretty clear picture of what to expect; it wasn't the first time. I'd been dreading this moment for hours. I stayed slouched in the passenger seat, trying to project indifference, but I knew he was right, again. He took his hands off the steering wheel and turned to me:

"You realize this is getting serious, right? If it was up to me I'd have kept you in Trois-Rivières. You could have stayed with me until New Year's, like it or not."

"Don't start. I'm not a kid, man."

"Actually that's exactly what you are. A little kid. And you have to get your shit together. I'm not going to be there to bail you out every time. You're dragging me into your lies, and it makes me sick."

I resisted the temptation to answer. It would have shown a flagrant lack of gratitude, and respect. After all, Malik hadn't said a word to anyone. And then there was all the money he'd lent me. But at that very moment, in his sweltering Golf, I was seriously tempted to get out and take off with a slam of the door. Though with everything he'd done for me, shutting my mouth and hearing the man out seemed like the least I could do. I sighed and nodded. My coffee had been cold for a while, but I kept taking bitter little sips, as if it might make this whole situation less awkward. I didn't look at him. Without really noticing I was examining the crap littering the floor between the two seats. Old McDonald's cups. Torn-up parking tickets with the university logo. Protein bar wrappers. CD cases mixed in with the piles like little squares of crystal: Stratovarius, Rhapsody, Dream Theater. Leftovers from meals wolfed down on the road. The inside of Malik's car was a dump for the detritus of a busy guy who spent his life driving between three cities, between his girlfriend and university in Trois-Rivières and his dad and friends in Sherbrooke and his mum and the rest of the family in Montreal.

It was 4:11 on my pager.

"I've gotta go. Dave said they were expecting me at 4:30."

"Think about what we talked about."

"Yeah, yeah."

"I'm serious. This shit's gotta stop."

Malik had raised his voice, but then he calmed back down.

"Okay," he said, pulling his lumpy, worn-out wallet from his leather jacket.

He took out four twenty-dollar bills and handed them to me.

I pocketed the money.

"This is the last time I lend you money. You have to swallow your pride and talk to your parents."

The hair on the back of my neck stood up. I didn't answer. I took another look at the pager. Through the windshield I could see a teenager begging. He was soliciting every person who went by. I sniffled, as if to grab a hold of myself.

"No need. I'll figure it out. Get my shit together."

Malik put his hands back on the wheel and lowered his head. He looked exhausted. Cars drove by on Mont-Royal. You could hear tires squeaking on the wet asphalt.

"Good, stop messing around. You're pushing your luck."

"All right, I get it."

I checked the time, yet again.

"I really have to go."

"Okay. I'll be back in Montreal after finals. You've got my number if you need to talk."

"I know."

I took another sip of coffee and grimaced. Opened the door. Montreal was warmer than Trois-Rivières. I turned back to Malik and tried to mean what I said:

"I'm sorry about all this hassle. And thanks for the money."

Malik started the car.

"Do me a favour, and be more fucking careful."

He held out his hand and I shook it. I took my bag and got out. His old Golf went up Mont-Royal, then turned on Mentana. After the snowfall, a light fog was lifting. Lampposts, car headlights, and storefronts stood out against the dense blue evening sky enveloping everything. I stayed still for a minute, taking the measure, though I tried to push it away, of the solitude I was returning to. The days at Malik's already seemed far away. I started walking toward the restaurant.

More and more people filled the sidewalks, their hurried shadows brushing by me. A dad pulled his two daughters out of a daycare, holding their hands while they told a story. Clearly it was an exciting one: they kept interrupting each other. A woman in a long cream-coloured coat cut me off and marched on, leaving a wake of vanilla perfume. She was talking on her cell in a caustic tone, and her high heels clacked on the wet sidewalk. A group of young teenagers with schoolbags slung over their shoulders were hanging out in front of their school. Under their open coats you could see their grey, white, and navy-blue uniforms. Their boastful, high-pitched, and inflected voices made me almost jealous to no longer be their age, with a little routine every evening, hot dinner waiting on the table at home, homework to be charged through before playing some video games. I would gladly have changed places with any of these people on the street. It seemed like every one of them had a better life that mine, not that I wanted to start feeling sorry for myself. I felt the cold deep in my ribs. I tried not to think about the situation, to concentrate instead on the here and now. But despite my best intentions I kept replaying the conversations with my cousin. It helped me steel myself and keep going.

I took out the stub of paper Dave had scribbled the address on. Dave was a friend who went to Cegep with me. He hated his job and wanted out. I absolutely had to earn some money, the sooner the better. I'd been looking for work for two weeks now with no luck. Searched the classifieds in the *Métro* free paper from top to bottom. Wasted mornings that should have been spent studying on soul-destroying trial shifts in a sinister telemarketing office. I'd frozen my feet off every evening in November, under chilling rain, going door to door in the suburban labyrinth of the West Island without managing to sell a single alarm system. My boss at my summer job had nothing for me. The guy who'd taken my place had his construction ticket.

Dave had taken care to warn me, as if he wanted to be certain I understood that his offer came with small print.

"You'll see, it's a lot of work. But the people are fun, and you get free food. Ever worked in a restaurant?"

"No."

I knew how to work with my hands, though. I'd been a labourer on renovations, cleaned houses on an army base, swept chimneys, done demolition. Sure, I would have rather spent my days reading and drawing, but I wasn't afraid of hard work.

"Whatever, do your training and they'll see."

"Anyway, I need a job."

In front of the drugstore a homeless man was buried under a massive pile of rags and wool blankets. I crossed over to the other side of the street, to move a little faster. I forced myself to forget about the eighty dollars in my pocket. But I was out of harm's way, for now. The two most dangerous spots in the neighbourhood weren't on my route. Bistro de Paris was to the west, on Saint-Denis, and Taverne Laperrière was on the corner of De Lorimier and Mont-Royal. Both were too far, I wouldn't have time. I walked past a stationery store. Every item in the window was decked with Christmas decorations. I passed a first restaurant, then a bar, already full. A grey-haired man came out, with a woman on his arm. They were both laughing. The woman's loud, melodic laugh rang out as the couple walked off into the distance, arm in arm. It made me think of Marie-Lou, and I missed her. The bar's seedy scent of cigarettes and beer was soon overpowered by the metallic smell of the cold mixed in with car exhaust.

I crossed two more streets and got to the restaurant. Four-thirty. It was already night. My heart started beating more quickly than before. I took a deep breath. The Bistro de Paris wasn't actually *that* far, when you thought about it. All I had to do was turn around, walk a few short blocks. I could always find another job later that week. I looked toward Rue Saint-Hubert and pulled myself together when I saw the place Malik had dropped me off. I managed to chase the image of the LCD screens with twirling multicoloured fruits and the tic-tac of credits accumulating as I landed on one winning combination after another.

CHAPTER 2

I SLUNK out of the bar feeling defeated and empty, turning my back on the machine I'd been glued to for nearly three hours, the machine I'd skipped out on my meeting with Marie-Lou to play with what was left of the money she'd lent me for rent two weeks earlier. Under the October sun I headed down Ontario toward Papineau, to meet the guys at the jam space. As I walked I listened to a mixtape I'd made with the best tracks of the last Amon Amarth album. "Risen from the Sea" had just kicked in. I turned it up to ten. I was trying not to think about how much money I'd lost today. How much had I lost since March? Who knows, I couldn't even round it to the nearest thousand. The mental highlight reel of my VLT sessions was always there for me to play back, the magic days and the big wins and the combinations that sent you flying through the air. Deep down I knew my little mental movie was lying like a used car salesman. But I was powerless to fight it. I'd win it all back next time.

Cité 2000 loomed in the distance between two rows of squat attached buildings. For Quebec metal bands, this was Mecca: a monolith at least four storeys high tucked between the Jacques Cartier Bridge and the Molson brewery, bathing in the pungent odour of yeast and fermented grain. The building overlooked the beat-up apartment buildings south of René-Lévesque Boulevard. When I saw I was getting closer I picked up the pace. I was late, and the three hours spent playing the machine had left me frustrated and a touch confused, so I was suddenly nervous as I came through the door. The cavernous lobby reminded me of an empty warehouse. In the middle was a big reception desk, behind it a grey-faced security guard dozing with his cheek on his fist. I went up and asked him to buzz the guys from Deathgaze.

"Room number?"

It took me a while to come up with the right number. He picked up the headset next to his register. He called one of the guys. I spent around ten minutes waiting, pacing.

Alex came down to get me at the front desk. He had his sleeveless black jean vest on with the sweatbands he wore at shows on his forearm. His straw-coloured locks cascaded over his broad shoulders. He'd let his beard grow out. He was only a year older than me, but most people would have guessed five or six.

"What happened, man, couldn't find the place?"

"Nah, sorry. My class went late."

I followed him to the stairwell, up to the third floor. He led me down long hallways littered with drywall dust. The sounds of bands practising all blended together and transformed itself as we went forward, screams piercing like needles, guttural growls rising from the floor, guitar riffs assembling like a swarm of giant bees, the muted, metallic bombardment of drums overlaying everything. I must have smiled like an idiot looking at the group names on the massive doors: Cryptopsy, Anonymus, so many more I've forgotten today. Finally we reached the Deathgaze practice space.

Alex pushed open the door and I followed him in, closing the door behind me. The room was small and packed tight with Marshall stacks and cases of empties. The walls were covered in some kind of black stucco, with holes here and there. Posters of Immortal, Cannibal Corpse, The Haunted. At eye-level they'd posted crumpled old set lists and school notebook pages covered with lyrics. Twisted or crushed pop cans littered the floor. The thick mats rolled out on the floor were stained and encrusted with crumbs of food and cigarette ash. A full ashtray crowned every speaker. A busted-up couch with a sweat-stained yellow pillow on one of its arms was wedged between two shelves overflowing with cables, extension cords, pedals, and drumsticks. High windows with metal grilles over them let in a trickle of grainy light. A hockey bag had been thrown into the corner of the room and forgotten, perhaps since the previous spring. A Tama drum, half taken-apart, gathered dust in one corner; another, as huge as Nicko McBrain's, towered in the other corner. When we walked in the drummer was messing around with his hi-hat, adjusting the height of the top cymbal. Beefy arms blackened by tattoos emerged from a Darkthrone *Transilvanian Hunger* t-shirt whose sleeves looked like they'd been cut off with a pocket knife. He gave me a nod. He had a crooked nose and a long goatee, like Dimebag Darrel. The other guy was sitting on an iron stool, noodling on an unplugged guitar. He raised his eyes to look me up and down wordlessly, then went back to the chord progression he was trying to nail down. He had a triangular jaw and a clean-shaven face and head. The neck of his guitar looked like a twig in his big, bricklayer's hands. I tried to find a place to put down my stuff. I stepped over guitar cases and patch cords connected to amps and a microphone plugged into some kind of PA. I took care not to snag anything.

Alex did the intros. The guitarist was Mike, the drummer Sébastien. The bassist wasn't there, he had his daughter that week. Alex was telling them about me, that I was "studying in the field." He probably thought I was an art student. I was too embarrassed to correct this misunderstanding, which didn't matter anyway. I'd brought a big sketchbook full of finished and unfinished drawings. The drummer snatched it from my hands. He gave me some enthusiastic compliments when he stumbled on my pastiche of the Iced Earth album cover, done in lines even thicker and rougher than Travis Smith in his Marvel phase.

"We're death metal, man," the singer said. "Not some shitty power metal band."

I looked at him for a second, unsure what to say. Perched on the little drummer's stool, Alex looked like a grown man on a child's trike. He raised his hand at the guitarist. Before talking, he tucked his long hair behind his ear, the way he'd always done.

"Man, this is just to give you some ideas. He's gonna make us something we'll all like. That's why he's here."

Alex was the one who'd convinced them to choose me to illustrate the EP they were bringing out early next year. My job was to draw them a band logo, make the files, and send them to the printer. Alex had made up his mind, and would stick to it like a sacred oath. Which it was, in a sense: back in high school he played in four bands and was always telling anyone willing to listen I was going to design the cover of his first album.

Alex grabbed the sketchbook from the drummer's hands and started flipping through it, like he was looking for something specific. He appeared to know my sketchbook better than I did. He showed them some Gimenez-style drawings I'd coloured in with watercolours, talking with the exact same confidence he had back in the day, when his pointless stories always had the whole room in stitches and made him the life of every party. The guitarist had laid down his King V, and the drummer was listening to Alex too, with his hands on his thighs. He held out my sketchbook and explained what they had in mind, pointing at certain drawings, almost tapping on the page. No one else could get a word in edgewise. He'd already talked to me about his ideas, and I had a sense of what he wanted, a sort of oceanic landscape with a giant octopus. The guitarist was poker-faced. When he looked at me I looked down. With his voice full of exhilaration, Alex kept haranguing us for another ten minutes. Then he turned to me and gave back my book.

"Show them your logo sketches."

I took out a Canson pad from my bag. He practically ripped it from my hands, and opened it straight to the page he was looking for. I'd made a logo kind of like Darkthrone's, with letters that seemed to be melting. The drummer swore appreciatively. The guitarist raised his eyebrows.

"That's not fucking bad."

Alex closed the Canson pad, a little smile in the corner of his eyes.

A week later Alex met me at Café Chaos after my first page lay-out class. We went there because he had to talk to the booking agent. When he told me the guy used to be the singer of Necrotic Mutation I was impressed. We took a while to drink a few pints and talked over the illustration, then he put an ATM envelope on the table, fat with money. Two thousand dollars: enough to cover printing, and my own work as well. I'd never gotten that much cash in one shot. Two thousand dollars, a million: it was pretty much one and the same to me. Maybe it wasn't that big a deal for the guys in the band though. Alex drove a forklift in a factory, the other guys worked construction or had other high-paying jobs.

The afternoon was coming to an end, it must have been four or five o'clock. It was going to be a cool night. We went to deposit the money in my account, at one of the ATMs on the corner of de Plessis and Ontario. My balance had suddenly leaped, like after an especially lucky sequence at the machines. My heart almost sky-rocketed out of my chest. I was floating, two feet off the ground, shivering all over my body. I almost withdrew two hundred dol-lars, out of habit.

Then, as if to seal the deal, we went to Pijy's Pub and drank a toast. We went there a lot. Two-for-one pitchers. Copper and varnished wood. A persistent odour of mothballs. We continued the discussion we'd begun at Café Chaos. He told me about the tour they had planned, might take them as far as Rimouski. I was having trouble focussing on his words. I kept looking at this old guy behind Alex's shoulders, playing a machine. He seemed to be winning a lot. It was unbearable to watch, with two grand in my account. My head was spinning. Alex's plans for the tour, his stor-ies about shows: nothing held my attention. My concentration was wandering. I was tracking the old guy's every move. He kept right on tapping the screen, adjusting his bets, and pressing the bright

yellow buttons. I stared at the box of his winnings at the bottom
of the screen. I couldn't stop thinking about all the money I'd just
deposited in my account.

We drank for another hour or two. Alex bought another round.
We'd put back two pitchers and a pint each. I was starting to slur;
Alex was barely affected. He could hold his liquor a lot better than
me. Back at the end of high school, when most of us were still just
learning how to handle our beers, he was tossing back Chemi-
neaud brandy.

We walked out into the blue sky of falling night. The smell of the
first cold snap tickled my nostrils. Alex said bye and disappeared
into Berri Metro station. I came back up Saint-Thimotée toward
Ontario, and stopped at a phone booth. I hung up and waited a
few seconds, then dialled Malik's number. He didn't answer. Then I
called up my old boss. I left a message asking if he had some work
for me. The next second, still holding the headset, I felt my soul
leaving my body. I was powerless. In a sweet moment of relief and
disappointment, I gave up. Dead leaves tumbled down the street
or lay rotting in piles next to the gutter drains. I set off alongside
the low-rise apartment buildings, housing co-ops and tiny, abandoned parks of the Centre-Sud neighbourhood. Looking discreetly over my shoulder, and sticking to the side streets, I went
back into the credit union on Plessis and Ontario. Three or four
years later, it turned into a Subway, but its physical disappearance
would do nothing to erase the memory of the acts I committed
that day. I took out three hundred dollars and went to Brasserie
Cherrier. I walked in without looking at anyone, and pulled up a
stool next to the machine that looked like the best bet.

It was October 5. I didn't know it yet, but three weeks later the
entire two thousand dollars from Deathgaze would be gone. Three
weeks religiously playing the machines and skipping every second
class. I wish I could say that was when I pulled myself together,
that the spiral of denial and loss had reached its nadir, but no one
would believe me. By the beginning of November I was totally
broke. I owed Marie-Lou almost six hundred dollars, which I'd

borrowed to pay my roommate August and September's rent, but gambled away instead. The last few weeks at the apartment were tense. I scrupulously avoided my roommate: I'd memorized his and his girlfriend's school schedules to know when I could spend time at home in peace. I'd stopped visiting my parents and going for beers with my friends from school.

When I realized I would never make rent for October or November, I moved out without saying goodbye. I filled a bunch of plastic bags from the art store with clothes and books and a box of drawing supplies, and shoved it all in the trunk of a taxi one night when my roommate was at his girlfriend's. I camped out at Marie-Lou's for a few days, said I'd got in a fight with my roommate. In the meantime, Vincent, one of the very last Longueuil friends I still saw, offered to put me up. He didn't ask anything in return. "You can crash in the living room for a few months. Between my girlfriend and school and soccer, I'm almost never here."

CHAPTER 3

YOU COULD SEE in through the glass panes of a garage door. On a sign above it, the restaurant's name was written in an elegant sans-serif: LA TRATTORIA. I pushed open the door and walked into a spacious slate-grey hallway. It wasn't what I expected. The fanciest place I'd ever eaten was Saint-Hubert BBQ chicken, my dad took us there all the time when I was little. But La Trattoria was nothing like Saint-Hubert, or the Normandin in Trois-Rivières or the Georges in Longueuil or any other family restaurant. It was nothing like the diners my friends and I hung out at after class or a night out. I was expecting some greasy fast-food joint. This room with its shimmering glassware felt more like an art gallery.

I tried not to think about it, told myself again that I was doing the right thing. At this point I didn't have a thousand options. The way Dave put it, there was no way they'd turn me down. No one took a job washing dishes unless they were desperate. I was desperate as hell.

I went into the hallway and pushed open a second glass door. From outside, the dining room had seemed cavernous and dark. Now I saw it was bigger than I'd thought, and even in the dim light everything looked polished to a shine. The chairs weren't normal restaurant chairs, more like what we had in the drafting studio at my Cegep, the junior college where I studied graphic design. The lacquered wood tables looked clean enough to eat off. The walls were exposed brick, with mortar oozing out of the joints as if someone had gone out of their way to botch the job. Two massive, ultramodern light fixtures hung from the ceiling like diamond-encrusted radar antennae. The dark wood floor made me feel like I should take my boots off before walking on it. A long, padded leather partition divided the rectangular room into two sections. Next to it stood a large wall of wine bottles stacked to the ceiling, at least fifteen feet high. There weren't any customers yet. My hands were sweaty. I dried them on my pants.

Back then I didn't know a thing. Were there twenty, a hundred and twenty, two hundred and twenty seats? I couldn't have told you. In fact the room held seventy diners, plus fifteen at the bar that stretched pretty much the full length of the room.

A handful of employees in black were gathered for a talk at the back of the room, next to the wall of wine bottles. They stopped for a minute and looked in my direction, then started talking again. A young woman was finishing up the table settings and bread dishes. When she saw me she put her little pile of dishes down on the corner of the bar and walked toward me. Her hair was blond and very short. She was also dressed in black: a skirt and a top that left her shoulders bare. She had prominent collarbones and pale skin. She said hi. I mumbled hi back.

"Yes?"

She spoke clearly in a tone that made it known I was an unwelcome intrusion. Obviously, I wasn't a customer. I stuttered that I was here for a training shift as a dishwasher. She sized me up in a second. I tried to appear determined and outgoing, as I'd learned at private school. She looked five or six years older than me, maybe seven.

"Next time, go around the back and ring the bell. The address is on the door, you'll see it."

I followed her through the dining room. Every single table was perfectly set. The cloth napkins were identically folded. I'd never set foot in a restaurant to do anything but eat.

The employees sitting around talking looked over at me as if I'd disrupted an important ritual. Only one of them dignified me with a nod. My nerves were starting to get the better of me. Everyone was blurring together, their faces somehow out of focus. The guys were all different ages, with the same chiselled features and GQ style, kicking back in fitted shirts and well-cut pants. The sound of the soles of my work boots on the hardwood echoed through the whole room. I felt like someone banging a hammer in a church.

The waitress led me through the front kitchen. The contrast with the dining room was stark. It was a kind of narrow rectangle, lit more brightly than a gym, with large growling hood vents above the ovens. A massive pizza oven was built into the back wall, throwing a dry, intense heat even through closed doors. Around the oven's legs a motley collection of receptacles had piled up: plastic buckets, buspans, and greasy containers that must have been chucked there during the lunch rush. The kitchen was divided into two stations by shelves stacked high with dishes. A cook was kneeling in front of the open fridges, writing on an aluminum pad with a black marker. He didn't say a word to me.

We passed a staircase down to the basement. The stairwell walls were painted a cheerless turquoise and covered with red, brown, and green splotches of sauce. The odd fly buzzed around the fluorescent lights above the stairs. I was getting hot in my coat. A strangely soothing smell wafted up from the basement. It took me a moment to place it: chicken broth.

The waitress stopped in the doorway of a room lined with shelves full of dishes. It was pretty big, maybe ten feet by twenty.

The left side was stacked with clean dishes; the right with the dirty ones. Between was a battlefield where the remains of the day's lunch lay in agony. A tall, grimy metal shelving unit was covered with piles of splattered plates. Pots stained with burnt tomato sauce harboured twisted ladles, tongs coated with unidentifiable sauces, plastic inserts with soggy julienned vegetables and viscous marinades, baking sheets spackled with fat and strips of scorched chicken skin. On the dishpit's long steel counter piles of crusted frying pans leaned precariously next to a dishwasher from which small puffs of steam emerged. At the bottom of one of the overstuffed shelves a mountain of cutlery soaked in a bucket of grey water. The tiled walls were filthier than a high school cafeteria after a food fight: knots of overcooked linguini, brown shreds of lettuce poised to come unstuck, unidentifiable lumps, soup splatters, and squirts of sauce covered the wall with a layer that grew thicker as it neared the ground, where it coalesced into a seam of sodden, oily black gunk. A large garbage can rose in the centre of it all like a sacrificial well, its black bag overflowing with what the lunchtime hordes had rejected, like the entrails of an animal with rumpled, slimy skin. The area smelled like disinfectant and something else I couldn't put my finger on, a greasy, fetid odour that filled my nostrils. A small hood vent was noisily sucking up the humid air that had long ago had its way with the ceiling.

Two cooks were hanging out at the back of the dishpit next to the open back door. Their black pants were stained with soup and the fronts of their white shirts were smeared, as if every kid at a daycare had wiped off their hands after an especially gross snack. They were smoking and speaking English. One held his rolled-up chef's hat in his hand.

"Renaud!"

They turned toward us. The waitress pointed her thumb at me.

"I've got a new one for you."

Her tone was even sharper than before. Her voice cut through the noise and the music coming up from the basement. This girl could have made herself heard in the mosh pit at a grindcore show.

Renaud clenched his cigarette between his lips and looked me up and down. His chef's hat fell over his oily forehead. Small grey eyes were set above bony cheeks. The way he had closed them to keep the smoke out of his eyes painted a mocking smile on his face. I couldn't say exactly how old he was, but he must have been at least ten years older than me. The waitress had snuck off unnoticed. The other cook pushed open the door with his hips and spat outside. The cold night air sent clouds of condensation drifting in. For a second I was tempted to slip right between the two cooks and run away into the dark alley. I checked myself. Because I was paralyzed by shyness, and because I knew that within an hour I'd find myself sitting in front of a video-poker machine. And then there was my cousin's warning, still ringing in my ears.

"So you're Dave's buddy."

I nodded. He looked at me without saying anything, as if waiting for the punch line.

"What's your name? We're not gonna call you 'Dave's buddy' all night."

I introduced myself. We shook hands.

"I'm Renaud. That's Jason."

The other cook was tall with close-cropped ginger hair. A very short goatee made him seem a few years older, and he looked like a red-haired Chris Cornell. He said hi with a little nod.

I rummaged through my bag and pulled out my resume. Renaud took a last puff of his smoke, and as he breathed out he said:

"Fuck that, give it to Christian. For your contact info. I don't give a shit."

He rolled up the sleeves of his chef's coat, tied his blood-stained apron back on, and headed down the stairs to the basement.

I followed in his footsteps. Once we got down we went into a noisy U-shaped room with fluorescent lights. Three other cooks were working away under a low ceiling criss-crossed by pipes. One was washing bunches of parsley in a large stainless-steel sink. The prep counters along the concrete walls were a jumble of plastic inserts of sauces and ingredients. Another cook, who I'd taken for a guy the first time I saw her, was methodically placing inserts into buspans, then carrying them upstairs to the front kitchen. A net contained purple hair too voluminous to tuck into her chef's hat. She was chewing a lettuce leaf and humming a song that definitely wasn't the Ice Cube blaring from the ghetto blaster tucked on a shelf between the spice jars, protected from flying sauces, vegetable juice, and clouds of flour.

A third cook was leaning over a big machine that reminded me of a table-saw, transforming big hunks of dried meat into thin slices he laid out on waxed paper. Another emerged from the cooler, slamming the door behind him. His apron was overflowing with eggplants and zucchinis. It was the guy I'd seen squatting in the front kitchen. He almost bumped into Renaud, who was making his way down a hallway with boxes full of tomatoes and big containers of vegetable oil. I followed him, stepping over further piles of dirty dishes: cake pans, fat-splattered baking sheets, cutting boards turned red from ten thousand nicks. The cook with the eggplant gave the leaning tower of dishes a kick in a vain attempt to restore balance, but it continued to collapse around the legs of the stainless-steel counter. I went back to see Renaud. At the end of the hallway we came to the staff room. It was fairly big, but the ceiling was even lower. In the middle of the room you could just make out a wooden table, like the ones in the dining room, buried under piles of empty cigarette packs, scattered newspapers, and crushed energy drink cans.

"Leave your stuff in the corner. You can change here, or in the bathroom over there."

The bathroom door was sandwiched between an ice machine and a shelf of steel scrubbers, clean rags, paper towel rolls, and boxes of soap. Beside it there were three other doors. One of them opened onto a dry storage room and the other some kind of boiler room from which issued a warm fermented smell like ammonia. On the wall across the hall there was a single door, identified on a plaque: OFFICE. It was slightly ajar. I could hear two voices, a man's and a woman's. They were arguing.

"It's okay, I'm ready to start," I said, relieved to finally take off my coat.

I'd come here in the work pants from my labouring job last summer, made of a fabric only slightly more flexible than sheet metal. I figured they'd be good for a job like this, was proud of my foresight. I hadn't counted on just how uncomfortable this material would get once it was soaked through.

"You'll need these."

Renaud handed me a clean white shirt, an apron, and two rags.

"It's all over there, next time you need it."

He pointed at a rod, with fifty or so shirts hanging from it.

"If you get too soaked during your shift, go ahead and change your shirt. It's hot in the kitchen and cold in the dishpit. Make sure you don't freeze."

A tall thin woman darted out of the office, ignoring us. She wore elegant clothing and her jet-black hair was up in a chignon. Her high heels hammered the floor and her key ring jangled in time to her footsteps. Her eyes were cast down, intent on her flip phone, and without slowing down or looking around she shouted, probably at the person still in the office.

"And Christian, tell your staff to pick up their shit. This isn't a hockey team locker room."

She disappeared down the hallway, gracefully sidestepping boxes of cans and vegetables. This woman exuded natural authority. She was thirty or thirty-five, not much older than Renaud at any rate. I heard her snap at the cooks I'd just walked by, and then hurry up the stairs, each footstep resonating on the metal steps.

A stocky man with a ruddy complexion came out of the office. His hair was dishevelled and greying at the temples, and he was dragging his feet like a guy getting out of bed at noon on his day off. In his right hand he held an empty beer glass. He walked over to his locker, with glassy eyes and a smile on the corner of his mouth.

"Hey Chef," Renaud said. "Did you do the Noreff order? If you want the bisque ready for the forty-five next week, it's gotta be done by Sunday."

I decided this must be the chef, and his name was Christian. He started unbuttoning his shirt and turned toward us, as if he had just noticed me. His beer belly was hanging out. He set his empty beer glass next to another one on top of his locker.

"I'll do it tomorrow," he said. "We're fine for Sunday."

I caught a glimpse of Renaud rolling his eyes. The chef took off his work pants and hung them up in his locker.

"Ever wash dishes?"

The chef asked me the question without looking in my direction.

"No," I said, surprised someone was actually talking to me. It was as if even I had forgotten that I was there.

"No worries, it's not rocket science. You'll see."

He kicked off his work shoes, which looked sort of like rubber clogs, and put on a pair of jeans and a faded shirt. You could still read the words, FORT LAUDERDALE, but barely.

"Anyway, Dave should be here soon. He'll show you the ropes."

"Dave's not working tonight, Chef," said Renaud.

"Who's the second dishwasher then? Carl? Eaton? Aziz?"

"Aziz left a month ago, Chef."

Christian was looking for something in the depths of his messy locker.

"You didn't schedule a second dishwasher," Renaud went on.

He nodded in my direction.

"He's on his own," he continued, not even trying to hide his annoyance.

The chef finally located his hat and slowly put on his winter coat.

"Whatever, get Bébert to train him. Make him earn that raise," he said, without looking at Renaud.

He came toward me and grabbed me by the shoulder. It was a weird version of a hug, as if he were knighting me.

"It's gonna be okay, man. Remember: It's just a restaurant."

He winked at me, then took his mittens off the table and walked off the way we'd come. You could hear him saying bye to the team before climbing up the staircase heavily.

"Okay, come on," Renaud said, cuffing me on the shoulder. It may be a little rough, if you're all alone tonight. We'll get you started on the mise right away."

I followed Renaud through the prep hall, more nervous than I'd been on my first day of school. I narrowly avoided tripping over a box. We walked by the person who'd been washing pars-

ley. He was on his way to the staff room, taking off his chef's coat
without giving us a second look. The cook who was there earlier
was getting ready to go upstairs with a final pyramid of backups—
I'd learn later that any container with ingredients or sauces for
restocking the line was called a backup. The pyramid looked like it
weighed as much as she did. The only person left downstairs was
the cook I'd seen coming out of the cooler. He was draping aluminum foil over a huge roasting pan full of big hunks of meat, still
on the bone, with little bouquets of fresh herbs and chopped carrots and onion. He moved quickly and confidently.

"Bébert," Renaud yelled over the music, which was louder now.

More gangsta rap was playing.

"You're training the new guy."

Bébert shoved the pan in the oven and closed the door with a
violent swing. It wasn't the same kind of oven as the ones upstairs.
I'd learn about this one soon enough, it was a convection oven.

"I don't have time for that shit. Dave's supposed to train him."

He was still trying to put some order in the piles of dirty dishes
on the floor.

"Dave's not coming in. Chef forgot to schedule him."

"Fucking chef." Bébert spat the words out. "Can't even make a
proper schedule."

Renaud was adjusting the temperature of a stainless-steel
stockpot as tall as he was, a roiling cauldron full of chicken carcasses that produced a huge cloud of pungent steam. He pushed it
with his foot as he placed a bucket under the stock pot's spigot.

"You're the sous-chef. New guy's your job."

"Give me the China cap," Renaud snapped.

Bébert, looking up at Renaud, held out a sort of giant conical
strainer that Renaud set on the edges of the stockpot. He poured
out a little stock, to check its thickness. He was grimacing in the
steam. He told Bébert to relax.

"I'll keep Jason late to give you a while to show him the prep
again."

They talked about me as if I wasn't there.

"Hustle up though. Jay's on his third double this week, and we're gonna be slammed tonight."

Without any attempt at gentleness. Bébert started slamming the baking sheets at the foot of one of the counters into piles.

"Did you call Canada Laundry? I hope so, we don't have enough rags to make it through the weekend. Think I'm gonna do my shift with a paper fucking towel?"

Renaud didn't answer. He set a digital timer and clipped it to his sleeve, next to the pocket where he had arrayed various differently coloured felt pens like bullets in a belt. He left me there with Bébert and took off, jumping up the stairs four at a time.

"So you're Dave's buddy. I hope you're a little faster than he was."

In a move to show some initiative I picked up some of the dishes lying on the floor and walked toward the staircase.

"Where the hell you going with that?"

"Uh, I'm bringing it. To start washing the dishes. Looks like there's a lot."

"Leave it, we don't have time for that yet."

I pictured the giant mess in the dishpit, and wondered what could possibly be more urgent than tackling the mountains of dirty dishes and pans sitting there waiting for me.

"Come with me, you've got something else to do first. I'll show you how to do the dishes later."

Bébert had a round face and fleshy cheeks like a little boy, but you'd have to be a brave man to pinch them. He was missing a tooth and his thick, solid mass filled out his chef's coat. A beer belly was beginning to grow. Rolled-up sleeves revealed three or four unfinished tattoos on his forearms. Instead of a chef's hat like the other cooks, he wore a Cleveland Indians cap over a shaved head. His pants were too big, sagging like the rappers of the day. He must have been twenty-four or twenty-five back then, but he gave the impression of an older man.

He flipped the tape in the ghetto blaster. A bad recording of Huey Louis and the News's "Hip to be Square" blared over the loudspeaker.

"Have you seen *American Psycho*?"

I was about to say yes but he didn't leave me time.

"I think this was my favourite scene."

I replayed the image of Patrick Bateman in a transparent raincoat, brandishing a fire ax in his loft, every surface protected by newspapers.

He opened the door to the kitchen and checked the shelves, reporting that the goddamn walk-in was a fucking mess.

From that moment on I tried desperately to keep up as Bébert listed off the thousand-and-one things I had to do. He tossed ten bags of spinach onto the stainless prep counter. My job was to pull off the stems and throw out any rotten bits. He came back out of the walk-in with two waxed cardboard boxes which he threw at the foot of the sink. I was to pick out twenty heads of romaine, and forty heads of leaf lettuce, pull off the leaves, wash them in ice-cold water, then dry them in an unwieldy salad spinner that I had to hold against my body as I turned.

"Make a dozen buspans, at least. Nothing fucking worse than running out in the middle of the rush."

Then I had to change the water and wash the arugula, which came in wooden crates, each bunch covered in a layer of sandy dirt. It was the same thing my mum used, but she called it roquette. At the same time—I was getting a crash course on multi-tasking— I had to put the parsley and coriander in the walk-in and make the calzones, bruschettas and focaccias, on the double. It took me a while to figure out the difference, but I just listened to Bébert without asking questions. I soon understood, though, that I'd have to convert each of three big balls of sour-smelling pizza dough into a dozen portions every night.

"On a night like tonight, you want to make around thirty per ball. I checked the reservation book and we're full up. Go fast, the dough needs time to rise one more time before the night starts."

I was trying to remember it all. Then Bébert explained how to use the giant electric pasta roller. He told me an edifying story about a pastry chef who crushed her hand by getting it caught between the machines rollers, laughing as if it was a funny joke. She had to have surgery, but they were able to reconstruct her hand. "Good thing she was young, or they would have had to amputate."

That night Bébert pretty much handled all the dough for me. He explained, patiently, that it wasn't really a technique you could learn on the fly, but it was important to get it down as quickly as possible, or I'd never make it through the batch in time. While I was finishing off the focaccias he looked up at the clock, which elicited a long string of curses at the dimwit chef who should have scheduled another fucking dishwasher.

"After the prep, you have to do a good cleanup of the prep room. Wash the counters, sweep and mop the floors, walk-in too, and soak your cutting boards in bleach."

Everything around me, at least everything in any way related to my work, was in the process of becoming *mine*: *my* dishes, *my* lettuce, *my* dough.

"And you're gonna have to get this shit done in under twenty minutes if you don't want your dishes to pile up too much."

Even rushing, it looked to me like a good hour's worth of work. I thought of all the dirty dishes probably multiplying as we spoke, growing into ever-taller stacks, adding to all the other dirty dishes already piled high in the dishpit when I got there. I tried not to panic.

"A little later, when you have time for a break," Bébert said, with a chin-nod toward the giant pot of stock and chicken carcasses, "you pour out the chicken stock in buckets like this—he indicated with his foot—then empty the steam pot and scrub her till she shines."

In the stairwell you could already hear the first customers being served. In time I would learn to read this distant rumbling

sound and its constituent parts. Oven and kitchen doors closing
with a muffled thud. Utensils and galvanized porcelain rattling
around in the buspans of dirty dishes. Frying pan bottoms scraping on stove elements. Cooks yelling out cooking times, coordin-
ating the hot dishes coming out with the coldside. And behind
it all, farther away, the swell of the already full dining room. We
could hear Renaud coming down the first staircases and yelling at
Bébert to get his ass in gear.

"Just doing your job, dickwad."

Bébert yelled this so loudly I imagined the customers could
have heard him clear across the dining room. Soon enough I'd
learn that that was the way of the kitchen: people yelled and
screamed, the customers never heard a thing. Bébert changed his
tone to come talk to me as he set off with a pile of dirty dishes.

"We're behind, so you better leave the cleanup till you get a
chance between two services."

I copied Bébert and picked up a pile of dirty baking sheets,
topped with a roasting pan full of gelatinous meat juice. It was
almost too much, and in this attempt to show my readiness to
work hard I narrowly avoided pouring it all out. Bébert didn't
notice. His foot was already on the first step.

"If you want," he said over his shoulder, "bring the radio over
and play your music."

Once we were upstairs Bébert tried to put some order in the
dishpit. He was cursing out the day staff so violently I didn't dare
talk to him. He told me what to do in a few quick half-sentences,
and quickly showed me where everything went, calling every dish
and kitchen item by its proper name, or at least the name the cooks
used. I had to learn them all, he said, they weren't going to spend
all night repeating themselves.

"You ever wash dishes before? It's easy like that."

He filled a new rack with dirty dishes, then took the sprayer
and gave it a cursory rinse before pushing it into the dishwasher.

Pulling down the door set the machine running with a loud
whooshing sound I'd soon get used to. Bébert explained that in

the time it took the wash cycle to run, about a minute and a half, I should fill as many racks as I could.

"If you lose the rhythm you're fucked. If you can hear the machine struggling and the dishes aren't coming out clean, check your soaps and the filter. Give everything a good rinse before you run it through the machine. And try to clean up all the crud in your dishpit as you go, so you don't plug the sink."

He played with the switches on the little control box on top of the dishwasher, to show me how to change the water.

"And this is super important. Any leftover oil or marinade you find in the mixing bowls or frying pans, or salad plates, scrape it in this bucket. Otherwise you'll fuck up the plumbing. And if it overflows, guess who gets to clean up the mess?"

From the front kitchen you could hear a voice yelling to come pick up the dirty pans and bring back the clean ones. It was Renaud.

"C'mon," Bébert said.

He tossed me a pair of tattered old gardening gloves from the trolley, steeped in years of grease. Then he grabbed a pile of clean pans in each fist and left the pit to take them to Renaud. I followed.

The kitchen was barely big enough for two people to comfortably circulate. Counting Bébert, there were now six of us, all moving around in a spectacular chaos. Twin rivulets of sweat were suddenly streaming down either side of my body. The cooks, in the heat of the action, worked around me and rubbed against me without looking at me. It was like trying to parse an argument in a foreign language. As he weaved in and out Bébert placed the pans under a stainless counter where the salads sat ready for pickup.

"Always put the pans here, in the right corner, under the pass."

The noise was confusing. The hood vents' breathing, the cooks yelling to be heard, the plates clanking together, the din of customers' voices, the door of the pizza oven that never stopped opening and closing.

And the stifling heat, enveloping everything.

Renaud was standing over the stovetop in front of ten pans full of sizzling veg or bubbling sauces. He picked one up and threw in a splash of white wine, and the flame shot up in front of him. He handled his pans with a clenched brow, sweaty forehead, and tense look on his face. Jason was standing in front of a shelf at the pass-through. With pinched lips he picked up the orders as they came out of the printer, and placed them on the correct strip on the two parallel stations, reaching out over the cooks in motion. He garnished the plates and slid them over to Renaud's station, right next to him, and he heaped them full of steaming pasta. The cook I'd seen downstairs worked with her back to Jason, at a station between the pizza oven and the ten open elements of the gas range. If she backed up even a single step, she'd bash into Jason. She was loudly tossing salads in big metal mixing bowls, plating them up a few at a time, and then holding them out for Jason, who'd place them on the pass-through. When he handed her order tickets she rearranged them on the ticket holder. Her face was shiny with sweat, her purple hair plastered to her forehead. As soon as an order was ready, Jason rang a little bell that pierced the ambient cacophony. The cook I'd seen using the slicer downstairs was checking the focaccias in the pizza oven and calling out how long each one had left to cook.

"Fuck, Renaud, what's up with thirty-two?" shouted a server between two stacks of clean plates.

Effortlessly weaving between his two coworkers, Bébert yelled at me to come pick up the dirty pans as often as I could. Three large piles had already stacked up under the shelf next to the range. He picked up a bunch of them, with a rag over his hands, yelling "Hot! Hot!"

The cook in front of the pizza oven pushed up against the salad girl to make way for Bébert, who weaved through the kitchen, and we went back to the dishpit.

I followed in Bébert's footsteps and slipped between Jason and Renaud. A pillar of flame shot up and I jumped back as I approached the dirty pans. I held out to pick up the smallest one, trying not to burn myself again.

"Don't touch!" Renaud yelled. "Leave it there. These are the ones you take" he said, tapping them sharply with his tongs. "That one's mine. Touch and die."

Instead of picking up the dirty pans I'd been about to make off with the ones he'd prepped ahead, full of ingredients and ready to hit the stove any minute.

"Move, dude. You're in the way."

Without bothering to answer I took off, with clumsy movements and a tingling in my scalp. The pans were still burning hot, I could feel them through the gloves. I got back to the dishpit, holding them at the end of my arms.

"Figure out a way to run through a rack of pans every time you're at the machine," said Bébert as he sprayed off the pans to cool them down. "And give them a real good scrub. Send them out dirty and they'll come right back. When you take them out of the machine, dry them and oil them right away, keeps them from rusting. All right, you're on your own now, I've gotta get back to my station."

Bébert went back to the front kitchen with a yell that they were going to rock this rush for real now. I focused on my work. I filled a rack of plates and coffee cups, which I sent through the machine, and started scouring the pans the best I could. After ten minutes of scrubbing away at burnt and congealed pan bottoms I was as soaked as a man trapped in a running car wash. My hands were starting to wrinkle from marinating in the dishpit stew, my fingertips were lacerated by the steel wool, and I was up to my elbows in oily brown water. The spray gun sent little chunks of food and burnt crud from the pans flying, and the steam plastered them to my face. I was beginning to understand why Dave wanted to ditch this job. But it was also working for me. I liked not having time to think about my own shit. The filthy plates, pots, and pans just kept piling up no matter how fast I scrubbed. It was enough to keep my thoughts fully occupied. It felt like I was wresting control of my life.

I still hadn't finished washing the pans from my first incursion into the kitchen when Renaud called me to pick up more. I was about to head off when I heard another voice.

"Yo Dave."

Someone was on their way up the hallway next to the line. You could hear the stress in his voice. We came face-to-face. He was the only member of the floor staff who'd acknowledged me earlier. A guy not much older than me, a little thinner, with the face of a male model. His black shirt was tighter than the other waiters', and his clean shoes looked like the ones we used to have to wear at private school, only shinier. He gave me a surprised look when he realized I wasn't Dave.

"Sorry, man. I'm Nick."

He didn't leave me time to introduce myself, just demanded that I wash the cutlery, which he made sound as urgent as a blood transfusion. He took off jogging toward the dining room.

"Yo dishwasher. Pans!" It was Bébert, bellowing.

I eased into the kitchen, with scarcely more confidence than the first time. The salad girl elbowed me out of the way, her hands balancing plates with colourful salads.

"Move!"

I just managed to avoid her on my way to the pans. I held my hands over the flame to pick them up. Renaud was checking a salmon filet to see if it was done, and had just dispatched portions of linguini and fusilli into four different pans, which he was sautéing with veg. He flipped his pastas without a thought for me, dodging around me as if I were part of the furniture. I set off with a burning stack of pans, dodging Bébert, who had taken over Jason's station. He was pushing off plates and throwing in little digs at servers who were slow to pick up their orders off the long stainless counter in front of him. I'd quickly understood that I was under no circumstances to touch these plates, not even to move them an inch.

Back at my machine, I soaked the thirty pans I'd picked up and emptied the bucket of greasy water that held a mountain of cutlery in the mire of the dishpit. I started sorting the cutlery, it was hard to imagine I'd ever get to the end of it. There must have been a thousand forks, knives, and spoons. I heard the sounds of pots clanging together and empty backups being thrown down under the pizza oven, which I didn't have time to pick up, and the yells of the cooks: every sound ratcheted up the stress taking hold of me. In the service kitchen they were picking up speed. I could tell that in an hour I'd be in over my head.

Finally I managed to sort all the cutlery, and while I ran it through the machine, for at least two cycles, I filled up a couple of racks with pans and dirty plates.

Once the cutlery was clean I hurried off to the dining room to take it to Nick. On my way back past the front kitchen Bébert ordered me to come pick up pans and "the shit under the oven," which a cook was sorting between two orders. The blond waitress who'd showed me around earlier intercepted me before I could find Nick and snatched the cutlery from my hands.

"About time!"

She was colder and snappier than earlier. She called Nick as she turned around.

Behind her I caught a glimpse of the dining room. It was totally full now, like a concert the moment before the headliners take the stage. The light was even dimmer than when I got there, all you could see was a swarm of shadows milling around, letting out peals of laughter and making extravagant gestures. Little lanterns on the tables illuminated the moving, blurry features of innumerable diners. Ghostlike smiles, implacable expressions, light-coloured shirts and plunging necklines, all in the warm yellow of the scarce light. You could see the silhouettes of servers gliding effortlessly between tables, vigilant and alert.

The woman I'd seen coming out of the basement office was up at the bar. She was settling up with two couples and ordering around the bartender, who was flying all over the place while this other woman calmly joked with her customers, as if they were old school-friends. I didn't know yet, but there was only one bartender,

Sarah, who took orders for the entire restaurant. The other girl, the barback, mixed cocktails and poured pints. Once the couples were on their way, the woman from the office noticed me and gave me a withering look.

"What, want to pull up a stool? Get to work. You shouldn't be out front."

Then she disappeared into the dining room with a bouquet of cheques in her hand. That was when I understood she was the owner. Nick gave me a thumbs up for the cutlery, which he was already polishing, in big handfuls.

I was on my way back to my pit when I got a feeling that one of the customers sitting at the bar was watching me. He'd left his sunglasses on: a massive bald guy in a light suit with a very close shave. He must have been somewhere between fifty and sixty. He was sitting in between two couples with a glass of white wine and a butane lighter in front of him. His hands rested on the first one and then the other cufflink adorning his thick wrists. No one, not even the bartender, seemed to be paying attention to him. I thought of Kingpin in *Daredevil*. It made me smile. I went back to the kitchen.

I manoeuvred between the salad girl and Bébert, and squatted down to pick up the stuff lying on the ground under the pizza oven. The heat was unbearable. Cooks were blindly chucking empty backups without a thought for the dishwasher struggling to gather it all up. I made several trips back and forth between the kitchen and the dishpit with my mess. I struggled to maintain the pace and keep the machine running. Bébert came back periodically with buspans of dirty dishes from the floor. He said he was helping me out because it was my first shift, but I'd have to get faster.

Little by little, I slipped into a sort of trance. As the night went on my every movement became instinctive. Like a machine, I converted dirty dishes into clean. When I checked the time on my pager, covered by an oily film in the pockets of my soaked pants, I could feel that I'd lost track of time a bit. It was already ten. I thought about the prep kitchen waiting to be cleaned, the counters to be washed—my counters—strewn with veg, flour, and puddles of oil, and the giant steam pot full of chicken carcasses I would have to empty and scrub.

It was dizzying. I'd never had so much to do and so little time to do it. Since my shift started there hadn't been a moment's calm, not one second when I felt that I'd gotten on top of the work and the countless individual tasks piling up one on top of the other, broken only by periodic crises, each more acute than the last.

I went down to the basement to tackle the prep kitchen. After portioning out the stock the way Bébert had asked me, I started emptying the steam pot. Little chunks of burning hot chicken crumbled between my fingers as I scrubbed the walls of the giant pot. I had to settle for scraping off the chicken bones with a big perforated metal spoon, the one the cooks called a "spider." I threw it all in a big garbage bag. The grease was splattering my face, and I had little bits of bone all over my skin. The smell of chicken broth at once repelled me and made me hungry. Through the stairwell I could hear Bébert yelling at me to come pick up the dirty dishes. I ran up the stairs, slowed by the two bags slung over my shoulders. Halfway up, one of them split, emitting a juicy gurgling as its contents spilled out behind me. Chicken rib cages, slices of veg, and strips of boiled flesh ran down the staircase like an oozing oily sea. I froze. My cheeks were burning. I ran a greasy hand over my face as I watched this puddle of waste spread out over the steps. I was seriously tempted to give up and run out the back door. I choked back a tear. I felt like an idiot. The voice of my old boss ran through my head, "If your shovel breaks, you use your bare hands." I pulled it together, and ran off to get a dust pan. Bébert appeared at the top of the staircase and swore. I was sure I'd be fired on the spot. He leaped over the spill and came back with the empty lettuce-box.

"Put a garbage bag in there, fast!"

I did as I was told. He started picking up the boiling hot chicken residue with his bare hands. I put down the dustpan and tried to copy Bébert, tried to go as fast as he was.

"Throw coarse salt down on the steps, that'll absorb the fat. Then sweep all this shit up and give the steps a good mop with degreaser."

He let me finish. Went to the cooler and came out with a backup of smoked salmon, and got back to the front kitchen, as if the accident never happened.

It must have been around midnight. The clamour in the dining room seemed to have died down. I was stacking clean dishes on the shelf while the cooks brought back the last of the empty backups and the rest of the greasy containers chucked under the oven during the night's final rush. It was time for one final push. A little later Bébert came back to my dishpit, now almost clear of dirty dishes. He set a pint of beer down on one of the shelves where I stacked clean dishes. His chef's coat was unbuttoned, exposing an old undershirt. With his lips, he pulled a smoke from his pack and lit a match with one finger. I was filling the mop bucket with hot water and degreaser. He watched me work for a minute. He held out his pack. I said I didn't smoke. He shrugged his shoulders. Then he started talking, holding in the smoke.

"The beer's for you, by the way. You earned it."

I reorganized a buspan of coffee cups.

"That wasn't half bad, for a first shift. You're gonna have to pick up the pace a bit, but you look like you'll figure it out."

Just as I was about to thank him, I almost dropped a pile of saucers.

Bébert started giggling. He was leaning against the door, opening it to exhale. Renaud called him from upstairs, said this wasn't Club Med.

"I'm not your bitch, man. Two minutes."

Bébert threw his half-smoked butt through the crack in the door, then slammed it shut. He gave me a tap on the shoulder.

"Seems like you've got some guts. I hope tonight wasn't too much for you."

"No," I managed.

He nodded toward the kitchen.

"Okay, I'm going to go shut that fucker up, then I'll help you finish up here. Kitchen's closed."

I waited till he was gone to take another sip of my pint. I was way thirstier than I thought, and tossed it back in two deep swigs. No beer ever quenched my thirst like that.

When he came back, Bébert scoped the empty glass, and laughed.

"Damn, you're a thirsty kid."

He put down a bucket of kitchen implements and a dented pot. His whole aspect changed. His light eyes were sizing me up.

"What are you doing after?"

"Who, me?"

"Yeah you, fucknuts."

"Uh, I don't know."

Of course I knew. I had to go back to Vincent's apartment. That was one of Malik's conditions. I had to go straight home after work. No setting foot in the bar.

"We're going out for a beer. You in?"

I hesitated. Bébert gave me a big, cocky smile, watching me struggle to answer.

"No, I'm gonna go home. I'm staying with a friend in Ahuntsic, it's pretty far."

The last bus was in under an hour. The eighty bucks Malik had lent me was tucked away in my wallet. The frantic pace of the shift had almost let me forget, but now I thought about it again. It was inevitable. I started cleaning my dishpit.

"Get the night bus, man. There's one that'll take you out there. Go finish your close. You're coming with us."

CHAPTER 4

THE DINING ROOM was empty save five or six couples talking quietly in the light of tiny lanterns scattered like dying embers. Behind the bar Nick kept right on drying wineglasses. The owner was gone. The waitress who had set me up at the beginning of the night was printing out sales reports and folding them into long stacks of paper. Her name was Maude. At one end of the bar a server sat in front of an ashtray, cashing out. At the opposite end the kitchen staff was standing around, finishing their staff drinks. All the tension had been released. Everyone's faces and bodies looked more relaxed, and their voices were softer and more poised. The bartender and the kitchen staff were trading wisecracks and talking about people I didn't know.

I discreetly went over to sit with them. My presence didn't make a ripple in the conversation. I leaned up against the bar and waited to see where the night would take me. My hands were chapped from all the water and detergent. I half listened to the overlapping conversations.

The girl cook was barely recognizable in her civvies. She turned out to be a little punk rocker and was wearing an Iron Maiden *Killers* t-shirt. Her hair fell down over her cheeks in long, spiky tresses, and seemed even deeper purple without her hairnet and cook's hat. Her name was Bonnie. I'd later learn she was an Ontarian who'd come to Montreal three years ago. She was telling a story I had a hard time following in broken, mumbling French. Sarah the barback was listening, and so was Jonathan, the garde-manger who worked next to the pizza oven, where I'd spent most of my shift getting in his way.

As far as I could make out, Bonnie's story was about one time she was walking up Sainte-Catherine and two idiots in a car whistled at her, so she threw her half-drunk latté into their window when the light turned green. While everyone laughed, Renaud said goodnight and buttoned up his coat. With brown hair greying at the tips, he looked like a prematurely aged teenager. Bébert gave him the finger, with a mischievous smile on his lips, which were wrapped around a lit smoke. While she talked I took a closer look at Bonnie's features. She had a little flat nose, and chewed on her bottom lip when she listened to a story. A scar ran down her left cheek to the bottom of her jaw.

Bébert slid his empty glass down the bar toward Sarah, expecting a refill. She rolled her eyes and asked the barback to pour him one last pint.

"You know I'm punching everything in, Bébert," Sarah said as she fingered the little screen.

She was around my height and had long black hair, up in a pony tail that fell right in the middle of her delicate shoulders. Little wrinkles lined the corner of her eyes and a natural pout gave her a bored look. She must have been around three years older than me, but treated me as if a decade or more separated us.

"What about Christian's beers. Do they all get punched in?" asked Bébert, snottily.

The barback poured two pints. She put one down in front of Bébert, and the other in front of me. I stuttered, unsure whether I should take it. I'd already had my staff beer. She smiled as she gave it to me. Her name was Jade, and she welcomed me to the team. Nick gave us a sideways glance as he swung a white cloth over his shoulder, for the glasses. Jade reminded me of someone. I thanked her for the pint and put my coat on. I chugged back my beer to feel the alcohol chase away my inhibitions. Jade asked Sarah something, then went down to the basement. You could hear Jonathan yammering on in a high-pitched voice about medieval role-playing. Bonnie was visibly listening just to be polite.

At the other end of the bar, Maude and the server cashing out were arguing about a cancelled order. She came up and gave us a dirty look, clearly eager for us to be on our way. Jonathan stopped talking and took a final sip of beer. Nick started moving faster, as he sorted and put away the remaining glasses.

"You all know what Séverine thinks about staff camping out at the bar."

Bébert emptied his pint in one swig, mumbling that it was fine, we were on our way out. I hoped Jade would come back up before we left, so I could say bye. Nick looked up to tell us he'd meet up with us after.

"Get moving, it's already almost one."

A few customers were still deep in conversation, lingering as if they had the whole night ahead of them.

Outside we were met by a wet cold. It was below zero again. Bébert took two king cans of Blue Dry out of his backpack.

"Roadpops?"

He passed the first one to Bonnie, and opened the other one. She took a big long sip and then passed it to me.

I grabbed the ice cold can in my ungloved hand, and murmured an inaudible "thank you." She didn't react. Light snow began to fall. There was still plenty of action on the avenue: groups of partiers hailing taxis, walking uncertainly from one street corner to the next, constantly interrupted by hiccups of laughter. The office party season was getting into swing.

From the first sip, the acrid, metallic Labatt Blue coated my mouth. Nothing could be further from the two red ales I'd had earlier. I looked up at the cottony sky. The alcohol was starting to soften me up nicely. The occasional fat snowflake crossed the streetlamps' yellow halo. I told myself that, wherever the night took me, I'd act as if Malik were right there beside me.

Bonnie and Bébert were talking and sharing a smoke. I followed in silence, feeling almost safe in their company. Jonathan was trying to draw me out, chipper as a camp counsellor. He had a baby face and a patchy, downy beard. He was telling me that for my first shift I'd done really well. I said I'd done my best. He asked what I studied, if I'd worked in another restaurant, where I was from. I answered him, newly nervous again and talking fast. But there just wasn't much to say. Graphic design; no; Longueuil. Jonathan looked at me, said, "Okay, cool." When the beer came back around to him he took the can.

I was walking forward, staring at the sky, trying not to think about the eighty dollars in my pocket. I could picture the bright colours of the LCD screen as if they were right in front of my face. I took another sip of the Blue and figured everything would be just fine. The top of the can stunk of tobacco. When you thought about it, Malik would have wanted me to go out and have a beer, see some people.

Our little crew ended up at a place I didn't know, the Roy Bar. As we walked through the heavy door a dozen customers greeted my new companions, as if they'd been waiting for them. Our arrival attracted a little too much attention for my liking, and like a third wheel I had no idea where to stand. One of the bartenders wrapped his tattooed arms around Bonnie and lifted her off the ground. He looked like a beefier version of the kids who used to spend the summer working on tricks and collecting injuries at the Boucherville skate park. The place actually reminded me of the skate park in a lot of ways. The walls were covered in graffiti, the speakers blared Pennywise. A massive plastic hammerhead shark hung over the pool table. The bar was full of baggie-panted dropouts with their hoods up playing eight-ball. The average age couldn't be over thirty. The real regulars, seated in a line along the bar, were in their mid-thirties. They looked like a punk band after the show.

We took our place at a big round table covered in skate stickers. I could feel my boxers, still soaked by the dishwater. Surely the fetid smell of grease was still clinging to me. I threw my bag between two chair legs, discreetly laid the book I'd been carrying in my back pocket on the table, and took my seat with the firm intention of holding my ground until the bar burned down or this night was sucked into a black hole. I was exhausted but almost felt good. The pressure had dropped again.

Bébert did a tour of the room, saying hi to pretty much everyone with handshakes and fist bumps and low fives. He moved from group to group, like a king making the rounds of his fiefdom. You could hear his deep laugh exploding all over the place. I had a look around the room, and was relieved to see not a single VLT. I gently breathed out all the air I'd been collecting in my lungs, and my back muscles relaxed. I unbuttoned the plaid shirt I wore under my coat for extra warmth.

The bartender who had hugged Bonnie was at our table now, placing pints of red ale in front of everyone. Bébert bought the first round.

Nick showed up twenty minutes later, bundled up tight in an $800 leather coat. Jade wasn't with him, nor was anyone else from the floor staff.

"How'd we do?" Bébert asked.

"Sixty-two hundred, man!" Nick answered.

"So you guys made coin. Shooters on you!"

Bébert laughed and called the bartender over.

"Yo Sam: ten vodka shots. On his tab."

Then Bébert turned to Nick.

"Man I can't wait till we get rid of Christian. We're gonna get ours."

Nick gave him the finger and made a face. Then he took off his scarf and coat, and threw them on the back of the chair, and sat next to Bonnie.

"You look nice tonight," she said.

For a second his confidence deserted him. I don't know why, but that gladdened me. At the same time, I figured it would have happened to me as well. And he must have had a good head start over me, with Bonnie. Maybe they were even seeing each other.

The bar was almost full now, and the hum of conversation was getting louder. Bébert and Jonathan were yelling, as if they were still in the front kitchen. The vodka shots showed up. Before we had a chance to put back this round Bébert had already ordered the next. Jack this time, his tab.

As empty pints and shots piled up and everyone around the table got good and drunk, I felt myself lifting off my chair, my body dematerialized. Everything had had the gravity sucked out of it. Bonnie was making a train wreck of a joke, in her crooked-ass French. Bébert and Jonathan were already cracking up. Nick was resting his arm on the back of Bonnie's chair. They were getting ready to toast, had already ordered a round of Irish Car Bombs. At this place they were called Val-Alain's, after the town where one of the bartenders ran off the road on the long drive home from a night drinking in Quebec City. The guys were swapping kitchen stories in voices hoarse from yelling all through the shift. They'd worked together at Tasso, Jonathan told me. Instead of medieval role-playing, he was telling me about his recipe for short ribs in stout. One of his friends was laughing his head off because some idiot server ordered a lamb shank rare. Bébert's obsession with Christian showed no sign of abating. He couldn't get over the man's incompetence. I was sure he was exaggerating. Nick just nodded along, while he ground up a bud in his hand under the table. I sat in silence, smelling like a dumpster.

I watched these people consumed by the joy of making it through another rush. I'd already drunk more than at my last Cegep party. But this was just an average night for them. Rancid was blasting on the sound system. Bébert turned to me, lighting a smoke.

"Is it good?" he asked, picking my book up off the table.

It was August Derleth, *The Trail of Cthulu*. I'd found it at the giant cheap used book store by the bus station. Tibor Csernus illustrated the cover.

"Not bad. You know Lovecraft?"

"I don't really read. But I had an ex who used to read all the time. She'd read all those Kun ... ends with an A ..."

"Kundera?"

"Yeah. That's it."

"I've never read him. I'm more into SciFi and Fantasy."

"Dave told me you draw comics. That true?"

"Dave told you that?"

I kept stealing glances at Bonnie over the dark pints on the table. She was staring at Bébert, and he was avoiding her glance. He was pretending to watch Rodney Mullen ripping through some L.A. skatepark on TV. Bonnie was starting to have a hard time sitting up straight in her chair. Nick now had his arm squarely around her shoulder. She wasn't even trying to speak French anymore.

"Yeah. He said you were an amazing drawer."

"He's exaggerating. I'm studying graphic design at Cegep."

"Oh, okay."

"I just got my first real job. An album cover."

"Cool."

"Yeah, for a group called Deathgaze. You know them?"

Bébert shook his head and blew out smoke.

"What Cegep you go to?"

"Vieux-Montréal."

Bébert broke out laughing.

"Did you go there too?"

"You could say that."

"What'd you study?"

"I majored in fucking up. I was dealing back then, and heavy into pills. That's pretty much what I did in college."

I couldn't think of what to say to that. The booze had more or less sucked all the life out of me. I forgot where I was for a second. Everything went dim; the lights on the ceiling and along the wall seemed to stop shining. The TVs showed nothing but snow. The air grew heavy. Cigarette smoke filled the room. A bartender stood up on the bar and yelled out Last Call. I lifted up my head, and wondered if I hadn't fallen asleep. Bonnie was up at the bar, on a stool, talking to the bartender. You couldn't tell who was hitting on whom. Nick was staring at his pint in annoyance, an empty look in his eye and a joint tucked behind his ear. Bébert slapped the table with open palms.

"Let's finish her up at an after-hours."

"How about the Aria?" Nick suggested.

I barely managed to get out of my chair. We all left together: Bébert, Nick, and me.

Outside the snow had stopped. A thin blanket covered the ground, crunching under our footsteps. The cold worked its way into my damp clothing. Jonathan and his friends were walking behind Nick, who had lighted up his joint. Bébert was in front, hands tucked into his unzipped coat and a smoke in his mouth. We could hear him rapping something. I couldn't really follow it. We crossed Saint-Denis. Bébert cursed out a cop car that had brushed him as we turned onto Roy. Three blocks up I caught sight of a night bus going my way. I said goodbye and stumbled over to the closest stop. The wind was buffeting me and my clothes were starting to freeze solid. I was relieved not to wait too long, I would surely have caught a cold. The massive, luminous form slowed and pulled up to the sidewalk. I got on and went to collapse in a seat at the back. Pulled my Walkman from my backpack and spent five minutes trying to untangle the headphones. My head was spinning. It wasn't unpleasant. I looked out the window. Even after three a.m., Saint-Denis refused to give up the ghost. Neil Young's weepy guitar was ringing in my ears, the instrumental bridge of "Change your Mind" went on and on. I was just lucid enough to make it home, and was proud of myself. I had a job, and I hadn't spent all the money Malik had given me, just twenty bucks, no more. And I hadn't gambled.

On the bench across from me two girls, not much older than me, were chatting, laughing at some interminable story. An old man stared at an invisible point in front of him, mittens lying forgotten on his thighs. A few seats farther on, a forty-year-old guy was slumbering, navy-blue coveralls open over a massive paunch, thick hand on a plastic lunch box. His tanned face was red from the cold. We passed Rosemont and I fell asleep, hugging myself, marinating in the smells of burnt olive oil and degreaser.

CHAPTER 5

THE TROUBLE started at the end of September, long before I was forced to skip my apartment and crash at Vincent's.

I started doing less and less work for school and instead gambled away my rent for August, and then September, and finally October in long, listless afternoons in front of video poker machines in deserted taverns and strip clubs. There was the Fun Spot on Ontario out past Amherst, and the Axe on Saint-Denis below Ontario, and when I left Marie-Lou's around one in the afternoon there was Brasserie Cherrier not far from the Lafleur hot dog joint. I drank beer that tasted like dish soap and burned through twenty-dollar bills until I was down to my last quarter, in the hope that finally, in the nine squares that filled the screen, the bells would align in a cross and the payout pour forth. I almost never won. What was worse, during those three months I lost more than the previous six. I still hadn't figured out that the more you gamble, the more you lose. I was gambling pretty much every day.

October was the low point: an agonizing month of alternating bursts of angst and surges of euphoria. There were schemes to avoid paying rent. Then two thousand dollars from Deathgaze. Then the gambling cravings came on stronger, stronger even than the ones that had made me lose everything I'd saved that summer. A crescendo of intensity followed by a precipitous comedown. November: Me fleeing the apartment under Rémi's threats. Me in the afternoon, alone at Marie-Lou's, searching through her stuff to steal her tip money to go out and gamble. Me desperately looking for a job. The skipped classes accumulating. Nothing able to sustain my interest. A single thing—gambling—able to hold my attention. Especially during those long rainy nights, lost on the West Island or out in Lasalle, going door-to-door, hoping to sell at least one goddamn alarm system and finally lay my hands on a commission. The team leader repeated it like a mantra: one sale, one hundred dollars; two sales, three hundred dollars. It was as simple as that. But I didn't sell a single system. I'd finish my night in a foul mood, coat soaked through by glacial rain, freezing from the roots of my hair to my toes, more spent than after a twelve-hour labouring shift, my mind numb and my ears, despite the silent headphones, filled with a mild but unrelenting buzzing that afflicted me from the moment the team leader dropped us off at Lionel Groulx Metro station until I got home to Marie-Lou's or Vincent's. It was then, when the day's possibilities were exhausted, that I would find myself empty-handed and haunted by my debts. In my mind there was no other answer. I had to gamble. I needed a fresh start.

One night, around November 10, I couldn't take anymore. I called Malik.

"Something wrong?" he said when he heard my voice.

Vincent was at his girlfriend's. I went and sat on the sofa with the cordless phone.

"Are you coming to Montreal anytime soon?" I asked.

Malik moved. I heard him fumbling through his kitchen drawers.

"Maybe next weekend. Why? Are you okay?"

I could hear a dish being set down in the sink, water pouring from the tap. My mouth was dry. I hadn't eaten since morning. I cleared my throat and asked him:

"Do you think we could hang out?"

"For sure. Since when do we not hang out when I'm in town? Man, you're being weird."

He was putting dishes away, opening and closing kitchen cupboards. I could picture his apartment. I wished I could be at his place, far from Montreal, far from my life. We'd make nachos, drink some beers, watch a movie, maybe play chess. I could hear him trying to figure out what to say next. There were no more sounds on the other end of the line.

"What's going on? What's up with you?"

I took a deep breath.

"I'm in trouble. I need some cash."

He stayed quiet for a little while. I heard a barely audible sigh.

"You need some cash, eh?" he finally said.

I had hot flashes. I was sitting on the end of the sofa. He asked me why.

"It's complicated. That's why I want to hang out. I got kicked out of my apartment. I'm kind of fucked here."

"What? What's going on? Where are you?"

"I can't really explain it all over the phone."

My voice started shaking.

"I'm at Vincent's. We have to have a real talk. Not long-distance, it'll cost too much. When are you going to be in Montreal?"

"Tomorrow if I have to. What time?"

"Uh, I don't know. Don't you have class tomorrow? I don't want to screw up your schedule…"

"My cousin's more important than my classes. Pick a time."

We decided to meet the next afternoon. He had some stuff to take care of at the university in the morning, then he'd drive to Montreal. He could be there around two. He'd pick me up at Vincent's. We'd go somewhere nearby to talk. I was relieved. Malik would definitely lend me some cash. I was almost looking forward to it. I was so exhausted I fell into a deep sleep, right there on the sofa, fully dressed.

The next day around noon I started waiting for Malik. He showed up a little late, around two-thirty. When I got in his VW Golf, *Symphony of Enchanted Lands* was playing for what must have been the ten-thousandth time. We went driving around town in the rain, kind of randomly. It felt like he was trying to cheer me up. We stopped at a red light.

"Do you know where you want to go? You hungry? I haven't had lunch."

I suggested getting out of the city and going to the Georges in Longueuil. I was hungry. All I'd had to eat was two pieces of toast and peanut butter, and a few sips of Sunny Delight.

He drove to Papineau to take the Jacques Cartier Bridge. I felt a shiver as we crossed Ontario. But as soon as we were safely across the bridge I felt better. He took the backstreets instead of the 132 to Roland-Therrien. We parked in front of what used to be the ice cream bar. It was drizzling here too. We went in. A waitress in a white shirt and bartender's belt was reading a newspaper next to the till. Aside from a few ageing truckers chatting over their club sandwiches we were the only ones there. We took a booth by the wall covered in framed photos. The owner fishing. The owner with Céline Dion, in front of a hotel. The owner with Ginette Reno. The owner with Claude Blanchard in front of a white Cadillac. The owner with Peter Falk in some kind of casino.

Malik ordered coffee right away.

"All right, what's up, man? It sounded serious."

He took two sugars and emptied them into his cup. I flipped through the menu for a while. I knew it by heart.

"You already know what you want?"

"Yeah," he said. "So are you gonna tell me what's up?"

I put the menu down on the table. The waitress came back. She took our orders. Pizza-ghetti for me; a sub for Malik. I looked outside. Across the 132 the St. Lawrence River looked grey and sad. In the distance the Olympic Stadium's tower disappeared into the rainclouds.

"Rémi kicked me out of the apartment."

I could feel Malik staring at me. I kept looking out the window.

"It's been messed up ever since school started, in the apartment. One of Rémi's buddies is always crashing in the living room. I asked him to pay me back a bit of rent from September and October, since this other guy is taking up part of my space, eating my food. He was all 'no way.' Said if I didn't like it I could leave."

Malik scratched his forehead and sniffled.

"Is your name on the lease?"

"No."

"Hmmm."

He put one more cream in his coffee.

"I'm in trouble, man," I said. "I'm totally broke and I've got no place to live."

I was fiddling with a corner of the paper napkin. My stomach was grumbling. I started sweating, could feel it running down my sides. I was overdoing it. Malik coughed a bit.

"And your friend Alex, didn't you say he was paying you for the album cover?"

"Yeah but they aren't going to pay me till it's done. That'll be like after Christmas."

"Huh."

Malik took a sip of coffee. He was calm, his face relaxed. I was nervous as hell, but trying not to let it show.

"So there's November's rent. What happened to December?"

I really wanted the food to get here. I started tearing my napkin into strips.

"I paid Rémi in advance. And he's not gonna give it back to me either."

"What was your share of the rent? Three hundred? Four hundred?"

"Around four hundred. With Hydro."

He nodded. He'd finished his coffee.

"What's with all the questions, man? I'm broke. Why are you asking me about money like this? I don't have any."

"You worked your ass off all summer. What'd you make? Four grand?"

"Nah, not that much."

My heart was beating at my temples. Malik put his empty cup down.

"Well, you were making eleven bucks an hour, forty hours a week, from May to August. After tax it must have been close to that. Four grand. I'm lowballing here. Even if Rémi stole sixteen hundred in rent, and you spent a few hundred to eat and go out for beers, I don't see how you could be broke already. It's not even December."

Outside it already seemed to have gotten dark. The air was thickening, compressing itself against us, against me. Clouds of fog were rolling into the restaurant and swirling around us. I looked him in the eyes.

"I need some cash, man."

"Why? You should have a nice chunk left in your account."

Images of *Crazy Bells* danced before me. I wasn't hungry anymore. I could see the bright colours rolling out before my eyes.

"Yo. I'm talking to you, man."

He was angry. His anger was quiet, undramatic.

"Anyway, I'm not lending you a penny unless you tell me how you managed to spend all your money. I need you to tell me what's going on. Before I lose my patience. Your story doesn't add up, man."

I couldn't see anything anymore. Outside, a foggy darkness had descended, engulfing the river, the highway and the parking lot and everything in its path. I felt at once empty and heavy. I looked down and said:

"I gambled. I gambled it all away."

Our food was getting cold. I looked up. I might have cried. I don't remember anymore. Malik scrunched up his eyebrows, as if he hadn't understood.

"You gambled it all away? What do you mean, you gambled it all away?"

I took a deep breath and then told him about the machines. He listened, with his arms folded, leaning against the table, flabbergasted. He'd been expecting some kind of confession, but not that. I told him I didn't know what to do. Malik rubbed his face and eyes. His lips were pinched tight. He sighed. He got up and went outside for a breath of fresh air. When he came back he started poking his sub with a fork.

"This is utter horseshit," he said, chewing his food. "Who knows about this?"

"No one." I hesitated a minute. "No one except you and Marie-Lou."

"Did you ask her for money?"

I still hadn't managed to take a bite of my food. I didn't answer.

"Does she know you gambled with her money?"

He was really chowing down now. He didn't take his eyes off me.

"No," I answered. "She doesn't know. She thinks she's helping me out of a jam. I promised to pay her back as soon as I could."

Malik wiped his face with a napkin.

"You have to tell your parents."

"No. I can't."

Malik thought about that. The waitress came by, and asked if I was enjoying my meal. I said I was.

"I have to go back to Trois-Rivières tonight. I'm going to lend you enough to live until Friday. But I need you to keep your receipts. You buy a fucking pack of gum, I want a receipt. On Friday I'm coming back to town. Then I'm going to take you back to Trois-Rivières for a few days. It'll be a change of scenery. We'll have a serious fucking talk. Between now and then, get your shit together. Get a job."

"I'm already looking."

"Look harder."

He asked the waitress for another coffee.

"Do you owe Vincent money too?"

"A little."

"Shit."

He looked bummed out.

"Okay, c'mon, eat, man."

The bolognaise sauce was turning my stomach while it whet my appetite. I picked at my food. He lifted his cup to his mouth.

"And don't you ever lie to my face like that again."

I nodded.

I managed to get through my meal. He paid for us both and drove me back to Ahuntsic without exchanging a word. We spent a few minutes in front of Vincent's apartment. You could see the light through the living room window. Malik was flipping through his CDs.

"Okay, try to get your head together now. Get going on your project with your friend Alex, catch up with your classes, draw, read, whatever man, do whatever you gotta do to keep busy. And stay the hell away from the bar."

"Okay, don't worry."

My voice was gone. My muscles hurt. I felt like I was catching a cold.

"Give me Vincent's number so I can call you. I'll call you Thursday."

"You've got my pager number."

"Just give me the number, man."

His tone was harsh again. I gave him the number.

I waited a minute in the warmth of the car. Our gazes got lost in the traffic lights farther off on Henri-Bourassa. I felt like crying. Malik could tell. He grabbed my shoulder.

"Hey, hey, hey. Don't start crying in my car. It's gonna be okay, man."

I thanked him for everything he'd done and got out of the car. Malik got out too.

"Hold on, come here."

He came up to me and gave me a hug.

"See you Friday."

"Yeah," I said. "Friday."

CHAPTER 6

I woke up feeling like I'd been run over by a steamroller. Grey daylight was creeping through the cracks in the venetian blinds. The fridge was growling like a lawnmower. I rolled over onto myself, still half unconscious. I could hear the cars driving by on Henri-Bourassa, making a swishing sound. I opened my swollen eyelids and rubbed my face and eyes at length. My pants were still wet and greasy. Three-forty p.m. I'd missed two more classes. It almost didn't bother me anymore. I chased the thought from my mind. Getting up was painful, so I sat down and pulled myself up with my arms. I yawned and looked around to see if Vincent was there. His boots weren't on the hall rug. My hangover wasn't as bad as I'd feared, but my muscles ached, and my back was all bent out of shape, like after my first construction shift last summer. I still reeked of cooking oil and mop water. I got up off the sofa with a frown and pulled on a pair of jeans whose leg was sticking out of my backpack. Spent a few minutes wandering around the empty, silent apartment. I glanced at Vincent's room. His bed had been made in a hurry, and then I remembered hearing him leave that morning. His bench press was covered in dirty laundry. On his bedside table was a bottle of Givenchy cologne, a track and field trophy, some gold chains and a photo of his girlfriend Janine. On the floor lay his soccer bag, a pair of beat-up indoor shoes beside it. The dreary day cast a feeble light on the messy room. I went to the kitchen and checked out the fridge—nearly empty. A shrivelled-up pepper, some old Chinese macaroni in a Tupperware, two Molson Drys and a two-litre of Sprite. I took out the green plastic bottle of pop and opened it, with almost no whoosh of carbonation, and took a few long flat sips as I searched through the cupboards for something else to eat. On the counter there was a little barrel of protein shake. No cereal, no bread, no fruit. I ended up grabbing a handful of Fudgee-Os from a cupboard and went back to the living room with the box.

After a few minutes' hesitation I sat down in front of the computer. I checked my Hotmail. There was an email from Alex, already a week old. I opened it and read it for a second time. "Hey man. Hope you're good, and 'inspired.' Ha ha. Anyway, looking forward to seeing what you've got. I sent you the lyrics you asked for. Mike wants to see how it's going. At least the logo?"

The last two sentences sent shivers up my spine. I read the email one more time, as if the answer to the riddle lay somewhere between the lines. Took a deep breath, clicked on "Reply," and exhaled a thin puff of air. "Hey Alex, I'm super busy with the end of my term but I'm making some progress on the illustration and the logo. And I called a few printers, and found one you guys can afford. I haven't scanned it yet, but I'm looking forward to showing you guys. See you."

I hit "Send" and closed Explorer, then got up.

The apartment felt emptier and even more depressing. Muffled sounds rose up from deep in the building, inaudible conversations, creaking floors, toilets flushing, ghostly rumours that were almost enough to convince me I wasn't the only person waking up in the middle of the afternoon while everyone else was off working or studying. I spent a minute standing in front of the living room window, with a view of Henri-Bourassa. The two-litre of Sprite was still in my hand, as I watched the sad snow falling and cars driving over asphalt covered by a layer of slush the colour of anthracite. Across the boulevard was a public housing project. Christmas decorations blinked joylessly on balconies the size of rabbit hutches. I was preparing to emerge just as the day began to fade to bluish dusk.

My body was at once numb and in pain. My stomach was growling, disagreeing with the artificial chocolate in the cookies. I went to pick my pager off the couch and came back to my perch at the window. 4:42. I pieced together the memory of last night at the restaurant. The faces of the various people I'd met appeared before me in a parade. I remembered Jade's. I felt stupid for stuttering in front of her. Then there was Bonnie, with her pouty grin and scars. Something about her reminded me of Marie-Lou.

I moved away from the window. The bottle of Sprite was empty. I tried to read a few pages of the Derleth I'd started, but just put the book down, unable to get through even a paragraph.

I went for a shower. My skin was still greasy from the oil, covered in crumbs of burnt food. I was searching for something deep inside myself, some ingenious feint or counterattack or firewall to counteract what I could feel bubbling up slowly within me. As the steaming-hot water poured over me, I voiced my thoughts out loud: "It'd be nice if Vincent came straight home after class."

When I got out of the bathroom the winter night had plunged the apartment into premature darkness. I got dressed and checked my pager. Marie-Lou had left a message, wanted to know how my training had gone. I couldn't summon the courage to call her. I sat down at the kitchen table and took out my Canson pad and graphite pencils. Tried to draw a bit, but every line came out ugly and wrong. I gave up after twenty minutes.

5:40. Vincent still wasn't back from school, and I was getting antsy, nervous. The crisis was brewing. Every once in a while palpitations started and I would feel something in my chest, and my temples would get boiling hot. No message. No Vincent.

It felt like I was choking. I went through the pockets of my pants from last night and pulled out the money I had left, around sixty dollars. I put my keys in my pocket and threw on my coat and my headphones.

The hallway smelled of washing, fried onions, and cat piss. My footsteps thumped despite the ancient, chewed-up, greyish carpet runner. I buttoned up my flannel shirt and went out of the building and into the cold, humid air. Then I turned the music on. With Maiden's "Killers" in my ears I walked quickly down Henri-Bourassa toward the Metro, as if pursued by an evil creature. I cranked the volume to drown out the car sounds, and maybe the voices in my head. I walked past wanly lit laundromats, hair salon windows with photos of models faded by years of sunlight, a tavern I'd noticed a few weeks ago. I walked past Haitian women bundled up in eight layers of coats, their faces three-quarters hidden under wool scarves, and past labourers smoking as they walked, frowning from the cold and looking generally pissed off. Their tool belts hung under their coats, and a clinking of metal marked the rhythm of their footsteps.

I kept my hands stuffed in my coat pockets and scrunched up my eyebrows, my face buffeted by heavy winds bearing melting snow. I walked past the tavern. I felt the rays of the " VIDEO LOTTERY" sign searing my skin. An overpowering wave of vertigo threw me off balance. It felt like sharp needles caressing me under the eyelids. I checked myself and kept walking down to the 99-cent pizza place by the Metro station.

I walked into the over-bright room. Behind the counter two dark-skinned guys were watching American soaps on TV. I ordered dinner and scarfed down two slices with bacon, trying to read Isaac Asimov's *Robots*. I'd borrowed it from my dad last time I went over for dinner. The cover was by Caza, an artist I liked.

Next to me a bunch of Grade Eight or Nine kids were having a high-pitched, animated conversation in a mix of French and English, while a mother in a sari was lecturing her eldest, who was running around one of the tables hyped up on sugar. I'd brought the Asimov to give me a break, but was finding it even harder to read than the Derleth. I felt my pager go off in my jeans. A voice message. I drained my root beer and headed out to the pay phone by the front door of the pizza place. Two new voice messages.

The first was Christian asking me to work the next day at four. Then came Vincent, who was hard to understand but wanted to make sure I had my key. He also let me know he was spending the night at Janine's. I swore and hung up without even clearing out my inbox. I pushed the glass door and found myself out on the sidewalk. It felt colder now. The humidity was working its way under my coat. I looked around at the people hurrying by, a parade of faceless creatures under the falling snow which had started coming down harder now. I'd so often sought out solitude, to draw and read and listen to music. Today it seemed the most unbearable thing in the world.

I started walking toward Vincent's apartment. In my head I was trying to organize my evening, the night ahead, fill it up with stuff to do. I'd work on the illustrations for the band. Catch up on my homework. I'd get started on Alan Moore's *From Hell*, play a little *Twisted Metal* on Vincent's PlayStation. Okay, I'd play a lot of *Twisted Metal*. I'd play *Twisted Metal* until I keeled over and fell asleep.

I was walking on the same side of Henri-Bourassa, being passed by buses trudging eastward in a spray of slush. The cold was biting now. I thought about the impending holidays, the family reunions that brought every year to a close. I thought about everything that no longer seemed to make sense anymore.

I gave the door a push. The soles of my feet clacked on the tile floor. I pulled up a stool, sat down, and pushed a twenty-dollar bill into the slot in the machine. It sucked it up on the first try. I kept another twenty handy for beers. On the first round not one seven or a single cherry came to rest in the squares. Nothing but fruit. Nothing that paid. But I stayed glued to my stool and kept right on betting.

The waitress pulled me out of my trance. Only then did I look around and take in my surroundings. A shitty bar without a shred of character, white walls plastered with Budweiser posters, a juke-box that spat out any coins you put in it, and, at the back, a melamine bar in front of a mirror that looked ready to fall over. Two taps, a few bottles of liquor—barely a starter's kit. Not a single customer. I ordered a glass of beer. She brought it on a tray. I paid with a twenty and left a big tip.

I bet with the recklessness that steals over you as you ride out the initial surge of momentum. I nearly lost it all, then won my twenty dollars back, then lost it again, then doubled my money. My credits seesawed up and down on the counter in front of me. I felt like I was somehow swelling up all over. Between bets I'd take tiny sips of beer. When the bells lined up in a cross formation, I drained what was left in my glass and ordered another. For the next fifteen minutes, every bell would compound my initial bet. Time dilated, like every time I went on a winning streak. The following minutes would be long, drawn out, electric. I was borne up on powerful waves of euphoria. My heart was pumping lava, my eyes were melting in their orbits, contracted to two small burning orbs unable to see anything beyond the lucky sequences stacking one atop the next.

Then it ended. I came back down to terra firma. I counted my wins and managed to pull myself away. It took a superhuman effort to turn away from the machine, like turning your back on the Garden of Eden. I printed my ticket and went to cash out at the bar. Two hundred and ten dollars. In a surfeit of enthusiasm I decided to do a shooter with the waitress, who was twice as old as me. She poured them without asking any questions, accustomed to stumblebums, crackpots, and sad sacks of every description.

I went outside. The boulevard now seemed calm as a sea of ice. Noises reached me from afar, as if muted by endorphins. I retraced my steps to the apartment, reinvigorated as if I'd slept three days on end. I was singing at the top of my lungs along with my Walkman. The anxiousness that had crushed me all afternoon was gone. I was incandescent, blissful. A single star had risen in the sky and was shining its singular light on me.

I returned to Vincent's with my money in my pocket. I didn't go out again that night. I read *From Hell* and drank two tall glasses of water, then turned out all the lights in the living room and stretched out on the sofa for the night wrapped up in a flannel blanket. It took a while to fall asleep. I tossed, and turned, and sweated before finally going under, after an hour or two, lulled to sleep by the bad movie playing in my agitated dreams. This slow comedown that always came on the heels of the violent ecstasy of a win was a familiar state. Twenty dollars, two-hundred and ten— it didn't matter how much you won. That's kind of the problem. For a gambler, the books just never balance.

CHAPTER 7

THE ICE CREAM STAND was wedged between the Georges diner and the Club International video store. In summer we'd stop in after dinner or on our way home from renting a Nintendo game for the weekend. Squeezed into the tiny room was a soft-serve machine that roared like an engine, a counter with a cash register, and a refrigerated display case of ice cream buckets. I always got pistachio. It was so cramped I never failed to wonder why they'd jammed what looked like an old arcade game into a corner, where it didn't seem to be doing much beyond taking up space sorely needed by customers waiting to order. Each side of the machine was painted with a big jack of spades, and on the screen, in eight-bit colour, a five-card hand refreshed at regular intervals. No one ever really played. Once, as I waited for my cone, I tried pushing a few buttons and my Mum told me to knock it off. She said it was a video game for grownups. The idea seemed preposterous. I thought it looked boring for a video game. Cards were boring to begin with, and turning them into a video game wouldn't make it any more exciting. I stared at the screen, with its strawberry-red hearts and king of spades flickering weakly. It all looked so drab and pathetic next to *Mega Man* and *Final Fantasy*.

In all the times we went for ice cream I only ever saw one person playing, a woman in her late forties. She was perched on a stool in front of the screen. Her legs were crossed and her elbows rested on the stool back. She was smoking Players. I could tell from the smell. One of my uncles who spent a lot of time at our house smoked the same brand. She was sipping coffee in a Styrofoam cup. Her hair was creped and her wrists weighed down by brace-lets that jingled together with every move, and she was tanned like a snowbird home for Christmas. The woman kept one eye half-closed to shield it from cigarette smoke. Every once in a while she'd press one of the buttons, unhurriedly, as if acting only after long and careful thought.

Just when we were about to leave with our ice cream cones, she picked up her yellow plastic lighter and pack of smokes and stepped down from her perch. Her flip-flops snapped on the tile floor. She spoke to the counter boy in a gruff voice. He handed her some money. She slid it into her purse. I asked my mum what was happening. She said the woman must have won. I took a long last look at the arcade game and we went out the door with our ice cream cones.

In time those early machines were replaced with new ones by Loto-Québec. The new generation looked more like slot machines than arcade games. Not the 100% mechanical kind with a big han-dle you pulled, like grandfather clocks in their shiny red lacquered metal case with a glass screen where you beheld twirling fruits and number sevens in the vivid hues of billiard balls. No: The first generation of machines Loto-Québec rolled out in bars all over the province looked like a video game version of the one-armed bandit you found at casinos. At the very least, they possessed the same hypnotic power. In the early 2000s they started cropping up everywhere. There they were one day, lined up along the walls of bars and taverns like pop machines.

The games would scroll by on the screen, each in its own radi-ant colours: crimson red, acid yellow, fluorescent green. It was enough to draw in gamblers and get them onto a stool in front of the machine. Just one game. That siren call was enough to reel me in and get my own ass parked on a stool in front of the machine for countless games. I'd insert a bill and it would be converted to credits, just like the way you got a certain number of lives in video games. Loto-Québec changed that over the years as well: it made it too easy to forget how much we were going to lose. Then, you chose a game on the touch screen, and the plastic buttons would light up like the dashboard on the *Nostromo* in *Alien*. You could set your bet and launch the game either by pressing the buttons or the squares on the screen. You could even bring the digital spin to a premature halt. Loto-Québec nixed that as well. It gave players a misleading impression that they could influence the game's random outcome, and that made the anti-gambling warnings above the screen even more hypocritical. The Loto-Québec machines took anything, from hundred-dollar bills right down to the last quarter you could dig out of your pocket. Because on those machines, unlike their ancestors in the ice-cream stands and corner stores, you could play lots of different games: *Keno, Poker, 7s Wild, Crazy Bells*, and plenty more. On some games the minimum bet was just a nickel. But no bet is so small it can't fuel the fantasy of new beginnings. I've won $184 after popping a single toonie in the slot. In the early years after Loto-Québec took over the VLT racket, machines started showing up all over the place. Today you don't find as many in bars. I'm pretty sure Loto-Québec has changed the algorithms so the wins are smaller and less frequent. It's not a theory I'm about to put to the test. There are things I'll talk about in this story I'd never be stupid enough to try again, even after all these years. At the end of the day it doesn't matter how much you win, or how often; every gambler pays the same price.

CHAPTER 8

I'D SPENT a futile night mulling over the same worries while the same images ran through my head. Christmas. Family time. My crazy new job. Malik worrying about me. The guys in the band waiting on me for drawings that were going nowhere. Marie-Lou pissed off when I admitted I'd been gambling. Debts, promises, lies; money, more debts. I'd need to win ten times more than I had the night before, but there wasn't a machine in the world that paid out that big. I could see that I was going to break my word, and somehow lie to Malik, and the guilt was eating away at me.

That morning, exhausted, I'd fallen into an uneasy sleep, with a dream cycling in a loop. In my dream I won, and then lost, and then won again, in bars I'd never been to but recognized as if I'd always known them. Marie-Lou was there too, trying to find me, but I'd always sneak out the back without even bothering to pick up my winnings.

I yawned and stretched. I didn't dare take out the wad of bills stuffed in my jeans pockets. The TV was still on with the sound off, bathing the living room in its blue gleam. You could hear the steady hum of traffic on Henri-Bourassa. My pager said 10:21; time to get moving. I got up off the couch and rummaged through one of my plastic bags, looking for clean clothes. The apartment's central heating was throwing that dry heat that makes your nose bleed. I wasn't sure working in restaurants was exactly right for me in the long run, but for now I didn't really have a choice. Above all it would keep me busy. There was no guarantee Vincent would come home tonight, and I'd lost his girlfriend's number. I tried his cell phone, but he was always out of minutes. No answer. I left a message and then took a shower. It seemed like my skin was still impregnated with the smells of the night before last, like I still reeked of that special blend of garbage juice, detergent, and fried food.

As I got out of the shower I saw someone had left a message on my beeper. I went to check, sure it must be Vincent.

Instead I recognized Malik's voice, and I had to sit down to take in what he was saying. He wanted to see how I was, and let me know he'd be in town sooner than anticipated. He'd be here the day after tomorrow, for sure, and wanted to see me. I could call him when I got the chance. I hung up and thought a minute. I decided to wait before calling him back. Last night's slip-up was still weighing too heavily on me, I wasn't ready to talk to him. I'd call him tomorrow, or later today.

I was hungry. I went to have a look in the fridge. Nothing. I would have to leave soon if I wanted to grab a bite before work. I thought about Bonnie. I put on my last clean pair of jeans and a Maiden t-shirt, to show my colours if I got the chance. I hoped she'd be working.

I started picking up my stuff. Went through my tapes laid out on the coffee table next to the PlayStation game boxes and my sketchbooks. I took the mixtape Marie-Lou had made me out of my Walkman—Dark Tranquility, The Haunted, In Flames, and Samael—and put in another, seriously worn out from hours of use, with my favourite tracks from Bruce Dickinson's *Chemical Wedding* intercut with a couple songs from Neil Young's *Sleeps with Angels*, and a long blues number by the Allman Brothers, "In Memory of Elizabeth Reed," followed by "Sleeping Village" and "Warning" from the first Sabbath. I changed my Walkman batteries and put in the tape.

I stuffed my work pants into my backpack—they were stiff with caked-on food—along with a pair of clean boxers, just in case

I was soaked at the end of my shift again. Also an extra t-shirt, while I was at it, to wear under my work shirt. I didn't want to make the same mistake as last time.

My hunger was giving me a migraine. In the pile of bus schedules on the hall stand I found one for the No. 69, and checked the time for the next bus. I did a final sweep of the living room to make sure I hadn't forgotten anything. By the sofa leg, next to an empty bowl of chips, I saw the Derleth. I picked it up and worked it into my jean pocket. Then I grabbed my flannel shirt and my coat. With my bag slung over my shoulder, I left the apartment, locking the door behind me.

The cold was harsh. Last night's humidity had subsided. The sun hadn't come out. It was one of those days when you start feeling the onset of night around midday. The snowbanks were blue; the building walls orange. A mum and her three kids were already waiting for the bus. I turned up my Walkman to drown out everything else. I couldn't stop thinking about the wad of cash in my pocket. The No. 69 eventually rolled up. Ten passengers got off, but the bus was still packed. I found a seat, shoved between a guy whose fat cement-coloured face stuck out of his peacoat like a shapeless excrescence and a Haitian woman around my age in leopard-print leggings, who was arguing with someone on her cell phone.

At Henri-Bourassa station I let the crowds sweep me along into the Metro and onto the platform, carried by the constant flow of the passengers. I managed to sit and tried to get some reading done, for the rest of the ride. I didn't even have time for ten lines when the shaking of the Metro car made me nauseous. Rob Halford's cover of "The Wizard" was winding down, and then "The Book of Thel" came on. The intro hit me just as powerfully as the first time I heard it. The rumbling in my stomach grew stronger, and a gnawing hunger was making me impatient. I climbed the escalator as fast as I could and headed out into the orange light. People were walking quickly, noses shoved in scarves. The Christmas-tree sellers had set up their stand, and the smell of fir trees filled the air all around the Metro station. City employees were putting Christmas decorations up on lampposts. I noticed the spot where Malik had dropped me off two days earlier. It felt like a whole week had passed.

I saw the Desjardins credit union almost across from the Metro, on the corner of Rivard. I decided to deposit my money. It would be safer in my account than in my pocket. There were no guarantees, but it was better than nothing.

I went inside. It was packed. Only one ATM was working. I joined the long line of people waiting. An employee was showing an old man how to deposit a cheque. Ten minutes passed and the line didn't move an inch. I let it go. I could come back after eating.

At the Fameux diner I ate an Italian Poutine and then, hunger sated, read a bit, enjoying the deli's warmth. When the waitress brought my bill I figured that, since I was in the neighbourhood, I may as well go check out the new arrivals at the record store. Free Son and Millennium were nearby.

It wasn't until I rang the bell at the restaurant, two hours later, that I realized I'd forgotten to deposit my money. I swore loudly just as Renaud opened for me.

"Calm down, kid. It's not that cold."

I stuttered something, tried to explain that I wasn't swearing at him.

"It's all good, get in here," he said, not listening.

I walked into the brutally lit dishpit. The machine was wide open, and you could hear a slow rain of drips falling into the water. A rack of dishes was drying. The pit was in an even sorrier state than last time. Everything had been stuffed in big stacks on a caddy whose sides were glossy with grease, varnished in dirty cooking oil, and dotted with dried, burnt bits of bread crust. The spray gun dangled over the sink like the broken neck of a giant turkey. A seafood smell rose up from the basement. Jason came and set a pile of dishes from the prep kitchen down in the one free corner of the floor. Under his chef's hat his red hair was soaked in sweat. He ran back into the service kitchen. You could hear the clamour of pots and pans rattling and fridge doors slamming and tickets squeakily printing. I was already dizzy.

"Good, you're early," said Renaud. "We're in the juice."

They'd been slammed for the lunch shift. We were already deep into office party season, Renaud explained, while I followed him into the prep kitchen, where it was also noisy as hell.

Jonathan said hi without stopping what he was doing. I said hi back and narrowly averted hitting a tower of baking sheets, salad bowls, and greasy buckets. In a plastic bucket held between his legs Jonathan was mixing salad dressing or mayonnaise with a mixer the size of a bazooka. With a roar like a Skilsaw, the machine drowned out the hum of the convection oven and the growling hood vent. The smell of lobster was overpowering, almost sickening. In among floating celery stalks red carcasses reared their head in the orangey scum bubbling on the surface. I was already dreading the cleanup.

Bonnie wasn't there. Or maybe wasn't there yet. A tall cook I hadn't met during my first shift was leaning against one of the prep counters. His long skinny forearms stuck out of a chef's coat with the sleeves rolled up, and he wore a Red Sox cap. He was busy placing balls of stuffing on strips of pasta, which he then cut into squares. Dave was standing next to him with his blond hair up in a ponytail under a net, swimming in a smeared white dishwasher's shirt far too big for him. He was trying to seal the squares to make ravioli, but was struggling to keep up with the cook, who set the pace. I watched the operation with a mix of reverence and fascination, like a kid being let in on the Caramilk secret.

When Dave saw me, his face first relaxed and then lit up, as if I was here to deliver him from a terrible fate. He wanted to shake my hand. His were sticky with egg yolk.

"Dude, watch what you're doing!"

The cook was flouring the counter, and said it with a friendly laugh.

I heard Renaud calling from the staff room. I nodded at Dave, who got back to work, and hurried back to see the sous-chef.

The hallway leading to the staff room made me think of the gangway of a spaceship, or maybe a mezzanine in a nuclear reactor, encumbered with piping, boxes of foods, and stockpots full of liquids of all kinds.

Renaud was sorting kitchen rags in the electrical room by the bathroom. The ones that were least filthy he was setting out to dry; the others he dumped in a giant jute laundry bag. Two servers were sitting at the table cashing out, concentrating like students at a final exam. The chef came out of his office in an undershirt, with his chef's hat still on. He started when he saw me, as if we were old friends who hadn't see each other in a long time. He came and gave me a limp slap on the back. One of the servers looked up at him with exasperation.

"I heard you saved the day, or the night I guess?"

His breath was sweetly alcoholic and his glassy eyes were shining over his red cheeks. The man was clearly soused. Half-hidden in the storage room, Renaud shot me an ironic smile in the corner of his mouth.

"Did you bring your contact info?" the chef asked me. "Come here, I'll enter it in the computer and give you a punch number."

He dragged his feet back to the office and threw himself onto an office chair on wheels. Despite his state, he typed fast. He entered the information I gave him, and as he gave me a punch card number said he was giving me a one-dollar raise on the spot.

"You seem dependable. Hardworking. We need good men like you."

I wanted to add something, to convince him that was why I was here: to work hard. It was painful to listen to, I was laying it on thick, but I couldn't help myself. The chef looked at me with his fishy eyes and cut me off.

"We're in the middle of a pay period. So you'll get paid next Thursday for your hours up to Sunday. The rest will be in the next period."

I said that was fine, occupied with mental calculations.

"Okay, I'll see you later, before I leave. Go get changed, there's a lot to do. Carl's coming in as second dishwasher."

"Carl?"

"Yeah, Carl. The other dishwasher."

It made me feel a lot better to know that this time I wouldn't face the onerous workload alone.

"Renaud!" he yelled. "Do a prep list when you finish tonight. Bob's coming in two hours early tomorrow morning."

Renaud, still sorting rags and aprons, didn't answer. Two servers had finished cashing out and were changing, and talking about their plans for the night. They were in their mid-twenties. They pranced around the staff room in socks and boxers. One was looking for deodorant in one of the lockers. The taller of the two was named Denver. The other one, a year or two younger, was Guillaume. His hair glistened with gel and he smelled strongly of cologne. You could tell Denver used Guillaume to prop up his ego. He chatted away as he brushed his teeth and kept going back and forth between his locker and the employee bathroom. They talked as if I wasn't there. Denver was going on about how he'd ended the night with one of the bartenders from the Diable Vert. Guillaume told him not to get his hopes up, she'd never call him back. Renaud was listening, looking annoyed. I watched them out of the corner of my eye, waiting for them to clear out so I could get changed.

Then Dave came in. He took off his hairnet, which seemed to pain him as much as a crown of thorns. He repeated what the chef had told me five minutes earlier.

"Anyway, you made a good impression on the team. Bébert was talking about you yesterday. He said he's happy you're the one taking my place."

I took his compliment as further reassurance. My position in the team seemed secure. Dave quickly undressed, revealing a skinny, pale body frozen somewhere before puberty. He threw his shirt into the dirty laundry bag next to the lockers, then put on a t-shirt far too big for him. He said he was sorry for leaving me so many dirty dishes, and asked if we'd be seeing each other at Cegep before the end of term. I said we would, and he wished me luck with an apologetic look on his face before disappearing down the stairs to an emergency exit I hadn't noticed during my first shift. It was almost as if he were running away from something.

I got changed as fast as he had, and rushed into the prep kitchen.

I wanted to get started on the focaccia dough right away, but the pasta roller was being used by the cook in the Red Sox cap. He introduced himself, with a big smile.

"I'm Robert. Call me Bob."

He could tell what I was going to ask him.

"No worries, I'm almost done."

He turned around to knead the balls of dough that were waiting in their buspans on top of the fridge.

"Anyway, the dough hasn't finished rising. Dave started them an hour late. Get going on your lettuces. I'll give you a hand with the counters once I'm done this."

Bob was deftly pulling long strips of pasta from the rolling machine, adding a sprinkle of flour to thicken it up. His movements were effortless, as if he was doing them for the ten-thousandth time. He'd calibrated the machine specifically for this job by taking out a few parts, and you could see all the rollers and gears turning away in the mechanism. I remembered Bébert's story about the girl who'd got her hand caught in the machine. It sent a shiver up my spine.

I got busy with my lettuces. Filled the prep sinks with ice-cold water and threw in the heads of romaine. The noise of the hood vent was added to the turning wheels of the pasta machine. Bébert snuck up behind me and yelled "Hey!" in a deep baritone, a couple of inches from my ear. I jumped, and spun around, dropping a few lettuce leaves. He was standing there with his coat open, a massive grin missing an eye tooth, and bloodshot eyes. He'd clearly been up all night, or not far from it. A little bottle of Red Bull in his right hand smelled like candy. He guffawed.

"Didn't mean to scare you, buddy!"

I picked the lettuce off the floor.

"Decided to keep the job? Good move!"

The chef, his greasy hair a mess, crossed the prep kitchen with his toque in one hand and an empty glass in the other.

"You're late, Bébert."

"I don't know, Chef. The schedule hasn't been posted for two weeks. Makes it hard to know if we're late or not, eh."

Bébert went to the staff room, walking by the chef without looking at him. We could hear him laughing as he made his way down the hall. The chef gave him a dirty look but didn't say anything. I went about my business, trying to keep a low profile. He didn't say a word to us. He trundled up the stairs, his heavy, tired footsteps audible over the bleating of the pasta machine and growl of the hood vents.

Bob finished his ravioli with a calm efficiency that made it look like they were making themselves. He handled the pasta with an assurance that only comes, I later learned, with years of experience. His movements had a mechanical precision, but his face was completely relaxed, as if he were kicking back in front of a hockey game on Saturday night. Bob was cool. You could tell right away.

As soon as the machine was free and clean, I started making the pasta, alternating with the salads. Up on the main floor they were already yelling for the first batches of focaccia and calzone. I picked up the pace and tried to maintain it so I wouldn't get buried under the wave of work that would inevitably crash over me soon. I tried to focus on the task at hand, without forgetting the long list of other things I had to do, a list that would only get longer as the night wore on. You didn't just have to get it all done: you had to get it all done in time, when you didn't have to get it all done at the same time. I'd only just started, and was already way behind.

While I was busy kneading my focaccias, Renaud, a few steps away from me, started swearing vociferously, as if he'd dropped an anvil on his foot. I turned to look at him. He was pouring out the contents of the steam pot into sixty-litre buckets. His eyes were wrinkled under his bony cheeks, in a mask of fury.

"Jesus Christ, that's not bisque, it's lobster Bovril. It's salty as fuck!"

He was yelling at no one in particular that it'd take a full truck-load of cream to dilute the salt content. Then he sighed theatric-ally, and mopped his forehead with the sleeve of his chef's coat. He kept on mumbling between his teeth, as if the chef were there in front of him, insulting him, repeating his insinuation that the man needed to lay off the booze.

Bob came through the prep room, clean and changed, with a different Red Sox cap on his head and a smoke in his mouth.

"Hey Bob, taste this."

Bob tasted it and broke out into a cheerful, loud laugh that was all the more striking next to Renaud's caustic rage. He was obviously used to dealing with mistakes like these.

"No worries, Renaud. I'll take care of it tomorrow morning. See you later."

He put a hand on Renaud's shoulder before setting off.

Renaud lowered his head in a gesture of discouragement. I ran up to the main floor with the first batch of pasta. I'd barely set foot in the kitchen when Jonathan yanked them from my hand, thank-ing me as if I'd come bearing water in the middle of the desert.

The noise from the dining room, which was already full to capacity, blended in with the cacophony of the kitchen. The first service of the night was in full swing. Every element on the range was covered with sizzling, smoking pans. I wondered how Bébert could tell them apart, and keep track of all the ingredients that went in each. He was yelling at a waitress to come explain the goddamn extra she wanted for fifty-three. Jason, with a furrowed brow and reassuring calm, was setting out plates on the pass-through.

It seemed more intense to me than the first shift, as if the novelty had worn off and I could now take the full measure of the chaos that obtained in the front kitchen. I already felt dizzy from the noise and the incomprehensible dance of the cooks' movements.

Bébert was tossing out instructions in his commanding voice, like the captain of a ship in a storm. He was always doing two things at once, if not three. He flipped the prawns in one pan while examining the ingredients in the others that stood lined up and waiting to be thrown onto the heat. Without taking his eyes off the pans, he asked Jonathan how his side was coming, and Jonathan would yell something back. Though he was on the hotside, not one plate left the kitchen without being inspected by him. Everything was coordinated with a military precision, to the sound of his orders ringing out over the noise.

I turned around to go back downstairs to finish the prep when Bébert yelled at me to pick up the pans, while I was here. His tone was sharp; he wasn't kidding around. Bébert was now fully immersed in the rush. Nothing else mattered.

I took all the dirty dishes down to the dishpit. That's when I came across Carl, my partner for the night. I hadn't seen him arrive. It was like he'd just materialized without anyone noticing. He had a round, hairless face, wore a backwards baseball cap, and looked around my age. He was casually putting away clean dishes. The stacks of dirty dishes had doubled since I started. I shoved the burning hot pans in a corner and introduced myself.

"Oh, cool," he said without looking at me or shaking hands. "I'm Carl. Can you finish this?"

He nodded at the caddy overflowing in every direction with dirty dishes.

"I've got to make a call."

He didn't wait for an answer, just put on a coat he had hung by the door, the one people used to go smoke outside. He pulled a flip-phone from his pocket and disappeared into the alley. I thought of my lettuces soaking downstairs and the lamentable state of the prep kitchen it was up to me to clean. I thought about the last batch of calzone dough I had to make. But I decided to make a start on the mountains of dirty dishes instead, until Carl got back. I ran through a first rack of plates and coffee cups, then tackled the pans. Not the load I'd just brought in, the ones that had probably been there since the middle of the afternoon, encrusted with cheese sauce. I hadn't even filled half a rack when I heard a menacing voice call out.

"Cutlery, motherfucker."

I turned around, startled, as if I'd been caught with my pants down. The guy was obviously older than me, by at least ten years. I could see patches of grey in his close-cropped hair. A two-day stubble darkened his cheeks, his shirt was askew, his open collar revealed a heavy gold chain, and a chunky watch hung from his wrist. He glanced at the shelves, to make sure what he was looking for was still there, then gave me a withering look. I was transformed into a pillar of salt.

"Where's your sidekick? I asked him for cutlery twenty minutes ago."

He kept looking at the shelves, shifting piles of dishes with angry, impatient movements.

"Who do I have to bitch-slap to get something done around here?"

Reflexively I almost answered that I didn't know, but stopped myself just in time. That was when I noticed the big plastic bucket overflowing with cutlery. It looked like every knife, fork, and spoon in the restaurant must be there. I could hear the pasta machine I'd left running, grinding away empty, along with pans clattering against each other and scraping the rings over the gas. The bell on the line was ringing incessantly, as if someone with Parkinson's had their hand stuck to it. I looked at the open door to the alley. Everything slowed down and I saw black for a minute, like when you get up too quickly. Then reality kicked in, and I snapped out of it. I turned back to the manager.

"Give me two minutes, I'll do it."

I picked up the bucket and emptied it out in the dishpit. The guy headed back to the dining room, furious as the moment he'd burst in, swearing at whoever cared to listen in a rough yet high-pitched voice. With fear in my heart, I frantically sorted utensils and ran them through the machine three times in the hope of removing all the spots. The last cycle had just finished when I heard a hurricane of fuck this and fuck that exploding into my dishpit. The manager grabbed the cutlery like the defibrillator needed to resuscitate his dying mother.

"I'm coming, you gang of monkeys."

One thing was clear: whoever this "gang of monkeys" was, I never wanted to be part of their crew. As soon as he was out of my field of vision airways cleared up and I could suddenly breathe again. My muscles and thighs relaxed. I let myself decompress a minute and then went outside to see what the fuck Carl was doing. The alley was deserted. I swore angrily at the cold air, and went back in, leaving the door half-open.

I got back to the prep kitchen: it looked like the smoking ruins of Rome after the passage of the Visigoths. I pulled myself together. Renaud was in the cooler arranging buspans of linguini and farfalle he'd pre-cooked. I didn't dare mention that Carl was MIA. I decided to finish the calzone dough quickly, figuring I'd have time to spin the lettuce after burning through the worst of the dirty dishes. I heard Bébert yelling something into the stairwell. I was pretty sure it had to do with me, but I was almost finished. I picked up the pace a notch, careful not to mess anything up. Bébert wouldn't think twice about sending me back to do them again if he found even one or two not up to snuff. The calzone dough was more delicate than focaccia dough, and would tear at the slightest jerk. Little puffs of heat kept hitting me while I started and restarted them, a little more nervous each time. Bébert yelled again.

"Renaud, quit wanking around and get up here. Fuck!"

The door to the walk-in slammed shut. Renaud yelled at him to chill out, he was coming. I stacked up my last batch of pasta just in time to follow Renaud up the stairs.

In the dishpit I found Carl, phone wedged between shoulder and cheek, putting away the dishes I'd washed while he was out. He was talking about quantities and prices in that coded language I'd heard before, from my first girlfriend's friends. He hung up, happy as a clam, and informed me that he was going out for another smoke. Just five minutes. I watched him walk out again, too taken aback to say anything. I just stood there, with my mouth hanging out. His shameless capacity to fully and completely not give a fuck was astonishing.

I threw two racks through the machine and went to see what was going on in the service kitchen. Renaud was on the hotside now. He was leaning against one of the shelves of the dessert station, which was empty for now, staring out at something in the warm dim light of the dining room. Bébert was back on the pass, filling up the fridge with fresh backups, singing a nursery rhyme that recounted the story of the castration of Renaud the guinea pig. The sous-chef had seen enough of Bébert's sense of humour to stop listening.

Jonathan was checking the croutons toasting in the pizza oven. Jason, tongs at the ready, was sitting on the garde-manger fridge, his gaze empty, lost in thought, dazed by the first rush of the night. There was something almost frightening about their calm. A storm was brewing. The air was charged, electric; the dining room a flurry of activity in an orange-hued darkness, a system gathering and ready to descend on us. Any moment now something was going to blow. But for now the emptiness stretched out . before us. Every movement partook of its usual precision stripped of its habitual speed. The service kitchen, like a self-regulating organism, was saving its energy. Under the powerful exhaust of the hood vents you could hear the faraway tinkling of cutlery on porcelain, and the hum of discussion.

I ventured a glance into the dining room, over the shelf Renaud was leaning against, and could make out, at the far end of the bar, a lineup of customers waiting to be seated. I took advantage of the lull to pick up as many dirty dishes as I could. I raided the space under the oven. Bébert, chill as ever, asked me to bring back clean pans and pizza plates "before we get juiced again." His eyes were busy counting the diners gathering between the door, while he

played with his tongs and started singing his nursery rhyme again.
I got back to the dishpit where I was greeted by a draft of cold
air. The manager came back in from the alley. He smelled like
tobacco and was rubbing his arms for a little warmth. Carl followed him in, imploring in a whiny tone.

"Come on Greg. Come *on!*"

"Forget it, man. What am I supposed to do with your sorry-ass
shake? I'm running a business, not a charity."

"Please, Greg. Come on."

"Fuck off, go back to your schoolyard."

Greg set off toward the dining room, laughing. It was one of the
coldest laughs I'd ever heard. I piled up buspans of dirty dishes on
the rack behind me and went back to work. I assumed Carl would
do the same.

Instead he acted like I wasn't there, and picked up the cell
phone lying on one of the shelves, then disappeared back out into
the alley. I looked around. Dude was seriously pushing it. I tried to
imagine the dynamic between him and Dave, and could see why
my friend had been so keen to palm his job off on me.

Bébert's bellowing reminded me that the cooks needed dishes
and clean pans. I brought up a big stack of each. I couldn't believe
how heavy the galvanized porcelain serving platters were.

"Don't drop that," Renaud said, still leaning against a shelf on
the line. "That's a week's pay you're holding there."

He was looking at me and furrowing his brow. The plates suddenly seemed even heavier, and I almost dropped a couple as I
shoved a pile onto the garde-manger shelf.

I went and did another batch of dishes in the hope of keeping
my head above water. Carl kept breezing in and out, disappearing
outside or back toward the kitchen with little piles of clean dishes.
He'd unhurriedly put away whatever came out of the machine, and
bring me back whatever didn't meet his standards of cleanliness.
He was far less discriminating when it was his turn to wash.

I kept working and didn't complain, my face hardened, abstract-
ing it all, trying to ignore my growing irritation. By concentrating

on the arrangements of dirty dishes in their racks, I managed to catch up after half an hour.

I ran the cutlery from the second sitting through the machine before Greg had time to ask for it. When he came and found them on the shelf, clean and sorted by type, he went out of his way to thank me and told me I was "a fighter, not a waste of space like your little friend there." I wasn't sure whether he meant Dave or Carl. Maybe both. Either way, I felt better staying in the man's good books. It was hard to say how exactly Greg's presence made me ill at ease. But when he was near I'd watch my every move. He exuded something akin to a total lack of empathy. And you could tell he carried an explosive charge on a short fuse, liable to blow at any moment.

The sprawling heaps of dirty dishes seemed to be regenerating less quickly. Carl had gone outside for the fourteenth time, to smoke or do whatever it was he did out there. I took a deep breath and went back down to the basement. I'd allotted myself fifteen minutes to finish the jobs I'd left half-done.

Just when I was starting to tell myself that the worst was over, I remembered the massive steam pot. It was a boneyard of charred carcasses, slices of boiled carrots, and burnt half-onions.

I attacked it first. To begin I pulled out the biggest pieces and threw them in double garbage bags, which I'd laid out in waxed boxes the way Bébert showed me. I soaked the pot in hot water and half a litre of degreaser. While it was soaking I spin-dried the lettuce and swept the floor, which was strewn with slices of vegetables, grey flour, and splotches of sauce. Then I hurriedly scrubbed out the steam pot with a steel scrubber that chewed away at my hands. The smell of seafood and detergent was more revolting than a rest-stop outhouse in the middle of a heat wave.

My pager started vibrating while my head was still buried in the steam pot. I glanced at the screen. Already 8:15. I had a new voice message. That was when it hit me that I hadn't called Malik back.

I was finishing mopping the floor when Bébert crossed the prep kitchen with a plate of pasta in one hand and a sweaty, greasy cap in the other.

"Isn't that your partner's job, usually?"

"What?"

I kept mopping furiously, the way I'd learned from my old boss when he caught me limply spreading dirty water around the floor of a room we'd finished renovating.

"The second guy in is supposed to clean the prep room, usually. Just before the first guy goes home."

I'd stopped mopping.

"We don't close together?"

"Together? Why not three or four of you? Nah, dude, first guy leaves at ten. Just after the second guy finishes the prep room, and takes fifteen minutes for dinner."

I didn't move. Bébert looked me up and down.

"What's wrong?"

"Nothing, it's fine."

I emptied my mop water in the sink and hurried upstairs.

The kitchen was in another lull. Hidden behind his oil and vinegar bottles, Renaud was checking out a couple women sitting at the bar, laughing into fluorescent pink cocktails. Jason, quiet as ever, had taken Bébert's place on the line and was portioning out pasta for the next rush. The buspans of dishes were full. Carl was joking around with Jonathan, both of them leaning against the garde-manger fridge. Carl saw me coming.

"Cool, man, you got that done fast. I can leave early."

Before I could get a word in he cut me off.

"I know it's supposed to be my night to close, but I talked to Christian. He said I could leave first tonight."

He pulled a calzone out of the big pizza oven and served himself on a big plate. The smell of crusty dough and grilled peppers made me salivate. He poured two big ladles of tomato sauce over them. My stomach was rumbling.

"I'll get you back, man."

He slid by me with his meal, giving me a pat on the shoulder on his way. I was starving to death. I heard him heading down the stairs to the basement. A feeling of rage and powerlessness welled up in me. Jonathan looked away. Renaud kept right on feasting his eyes on the two women.

I went back down to the dishpit, dizzy from lack of food. The dishes had piled up in my absence. Carl couldn't have washed more than two plates and maybe a pan. Tops. I changed the garbage bags, which were full already, and got ready to get back to the work Carl had never really started. Bébert walked into the pit and put his empty plate on the rack. He made some room on the clean dish shelf and set up the little boom box from the prep room, and tuned it to the alternative rock show on COOL-FM.

"Here, put some music on and I'll give you a hand with this shit."

He stumbled over to the door and opened it a bit. Lit a smoke and watched me work for a minute. Despite the hunger gnawing at me I tried extra hard to pick up speed, to prove that I wasn't lazy.

"He's a bit of a dogfucker, eh?"

I was scrubbing an aluminum pot. The bottom was plastered with a layer of burnt gorgonzola. My sweat was dripping into the stinky brown foam loosened by the scrubber.

"Who?" I asked without stopping my work.

"Don't give me 'who.'"

He crushed out his smoke in the ashtray on the shelf by the door.

"I'm gonna talk to Renaud."

As he turned back toward the kitchen he turned up the stereo. It was "Aerials," by System of a Down.

"Stay strong man. And next time he tries to pull a fast one on you, put your foot down."

Bébert came back ten minutes later with a big plate heaped with steaming hot pasta.

"Here, take five minutes and eat."

"What is it?" I asked, just to be polite.

I was so hungry that if he'd waited another moment I would have grabbed the noodles with my bare hands, fuck cutlery.

"Linguini Carbonara. It'll put a little lead in your pencil."

I looked down at my plate. The richest pasta on the menu, with three big ladles of reduced cream sauce, parmesan, bacon, grilled chicken and egg yolk.

"Eat, boy, eat!"

I got a clean fork and cleaned my plate in a matter of seconds. Bébert watched me wolf it down.

"Dude. Chew!"

We could hear Renaud bellyaching, yelling at Bébert from the service kitchen.

"All right," Bébert said, "last push! Give 'er!"

This marked the start of the most intense part of the night. Every dish from all four corners of the restaurant, from the prep room and the front kitchen and the floor, began to pile up in incredible heaps as the shift neared its end and the kitchen got ready to close. Between eleven and one I had a massive list of tasks to frantically work through.

It started with the floor staff coming back to badger me to wash the night's final load of cutlery, because otherwise they couldn't polish them and finish off their other final duties. If Greg was working I'd start with the floor jobs; if it was Nick, I'd get the worst of my own work out of the way first. Even the busboys and bar-girls, on the floor staff's bottom rung, earned at least twice what I made in a night. So I wasn't about to make my life miserable just to make theirs easier. On my second night I still hadn't really pieced together how the whole thing worked, but I figured it out quickly enough. You had to. So I flew along at warp-speed to get the last few sets of dishes out. It was done before anyone in the restaurant could ask me for anything. The endgame was to avoid the wrath of Greg.

Next came the random batches of kitchen dishes, and big piles of tongs and ladles and pizza cutters. Jason and Bébert would also come back to bring me a puzzle of stainless-steel containers—the inserts—and a metal plate with round holes in it, all the parts of what Bébert called the steam table, a stainless-steel basin within a large metal frame where the inserts were kept warm.

They brought me the cutting boards from the garde-manger and the line. They were long, cumbersome, and hell to clean. Next came ashtrays from the smoking section, a thousand espresso cups, the coffee grounds container Sarah dropped off right on top of my overflowing buspans of dirty dishes. The icing on the cake was the cast-iron rectangles that covered the gas range—the piano notes, Renaud liked to call them. Once I had powered through all that, I swept the front kitchen floor—the cooks only ever did a symbolic sweep after finishing—and the dishpit floor as well. Then it was time for a wet mop, with plenty of degreaser to unstick the layers of grease that accumulated on the floor tile in the course of the shift, and break down the crud that had gathered between the dishpit tiles. Of course I'd have to redo this five or six times, since someone inevitably walked over my clean wet floor to go back and get a buspan of clean cups or bread baskets or something. It was almost like they did it on purpose.

The front kitchen lights were dimmed now and the exhaust fan turned off. I went around emptying the garbages to take them out. The kitchen staff was chatting at the end of the bar, drinking staff beers. I couldn't wait to finish. I went out to heave the last few bags into the dumpster and the cold throttled me—my arms and shirt were soaked in greasy water and chunks of burnt food. I was fantasizing about taking a long, soapy shower.

I got back inside as Jade was bringing me my own beer. She gave me a smile that stopped me in my tracks in the doorway.

"Didn't see you there. Doing all right?"

I have no idea what I answered. Probably an unintelligible agglutination of vowels. She burst out laughing.

"Here, have a beer. You deserve it."

She sauntered back over to the bar, curly hair bobbing from one shoulder to the other. The fragrance of her perfume wafted through the air a moment before being overpowered by the smell of floor soap. The spell eventually wore off, and I took a long sip of beer.

Bébert came across the dishpit with his gangsta limp, ready to leave. Greg was following him, just as pumped up as in the middle of the shift.

"Can't trust a single one of 'em," he was saying. "Fucking monkeys."

"You know how these kids are. Wannabe big shots."

Bébert was looking for his smokes. Greg was wearing a black leather jacket that came down to his knees. His silver watch gleamed in the chink between his sleeve and his gloves, which were also leather. I could see, through his brush cut, a scar that criss-crossed his skull. A smell of peppermint followed him. In his evening wear he looked just like the restaurant's well-heeled customers. He winked at me and said "Bye, fighter" in a voice hoarse from yelling. Bébert gave me a fist-bump, wished me luck, and lighted a smoke before venturing outside. When they opened the back door I saw Bonnie waiting in the orange and black night with a friend of hers, a punk chick with a scarf and a Perfecto leather jacket. They looked at me, not without amusement. I pretended not to see them. In my ridiculously filthy state I was in no mood for chatting with people dressed up for a night out, while I walked around in an aura of garbage juice.

The door closed. Their shouts faded in the distance. I turned off the stereo and exhaust fan. Faint sounds of laughter and discussion reached me from the bar. I went down to the basement. In a moment of weakness I stopped in the middle of the hallway. A feeling of loneliness and sorrow crept over me, and I took a deep breath. I tried to shake it by laughing, but it came out ominously hollow. The prep room was empty, and looked much bigger now that it was clean. I walked by the white board. The prep list was staggering. I couldn't believe the cooks could get through that much prep in a single shift. I'd closely read the list of what Bob had to get through the next day, and it made my head hurt for him. In the "instructions" column, someone had left him a note. In poorly spelled French, it said the bisque was fine. Signed Renaud.

I shut myself in the staff bathroom to wash my arms and face. The room was so tiny and the sink so miniscule it took contortions to give myself a scrub. It was no use. I still felt like an oily, putrid mess. I threw on my dry underwear with a sense of deliverance. As I transferred my pager from one pair of pants to the other I remembered that there was a message to listen to, and reminded myself I had to call Malik, but couldn't bring myself to do it.

Since I was working the next night, I left most of my stuff in a corner of the staff room.

I went back to the main floor. There weren't any customers left in the dining room, and some of the floor staff was hanging out at the bar. The entire kitchen staff was gone. Maude was relaxed and smiling, transfigured. One of the night servers, a guy named Julien, I think, was smoking, sitting on a stool, with his shirt collar unbuttoned. He looked around five years older than me. Sarah was talking about a guy she'd met the night before at Café Central, and brought home. Denver, who'd just gotten back from the Diable Vert and hadn't even had time to take off his leather jacket, was swirling the wine in his glass and following the discussion, looking amused. Jade was polishing champagne flutes and humming to herself. There were too many people around for me to talk to her. The boss was there too, and that was enough to make me want to get moving. She wore a loose-fitting white blouse with tight jeans tucked into leather boots. With her hands on the bar and a bottle of wine in front of her she was teasing Sarah to tell her story about the guy, making everyone laugh. She caught me as I was walking toward the front door. I thought she was going to ask me to go out the back.

"Aren't you going to punch out?"

"Punch out?"

"Yes. Punch. Out."

Her look was withering, as I grappled with what was clearly an elementary concept. Pretty much the entire staff was staring at me. Jade had put her head down, and Maude's stare was seesawing between Séverine and me, like when you watch a tennis game. Julien and Denver stared at me with a slightly mocking smile.

"Christian gave you a number, right?"

I thought back to the beginning of the night. It was true, the chef had given me a number I was supposed to enter into the order computer at the beginning of my shift. I had to punch it in again when I finished. Except that as soon as I started work I'd forgotten all about it.

"He did. But he didn't show me how it worked."

Séverine looked suddenly tired. She sighed. Denver and Sarah started talking again. Julien lit another smoke, which he shared with Maude. Séverine poured them a glass of wine. She served herself too, then went over to the computer at the end of the bar.

"Come over here."

She rolled her sleeves up over slender yet muscular arms, and showed me how it was done. Her instructions were clear but her hand was flying over the screen, which made the bracelet of her little gold watch slide over her wrist. She wasn't the most patient person I'd ever come across. Her *eau de toilette* must cost as much as my paycheque. She didn't react to my smell. I could picture the collision of our two olfactory auras: hers lemony fresh, almost sweet; mine musky and redolent of kitchen smells, burnt food, garbage, and detergents. Her heady perfume enveloped me like a flock of angels unsticking the sulfurous emanations of my own grinning devils, one molecule at a time. She was suddenly serious.

"If you forget to punch out, I'll forget to pay you those hours. Give me the ones you did this week. I'll punch them in now. Just this once."

Maude and Julien were still watching. Jade too. She'd finished wiping glasses. The feeling of her eyes on me was the hardest thing to take.

"All right. You can go."

Cheeks burning with shame, I set off to the entrance and pushed the first door. The second door at the end of the hallway

wouldn't budge. It was locked. My scalp was tingling, as if har-
rowed by thousands of microscopic needles. I made my way back
into the dining room. The staff was chatting, drinking wine. The
boss sent me a withering look that reduced me to a little cloud of
grey smoke.

"What's up now?"

I muttered that it was locked.

"What?"

She was coming toward me taking sharp, loud steps. My ears
were as red as my cheeks, I could feel it. I cleared my throat and
said it again, cursing my shyness.

"Uh, key's in the door. Open your eyes! Bye!"

She gestured, as if to shoo me away, then turned back to the
others.

Sure enough, the key was in the lock. I unlocked it and set out
into the clear night. I walked between the people on the street until
I found a phone booth. Flipped a quarter into the slot and then
dialled my voicemail.

"You have. One. New message. Three. Saved messages."

I listened to the most recent. I was expecting Malik's voice, but
it was Rémi, my old roommate, whose voice exploded into the
headset. "Fuck, man, are you gonna call me back one of these days?
You owe me three months' rent, it's been like years, and you're
gonna fucking pay me, man. Then you just disappear? You better
call me back..."

I hung up without listening to the end of the message. Or else
what, Rémi? I thought. Or else what, huh?

Since I'd washed up at Vincent's with my made-up story,
I'd been hoping Rémi would give up and leave me alone, not go
searching all over town for me. I guess I figured this was one more
thing that would go away if I just kept ignoring it. It was a strategy
I'd been trying out with lots of things.

With my hand still on the frozen headset, I gave another
thought to the thing that had been bothering me all night. I took
the money out of my pocket and counted my wad, keeping it

hidden from the people in the street. The payphone screen read 00:27. My heart started beating faster and I felt a wave of numbness spreading from my chest to the very tips of my toes and fingers. My feet were shaking, my arms felt like wet blankets. I hailed a cab. He stopped ten feet ahead, his taillights a smear of red in the amber night. I jogged through the slush to the car, opened the door and slumped down in the seat. I gave the cabbie directions, not even hearing them, as if another voice had pronounced my words, like in a silent film.

The taxi rolled down the avenue. The light of the neon signs, storefronts, and fast-food marquees made me feel like the lead ball in a pinball machine. The darkness of the car interior resolved into something more living and colourful as we progressed. Classical music seeped out of the speakers, at a low volume, filling the car with the even notes of a cello. On the dashboard I saw the illuminated cover of a well-thumbed miniature Koran. My aunt had one like it. The driver turned onto Christophe-Colomb and sped up, we passed Rue Rachel, full of young people out partying, and went down to Ontario. He was taking me to the eastern reaches of downtown, where there was no chance of running into anyone I knew, and where, I lied to myself, I would be at peace.

CHAPTER 9

THE BOUNCER always recognized me. I never failed to tip him when I paid my cover, but I also stood out from the other regulars who filled the club on busy nights. There was something fishy about a guy my age coming in as often as I did, especially one immune to the charms of this place's main attractions.

The bouncer had the body of a porn star who could bench three hundred pounds. His white polo shirt clung to his chest like a cyclist's jersey, and his close-cropped platinum hair took on a fluorescent hue in the ultraviolet glow of the black lights. Once my five-dollar bill disappeared in his fist, a mitt like the paw of a furless bear, he'd give me a nod and an affable smile that made it hard to imagine the brute force I'd seen him marshal to toss out unruly or troublesome customers. He didn't ask where I wanted to sit. He knew why I was here.

I crossed the room without paying much attention to the stage around which the other patrons clustered with craning necks. Their indistinct faces blurred into the shadow like a Francis Bacon painting. From the corner of my eye I could see myself reflected in the mirrored walls as I moved through the club, my shimmering cornea riddled with dark spots, my silhouette's dark, hazy outline diffracting against that of the two naked women in white latex boots whirling around on the chrome-plated stage. The place reeked of disinfectant and drugstore cologne. A short version of Ozzy's "I Just Want You" was blaring with the bass cranked to eleven, drowning out everything. My heartbeat quickened under the peaks of adrenaline that spiked up even more precipitously as I neared the bar. While I waited for the bartender to come over I took in snippets of the conversations around me. One guy who was just a touch older than me and not quite at home in his suit, was leaning into the flowing hair of the stripper sitting beside him. She was straddling the line between flirty and cheeky as she fended off his advances and dodged his inane questions and probing yuppie hands, while at the same time trying to lure him back to a booth for a more intimate chat. He was almost screaming in her ear in a plaintive voice, "C'mon, tell me your name, honey. You can tell me, I'm not like the rest of these losers."

I tuned him out as the barmaid approached, taking giant strides behind the bar. She was taller than me, and blond, with crow's feet her makeup couldn't quite conceal. She always greeted me with a, "Hey, dear." I ordered two beers and finally made my way over to the machines. My body relaxed, as if the ties that kept me trussed together had snapped. I felt a mild euphoria. Everything around me was suddenly clean and sparkly.

Only one of the machines was in use. I checked the bonus jackpot on all three, and took the highest, the one most likely to pay out. I set one of my Buds down on the counter, next to the ashtray, and took a long sip of the other. It was ice-cold and thirst quenching, a taste of unadulterated pleasure. I pulled the wad of bills from the pocket of my jeans and took a seat on the stool. The two-hundred-fifty-six-colour screen set something deep within my skull alight. My cheeks were burning now. I unfolded my wad, pulled out a first twenty, and inserted it into the machine. On the touchscreen I selected my favourite game: *Crazy Bells*. I started with small bets, to get a sense of how often the right combinations were coming up. My trick was to keep playing as long as I possibly could, patiently waiting for the winning combinations to start popping up more regularly. Obviously the same strategy as every other video lottery junkie. Then I'd work my way through one or two twenties, before ratcheting up my bets. I could feel the trance deepening and, after another long sip of fizzy beer, I started betting a little more recklessly. A nymphet in a fluorescent dress came and sat down right next to me. I didn't take my eyes off the screen.

"What's your name, honey? I'm Sandra."

My bet was up to five dollars on that turn, the maximum. I pressed on the screen.

"You look lonely. Why don't we go to the back for a while?"

She held out her hand for the taking.

With superhuman effort I managed to answer, but it came from a place very far away. On the screen, in each of the nine squares, lemons, sevens, bells, cherries, and oranges flew by at breakneck speed. My eyes were trained on the screen for the red of the sevens and the yellow of the bells. I bit my tongue, hoping with all my heart they'd stop spinning in every box on the screen. I pressed the button again, to stop the spinning. The girl shrank away into the deep purple room, fading into the crowd of shadowy figures sitting at tables. In each of the nine squares the symbols had come to rest. I saw sevens—two or three of them. A cherry, which meant a bonus if I won. Another seven, and then a fifth. A hot flash shot through my whole body. My eyelids thickened and I felt my eyeballs pulsing behind them. My arm hair stood up on end. The numbers on the counter were still illegible, still spinning at full speed on their digital axis, as the total of my credits climbed higher and higher. My jaw contracted. I breathed in deeply, then upped my bet to the maximum. Another sip of my second beer, then I pressed the screen again. The reels started spinning. I hit the glass with my index. Bar, orange, orange, grape, seven, bar, lemon, bell, cherry. No win, but at least my bet wasn't lost, thanks to the cherry. I set the reels spinning again without touching the bet, then held my breath for a while. I stared at the screen, as if standing guard. I gave the screen another quick tap with my fingertips to get the reel spinning again, followed by a second to bring it grinding to a halt. My nails made a dry clack on the screen. The symbols slowed and resolved in their boxes. My back muscles tightened. I let out a long sigh, then pounded almost my entire beer. I looked around without seeing a thing. Everything was suffused with a dewy, ultraviolet light. On the screen six of the nine squares had sevens in them. My credits had leaped to three-hundred-twenty dollars—two-hundred-forty more than I'd fed into the machine. I was on a roll. A silent euphoria heightened every one of my senses, but I controlled myself, playing it safe with smaller bets: enough for a pretty big win if I hit a combination, but not enough for a serious loss if nothing paid out. I went for one last round. Nothing. I stopped there. Got up hurriedly and printed out my wins. I floated to the bar, unable to contain my excitement. I handed the ticket over to the bartender, and she came back with the money from the till. She stacked the twenties onto the counter. I ordered another beer, and gave her a twenty, and another twenty to the bouncer who'd come back for a coke. At the end of the bar I recognized Cherry. I felt a pang in the chest, and looked down for a minute. She was sitting with a customer. Tonight's wig was pink. She was sipping her usual gin-and-7Up, sucking the straw like a cigarette holder. She said hello with a subtle nod, while listening to some fifty-year-old guy's story. The guy ordered something else from the bartender. The bar's lighting revealed all the dandruff that had fallen onto the shoulders of his dark jacket. I took my beer and went to sit in the corner, to leave time for the adrenaline to dilute in my bloodstream and enjoy the slow wind-down that always followed a climax.

In this state of profound relaxation I collapsed into a plush booth, as exhausted as if I'd swum two-hundred laps, and saw Cherry leaving the bar stools, followed by the guy. They disappeared into the booths at the back. My vacant look swept this room full of working girls. The dancer who'd come to see me while I was gambling didn't bother trying her luck again. She was also going from table to table, perched on four-inch heels, taking small, fast steps.

At the next table over, three dealers from Rue Berri were polishing off their third bottle of vodka, which lay on ice in a bucket like champagne. Two dancers were drinking with them. They'd break into laugher pretty much every time anyone said something. One of them had clearly had a boob job, and adjusted her hot-pink bra every thirty seconds. The other unconsciously rubbed her nose at regular intervals.

I drifted off, staring at multiple reflections of myself in the mirrors as if they were other people. In the ultraviolet light my skin was luminous, like a deep-sea fish, my hair hung down over my temples like dripping tar, and my features were indistinct as if wrapped in glutinous film. I blinked and shivered. I could barely recognize myself. The guys next to me yelled something. I turned around slowly, taking a long swig of phosphorescent beer. The stripper in pink had a shooter jammed into her cleavage. One of the dealers grabbed it in his teeth and knocked his head back, gargling in his throat. I took a final sip of beer in the company of that feverish kid slumped in his booth and reflected in multiple versions in faraway mirrors all over the room.

CHAPTER 10

ON THE WEEKEND when my dad took me to Sam the Record Man on Sainte-Catherine, we'd leave Longueuil early to be sure to find parking. It was usually a Sunday morning, just after my dad's rounds at the hospital. One trip in particular is etched in my memory. I couldn't have been more than twelve. We walked the downtown sidewalks in silence in the cold late October sun. I could feel the stiff twenty-dollar bill in my jean pocket. That was my budget: one CD.

The store's front windows were littered with boxes of promo materials and faded posters. It smelled like an old drawer or dusty church basement, mixed in with cold coffee, like the teachers' lounge at school. The guys who ran the store looked like Irish bluesmen. The floor was buckled and full of soft spots, covered in old lino that shooshed under our footsteps. CD and record bins lined the walls. The overall feel was more flea market than record store. Rooms seemed to have been tacked on over the years, each expansion more improvised than planned, as if new inventory had one day showed up and colonized the neighbouring rooms. My dad walked around the record store like the creator surveying his domain. He knew where everything was, stopped to check out new releases and imports, flipped through the bins, sometimes pulling out a rarity for closer scrutiny, running his fingers through his beard with a serious, concentrated expression. Then he would disappear upstairs to the jazz section that dwarfed all the others put together. I'd browse the Alternative Rock section where all kinds of Big Wrecks and Third Eye Blinds and Marcy Playgrounds went to die along with the rest of the bands that sprung up in the second half of the nineties only to get flung back into obscurity as the new millennium approached. I was trying to choose between the most recent albums from the groups my school's five or six skaters listened to on their discmen as they smoked in the back stairwell. Pennywise, Rancid, NOFX. The problem was I didn't really like that stuff. I waited for my dad to go upstairs, so he wouldn't see me, and then headed over to the metal section.

I'd always been impressed by the album covers. They reminded me of my dad's old paperbacks, the ones I didn't yet read, because they were in English, but would flip through for hours on my dad's bookshelves in the basement, trying to imagine the universe depicted within.

Metal was in a dormant phase. A lot of groups had broken up in the nineties. American thrash had softened up and sold out, losing a lot of fans in the process. The Scandinavians still weren't very well known in North America. Everyone was into Nirvana, punk was exploding. And then there was gangsta rap: Tupac and Ice Cube were knocking Axl Rose and Peter Steele off their pedestals.

Sam the Record Man had a much better selection than the Music World at the mall in Longueuil that my friends and I sometimes went to. Or maybe the Metal section at Sam's just seemed well-stocked because I was twelve years old and didn't know shit. I essentially knew three things about metal: the last Metallica concert had turned into a riot all because of Axl Rose, one of my friends listened to Helloween under the covers because his mum thought it was too violent, and as far as my cousin Malik was concerned only one band mattered: Iron Maiden. As I flipped through the Cannibal Corpse and Mercyful Faith, I kept coming back to Maiden. I was drawn to the name, of course, but also the album art, with a recurring skeleton character. Eddie—my cousin had told me his name—was there in all kinds of fantastic scenes. On one cover he was a cyborg brandishing a laser gun; on another, a statue of Pharaoh, eyes aflame; yet another had Eddie yanking a fetus from his stomach while coming apart in a sea of icebergs. I was as excited as a kid pouring over Jack Vance's *Tschai* cycle, or the Philip K. Dicks illustrated by Tibor Csernus.

Before my dad came back down with his usual pile of CDs in hand, I chose the album with Eddie climbing out of the ground in front of a tombstone while being struck by lightning in a blue and yellow dusk. I hurried over to line up at the till, driven by an unknown impulse, as if I was up to no good. I was buying my first metal album. It felt like stealing a *Playboy*.

The ten-minute wait for my dad was spent nervously shifting my weight. I'd slid the CD into my raincoat pocket. I couldn't wait to listen to it, but was afraid of what my dad would think.

He approached the counter with five or six multicoloured CDs. The clerk, who was older than him, questioned him on his choices. Had he seen Jack DeJohnette live? I stopped listening when I realized they were talking about jazz. Finally my dad was done paying, and he turned toward me. He could see the little plastic bag sticking out of my pocket.

"What did you get?"

My mouth was dry.

"You wouldn't know it."

The Offspring and Bad Religion albums I'd bought the last few times hadn't registered with him. He held out his open hand. I pulled the bag out of my pocket and handed it over hesitantly. He took out the album and furrowed his eyebrows in a way I found hard to read. Then he put it back in the bag and gave it back to me, with no change in his facial expression. I'd expected him to say something. I was boiling hot. He looked at me. I was sure he'd send me to return the CD.

"Don't play it too loud, you don't want to upset your mum."

He opened the door and I followed him out, legs numb, apprehensive about learning what he really thought of my purchase.

As soon as I got home I shut myself up in my room and put the CD on my stereo, with headphones on to be sure I wouldn't bother

anyone. I pressed play. A whistling, screaming crowd filled my
ears. It was a live album. That surprised me. Over the cries of the
fans you could hear a speech in English and the sounds of planes
taking off. The first notes rang out dramatically. The crowd started
yelling louder. The hair on the back of my neck stood up. Then the
song started in earnest, and the crowd yelled even louder, and I
was part of it too. It felt like I was there. From that moment on the
idea of seeing a metal show became an obsession. I listened to the
album from beginning to end, at least three times in a row, without
moving, almost without blinking, as if my body were a conduit
for the electrical current that kept me lashed to my stereo. I didn't
open a single one of the comic books I'd planned to read, I just sat
there listening to the album. Though I didn't know it yet, I'd pur-
chased the most legendary live Maiden album, *Live After Death*,
from the World Slavery tour, an epic one-hundred-twenty-seven
shows in three-hundred-one days. I wished I hadn't been born too
late to see a single one of them. Especially since Bruce Dickinson
had already left the band. Just twelve years old and already my
musical tastes were out of phase with the times.

A few days later, mid-week, my dad came home from his clinic
around nine. He was heating up his dinner in the microwave and
asked me to follow him downstairs to the basement, to the library,
which he also called his music room.

"Sit down, we're gonna listen to something."

I sat down on one of the armchairs. He pulled a record out
of the chest that held his collections. He held out the big album
sleeve. The first thing you noticed, standing between trees that
had lost their leaves to autumn winds, was a woman with green
skin, dressed in black, standing in front of an old canal. In the
background there's an ivy-covered watermill with darkened windows, and a stone wall; above her a grey sky. I looked closely at the
image while my dad placed the record on the platter with the same
care he'd use to stitch a wound or pull a glass shard from a child's
hand. He eased the stylus into the groove, then rubbed his hands

together—an unconscious tic—before picking up his plate again to take a bite of chicken and rice.

In the speakers the sound of rain and a faraway ringing bell rose over the scratching of needle on the vinyl. Then a first epic chord thundered forth. I jumped.

It wasn't the same high-voltage galloping as Maiden. The melodies weren't as catchy; it was more muffled and bassy, and the heaviness of the guitar gave me the shivers. I felt like my whole body was vibrating, and I was being filled with a strength that had always been latent in me without my ever suspecting its presence.

"What is it?"

"Black Sabbath," he said, over the music filling up the room.

I took another look at the album cover.

"They invented heavy metal. Without Black Sabbath, there'd be no Iron Maiden."

So he had heard of them. Of course he had. He turned up the volume a bit. One of his hands followed the chord changes on the neck of an imaginary guitar. The rhythm gathered speed, it was starting to make me want to throw myself around.

"Aren't you afraid of waking up Mum?"

My dad turned back to me. He was smiling. At that moment he was transformed into the fourteen-year-old kid who used to hurry off to hang out at Phantasmagoria the second his classes at Stanislas College finished, impatient to flip through the stacks of psych or prog rock, in the hope of finding the album that would spend the following weeks glued to his turntable.

The next evening when I got back from school I found, right next to *Live After Death*, a CD of *Black Sabbath* by Black Sabbath. Since my mum wasn't home from work yet, I listened to it as I did my homework. When she got home I put my headphones on and kept right on listening.

CHAPTER 11

I MIGHT have heard Vincent getting ready that morning. Or maybe it was afternoon. I was deep in unrestorative slumber. When I opened my eyes a thick paste lined my mouth. It was already dark, and I was alone in the apartment again. I was all curled up in a ball, my lower back stiff as a board. 3:34 pm. I started at six. I felt hollowed out and depressed. Hostile creaking sounds were all around me. I thought about the wad of twenties in my pocket. I thought about my relapse, about the indelible colours streaming by on the screen. It hurt to force myself into sitting position, pushing with my arms. I had to call Malik. If I didn't do it now, he'd think something was up. My head filled with pictures. Call him, I told myself weakly. I collapsed onto the sofa. The sound of a chair scraping reached me from the next-door neighbours'. A voice emanating from the kitchen kept repeating its message: "Call him!" "Call him!" I was standing at the living room door, looking toward a kitchen bathed in violet. I still had my dishwashing clothes on, like a heavy weight paralyzing me. Video lottery tickets stuck out of my pockets. I still had to cash them in and collect my winnings. I heard the voice again. It was my voice, but the words were out of sync with the lip movements of my doppelganger perched in front of a video lottery terminal that had taken up residence where Vincent's microwave once sat. "Call him," my face said to me, in slow motion. I didn't know who I had to call. Imprisoned in clothes that grew more and more constricting, I tried to move. I struggled to stick a hand in my pockets, to take out the tickets before they got so soaked by my sopping wet pants that they disintegrated. I jumped up under my covers and opened my eyes. It was like waking up for a second time. Gradually I came to my senses, and felt a touch less numb. I reached for my pager. It was almost 4:30. There was no one in the apartment. The living room was completely dark. I got up for good, opened the curtains, turned on the light, and started tidying up a bit. I gathered my dirty clothes in a heap, ready for a load of laundry. Comic books and paperbacks were scattered all around the couch. I began arranging them into some semblance of order, the reprinted *Ghost Rider 2099s* I'd found at Millennium, the first *Meltdowns* illustrated by Kent Williams, the last *Sandman* still in my possession—I'd lent the rest to Marie-Lou—a Clive Barker, Volume Two of the *Imajica* series, and a Richard Matheson I was struggling through in English, a few pages at a time. The Derleth was still in my bag. I put the PlayStation games back in their cases and threw away the gravy-encrusted poutine containers. I flipped through my sketchbooks, then stuffed them in the bottom of my bag of clothes.

I decided to call Malik right away, to get it over with before showering. Pretty soon I'd have to leave for work. You couldn't even see outside, it was so dark now.

A chipper-sounding Malik picked up right away. He told me he was going to Cuba with his girlfriend for Christmas. The news came as a relief, and that relief brought a sense of guilt. I talked about the Iced Earth show in April, and said we should go together. Good idea, he said, promising to take care of tickets. Then he cut our conversation short. It felt like he might not be alone. We made plans to meet at Henri-Bourassa Metro station, at noon the next day. He didn't mention the eighty dollars he'd lent me three days earlier. I hung up with an ominous feeling of unease. I was already dreading our meeting.

CHAPTER 12

I T WAS SIX O'CLOCK when I got to the restaurant. I hadn't seen daylight since noon the day before. I went in through the back door, left open by the last smoker. The smell of chicken stock again wafted through the alley, but gone were its pleasant associations. It no longer brought to mind my parents' kitchen in the winter dusk, when I'd come home from school or a day of snowboarding. Now it was the smell of a steam pot to be emptied, of garbage bags to fill as grease streamed down my face and arms, of pans to be scrubbed until the steel wool yanked the nails from my fingers.

I crossed the already full dishpit, went along the service kitchen to the dining room, and stopped by the computer to punch in.

The dining room was already half full. I envied the people who had the luxury of sitting around chatting while they waited for their meal, sipping on a beer or glass of wine. Servers circulated between clusters of customers and the still-empty tables, wine bottles in hand. Nick was polishing cutlery, and asked how I was doing. I said hi and punched in my number the way the owner had shown me. Then I turned around. I saw Bonnie in the service kitchen, taking inventory in the fridges, explaining to another cook which backups to do first. The guy's name was Steven. He'd worked with Renaud somewhere else, and been brought in for a trial shift. I acted as if I hadn't seen Bonnie. She intimidated me so much I couldn't address her without mumbling. I went down to the basement, but the owner appeared out of nowhere and harpooned me as I was stepping onto the first stair.

"Next time don't punch in till you're dressed and ready to work!"

Her tone was sharp, her judgement final. She was off to the dining room before I even had time to agree. I slipped down into the basement and saw Bébert arguing with Jonathan over some instructions left by the chef. They said hi at the same time without interrupting their argument. Renaud was prepping veal for a group of 45 that had reserved for later that night. A copy of their menu was hanging by the prep counter. Salade composé. Lobster bisque with seared scallops. Osso bucco or mushroom ravioli in a blue cheese and walnut sauce. The kinds of things I'd never tasted in my life. At home my mum made pasta, but nothing like this: there was spaghetti, lasagna, sometimes tortellini in rosé sauce. She also made pork cutlets, meatloaf, roasts, steak of course, lots of white fish, salmon and salads sometimes, chicken and fried rice. That was pretty much that. On the group menu, Bébert had scribbled a picture of a dick next to the prices, as he often did next to instructions and notes the chef left on the prep counter. I had a hard time understanding how he managed to get away with all his little pranks and the trouble he couldn't help stirring up. I especially wondered how he slid it by Renaud, who seemed to run a tight ship and was strict with everyone—except Bébert, who was constantly testing his sous-chef, when he wasn't outright laughing in his face. Only much later, after years in the kitchen and on the floor, would I understand that an employee like Bébert can keep his job as long as he can soldier through the rush and get everything done by the end of the shift. And no one could soldier through a rush quite like Bébert. It didn't matter how wasted he was, and he was most of the time. The truth was that Bébert had charisma and leadership in spades, and that was what let guys like Renaud and Christian take it easy.

Carl was sweeping the floors without an ounce of conviction. He checked his flip phone almost once a minute. And ignored me.

I hurried off to get dressed so I could tackle the dirty dishes as quickly as possible.

Upstairs the first order of business was to change the garbages. There were the clean ones, out front, and the greasy, oozing ones, back in the kitchen. And of course there was the dishpit garbage, overflowing with scraps from the lunch rush. Bonnie was showing the new guy how to organize the order tickets on the rack. She gave me a little nod to say hi, between two sentences in her halting French. I went back to the dishpit, galvanized by even this tenuous acknowledgement of my existence.

I cleaned the dishwasher filter and checked my soaps the way Bébert had showed me on my first shift. I sorted the buspans of dirty dishes so I could alternate floor dishes, pans, and prep room utensils. I rinsed off baking sheets slathered with chicken fat and roasting pans smeared in gravy and scorched with rosemary. I ran everything through the machine and scrubbed out the pans, eight or ten at a time. I did my best to keep my machine running the way Bébert had taught me.

Nick came over to chat. I was almost happy to see him. He looked exhausted. He sat down on an overturned bucket next to the slightly open door at the back of the pit. He stretched, then let his arms fall with a sigh. He scrubbed his face with two hands. His eyes were puffy.

"Big Friday night?" I asked him as I put dishes away.

"Hell of a night, yeah. I just got up two hours ago."

He took the smoke from behind his ear and dug through his pockets for a light. His immaculate clothing stood in stark contrast with the filthy surroundings. I asked him if the manager was working tonight.

"Manager? What manager?" he asked, eyebrows raised.

"Uh, Greg?"

Greg's unpredictable, explosive mood made me nervous. I felt better knowing whether he'd be there or not ahead of time.

"Greg's not the manager, dude. He's the other busboy."

"Seriously?"

"Seriously," he said, before lighting his smoke. "There's no manager here."

I felt stupid. Obviously I had no idea how to tell one floor job from another. They all looked the same to me. Plus Greg looked too old to have the same job as Nick.

"And good fucking thing, too. Greg, manager? Ha."

We kept talking while he smoked, and then I heard a clear voice addressing me.

"You like coffee?"

With an open smile that exposed all her teeth, Jade set a little cup down on one of the shelves of clean dishes. Her dark hair was up in a chignon, so you could see her entire face. Little dimples appeared when she smiled. I thanked her, a little shyly.

"Drink this. It'll put some colour in your cheeks. You look bummed."

She set off nimbly back to the bar. I dried my hands on my apron, and picked up the tiny cup of coffee topped with coppery foam. I sipped with the tips of my lips. It was at once bitter and creamy, nothing like the Nescafé Rémi heated up in the microwave or the drip coffee my parents drank. Jade turned around when she reached the order computer at the end of the passage, and smiled at me again. Nick laughed. I didn't respond. He might have been testing me. He stubbed out his butt in the ashtray, washed his hands in one of my sinks, and jogged back to the dining room.

That night started off slower than my previous shifts. By now I knew not to expect much from Carl, and since I was second dishwasher and didn't have to prep for the first seating, I'd managed to get a touch ahead. I'd ripped through the remaining lunch dishes and made sure no new ones piled up. Over time I was learning how to manoeuvre through the kitchen in the middle of a rush without getting in the cooks' way, and developing an intuitive sense of when to go pick up dirty pans.

Every time I crossed the threshold I caught little glimpses of how it all worked—the electric intensity, the constant razzing, Bébert's junkyard soliloquies, Bonnie shoving against Steven as he put out the first appies, Bébert mocking Nick for his cold sore, or taking exception to Renaud's handiwork.

"Man, you're gonna be chef and you can't reduce a sauce?"

He pushed aside a heap of pasta with his tongs to show Renaud the pool of runny sauce at the bottom.

"Sauce gotta to stick the noodles, dude. Pasta 101."

Renaud ignored him as usual, with an enigmatic, almost satisfied smile.

Every second time I brought them a fresh stack of pizza or salad dishes Bonnie thanked me. And with each of these "thanks," uttered without looking up, my mood improved a little. Bonnie wielded her tongs like an extension of her hand. In a series of movements that had become automatic she'd dip them in the garde-manger inserts and pull out little slices of zucchini or eggplant and a couple chunks of peeled tomatoes, then toss it all in the stainless-steel mixing bowl held in her other hand. She hummed quietly while she worked, to herself and for herself alone.

Back in the pit I was getting faster. Carl emerged from the basement looking like there was nothing on this terrestrial plane that could faze him, and didn't even bother making excuses when he went back out to make yet another call. His disappearing act was starting to seriously grate on me, but I didn't do anything. It was easier to work around his unrelenting slackery than to confront him.

From the moment I'd first set foot in the dishpit, I'd never once felt in control—until now. This night was rolling smoothly and rapidly down its track. The cooks were asking me to go downstairs to grab backups from the cooler more often than they yelled at me to pick up dirty pans. I'd started bringing them clean pans as they came out of the machine, instead of waiting for them to pile up.

As the indistinct mass of work resolved into an organized system in my head, my worries left me for a while. The restaurant was becoming a sanctuary of sorts, a place where everything—my money problems, my debts, my gambling—could be forgotten.

Carl took off halfway through the shift again, rightfully so this time as the first dishwasher in. Jonathan and Renaud had knocked off early too, leaving Bonnie and Bébert to finish the night with Steven, who was facing a relentless barrage of mockery, digs, and random shit talk. I felt fortunate that I hadn't been subjected to the same treatment when I started.

Carl had of course managed to leave plenty of his work for me, but against all odds the prep kitchen had been cleaned.

The stereo was back in the dishpit and I'd put on a mixtape that hadn't been selected by chance. When she came to the pit to bring me a focaccia for dinner, Bonnie picked up on it right away.

"You like Maiden?"

She looked kind of amused. For the first time, I felt she was taking an interest in me.

I said I did. *Seventh Son of a Seventh Son* was playing. I told her it was my favourite album.

"I don't really like *Seventh Son*. The sound is kind of cheesy. I like the first albums better."

Before I could get another word in she set off for the kitchen, in her baggy whites. I shrugged my shoulders and started eating my focaccia. The doorbell rang. I stopped eating to answer it. I opened the door. A skinny guy, a little taller than me, stood in the orangey light of the alley. He was shivering in his Avirex bomber jacket, hands in the pockets of his phat pants. He lifted his chin out of his neck warmer.

"Carl here?"

I was about to say no when Bébert popped up behind me out of nowhere.

"And what the fuck do *you* want with Carl?"

I let Bébert walk by. The guy backed up, hands still in his pockets.

"Uh. He has my keys."

"Yeah, I bet. How about you get the fuck out of here, and tell your buddy Carl not to shit where he eats."

Bébert slammed the door.

"I'm getting sick of this shit. That's the fourth time this week."

Then he turned to me and smiled again.

"How's the focaccia?"

He checked out my plate, which was already more than half eaten.

"Enjoy it, buddy," he said, and went back to work.

What was left of the shift slipped by without a hitch, until 11:30. As we were lining everything up for the close a group of twenty people showed up out of nowhere to join the last tables still being served. I caught wind of it through Bébert's hail of curses when he came back to the dishpit in search of pans.

"Twenty fucking goofs walk right in like it's five in the afternoon," he said, as he stacked clean pans, "and I'm alone with a new guy who doesn't know the menu."

I was pretty far ahead with the dishes. I asked if I could help with something.

"Don't worry, man, you're gonna be in the juice too."

Over the groaning of my exhaust fan I could hear the printer grinding away, spitting out order tickets. I sent a rack through the machine and decided to go see how things were shaping up in the kitchen.

The group ordered haphazardly, a couple dishes at a time, nearly all graced with complex substitutions. Bonnie was on the pass, and doing here best to prep pans for Bébert to throw on the stove. But she didn't really know the hotside menu, and had to search around to assemble the ingredients. She was checking an old menu stained with sauce and oil for guidance. But things were going sideways: she'd forget the broccoli in one dish, put green onions instead of garlic in another. Every couple of minutes she let out an impatient sigh. Bébert was putting out the final tables before starting on the new the steam table where his sauces lay warming. He was setting up and plating his own food, leaving Bonnie free to prep the pans for the group and keep an eye on Steven, who was sweating like a pig as he wrestled with salads and appetizers. He kept wiping his forehead to keep the sweat from dripping into the food. The restaurant had gotten loud again. It wasn't the steady thrum of a full room, but another kind of racket, a cacophony of shouty voices clamouring to be heard over boozy laughter, a sound I was only just beginning to recognize as the swan song of end-of-the-night groups. House music was pumping from the speakers, and Séverine had turned it up. Practically empty twenty minutes ago, the room had turned into a party. Customers who'd eaten earlier were joining the group. Behind Bébert, who was thundering full steam ahead, I could see the dining room through the dessert shelves. A group was gathering at the end of the bar. Everyone was glamorously dressed, and they all flashed the gleaming smiles of wealthy forty-somethings. They were deep in flirtatious conversation with Jade and Sarah, who seemed to have no problem holding their attention while keeping the drinks flowing. I looked away. It felt like I was in an aquarium, watching the rest of the world living through a glass wall without end.

"Nick, tell your servers to pick up their fucking food. I don't have all night!"

A guy with a fulsome tan and Tintin hair came up and leaned over the dessert pass-through. His muscles were straining to pop out of a clingy turquoise V-neck, and his eyebrows were concealed behind chunky statement glasses. The smug smile stamped on his tic-ridden face made it apparent he had no idea what he was getting into. He leaned almost his entire body into the kitchen, between two pass-through shelves. Watching him reminded me of the idiots who venture into tigers' cages to prove their fearlessness. Typical pal of Séverine's, coked to the gills.

"Hey, Ti-Bert! Got time to cook me up something? If I order here you could do it quicker, right? Your waiters aren't exactly breaking records tonight."

Bébert didn't answer. He deglazed a pot with white wine. A two-foot flame rose up out of the elements. Then he shoved the pan up in his new friend's face. The cretin jumped back and knocked his head on a shelf. He let out a whimper, and caught the glasses that had been knocked off his face just in time.

"Sorry, man, I'm busy!" Bébert yelled without looking at him. "Go tell Séverine your sob story. Shit, you should be able to see how busy I am with those two-thousand-dollar glasses."

He lifted his head without looking at the guy's beet-red face. His gaze was directed behind him, in the dining room. He was looking for someone.

"Where the hell are you, Nick? Ring the fucking bell, Bonnie!"

His voice rang out like cannon fire. The dampened purring of the hood vents and clanging of pans all augmented the pressure Bébert brought to bear on the world. Then Nick popped up like a jack-in-the-box and yelled at me over the cacophony to get a mop. There was something in his tone I didn't like, and he could tell.

"We've got a situation in the washroom, man. It'd be awesome if you could take care of it."

Nick grabbed a pile of steaming hot dishes and set off into the dining room, weaving between customers. I went to get a mop, rolling the bucket to the dining room and then finding a path through the customers and their cloud of expensive perfume. No one deigned to get out of my way. I had to keep saying "excuse me" and try to carve a path around them, interrupting their discussions, sometimes clearing a bit of a path with the mop bucket. Séverine had witnessed my entrance and was watching me like a hawk. I kept my eyes on the ground in front of me and made it to the bathrooms without spilling too much mop water. I heard voices coming from inside but pushed on the lacquered door of the first washroom anyway. I walked in on two guys with movie-star haircuts in t-shirts and suit jackets, doing keys of coke. When they saw me they froze with dazed looks on their faces, then got right back to their conversation, giving me a look of disdain that made me want to leap up and throttle them. Evidently the "situation" wasn't in this washroom. I went into the other one. One of the toilets was overflowing. I hadn't brought a plunger. I crossed the dining room again in my filthy uniform soaked in dirty dishwasher, and did my best to steer through the crowd of people happily chatting and drinking cocktails. I looked like a homeless man crashing the Oscars.

When she saw me walk by with the plunger Bonnie yelled at me to grab a buspan each of spinach and leaf. I registered the info and ventured back into the melee of customers, concealing the plunger against my leg. I was trying to ignore the feeling of humiliation mixed in with contained anger, but it was bubbling over despite my best intentions. I felt as if everyone was staring at me, though no one noticed me at all.

A young woman walked in to do her makeup while I was unclogging and cleaning the toilet. Another came in and, when she saw me, sighed in exasperation. "Take your time, why don't you? Are you almost *done* yet?" I quickly gathered the wads of soaked toilet paper, sponged up the water as best I could, and glided back with my mop bucket like a gondolier of grime.

I beat a furtive retreat to my home base, trying to clear my head and dispel the shame taking over my headspace. I parked the bucket and mop in the dishpit and ran to the basement to grab the spinach in the cooler.

That was when I cracked. I started yelling, calling Carl every name in the book, trembling with rage as I fantasized about breaking that ass-picking dogfucking midget's snotty little face in half.

Carl hadn't prepped a single buspan of lettuce. All I had left was one romaine and one leaf. No spinach, no arugula. I shouldn't have been surprised. It meant I couldn't bring up a buspan now, as Bonnie had asked me to; it meant she'd fall behind on the appetizers; it meant everything would fall behind. I felt like punching the wall. There were tears in my eyes. I grabbed the buspan of lettuce and two bags of spinach and ran upstairs. I had no choice but to quickly destem and wash them right in the kitchen.

"Bonnie, I ..."

"What?" she snapped.

She looked at me and scrunched up her face when she saw the unwashed spinach.

"It's Carl. He didn't ..."

"What the fuck is this?" she asked as she yanked the bags from my hand and held them up under my nose.

"Carl he ... didn't finish the prep ..."

"Not my problem," she spat. "I asked you. You fucked up."

"I'm gonna wash them quick right here."

"Don't get in my way," she said, as she gave me a withering look. "And hurry the fuck up."

She was throwing utensils and swearing bilingually. I rolled up into a little ball and found a spot by Steven to sort spinach. He had seven spinach salads along with fifteen other appetizers, all going out at once. I started tearing the dark green leaves and felt the sweat running in channels down my sides. My hands were trembling, but I was going as fast as I could, with my jaw clenched until my teeth were ready to break. Bébert had been watching what happened and said to me:

"Just rip through that spinach. Don't worry about that little shit, I'll handle him."

For good measure he cursed out Christian the drunk and Renaud the eunuch. I passed the spinach over to Steven the second it was ready, so he could finish off his plates. Séverine was standing by the till, casting interrogative glances in our direction. She settled up with one of the last couples that had come in before the group, then came over and stood in front of the pass-through. She had let her hair down, as at the end of the previous night, maybe because the people who had shown up out of nowhere were friends of hers. Her hair was straight, almost darker than Sarah's, and longer too. It fell over her naked shoulders. Though she was trying to keep a lid on it, you could see that she was furious. The moment she opened her mouth, I could tell this was no time to talk about our problems.

"What's up with my appetizers?"

Bonnie didn't answer and neither did Steven. Both were waiting for the other to speak up and take the first blow.

"Hey! Bonnie Evans. I'm talking to you."

"It's your fucking goof Christian's fault," Bébert cut in in a nasty tone. "He hires incompetents who don't do their prep."

"Did I ask you? I'm not talking to you. Flip your pans and don't make me come do it myself."

Bébert kept working, ignoring her. He was stone-faced and there was violence in his movements.

"Hurry up, people!"

She smacked her palm down on the stainless-steel pass-through shelf and strode furiously off. Even after she had disappeared you could still hear the echoes of the sharp *ping* her ring made when it hit the steel. Bébert's cheeks were scarlet.

"Fucking bitch!" he said.

He turned to me, already almost calm, and said:

"Help us with the focaccias, it's not that hard. Steven, what you got for focs?"

Bébert kept right on tending to his pans. Steven looked up from his salads. He wiped his forehead and scrutinized the tickets in front of him.

"Uh. Chicken foc, goat cheese foc, and . . . yeah, just three. A basil foc too."

"Good. Dishwasher'll make them. You do crostini and salads. Everything's gotta go out right fucking now."

I felt dizzy, as if I'd been tossed several feet in the air. I took a deep breath and focused on Bébert's instructions. Now I was sweating almost as profusely as Steven, and I too had to wipe my forehead at regular intervals. Bébert pointed out the ingredients for each focaccia with his tongs, while sautéing pastas. He threw tuna steaks on the grill and turned the smoking veg in the pan with his bare hands. He'd given me a plastic bucket of tomato sauce, to ladle over the chicken focaccias. Bonnie was prepping the plates, with expressionless eyes and lips clenched tight as if she were choking back tears.

I made the focaccias as best I could while Bébert barked out instructions. Bonnie elbowed me out of the way and grabbed them to throw into the pizza oven. In an attempt to scoot around Bonnie and the oven door that was about to open Steven bumped into Bébert, whose tongs held an osso bucco dripping in sauce. It did in fact seem to fall to the floor in slow motion, in some kind of bullet time, while the four of us all stood around in a freeze-frame. The osso bucco hit the dirty kitchen floor with a muffled slurp. There was a moment of stunned silence in the kitchen, broken

only by the growl of the hood vents noisily sucking and the roar
of the crowd in the dining room. Bébert kicked the osso under the
oven, without even swearing. In a single movement he leaned over
his fridge and took out another one. He pulled the meat from its
sous-vide and threw it in the microwave. The servers were already
leaving with the other plates for the same table. He told them two
more minutes for the osso. With some chicken stock he extended
the sauce left in the pan from the first osso. He took the meat out of
the microwave, felt it, seemed satisfied it was tender enough. Then
he said, between clenched teeth, as if talking to an imaginary diner
in a snotty, disdainful tone.

"It'll still be better than if Renaud made it. And you won't
notice a thing all coked up like that, will you. Fucking chump."

He dropped the meat into the makeshift sauce, added a splash
of tomato sauce, then asked Bonnie to plate it up.

"Yo Bébert. The osso coming?"

"Nick, bring me a beer."

"Bébert...I..."

"Beer, motherfucker. And yeah, your shitty osso's coming,
Bonnie's plating it."

With smooth, quick movements Bonnie had placed the meat
on an angle, over a curl of linguini, doused it all in sauce, and
planted a sprig of thyme in the marrow of the knuckle, before
wiping the rim of the plate.

Bébert turned toward me.

"Go to the walk-in and bring me the blue cheese sauce. It's with
the other sauces in a bucket like this, under the lettuces. If you're
not sure, taste it."

I ran down to the basement, four steps at a time. Another surprise awaited in the prep kitchen: I hadn't noticed earlier when I'd
gone for the backups, but Carl hadn't cleaned the steam pot. The
strips of meat had been baked onto the walls of the pot, which was
overflowing with chicken carcasses. For a few seconds I seriously
contemplated fleeing through the staff room emergency door. It
would be ten minutes before anyone noticed. I heard Bébert from

upstairs, bellowing to hurry up. The stairwell amplified his voice like a megaphone. I heard him stocking up on pasta bowls. If I took off, the evil forces within me would win again. I took a minute to calm down, then went into the walk-in.

I couldn't tell the cream sauce from the goat cheese sauce from the blue cheese sauce. I may as well have been looking at three buckets of white glue. The only way to figure it out would be to taste them. Other than industrial cheddar, Kraft Dinner, and Pizza Hut mozzarella, all cheese grossed me out back then. The prospect of tasting a cheese sauce, let alone a blue cheese sauce, turned my stomach.

I picked up the two buckets I thought looked about right and brought them up to Bébert. I told him that not even by tasting could I tell the difference. I waited for him to lose it. But he didn't say anything. He could tell them apart by looking.

"That one's the blue. See how the chèvre always has a crust on top."

Nick had brought him a pint. The smile returned to his big cheeks, and he sent me back to the dishpit. He was having fun teasing Steven, who was checking out the focaccias I'd made. We had weathered the storm. It had now moved on to the dining room.

CHAPTER 13

J ADE came back with a beer while I was digging my way out
from under the mountain of kitchen dishes. She didn't look
remotely rattled by the end of her night, seemed as fresh as she
had been at the beginning of the shift.

"Not so bad, out front?" I asked.

"No," she said sweetly. "They're a lot of fun. I like when it gets a
bit crazy. Otherwise it's boring."

I saw her heading for the rack of clean cups, and tried to pick
it up for her. We gently bumped into each other. She burst into a
laugh, with her hands on my shoulders, as if ready to push me out
of her way.

"Drink your beer. And try not to break anything."

She went back to the dining room with the rack of cups. The
porcelain chimed in time with her footsteps as she headed away
from the dishpit. I took a sip of beer. It was sweeter than honey.
I was probably bright red to the roots of my hair.

When I came up from the basement to clean up Carl's mess
I found Steven and Bébert scrubbing the steam pot. They were
attacking it with gusto, as if it were another of their jobs to be dispatched as swiftly as possible. I stuttered out my heartfelt thanks,
feeling a gratitude akin to being given a heart for transplant.
Bébert laughed.

"How about less talk and more taking out the garbage?"

I took the garbage bags upstairs, then went back down as Bébert polished off his second pint. He pounded the bottom of his glass on one of the prep room tables. Steven was washing off his arms with the powerful fluorescent green degreaser in the prep sink. That's what I should have done myself from the beginning, instead of trying to fold myself up like a contortionist in the miniscule staff washroom.

"Where we drinking?"

Bébert was unbuttoning his chef's coat.

"How about it, Steven? Gonna man up and come for beers?"

The new guy unrolled his sleeves as he mulled it over, as if Bébert had given him a trigonometry problem to solve. Bonnie was coming back from the staff room. In her street clothes she looked ready to climb onto a stage somewhere and scream into the mic. Her purple locks poured forth from a burglar's toque and her unbuttoned army jacket revealed a tatty Ramone's sweatshirt. You could see skin through the holes. A king-size smoke was clenched between her teeth. She told Bébert anywhere but Roy Bar was fine. She didn't want to go back there. He asked why. You could tell from his cocky smile he already knew the answer.

"I'm getting tired of that place," she said in English.

"Yeah right, Bonnie," he answered in her language. "Sam told me what happened."

He laughed. She rolled her eyes. I remembered the bartender who'd held her in his arms, last time.

"But don't worry," Bébert said, "he's not working tonight."

She gave him a punch in the shoulder.

"Fuck you, Bébert. I don't wanna go there."

Steven took off to change after agreeing to come with us, wherever we decided.

We heard Nick bounding down the stairs.

"Yo Nick. You with us?"

He headed down to the wine stockroom, with a big ring of keys.

"I don't even know what time I'll finish, man. They're hitting it hard upstairs." Bonnie said we should go across the street, so

Nick could meet us later when he got off. I'd be happy not to see the tattooed barman, though Nick wasn't my first choice to take his place. Bébert told Bonnie he and Nick were banned across the street. One time, just before last call, Bébert ordered a "Canada" of JD—one shot for every province and territory—and by the time he made it to Saskatchewan he was throwing his shot glasses around the bar as he emptied them. Bébert told the story as if he'd been caught talking too loud at the library. Nick came out of the wine room with a milk crate full of bottles held out in front of him, arms straining under the weight. He put the crate down and locked the door, then put the key ring back around his wrist, bent his knees, and picked up the crate again. It all took around three seconds. He didn't even seem to be in a hurry.

"Let's go to the Zinc," Bébert said. "You can meet us when you get off. And I'll kick your ass at pool."

Nick said, "Okay, cool," over his shoulder as he climbed the stair, bottles clinking together with every step.

Steven came back changed. He looked older. In their whites a lot of cooks looked like overgrown teenagers in pyjamas. I went to wash my face, arms, and chest in the staff washroom, and quickly changed.

Bébert was in such a rush to get to the bar I didn't even have time to say bye to Jade. We went out the back door. The cold was biting. I was happy to be changed. Bonnie in her cook's outfit and Bonnie in her jeans full of holes were two distinct, twin creatures inhabiting parallel universes. Her look reminded me of Marie-Lou when I first met her.

We walked a while through the snowy alleyways, with curls of steam rising from our heads. An open bottle of wine magically appeared out of Bébert's bag.

"You jack that from work?" I asked.

"What, you think I can afford this Chatêau Asshole? Wait till I'm sous. Then we'll really get into the good stuff."

We shared it three ways, since Steven passed it along when his turn came up. I didn't usually drink white wine. It tasted like sour apples, but out there in the snow at one in the morning it went down easy. A little touch of warmth rose up in me every time Bonnie passed me the bottle. I had stopped thinking about the twenty-dollar bills in my pockets; my head was no longer playing the highlight reel of every spot I knew in town to gamble. Bonnie was laughing at Bébert's barbs. He was really going to town on Séverine. Steven followed us in silence, hands in the pockets of his Kanuk parka. Bébert stopped every once in a while to tag a wall with the can of the spray-paint he carried in his backpack. Bonnie told him to hurry up.

"Move it, Bébert, it's fucking cold."

By the time we got to the Zinc we already had a nice buzz on. I glanced around the room. No machines. The place was exactly what the name suggested: a long zinc bar stretched from the front door to the back of the room. The windows were steamed up. The oxblood walls and low-hanging lamps gave it a cozy vibe, like a grandparents' basement. The floor was tiled like a shopping centre, and the tables were wobbly. This tavern had been part of the Plateau of the seventies, and the eighties as well.

Bébert ordered two pitchers and put himself up for next game on the pool table. I wiggled into a booth. Bonnie sat next to me. Bébert poured us all beers and began submitting Steven to a rigorous interrogation. Where did he work before? How did he know Renaud? How had he found the night? Bonnie stubbed out in the ashtray at the centre of the table and looked at me.

"Hey. So . . . yeah, I kind of yelled at you back there. I'm sorry about that."

She picked up her glass.

"Cheers, man."

I clinked my glass against hers.

"That's all right," I said in halting English. "Carl, he leave without doing his job. I was hungry."

"Angry, yeah," she answered after a long swig of beer. "Nah, really, you did great tonight."

While Steven and Bébert were hashing out their past jobs and trading gossip about people they knew, I got back to our talk about Maiden, under more propitious circumstances. The scent of her shampoo was discernible over the smells of tobacco and cooking grease.

"So you're a diehard Maiden fan, right?"

"Yes, I do!"

"*Tu peux parler français*, you know. I understand it well enough. Can't speak it for shit though. But you already know that, right?"

She pushed a lock of purple hair back behind an ear riddled with piercings and held out her pack of smokes. I declined; she lit another. She threw her pack of matches on the table. The Café Chaos logo was printed on the front.

"Oh. You know that place?" I asked, still trying my English.

"Yeah, why? What do I look like, a tourist?"

She gave me an insulted look, until I turned red and stuttered some semblance of an apology. Then she burst out laughing and put a hand on my shoulder.

"Just kidding!"

She laughed, with her other hand over her mouth. I smiled and took a sip of beer.

"I really like that bar. It's one of the only places I know that plays metal all night long," I said, switching to French

"My friends and I always go Mondays. That's the best night."

"*Tu y vas lundi prochain?*"

"Next Monday? No, I work. But we can go some other time."

She threw a cardboard coaster at Bébert, who was still chatting with Steven. He shot her a middle finger, without looking at her. She let out a little laugh, and threw another at him. I took another sip of beer and watched them. She turned back to me.

"What else do you listen to," I asked, "other than Maiden?"

"*Plein de choses.* Older Megadeth and Metallica. First band I saw live."

"Oh yeah? When?"

"Lollapolooza '96. With these fuckers."

She showed me her shirt. My eyes widened.

"You still have the shirt?"

I didn't really know the Ramones. She took a puff of smoke.

"One of the best shows I've ever been to."

"Ah lucky you. I was too young to go there."

"You know Suicidal Tendencies? Man, the guitarist is such a babe!"

She said it in a low voice, eyes turned heavenward and hands clasping an imaginary version of the dude in question. I tried to visualize him. I'd heard a couple Suicidal Tendencies songs. It sounded a bit like Anthrax, or maybe Slayer.

"You like Slayer?"

"Some tracks are okay. I'm not so into their heavier stuff."

I must have looked a little surprised.

"I know I dress a bit like a metalhead, but . . . *je suis une hippie* inside. I listened to metal . . . *à cause de ma big sis*. She always made fun of me for the stuff I listened to: Pat Benatar, Heart, Fleetwood Mac, CCR, Jefferson Starship, shit like that.

It reminded me of the songs that played on CHOM FM in my dad's car when he'd pick me up after primary school. Bonnie pulled the pitcher closer to her glass and then took up a new position in the booth, to get herself another. A look of concentration came over her face as she poured beer, a long cigarette dangling from the corner of her mouth. It foamed up and she spilled a bit. She giggled as she wiped the table with her coat sleeve. She stayed there a minute, zoning out, then said:

"I was born two decades too late."

I smiled, without her seeing. I told her that the hippie part of me loved Neil Young.

"Oh, my mum is such a huge fan!"

Her mum used to listen to Neil nonstop at home, when Bonnie was little. On vinyl, on an old turntable. I tried to imagining her childhood, growing up in a bungalow in suburban Ontario. Her dad was great, she said, he liked everyone, could fix anything. Her mum was an old hippie, and was actually at Woodstock, or at least that's what I think she said. I wasn't catching it all. But I came away with a series of images in the faded colours of eighties photos. An eight-year old Bonnie with bowl-cut hair and grass-stained knees, riding a BMX in an empty lot or running around with her brothers and sisters and the neighbour kids.

"She would put on *After the Gold Rush* or *Everybody Knows*... and sing all those songs while she cooked."

Her mum also listened to Janis Joplin, "when she was feeling bluesy."

I started getting wrapped up in the story. I said there was more intensity in Janis's voice than in any metal guitar solo. She talked about Freddie Mercury, and the Queen songs she used to sing at the top of her lungs in the shower.

"Singing in the shower is the best!" she said, before correcting herself. "Singing *and* drinking beer in the shower is the best!"

That's how we got back to Maiden. I went off about Bruce Dickinson. At that time he was my idol. I started explaining how, during the recording of *Chemical Wedding*, he'd ingeniously replaced the low E on both guitars with bass strings, for a heavier sound. Then I got going on the overall album concept. It was based on William Blake's poetry. I went track-by-track through the entire album, with extravagant hand gestures to drive home my point. Bonnie listened, sort of paying attention, perhaps more out of politeness than genuine interest in what I was saying. But I just couldn't stop. The alcohol was going to my head. At the end I could actually hear myself getting carried away, and feel Bonnie inching away as friendly mockery took the place of the genuine enthusiasm that had been there moments ago.

"Have you seen Maiden live?"

"Two times, *oui*."

Her eyes widened. Then she opened her mouth when I told her I'd been there for Dickinson's return to the stage, in '99. They'd pretty much stuck to their early stuff.

"I'm so jealous."

On that tour she'd tried to go see the Toronto show, but the guy she was going out with hadn't been able to get tickets.

"We should've tried for another city, Montreal, even Quebec City. Man, I would have killed to see that show."

I took a sip of beer. My excess of enthusiasm was dissipating. Steven and Bébert were playing pool. Bébert was striding around the table like a hunter, deciding which ball to pounce on next.

"Why'd you move to Montreal?"

She took a final puff of her smoke and stubbed it out in the ashtray. She scrunched up her eyebrows, gave a serious look.

"To study. I wanted to get into journalism, at Concordia. But I dropped out. You know Montreal: too much drinking and partying."

"Journalism. So you like writing?"

She pointed at her glass.

"I like booze more!"

She started laughing again, and shot me a knowing look. At that moment you never would have guessed that the girl beside me and the cook who shoved aside everything and everyone in her path were one and the same person. I had never seen her so happy. I was about to ask her what she liked to read.

"Ahh, young love."

It was Nick's voice in the distance. Bonnie turned to him.

"Yo bitch. What's up?" she said by way of a greeting. "Why are you still wearing that suit? You look like a fairy."

She was pulling on his too-tight shirt. He yanked it back, with an annoyed look. Nick reminded me of the hockey players I'd gone to school with, who wore clothes two sizes too small so their polo-shirt sleeves cut into their biceps.

Bébert was holding court on the pool table. Anyone who challenged him was swiftly sent packing. It never took more than three or four turns. Steven was watching, and commentating his shots. I checked out Bonnie, discreetly, as she talked with Nick. He went up to order a round of shooters.

Bébert came back to the table with a pitcher of ale. Behind him, Steven was playing against two guys around my age. In their immaculate white baseball caps they looked like they'd been teleported in from a suburban nightclub. Steven had them up against the ropes.

I was gently slip-sliding into drunkenness as my exhaustion caught up with me. I could feel the layer of grease coating me from head to toe, except of course my hands, scrubbed clean by abrasive soaps and steel wool.

Bébert turned toward me and asked if I was okay. I gave him a thumbs up. He came in closer.

"I know it was a rough night, man. We'll deal with Christian, leave it to me. We'll find you a real partner."

I shrugged my shoulders and told him again that I was fine. Though the signal was still weak I could feel something welling up inside me, a hint of that fever that always preceded a relapse. I caught a glimpse of Bonnie's white neck through her purple tresses. She was digging for a smoke. I looked away.

Nick came back with the shooters. He handed them out, one apiece. We shot them back, screeching like banshees. The booze hit me like a fist to the jaw. The fever dissipated, the noise drowned out the signal. I was numb enough to be out of the danger zone.

The pace they kept was a far cry from the drinking I'd done as a teenager, or the crash-and-burn style of my Cegep friends. I was having a hard time getting used to my new friends' bottomless thirst and the pace at which they raced full-speed ahead to oblivion.

Bonnie had moved her chair next to Bébert's and they were setting in on Renaud, clearly well-trod common ground. She kept touching him, sometimes on the shoulder or even the thigh. The alcohol she guzzled seemed to have no effect whatsoever beyond adding a dash of colour to her cheeks.

Nick was chatting with Steven now, about some guy named Gaétan—or maybe Gates?—a Champagne-and-amphetamine-fuelled restaurant boss who slept no more than three hours a night.

The kind of boss who'd bust into the kitchen and do half the rush, throw some pans and make the servers cry, then go right back out to the floor to lay down the red carpet for friends who'd show up out of nowhere. They'd both worked for him before. Nick still had nightmares.

"I spent three months in that kitchen, man," Steven said, "and lost fifteen pounds. Fuck, we were always understaffed, doing two hundred covers a night. As if that wasn't enough, dude would show up at the last minute and grab stuff for his other events. One time a line cook told him he couldn't just take off with the batch of brochettes, we were running out. So Gates, man, he throws them in the garbage, right in the kid's face. Says all he has to do is make more tomorrow."

As they fleshed out their portrait of this guy I wondered how Séverine stacked up in the ranking of slave-driving restaurant owners. I still hadn't seen enough to get a proper sense of her character. I hoped she wouldn't turn out to be a wingnut like this guy.

"Yo Bébert. You in?"

Nick held a little chunk of hash hidden in his palm. Her eyes shining from the alcohol, Bonnie said she'd join them, then got up to go pee.

"Who'd you get it from?"

"Greg," answered Nick.

"Okay, I'll have a puff."

I turned toward Bébert to ask him if Greg was really just a busboy.

Bébert laughed a bit, as if he was remembering an old joke.

"Isn't he a little old to be a busboy?"

"What's it to you, man?"

"Uh, I don't know. Just seems like something's off. What is he, thirty, thirty five?"

Bébert wasn't smiling anymore. He leaned toward me.

"What exactly do you want to know, man?"

I leaned back a bit, putting up my hands.

"Nothing. Just seems kind of weird, that's all. I was sure he was a boss or something."

The bar was getting noisier as three a.m. approached.

"Let me give you two pieces of friendly advice. One: If you got questions about Greg, ask him yourself. Don't go around asking other people. Two: Don't ask any questions. Greg really hates people asking him questions."

That sobered me up a bit. Bébert was staring at me. Clearly, I'd said something wrong. I didn't really see what the problem was.

"All I wanted to know is if he's really a busboy. Nick said he was a busboy, but it didn't seem like it. He makes me kind of nervous, that's all."

Bébert leaned back now and took a sip of beer. Bonnie was telling an intense story that involved lots of punching in the air; Nick was listening to her, falling over laughing. I got up to leave, and tried to pay Bébert for my share of the pitchers, but he wouldn't let me. He told me to have a good night, and not to worry about Greg.

I staggered out of the bar. The cold caught me off guard. I walked a while up Mont-Royal, which was quiet except around the doors of the bars closing one after another. I hailed a cab. It stopped and I sacrificed one my twenties for a ride back to Ahuntsic. Replaying my conversation with Bonnie, I hoped I hadn't come off like too much of a kid. For a pathetic second, I imagined she was in the taxi with me, and we were on the way to her place. In your dreams, man. But I let myself dream. Sometimes you've got to. For sure I was sad that our conversation had dead-ended right when Nick showed up. I guessed they'd known each other a long time, there was no way I could be as comfortable as they were with each other. I lacked their confidence, their comic timing. The taxi rolled north, sometimes catching three green lights in a row, the car seemed to be sailing on water, swept along by a powerful swell through a white city sleeping frozen under amber, and I let myself drift off to sleep, on my way toward the end of it all, to the very end of nothing at all.

CHAPTER 14

I AWOKE, puffy and swollen, from unrestful sleep. My back was
even more bent out of shape than the night before, as if I'd been
beaten. I checked the time on my pager: 10:53. With Hercu-
lean effort I pulled myself from the sofa and started pacing slowly
around the apartment, to get my creaky bones moving again. I
wandered aimlessly from room to room like a person who's forgotten what they're looking for. Vincent's room was empty and
the mess was piling up. As always it smelled like deodorant and
shampoo.

The cupboard was dolefully bare as always, the kitchen
depressing as ever. I recalled my parents' kitchen, with bread set
out on the counter alongside a basket of fruit and a fridge full of
eggs and bacon, jam and fresh-squeezed juice. I used to love frying
up toasted sandwiches with eggs, bacon, and mayo. I told myself I'd
have to buy at least the basics—milk, bread, peanut butter, coffee.
Another time: it was already late and I had to get moving. I had to
meet Malik at Henri-Bourassa Metro station in less than an hour.

I read the note Vincent had left on the kitchen table, tucked
under my Walkman to make sure I'd see it. He asked if I thought I'd
be staying through the holidays, and whether I could help out with
the rent and Hydro if I was. Whatever I could afford.

I took a shower, still hoping to chase the stench of cooking oil
clinging to my hair and body. I hurried out of the bathroom and

packed my bag with all the stuff I'd need for my shift, then ran out
the door to the bus stop. I just barely caught the No. 69.

It was a beautiful December day. For a week now the grey grass
had been covered over with a blanket of white, dazzling against
the blue sky. It squeaked under my footsteps.

I got to the station ten minutes late. In my current state that felt
like a triumph of punctuality. Malik's Golf was parked in the lot
beside the station. I opened the door. The epic riffery of the latest
Nocturnal Rites greeted me. I got in and leaned back in the passenger seat. Malik was reading over his class notes. They were full
of equations.

"Nice. It's a change from Rhapsody."

I just couldn't get one hundred per cent behind bands who
dressed up as knights and posed for photos holding Claymore
swords.

Malik admired their chops, but I balked at the lyrics. When it
wasn't a pale imitation of Middle Earth, it sounded like the debrief-
ing after a scintillating game of D&D, in rhyme. Malik turned it
down a bit.

"Where we going?"

I suggested we take Berri, then Saint-Denis. We could go somewhere close to the restaurant since I had to work at four.

The sunny streets, low sun, and people taking over the sidewalk made me nostalgic for the holidays. I wished I could go ten
years back in time and recover the excitement I would feel as a
kid when December rolled around. Malik had turned the volume
back up and was tapping along with the beat on the steering wheel.
I could almost imagine I heard myself asking him to take me back
to Trois-Rivières, and was worried the conversation might take a
sharp left turn. It wasn't a good time. He had exams to study for,
and it was dawning on me that my college semester was more or
less a write-off. Since I preferred not to think or talk about it, I
kept quiet. I wiped the steam from the windows and watched the
parade of facades, already darkening in the winter sky. "Hell and

Back" was playing, the only Nocturnal track that had made it onto any of my mixtapes.

We took a seat in one of the booths along the window at the Fameux. Malik ordered a club sandwich and coffee. I had an Italian poutine and a Coke. I had to fill my stomach. I was getting dizzy.

"When are you leaving for Cuba?"

"The 21st," Malik answered, rolling up his sleeves. "I'll be back the 28th or 29th."

The waitress brought our drinks. I took a long swig. The sugar helped. The place was two-thirds empty. A few customers stared at the *Journal de Montréal*. A student sat at the booth across from reading a thick collection of spiral-bound notes. Outside, across the street at the entrance to Bily Kun, guys in navy-blue jumpsuits were drinking coffee, smoking, and chatting.

"You're gonna spend the 24th and 25th with your parents."

"Yeah, I guess."

"It wasn't a question, man. You're gonna spend Christmas with your parents."

He took a sip of coffee, gingerly. Frowned, added sugar.

"I don't really want to."

"And that matters because…?"

His elbows were on the table, fingers interlaced. Despite the dark circles under his eyes Malik looked good. He was freshly shaved. He turned and looked me in the eye.

"Your mum keeps telling my dad she never hears from you. Make a fucking effort, man."

I looked away to hide my irritation. I decided to pay him back his eighty dollars before he mentioned it. I put the ATM envelope down on the table. He reacted exactly the way he did when I made a reckless move during our chess games.

"Good," he said.

"See. I'm not a lost cause."

I took the straw out of my drink and drank from the can.

"I never said that."

He didn't touch the envelope. He was holding his cup to his lips, taking small regular sips.

"Sure you don't need it anymore?"

"No, it's okay, they're paying me now."

"Already?"

"Yeah, I started right in the middle of a pay period, so the chef paid me my first week in cash."

"Seriously? They're paying you under the table?"

"Nah, it's not like that. The rest of the hours will be on a normal paycheque."

I was fiddling with the plastic straw as I talked. The sky was already darkening, and the dry electric heat made me feel better. You could tell it was a bone-chilling cold outside from the way the people walking by were retreating into their coats. Malik's coffee cup was already empty. He'd always drunk his coffee fast. He liked it boiling hot.

"I'm getting it together, slowly," I said. "I'm paying Vincent my share, too."

The waitress came by with a coffee pot. Malik cleared his throat, with the same sound our grandfather made to invite us into a conversation.

"How're your classes?"

"I'll be fine, I'm pretty sure. My job is helping me stay organized."

"Seems like a whole lot of progress in just a week."

"Yeah well. I'm getting my shit together. It was time."

A car horn honked repeatedly. We turned around. A beggar was doubled over on in the middle of the road, as if he was looking for his glasses, while cars angrily drove around him.

"You don't think it might be too much for you, both at once?"

"No, it'll keep me away from the machines. Keep me busy."

Our food showed up and we dug in. I asked him how the end of his semester was going. He said he already had an internship lined up for next summer. He was working on armour for bomb-disposal units, a big project that would stretch over his fall and spring terms. I imagined the Power Armour used by the Enclave forces in *Fallout 2*. I wanted to see it. He asked how my projects were going. Now that I was digging myself out of my hole I'd be able to get to work on them again. Alex was super excited about my drawings, I told him, and was talking about it to all the other groups he knew. Malik lifted up his cup, with a proud look on his face.

I ordered coffee after my poutine, and we had a good long talk that stretched out a couple hours. We made plans for spring, shows we could see, and he gave me my Iced Earth ticket. In Flames was coming to town soon, too. We talked about going to spend a weekend at his dad's place in the Eastern Townships, maybe going out snowshoeing. He kept saying it would do me good to get out of the city, spend some time in the woods. These faraway projects opened a door to a happy place in my mind, where I could imagine a future free of worry and untroubled by the need to gamble. He asked me if there were any girls in the picture. I said not really.

"Wouldn't hurt, hey?"

"Yeah. It's not that, though."

The homeless guy who'd been out in the street was back. Now he was climbing on the roof of a parked car. You could see he was yelling something. No one paid attention. I turned back toward Malik.

"Anyway, I don't want to talk about girls..."

The waitress brought our bills. I felt a momentary panic. There was no way I could pay without exposing my wad of money, grown fat from my recent winnings. But before I was forced to attempt some sleight-of-hand Malik paid for us both.

He dropped me off at the restaurant and kept going up Mont-Royal, on his way to Papineau and the bridge. The sky had turned deep indigo. People's breath formed little frozen clouds. I shivered and took out my pager to check the time. I had a message. I went to phone booth in front of the Second Cup and dialled my voice mail. I recognized Alex's voice. Suddenly my saliva turned acidic and I could feel my heart rattling around in my chest.

"Hey man, we wanted to know when you were planning to show us the drawings. We want to see how it's coming. Mike's getting a little sketched out, especially since you didn't show up last time. It was a lot of work to talk him down, man. I can keep them calm but you've gotta do your part. C'mon. I know you've got this. Give me a call. We're out of town this week, come by the practice space next week. Okay? Bye, man."

I erased the message as soon as it was done, as if doing so could erase the pressure, the deadline, my debts, my lies, my bullshit, the whole world. I took a deep breath. I felt like calling Malik and coming clean. I took another long deep breath, and felt a touch of my sang-froid return. I hung up and crossed the street.

CHAPTER 15

I RANG THE BELL and a jolly little man opened the back door. He must have been about five-two, with ink-black hair and olive skin that was a touch darker on his closely shaved cheeks. The way he was stacking the dining room dishes made clear that he was exceedingly organized.

In rudimentary English, the man told me that his name was Eaton. I introduced myself as well. He repeated my name several times, as if to commit it to memory, without managing to get it right. Over the next weeks I would see that Eaton had a particular way of messing up everyone's name. Bébert was Cuckoo Guy; Bob was The Bob—he often placed definite articles before proper nouns—Jonathan was Chinatown, Bonnie Bobbie, Steven Estevan. He must have done it to get back for all the times his own name had been massacred, before he replaced it with a nickname. My own handle was Laloo. Every time we worked a shift together I'd ask him his real name, more than once. He'd always skirt the question with a mischievous smile or jokes whose gist I could grasp though their specifics eluded me. After a week he finally revealed his real name to me: Bramata Burudu.

That evening I asked how he'd chosen "Eaton," and, as he dried dishes, he told me. In one of the first restaurants he'd worked at when he got to Quebec, they'd asked him to find a "less complicated" name. The day after this barbaric request he was walking through the McGill Metro station and, as he emerged onto Sainte-Catherine, had come across "this big tall building" inscribed with large letters reading "CENTRE EATON." Crowds of people were clamouring to get inside. He'd figured that this must be an extremely important place, clearly named after a great man, and decided to take that name as his own.

He'd finished his shift and put everything away. The stainless-steel dishpit was so clean you could almost see your reflection in it. I'd never seen the pit like that. It seemed twice as big.

In the basement I ran into Bébert. He seemed to be adjusting the temperature of the convection oven, with a bottle of Bawls in his hand. I could smell the guarana of his energy drink even over the detergents and grilled peppers and pungent basil pesto. Bébert gave me a big slap on the back and asked how I was doing.

"A-one."

The prep kitchen was in the same condition as the dishpit. Eaton and Bob hadn't forgotten a thing. The whole room had been scrubbed from floor to ceiling. In the break room Greg was getting changed while he chewed someone out on his cell phone. He had a way of yelling, like he was fighting not to lose his voice. In the unforgiving fluorescent light his premature wrinkles were more apparent, his hair a little greyer. Not the face of a guy coasting through life. Bébert burst into the room with his Bawls, tossed a bottle to Greg, and asked me and if I wanted one.

"Way better than coffee, man."

Renaud came rolling out of the office on his chair, with papers in his hands. He'd been doing the schedule.

"Get ready," he said to me. "Tonight's gonna be intense. I hope you're ready to hustle. We've got the forty-five. You might finish kind of late, they're coming in at ten-thirty."

He was chewing on his pencil like a stick of liquorice. He suggested I get through my prep list as quick as I could, because after eight they weren't expecting anyone but the group, and they wouldn't be having calzones or focaccias.

"Yo, Renaud, is Christian gone already?" Bébert asked, as he looked for something in his locker.

"What do you think?"

Renaud pushed off with his feet and rolled back into the office, all the way to the computer.

"Don't listen to that goof," Bébert told me, nodding toward Renaud. "Tonight's just another shift. Groups of fifty don't scare us."

Bébert walked out of the break room, looking relaxed. Greg went right on channelling his rage through his phone, shirt unbuttoned, staring intently at something that wasn't there in front of him. He stayed silent a few seconds, then cut off the person on the other end of the line:

"Now you're talking about shit that don't concern me, bro. No way. Absolutely not. You call him back right now, and . . . I don't have fucking time for your bullshit, man. . . It's ten or nothing. Tell him that. And don't even fucking think about calling me back with another problem."

While the other guy sputtered away he buttoned up his shirt and tucked it into his pants, in sweeping angry movements, then picked up the bottle of Bawls as he went up the stairs, shirttail flapping behind him.

"Yeah, or maybe you want to spend a relaxing weekend in hospital."

He took bounding steps and seemed about to lose his voice. On his way up the stairs he dodged Bonnie who was dragging her ass into the break room. Though it was well past dark she had big sunglasses on. Purple tresses cascaded over her cheeks like long luminous claws. Bonnie looked like Molly Millions, the cyberpunk heroine of *Neuromancer*, or Kei after his duel against Tetsuo. She also looked like she'd spent the night in a bathtub, or maybe on a doormat. Sipping on a giant coffee, she opened her locker and threw her keys on a table, then peeled off her coat as if painfully removing a spider's cocoon or cumbersome armour. She didn't say hi to me. I didn't say anything to her either.

"Morning, Bonnie," Renaud said, still behind the computer. "Kind of late, huh?"

"Yeah, whatevs," she said in a hoarse, barely audible voice.

I finished changing, put my stuff in Dave's old locker, and went to join the team in the prep kitchen.

Despite all the cleanup Bob and Eaton had done before leaving, the room was now littered with produce crates, broken-down waxed boxes, empty containers of oily pesto and smeared cream cheese, baking sheets, buspans of pasta, mandolins with bits of carrot stuck to them, and dirty spatulas (which Bébert called "spazzulas").

Jonathan was running back and forth between prep counter and cooler with loads of vegetables to chop. He'd shaved his patchy beard since I last saw him. I watched mountains of tomatoes, zucchini, and onions rise up on his counter and the next one over. It seemed inconceivable that he could get through all that before the rush. The prep list for the forty-five kept getting longer, and he kept voicing his feelings under his breath like a mantra, "what kind of idiots take a group that late, what kind of idiots take a group that late, what kind of idiots line up two services before a forty-five." I washed twice the usual lettuces to make up for what Carl had left undone the day before.

Renaud came over to see how it was all progressing. He just stood there in the middle of the prep kitchen, rubbing his head under his chef's hat, not sure who to ask to do what. Then he disappeared into the cooler, to do god knows what. I heard plastic lids opening and shutting, and the bottoms of sauce buckets being pushed back into place on the cement floor. Every once in a while he'd call Jonathan, who'd come help for a minute and then get back to his prep, with impatient, rushed movements. I focused on my lettuce, as if it might keep me safe from whatever lay ahead.

Bébert and Jason were running around upstairs. By now I could clearly picture everything happening above me from the sounds that reached me below—pans being slammed onto elements or dropped under the pizza oven, plates clanging down on the pass-through, the bell ringing—and I unconsciously took mental note of instructions yelled out in my direction. They were burning through the first round of reservations, which Séverine had grouped at the same time to maximize volume before the group arrived. She was also squeezing in walk-ins. You could distinctly hear Bébert swearing from the basement.

The chef hadn't left clear instructions, and it showed. Bob had spent the whole day doing prep but hadn't been given the right information, so he'd focused on certain parts of the menu while totally neglecting others. Christian had prepped for the group, oblivious to the fact that we'd have to make it through two full services first. It wasn't even six when we ran out of marinated veg, the buspans of mushrooms were empty, and we were down to our last backups of chicken and shrimp. Jonathan was trying to fill holes, and I was giving him a hand in between batches of lettuce. I tore up the rest of my pleurotes, then helped him portion chicken strips that we had to get marinating asap. Handling a knife that big made me nervous, and the gelatinous texture of raw chicken grossed me out, but this was no time to be picky. After what seemed like an eternity in the staff room, Bonnie had joined us. Her whites brought out the green of her face, and she seemed even more lost than Renaud. Carl slipped by like a ghost, or more like the sulky slacker he was. Late as well. We ignored each other.

I tried not to get annoyed as the work piled up. I could hear the dishes clinking upstairs. But with one of the prep sinks full of thawing scallops, there was no way I could do my lettuces any faster.

Upstairs the first rush in full swing.

"I don't give a fuck if it's not your table. Take it out!" Bébert yelled. "I ain't cooking that shit twice."

"I don't even know where it goes." Sarah answered.

"Read the fucking ticket. And take out the table."

"No, but I mean—"

"Hey! Take. It. Out!"

Sarah snapping, Bébert barking, servers' voices rising above the crowd, Greg swearing, dishes slamming onto the pass, the muffled opening and shutting of the pizza oven: it all worked its way down to the basement like a series of tremors portending the thousand-and-one blasts to come.

Jonathan was running out of patience. The tension seemed to be eating him alive: he was swearing and irritated at everything and nothing. Bonnie always had a short fuse, but tonight Jonathan seemed even more irascible. It wasn't like him at all. As for Bonnie, she was wordlessly finishing her mise, laboriously piling buspans and inserts of ingredients for focaccias and salads on clean baking sheets to carry upstairs in a single trip. But before she could finish she had to run off to the bathroom. As the contents of her stomach poured forth into the bowl, you could hear Renaud asking if she wanted a little shot of Apple-Jack.

I finished slicing the chicken. Jonathan calmly let me know that the strips were a bit thick, but they'd do. He explained how to mix up the marinade, but Bébert's bellowing from upstairs was throwing off my concentration. He was yelling at Bonnie to get her shit up here, today. The tension just kept ratcheting up. Upstairs it sounded like a madman was pounding pots and pans while a jailhouse choir sang a song consisting in equal measure of elaborate curses and the names of dishes over a beat of steal cracking against tile. A poltergeist had taken over the service kitchen, and everything seemed to be flying and banging around every which way. I went to search the walk-in for marinade ingredients. I was sure that while I was downstairs Carl would keep lounging around in the dishpit with his goddamn cell to his ear.

I came out of the walk-in just as Jonathan cut himself peeling tomatoes. He let out a couple angry "goddamn motherfuckers," then cleared some room in the sink to wash his cut.

"C'mon, fuck! Hot water, let's go, fuck."

Renaud dropped what he was doing on the other prep counter and went to find the first aid kit. Because he was afraid of blood

Renaud asked me to find Jonathan and bandage his cut. Jonathan was holding his finger under a trickle of water dripping from the tap. He dried his hand and I wrapped his index finger in gauze, then put a latex finger cot on—it looked like the end of a surgeon's glove—and went on with his work. He hadn't noticed that I'd made the marinade with cinnamon instead of chili powder. I said nothing, since I didn't want to see him really blow his top. This night was already such a clusterfuck I figured no one would notice anyway.

I left Jonathan and Renaud to fend for themselves and went upstairs for a load of dirty dishes. When I got to the dishpit, Surprise! No one was there. Twenty bucks said Carl was out in the alley again. At least the dishes hadn't piled up too high. Three racks full of washed plates and saucers were sitting on the clean side of the machine. I went to put them away, but they felt greasy to the touch. I loaded another rack in the machine. Halfway through the cycle I realized the water in the dishwasher was cold. I emptied it and filled it again. Still ice cold. I ran another cycle through. Nothing seemed to work. The water wasn't changing temperature. I went to look outside, to tell my teammate. He was all wrapped up in the smoking coat, cell phone to his ear, kicking back on the wrought iron staircase of the condo next door. I beckoned him over. He gestured toward his phone. I'd never met a worse slacker in my life. I went back in.

On my way back to the kitchen a new feeling was coming over me, something in the neighbourhood of panic. I had no idea what was happening. I imagined the hot water could be easily fixed by opening or shutting the right valve. But somewhere beneath this surface confidence an alarm bell was tolling faintly. After a rocky start to the night, the service kitchen was firing on all cylinders. Bonnie looked like a gnarly old eggplant, she was dancing like the devil in a cauldron of holy water. She still wasn't acknowledging my presence. Jason was helping with her salads, but her movements were far less nimble and controlled than usual. You would have expected Bébert to be stressing, but the man was just calmly putting pans of ingredients onto his elements, singing to him-self, with a headphone in his left hear. He kept a Walkman hidden under his chef's coat. I had to call him twice before he turned to me and chanted a snippet of Notorious B.I.G.'s "Ten Crack Com-mandments."

"Bébert. Listen, Bébert," I cut him off. "Is it normal for the water in the machine to go cold?"

He ripped out his earbud.

"What?"

I repeated my question.

He yelled at Jason to take over for him, pushed me out of the way and stormed down to the basement. I ran down the stairs after him.

Jonathan was still in the prep room, eyes red, working on the prep. He was sniffling. Before we had time to say anything about it he told us that it was the shallots.

I went to see what Bébert was doing. He was leaning over the hot water tank, playing with something covered in peeling paint, underneath the tank. Renaud came over, looking like a guy who'd been woken up at three in the morning over some bullshit. Bébert looked up at me. A big vein was pulsing on his sweaty forehead. His earbuds were dangling over his gut, spitting out Biggie. Fun time was over.

"Fuse is blown, man. Pilot won't light. No hot water."

"Fuck. I hope Séverine has the number of the repair guy."

Renaud ran off to the office. Bébert turned around and sprinted back up the stairs. I decided to go get some dishes done. I ran every rack through twice, while Carl brought back dirty pans and took cleanish ones out to the cooks.

When Greg came looking for a rack of coffee cups, I tensed up. He was complaining about a customer. He sprung across the dish-pit in a single bound, quick as lightning, saying that he was going to "throw it in your face, your fucking herbal tea, old bitch." Carl tried asking him a question but Greg just answered with another question, something about whether Carl was going to shut his

goddamn mouth one of these goddamn days or whether he'd have
to do it for him. He turned toward me just before he got caught in
the hallway. And yelled at me:

"Tell your little friend I better not run out of cutlery."

I started working twice and fast, but after a couple racks I saw
that it was futile: no matter how many times I ran them through
the machine, the plates were still coming out greasy and covered
in sauce.

"Stop, guys."

Renaud had come back to bring us the rest of the dirty dishes
and was watching us go, with a face I didn't like much.

"The soap doesn't work in cold water. Go heat up water in the
steam pot, then dump it in that big sink, and wash everything as it
comes in."

"You mean by hand?" I asked.

"Yup."

"Are you kidding?" Carl asked.

Renaud acted as if Carl hadn't spoken.

"Get moving" he said in closing, "or you're gonna get buried
alive."

It was already clear to me that we were going to get buried
alive, one way or another. Hot water, cold water: what difference
would it make in the end? It was almost seven. We still had an
entire service to get through before the group showed up. At the
rate we were going, washing everything by hand, the entire group
of forty-five would be eating off dirty plates. There was no way we
were going to make it. My stomach was tied in a painful knot, as
if I'd swallowed a massive burning coal or a hornets' nest. As soon
as Renaud turned around I went down to the basement to turn on
the steam pot and finish my salads.

Fifteen minutes later I was on my way back up. The heavy buckets of boiling water bashed against the stairs. Carl was back in his
favourite position, watching the dishes pile up with his dead fish
eyes, having a smoke and playing *Tetris* on his phone. When he saw
me he got up and put his phone back in his pocket. He pretended

to get to work around the rack of dirty dishes, with his smoke still in his mouth. I brought the baking pans that Renaud had pulled the osso bucco out of, and asked him to soak them right away in straight degreaser.

"That'll be one thing done at least."

"Whatever, man, you're not my boss."

He answered without looking me in the eye as he stacked dirty dishes, organizing the work according to his sophisticated system of camouflaged indolence. I took a deep breath and didn't say a word.

The second service overlapped the first. I was making strategic incursions into the kitchen, where a new flurry of orders had caught the cooks off guard. Séverine was determined to fill every seat in the restaurant at any cost. Just watching her was exhausting: she was everywhere at once, smiling at new customers as they came in, moving around the room with a bottle, mixing candy-coloured cocktails behind the bar, storming into the kitchen to help take orders out. Nothing distracted her. Watching her make her way from one side of the restaurant to the other in rapid-fire staccato steps, without ever seeming to tire, it was easy to conceive of the restaurant as an outgrowth of her mind, a living map, an Edenic simulacrum she floated through while we remained confined to the red-hot lower rings of hell. Renaud had taken Bébert's place on the hotside, and Bébert was more hindrance than help as he spurred him on to reach levels of speed Renaud couldn't manage even on his best days. Bébert was throwing out plates faster than ever, barking periodically: "Ain't no one gonna put me in the juice!" He was riding Jason hard, though the guy was doing his best to make up for Bonnie's zombie torpor; she seemed poised to faint, or maybe bite someone. Even in this sorry state I couldn't take my eyes off her. In her shoes, I would have collapsed at the start of the shift. I probably never would have even made it out of bed. Bébert was going through Renaud when he had something to ask her: she wasn't talking to him either. Though they were less than three feet apart, each was managing to pretend the other didn't exist.

The stacks of clean pans and dishes were shrinking before my eyes. We'd have to pick up the pace to have any hope of equalling the speed of the machine. I came back from spinning my last batch of leaf lettuce and the arugula, which was running low. I passed Jonathan in the stairwell as he slowly climbed up, with an empty look in his eye.

The scallops were still thawing in a bath of cold water. That left me just one sink. Even going as fast as I could, washing and rinsing the arugula was taking forever. I had to be extra careful to avoid the wrath of Séverine, who'd once found a batch still covered in sand and made it crystal clear to me that this was a restaurant, not the beach.

Someone came flying down the stairs. Greg showed up looking for wine for "those idiots who don't know shit about wine." I was checking the time every ten minutes. I wanted to get my prep out of the way, so I could help the others faster. Then, over the cacophony of the service and the clatter of pans, I heard Carl's whiny voice:

"Yo Bébert, I'm not gonna do all the work while the other guy's playing with his dick downstairs."

I felt the hair on my neck stand up and started shaking.

"Quit bitching. Not a good time." Bébert yelled at him.

I stopped what I was doing and listened. Carl upped the ante, saying he wasn't about to do the work of two just because I couldn't keep up.

"Shut it, dude!" Bébert said again.

My cheeks were burning. I could feel that something bubbling up in me, my heart was beating fast enough to burst. I heard someone coming down the stairs. I recognized Carl's footsteps. He appeared at the foot of the stairs. I saw his smug lazy face, and his fucking cell in his hand. Overwhelmed by an untenable pressure, something in me popped. Carl went to say something but I grabbed him by the collar and dragged him over to show him the sink full of arugula, and asked him if it looked like I was playing with myself.

"Let me go, you little faggot," he said, fighting to free himself.
He pushed me with surprising strength. I pushed back. He
flew into a pile of baking dishes and sauce buckets lying under one
of the prep counters. He stood up and threw himself at me, his
face purple with rage, threatening me like the cocky little punk he
was. He caught me around the neck and I wrapped my two hands
around his throat, pressing on his Adam's apple. I could feel his
strength, and also my own powerful, visceral desire to kill him
then and there by pressing on his windpipe until he shat his pants.
His hands dropped from my dishwasher's shirt and locked on my
forearms, but it wasn't enough to make me relinquish my grip. The
pockets under his eyes were turning blue.

"Let me go, you crazy fuck," he managed to gurgle, spitting on
me.

He started slapping my forearms and I squeezed tighter. I
couldn't feel a thing, but it felt like I was swelling up all over.
Adrenaline flowed through my body and my blood vessels dilated
as I crushed Carl's trachea.

"If I ever hear you say I'm slacking off again," I said in a muffled,
raspy voice. "Get it, you fucking germ?"

Probably alerted by the sounds of our struggle, Greg came out
of the cellar to break us up. He pulled Carl far away from me and
told him in a firm voice to calm down. Carl was bent over, sucking
air, wheezing and holding his knees, his face scarlet. It was almost
enough to believe his shiny, purple face was going to pop off and
send blood gushing in every direction. I would have rejoiced at the
sight. He ripped off his apron and started insulting me, it was his
turn to shake with rage, barking out whatever came to his mind,
completely absorbed in his starring role as a two-bit gangster. He
was yelling at me over Greg's shoulder, while Greg, like a hockey
referee, pushed him into the staff room. He kept right on yelling at
the top of his lungs that I didn't know who he was, but I was going
to find out, believe it.

Greg pushed him again. "Calm down, little man." I was coming back to my senses, with nerves on edge and a surge of nausea.

I could still hear Carl swearing and threatening me like he was some serious gangster, and throwing shit all over the staff room and pounding on lockers.

"Just relax, man." Greg said. "Before I start laughing."

Carl kept right on kicking up a fuss until the sharp sound of a slap rang out, followed by a silence broken only by the growl of the hood vent.

"That's enough, you little fuck," Greg said in the same tone, firm and final. "Scram!"

I heard Carl quickly gather his stuff and head out the back door.

By the time Greg came back and stood in front of me, anger had given way to shame. I was breathing deeply, to chase the sick feeling from my stomach.

With a smile on his face, Greg asked if I was okay. He said again that I was a fighter, and thanked me for giving him the opportunity to slap Carl.

"I've wanted to slap that little punk for a long time," he said. I tried to stand up again, but I was short of breath. I realized I was dripping with sweat. Greg left me alone with my thoughts, picked up his bottles of white wine, and headed back up the stairs. When he got there I heard him break out in laughter.

"You'll never guess what happened. New guy beat up the little slacker."

He started laughing again.

Thirty seconds later Renaud came bounding down the stairs. He found me leaning against the steps, still trying to calm down. He surveyed the scene, eyes wide and mouth agape. His sleeved were rolled up over ropy forearms. He put a glass of beer on one of the prep counters. I longed to disappear.

"That's for you," he said after looking at me in silence a few minutes.

I didn't move.

"Sorry, man. I should have dealt with him a long time ago." He tapped me on the shoulder.

"The repair guy's on his way. You're gonna have hot water again. In the meantime do the best you can. Jonathan and I will give you a hand between rushes."

My throat was in a knot. I felt completely drained and on the verge of tears. I choked back a sob, just in time. Renaud looked at me, as if he had all the time in the world for me. I don't know why but at that moment I thought of Marie-Lou, and Malik, and everything else. Somewhere deep inside a sort of animal stress had been unleashed, and I started thinking about money, and my debts, and Alex and Rémi, and the myriad lies I'd gotten into the habit of telling everyone I knew.

"I'll finish the lettuces and then I'll be there," I managed to spit out.

"Good."

Renaud looked reassured. He squeezed my shoulder, looking down at me this time. Then he turned around, checked on the scallops, and went up slowly. I heard him sighing in the stairwell.

CHAPTER 16

THE DISH SHORTAGE caused by the hot water outage left little time to dwell on the possibility Carl might burst into my dishpit with two or three buddies and kick my ass. But my hands were still shaking when I got back to work.

Whenever he got a chance, Jonathan came back with fresh hot water. You had to change the water in the sink after every batch of dishes. Even with institutional soaps powerful enough to wear away the skin on my hands, the water quickly grew dirty. We were using the machine, hand-filled with hot water, for the toughest pots and pans. Bébert would bring them to me, rapping away, all hopped up on something that gave him the power to float above the confusion. Jonathan looked perpetually bummed out, and when he did break his silence you could tell he had a lump in his throat. He dried dishes, to give his cut finger a chance to heal. I scrubbed and rinsed.

We individually washed each fork, knife, and spoon. Servers were begging us for cutlery. Some set up little caches, others hoarded it in their aprons. Most of what I washed went to Greg. He'd pick up each item like a nugget of precious metal, congratulating me on each clean handful and calling me "fighter." Then he'd slip off into the dining room like a smuggler with a new shipment, distributing the contraband to whichever server was paying top dollar. Forks and knives had become a coveted staple. In every section of the restaurant the floor staff was struggling to set new tables, and until they did they couldn't seat new customers.

At a certain point I stopped noticing the mountains of dishes piling up around me, and my focus trained on whatever was most urgently needed at any given moment. Jonathan did what he could.

From time to time I'd take a load of clean dishes to the kitchen. The lack of hot water hadn't slowed them down one iota. The sizzle of meat, garlic, and onions in the skillet, the sputtering of cooking wine or cream in the hot pan, the growl of the hood vents, the orders shouted in a mixture of French and English: everything was coming together in a cacophony that would drive you crazy if you spent more than five minutes being mercilessly buffeted around by the cooks.

Everything was happening at breakneck speed. Without a single wasted movement Renaud was carefully setting up plates, which were going out to the dining room twelve at a time. Humming along to his music, with glassy eyes and dilated pupils, Bébert had his hands right in the pans, manipulating the food as it cooked. The stifling heat kicked up a notch every time the oven door opened. As the sweat streamed down their temples, everyone kept right on working. Through the pass-through I could see Maude and Sarah's eyes shining in the warm dim light of the dining room when they'd come pick up their orders. Farther off toward the front of the dining room, in the hopping section of full tables with servers dancing around them, Séverine welcomed new customers with a warm smile. She was relaxed, a side of her personality we rarely got to see. Leading diners to their tables, she elegantly manoeuvred through the crowd, impervious to the ambient chaos. Out front everything was proceeding without incident, while in the back we had no hot water and the repairman squatting under the water heater was clocking double-time and the work was piling up and I was packing a paring knife in my pocket in case Carl came back with his crew to teach me a lesson, while Bonnie ran to the kitchen bathroom to throw up between orders and Bébert took long regular swigs from a paper-bagged King Can of Blue he kept under the bottles of olive oils. He'd seen that I'd seen him and, before sending me off for a backup of blue cheese sauce he shot me a pirate's grin that exposed his chipped teeth.

"And bring me the right one this time, hey?"

The hot water's return had the psychological impact of the power coming back on after the 1998 Ice Storm. Or at least to me it did. I set up the ghetto blaster in the dishpit and put on the most brutal mixtape I could find in my bag, to help me attack the strata of dishes and pans that had amassed. Jonathan went back to the kitchen to take over from Bonnie. Renaud had sent her home. He wasn't overly scrupulous about that kind of thing—about a lot of things really, as I'd later find out soon enough. He'd let Bonnie break one of the tacit rules that binds the staff of every restaurant, a cardinal principle of solidarity: no one misses a shift for a mere hangover, particularly when said hangover was earned in the company of co-workers, and especially on an unusually busy night.

I was in the scrubbing pans when someone cranked the volume as Slayer's "Killing Fields" kicked off.

"What do you know? A young kid who listens to decent music."

I turned around. Greg was headbanging as he sorted clean cutlery and put it back in the rack. He seemed relaxed, as if we hadn't narrowly averted catastrophe.

"I saw them in '95. Verdun Auditorium. Crowd went off. Moshing so hard people got hauled away in ambulances."

I never would have pegged Greg as a metalhead. But knowing this made me somehow less afraid of him. He told me later he'd played bass for a few years. His band even had a few shows at Café Chaos.

It was getting close to ten, and I'd worked my way through the worst of the dishes. It helped that Séverine had stopped taking new tables around nine-thirty, to make room for the forty-five.

I hadn't heard her come up because of the music, but when she materialized in the dishpit I turned around. It felt like a member of the royal family had deigned to visit my hovel. I went to turn down the music, almost embarrassed to be listening to it in front of her. Her hair was pulled tight over her head, and pulled up in the back in a Samurai bun. Her thin eyebrows were furrowed. She surveyed the shelves with an annoyed look. I felt like an impotent child. I expected her to scold me for the state of my dishpit, or for getting in a fight with Carl. Instead she began rearranging the stacks of clean dishes in a few quick, methodical movements.

"Give me a hand," she said without looking at me.

I wiped my hands on the last clean rag. She explained which service plates I'd have to take down to the prep kitchen. That was where they would plate the salads and bisque. She picked up a heavy pile, then looked at me. Her forehead relaxed, her perfume refused to yield to the nauseating odours of the grease trap and garbage can. She smiled at me. Little dimples appeared in her cheeks, which looked paler because of her hair.

"When the hot water went out... You did a good job."

She had already turned on her heels and was walking away toward the service kitchen with her pile of dishes, taking long steps like a sprinter.

"Bébert," she said. "Plate the osso bucco in these."

I got to work. I brought the soup bowls and salad plates down to the basement. Renaud was heating the bisque. Jonathan's finger had swollen up like a lightbulb, but nothing seemed to bother him or slow him down. He was tossing lettuce leaves with dressing in the big stainless-steel salad bowls. Maude had arranged long trays on the prep tables.

"Put the salad bowls on these," she said. "Nine bowls on each tray."

Séverine went downstairs. I set the bowls on the tray, Jonathan filled each one with a portion of salad, and Renaud garnished them with a colourful julienne of veg and a monk's cress. Maude wiped the rims of the bowls to catch any splashes of dressing. We all swirled around the prep counter without ever bumping into each other, our movements coordinated in a bizarre spontaneous choreography. Séverine inspected every salad before Denver and another server I'd never seen before grabbed a tray each and lifted it seamlessly onto their shoulders. They went up with the first salads. Denver had barely returned for the second tray when Maude asked me to lay out the soup bowls. She wiped off the trays as they came back, and helped me place the bowls.

"All right, people. Bisque. Go!"

Renaud had finished garnishing salads and was about to go upstairs to get the thawed scallops to Bébert, who would sear them. Séverine stopped him in his tracks.

"Renaud. Did you taste this?"

His face was impassive, his cheeks hard as ivory. The hood vent stopped growling of its own volition, and it felt like the fluorescent tubes might explode from the tension in the air.

"Taste."

I saw Renaud tasting the bisque exactly as he had the first night, when he was portioning it. At that moment I saw exactly what kind of person my sous-chef was. He acted surprised and disgusted—exactly as he had a few days early. The man wasn't a bad actor. He recited the same lines, in the same order, as if he were tasting the bisque for the very first time. But this time he added that Christian had told him it was fine. Maude tasted it too. She screwed up her face. Renaud kept laying it on thick.

"Damn, you just always have to check up after him."

It was like watching the teacher's pet ratting out a classmate.

"But this time you didn't check, did you?"

Renaud muttered something, but Séverine had already stopped listening and was no longer looking at Renaud. Her attention had turned to the stockpot full of bisque. Séverine ordered Renaud to bring her a bucket of cream sauce and started fixing the bisque herself. She didn't bother with an apron, just perched on her high heels in her tailored jacket, her necklace clinking over her silk top. Renaud watched her with an idiotic, forlorn expression on his face and in his deep-set insomniac eyes.

"Maude, tell the guys to slow down the appies, then wait at least ten minutes to clear. Sell a little wine while they're waiting."

Maude darted upstairs. Séverine turned toward Renaud while she added cream to the steam pot. I was sure she'd get splattered but her movements were so assured and precise you would have felt safe if it was nitroglycerine in her hands.

"What are you waiting for? Take the scallops up."

Renaud snapped out of it and hurried upstairs with the scallops.

That left just me and Jonathan with her. I was worried that any minute I might become the designated scapegoat for this gong show, and looked around for a dark hole to crawl into. Jonathan found something to do before Séverine had to ask: he rinsed out the salad bowls, then started searching around in the prep kitchen for graduated plastic pitchers. I was about to ask Séverine what she wanted me to do. She beat me to it.

"Keep stirring this for me," she said calmly. "I'll be back in thirty seconds."

She climbed upstairs at full speed, footsteps clacking loudly on the iron step covers. Upstairs the hum was swelling into the roar of a full restaurant, almost loud enough to drown out the sound of Bébert laughing and Renaud talking.

In exactly thirty seconds Séverine was back, in a percussive storm of high heels. She sent Jonathan upstairs to help Bébert get ready for the mains.

"You have to do everything yourself. You always have to do everything yourself. Unbelievable."

Maude came back to the prep room.

"It's all good, Séverine. People are relaxed, no one's really noticing the delay. They're drinking a lot, having fun. All good."

Séverine kept me by her side to help serve the bisques. Renaud came back with the scallops. They looked like a bunch of little yo-yos sizzling in the big pan. It smelled delicious. With a pitcher of pink liquid in each hand, we were filling up the bowls in which Renaud had placed a single scallop. Maude loaded the trays and they disappeared upstairs on the servers' shoulders. The assembly line was so engrossing I stopped thinking of anything else and occupied myself pouring pink bisque into the white bowls, like a robot dressed in stinking rags. As soon as the last tray of bisques had been whisked upstairs on Maude's shoulders, Séverine asked me to clean the tables we'd used and then see if Renaud needed help.

Five minutes later a similar assembly line had formed in the service kitchen for the osso bucco and ravioli. Jonathan's mood had changed, he was going even faster, as if he and Bébert had been swept up in the same whirlwind. Only Jason was still stone-faced as he sorted garnishes for the final plates. Renaud was putting up orders on the hotside, with help from Maude. A lock of oily hair plastered to his oily forehead made him look like a rockabilly swell who'd grown old a touch too fast. He was organizing tickets by table. It was Maude who had to make sure everything went out in the correct order, to the right people.

Greg was touring the kitchen from one end to another, peering through the pass-through where they were heating plates for the osso, asking whether "it was working." I wondered what he meant.

"Hell yeah!" answered Jonathan.

His soprano was even shriekier than usual, and he looked like he'd jammed two fingers in an electrical socket. Greg winked at him. Renaud turned toward the team.

"Okay, ladies, focus. Table 50, seven ossos, nine pastas. Table fifty-one, three ossos. . ."

I let them get on with their orders and went back to attack the empty bisque and salad bowls already piling up on the rack.

A little before 11:30, Bébert came to find me in the dishpit and handed me some leftover osso bucco with a double portion of linguini. Between my fight with Carl and the subsequent rush I'd failed to notice how hungry I was. Now my stomach almost cramped up at the sight of the food. There was nothing worse than working surrounded by leftover foods when you were starving. The meat was so perfectly cooked it almost melted in my mouth. I scarfed down my meal in a few scorching mouthfuls, then got back to work.

It was around one a.m. when I finished up my mop. Bébert and the others had changed and were having their staff beer at the end of the bar. Silence had descended on the kitchen again, but the group was still partying away in the dining room. The music was pulsing and deafening, pierced only by the patrons' voices. Séverine was giving the bartenders a hand while the other servers cleared the places of other customers who, one by one, were abandoning their seats to walk around the restaurant chatting or head to the bar for more drinks.

I finished cleaning the kitchen, and took a moment to peer through the pass-through. The crowd looked straight out of a fashion magazine or an ad for a dating site. Handsome men, beautiful women. My soaked, grease-stained clothes suddenly bothered me. I imagined that I'd never be part of their world, just as none of them would ever find themselves on all fours with their arm down an overflowing grease trap, or scrubbing pots until the wee hours, face spackled with food. But what did I know about it, really? I snapped out of my reverie and finished closing.

As this interminable shift neared its end and the kitchen and dishpit grew cleaner, I started fantasizing about one possible end to this night. Visions of combinations slotting into place stole over me, sending long shivers of anticipation shooting through my body, while another, much number part of my mind ordered me to go straight back to Vincent's after work. But somewhere deep inside me plans were already being laid, preparations drawn up for the only possible outcome of all I had just suffered through. I feared the moment I would close the back door behind me and find myself out in the alley with all my money in my pocket. It was the ending that I was dreading while doing everything in my power to hasten its arrival.

"You coming?" Bébert asked, popping into the dishpit.

"Depends. Where you going?"

"Somewhere fun."

I finished putting away the dishes.

"Okay, why not."

A wave of relief surged over me. I almost had tears in my eyes. I started piling up the empty racks.

"You okay?" asked Bébert. "You're making a funny face."

Greg appeared in the dishpit. He had changed as well, into a basketball team t-shirt under his leather jacket.

"C'mon, kid. We're out of here."

A joint trembled in his lips while he talked. He crossed the pit and opened the door with his back. When he sparked the joint a skunky odour filled the space between us. Bébert followed him outside, and Jonathan, too, almost skipping.

"Okay, I'm coming," I said, turning off the dishwasher.

I changed even faster than usual and set off to catch up with them. When I went to punch out Renaud was at the end of the bar, finishing his staff beer. He called me over. Jason was next to him, smoking in silence, forearms crossed like a big cat after a meal.

"You're off tomorrow, but the day after we're gonna need you for the day shift and the night too. I'll try to find a new dishwasher as fast as I can. But in the meantime we'll need you to fill some holes."

I nodded, as I punched my employee number on the screen.

"Hey, you okay?"

"Yeah, yeah. I'm fine."

I waved bye and took off.

In the alley a black Monte Carlo was purring, with Greg at the wheel. I could see the rings on his fingers, gleaming through the tinted windows. The bass shook the whole car. The passenger door was open, and there was no mistaking the loop from Biggie's "Big Poppa." Bébert breathed out a milky cloud of smoke.

"Fuck, man, take long enough? What'd you have a book to finish?"

I got in and we drove around ten minutes. It felt like I was in a rap video. The guys were yapping over the beat. Jonathan was telling the story of the bisque, on the edge of his seat, almost losing his shit, even more cranked up than earlier. He was leaning forward, with his hand on the driver's headrest, wearing a fresh white bandage that gave him a Mickey Mouse hand. He seemed to be pointing at something outside, in the night.

"You should have seen the boss's face."

"I'd have rather seen Renaud's face," Greg said, as he passed another car. "Dude must have shit his pants."

Bébert said that was it: Christian's days were numbered. You could hear the scorn in his voice. Greg said we wouldn't be any better off with Renaud.

"Two-faced rat. You can smell it a mile away."

"Hey Bébert, is it true Christian drinks cooking wine?" Jonathan asked.

"Yeah, man. Mixed with Coke."

Bébert moistened the joint, which was burning too fast.

No one brought up my fight with Carl, and that was fine by me. I played the episode back in my mind, with an ill-defined but unshakeable sense of shame. My next shifts would be haunted by the fear that he'd pop up out of nowhere to exact his revenge. Sure, I could tell he was just a two-bit low-level dealer, but he must know some bigger players capable of messing me up just for the fun of it.

Greg turned down a side street, and passed a double-parked taxi, calling the driver a monkey.

"What time's your friend's set?" asked Bébert, holding in a toke.

"We missed it. But the other guys are pretty good."

"Check it. There's a spot."

The doors of the Monte Carlo opened in unison like black steel hindwings. We got out. It wasn't too cold. We headed up a side street and came out on Rachel. The street was bathed in light from cars and restaurants, reflecting off the wet asphalt. Greg and Bébert were walking toward me, while Jonathan chirped away behind them like a comic book version of himself. Greg whistled at chicks on their way to the all-night poutine spot, and joked around with Bébert, his deep, cavernous laugh taking its place in the nervous chorus of car engines and horns. Greg was talking about the three girls he was seeing. Bébert said he couldn't find one who could keep up with him. It felt like the bad kids at school had brought me into their crew, it reminded me of when we used to sneak out and go to the Exclusif in Longueuil, with the Hubert brothers and their little goons who no one dared look at funny.

When we got to the bar there was a short line. The doormen said hi to Greg, had a little chat, and we were in. The place was hopping. It was a far cry from the Zinc or the Roy Bar: the lounge was full but the lighting was dim and the vibe was smooth. You could see silhouettes gathered in plush booths over low tables that held bottles of liquor or Champagne. Lamps like science-fiction fireflies emitted cool light. A central bar bisected the room. In front of bottles that shone like rockets, the bar staff floated in a bluish haze of light misting down like vapour. Customers gathered at the bar in clusters that formed and then dissipated. They looked like younger, more chilled-out versions of the people who ate at La Trattoria. I followed Greg and Bébert who were shouldering their way through the crowd. I apologized to every third person, sweating all over. Jonathan, who was even more awkward than me at pushing his way through the crowd, was falling behind, with his bandaged finger pointing in the air in front of his face. I almost bumped into a waitress with a tray of twenty-dollar drinks. I felt clumsy and filthy, like someone parachuted into a foreign land with unfamiliar customs and an incomprehensible language.

Greg was saying hi to people who must have been fifteen years older than me, in his element like a cool kid in the high-school cafeteria. He shook hands with the bartender, who looked like a Minotaur who took the time to pluck his eyebrows. Greg kissed the two barmaids on the cheeks. They looked thrilled to see him, like groupies with Lemmy Kilmister's arm around them. He ran into two other girls he knew, chatting at the bar: slender beautifully dressed visions with come-hither smiles. They seemed to greet Greg with a languorous slowness. Never in a thousand years would I imagine that girls like that might talk to me. He said a few words first to one, then to the other, with his hand still on the rib cage of the one who'd just kissed his cheeks. He hugged five or six black guys chatting at the bar. We went to a booth. Some friends of

Greg's were already there, with three girls. Greg leaned over to kiss the girls' cheeks, then shook hands with the guys. Greg gave me and Bébert a sign to take a seat here, then continued on his rounds toward the DJ booth. He seemed to know everyone in the club. He'd already said hi to three times more people than I had in my address book.

The low table held two bottles of Champagne on ice. I almost knocked one over with my boot when I moved to cross my legs. Jonathan served as a sort of wall, protecting the girls from my garbagy odour. They said hi to Bébert and shook hands with Jonathan and me, without really asking our names. I started feeling like I might die there, and couldn't help thinking that the cost of a beer in a place like this would ruin me.

Bébert was chatting with friends of Greg's with his arms straddling the back of the booth, relaxed as can be, as if this place was his kitchen. One of them, a two-hundred-eighty-pound Haitian guy named Ziggy, held a miniscule gin-and-tonic in hands the size of baseball mitts. The other guy, Kasper, was Haitian too. He wore diamonds on his wrists and ears and a whole lot of cologne. It was probably enough to overpower my own smell. Bébert seemed to know them pretty well. They were talking about the end of a recent night, some guy named Rick who'd gotten what he had coming.

Greg came back, threw his coat over the back of the booth, and went to sit in the middle of the group of girls. A waitress emerged from the crowd with a bottle of Belvedere vodka in a bucket of ice, and put it on our table. Greg poured it over ice in little glasses. Jonathan kept looking around in amazement. He drank down his first glass in one shot. Bébert, who'd been running around like a maniac all shift, finally seemed relaxed. It might have been all the weed. He and Ziggy were talking music. Greg was chatting with Kasper and the girls. He even slipped in the odd word in Creole. Bébert eventually turned toward me. I was holding onto my drink like a life buoy, making myself small and invisible. He asked if I was so quiet because of the fight with Carl.

"No, no. It's not that."

He took a sip of vodka, without taking his eyes off me.

"Think he'll come after me?"

"Don't worry about that," he said. "That guy won't even have the balls to pick up his vacation pay."

I was sipping my drink, fighting off the shivers it gave me. I couldn't place the taste. It actually didn't really taste like anything, beyond alcohol. I hoped that if I got drunk quickly it would get easier to swallow. Jonathan wasn't pacing himself at all, he was really throwing it back. Greg let him serve himself, he was too busy with the girls. One of them looked like Lauryn Hill, and it took a conscious effort not to stare at her too much. Jonathan started talking in a voice that was somehow both rapid and limp, saying whatever popped into his mind, like a highlight reel of his life in fast-forward, spinning out of control like a drunk with ADHD. He'd grown up in Val d'Or and he was finishing cooking school and he made his own Styrofoam weapons for the re-enactment battles on Mont-Royal on Sunday mornings, he was into Rush and Eminem and Radiohead. As he spoke his eyebrows formed little chevrons over his wide eyes. From time to time he scratched the back of his head, ruffling his greasy light-brown hair. He just kept jumping around like that for twenty minutes or so, barely taking the time to catch his breath. Then he was onto *The Fellowship of the Ring* and *The Two Towers*, which were coming to the theatre in a few weeks. I brought up the first film adaptation, Bakshi's 1978 version, but that drew a blank. He looked at me for a few seconds with his hangdog lip, then polished off his vodka and poured himself another. He'd tap on the chest and interrupt me, which made me stop talking, and then he was off again, telling me all about his re-enactments and the coat of chainmail he'd assembled, one link at a time. I had nothing to add and was only half listening. I could hear Bébert discussing ounces and pounds. He looked chill and talked loud to be heard over the slow, sensual beat, some kind of reggae with no words, swirling in bass and echoey sounds from outer space. I envied Bébert for being so comfortable with such a slick crew. His Cleveland Indians cap covered his eyes, his scruffy beard made him look a few years older than he was, and his Everlast t-shirt and spray paint-splattered jeans wouldn't pass muster with any dress code in town.

The sharp smell of tobacco mixed in with the sugary vodka and coated my mouth. The girls got up to go dance. Ziggy and Kasper too. Jonathan turned toward Bébert and started telling him all about who knows what, he was even more skittery than before. I remembered his pissy mood at the beginning of the shift, and wondered what had happened. I leaned over toward Greg, who was listening to the messages on his cell, covering his other ear with his palm. It took a good two minutes to screw up the courage to ask him my question.

"So what was it like? The Slayer show?"

"The Slayer show?"

Greg poured himself a vodka and threw two ice cubes in the glass, splashing a little on his hand.

"Yeah, you know, uh. The one you told me about. Verdun Auditorium."

Greg was about to answer but his phone buzzed. He flipped it open, got up without excusing himself, and disappeared into the crowd. I was left feeling stupid.

One of the girls came back to sit on the booth across from me. She smiled at me and smoothed out her dress in one seamless motion. I had a nervous reflex, fortunately not acted on, to give her a little wave, like when you see a friend in the metro, across the tracks. I felt my face going crimson. The heat didn't help. I was keeping my flannel shirt buttoned up over my t-shirt, to keep the foul odour of the dishpit contained. I was dying in all that clothing though, soaked like a mop.

"Nah, nah, man," Bébert was telling Jonathan, making the same "cut it out" gesture over and over again. "Listen, dude. Shut up and listen for a second. You can't let her walk all over you. Give her a yard and she'll take you for a ride around the block. Calm down, give her a couple days, then try to patch things up. And quit bugging her with your stupid stories about foam swords and forts. She's a skater, man."

Bébert had taken Jonathan's shoulder in his massive hand. Pretty soon Jonathan was looking bummed out again. His big bandaged finger lay in front of him, gleaming white, and his head stooped like a man defeated. He was leaning over on his knees, his body gone limp, equal parts groggy and drunk. They might have been talking about Bonnie, but I couldn't be certain.

I pretended to watch the dance floor. People were moving as if swept along by the same hypnotic wave, under subtle lighting that bathed everything in a sapphire glow. I decided I didn't totally hate trip hop. I almost thought I caught a glimpse of Marie-Lou in the crowd, hair spilling over her cheeks, but it wasn't her after all. I told myself that I absolutely had to call her. Greg was at the bar, doing shots with a tall thin guy whose biceps bulged under his jacket. He looked like a boxer in the twilight of his career.

"What's your name? I'm Mélissa."

Lauryn Hill's friend was holding out her hand to me. I introduced myself.

"Come again?"

I said my name again, a little louder, and she said once again that it was nice to meet me, though she hadn't had any better luck catching it the second time.

"So you're Greg's friend?"

"Well, we work together at the restaurant."

I heard Bébert telling Jonathan to take it easy on the drinks, those pills wouldn't make him invincible.

"You a waiter?"

Her big dark eyes shone under her bangs.

I didn't find her as pretty as her friend Lauryn Hill, but it still seemed inconceivable that a girl like that would start talking to me out of the blue.

"No . . . a cook," I said, hoping the guys wouldn't hear me.

"Cool. I like a guy who knows how to cook."

She must have thought I was older. Then she asked me to dance with her, but I wasn't drunk enough to say yes.

"Too bad."

She winked at me with a little laugh, and went off to meet her friends. The vodka was going down easier and easier.

Jonathan was starting to fade and slump over. He focused on something on the varnished tabletop, a reflection or maybe a mirage, the shimmer of a fainting ghost. I asked Bébert what was wrong with Bonnie today.

"She's partying a little too hard these days."

I took a big sip of ice-cold vodka. It went down like water.

"Is it serious with the guy at the Roy Bar?"

He looked at me with a face that was half surprised, half mocking.

"Why you want to know, man?"

"Uh. Just to know."

He started laughing, like chainsaw firing up, and lit a smoke. I took another sip. This time it burned. It was all I could do not to cough, and to keep my calm. I coughed into a clenched hand. My eyes filled with water.

"Don't go there, man."

"Go where?"

"You really got your eye on her?"

His laugh had sputtered out, leaving only the trace of a sardonic grin.

"Bonnie? Well...uh..."

"Stop it. You're not the right guy for her."

I looked at Jonathan, who looked lost in meditation. He was on the verge of passing out.

When he held in his smoke to talk, Bébert always seemed a touch more serious.

"Is that what you were asking Jonathan about just now?"

"What?"

"You know, about Bonnie..."

"Nah, dude. We were talking about his girlfriend."

Greg came back to sit down again, looking pumped. He leaned over the table, poured himself another drink, and started talking to Bébert. I pretended not to listen.

"Tell your buddy to leave the door unlocked. If everything works out we'll leave him ten. And tell him if anything goes wrong he better forget about us. Never heard of us. 'Cause we don't exist."

Bébert nodded a couple times, to the beat.

"All right! Cheers, B-Bert," said Greg, filling up our glasses. "You too, Tom Araya."

He raised his glass. We drank a while. The vodka was going down. Each new sip tasted better than the one before. Greg got up after that and went back to working the room. I was starting to get seriously loaded, but not as bad as Jonathan, who was more or less sleeping in the booth. Bébert and I decided it to call it a night. He got up. I did too, careful not to knock over the glasses on the table. He took his coat from the booth. He looked around for Ziggy and Kasper, and said bye by touching his temple with his index and middle finger. We helped Jonathan stand and managed to get him out of the club without his state showing too much and before he threw up all over himself. He was cooperative and chattered away unintelligibly. We put him in a taxi. Bébert paid the fare in advance, and we went for late-night falafel.

We headed up Saint-Denis toward Amir. Walked by a twenty-four-hour deli that I'd never noticed before. Through the fogged-up window I saw a man whose appearance held me riveted. I let Bébert go ahead and slowed down. He wore a black suit and had long, straight black hair like an Asian woman, tucked behind his ears and falling over his shoulders. He sat across from a beautiful blond girl, my age or maybe a touch older, with a pit bull's collar around her neck. A bowl of soup sat steaming in front of her. Her eyes were swollen with tears. She rubbed her face with a hand, as if trying to get the better of a persistent itch, or stop crying. He had an elbow on the table and his face resting in his hand, with a cigarette between his index and middle fingers. His skin was deathly pale, maybe from the fluorescent lighting. The girl's soup was untouched. The young woman started talking, gesturing with her hands. That was when he turned toward me. Scarcely six feet separated us, and the glass was half fogged-over. His cheeks bore visible scars from burns, or maybe knife marks, it was hard to tell which. His eyes disappeared into their orbits and it looked like his entire temples were covered with black ink, or tar, which blended in with the fabric of his jacket. The guy looked to my right. I followed his gaze and I jumped a little. Bébert was standing next to me on the sidewalk. He'd turned back and grabbed me by the arm.

"Dude, don't stare at people like that."

I snapped out of it. We took off with our hands in our pockets, but I couldn't help looking back. The blond girl gave me the finger.

The line at Amir seemed interminable, probably because we were so hungry. I ordered two pitas, and Bébert had one with garlic potatoes. We took our food to go, and started eating right out of the bag.

We went by the deli again. All that was left was the bowl of soup. That was when I started thinking about our paycheques, which came tomorrow. And about the casino. Apparently it was open all night. I could make way more there than at the machines. Bébert disrupted my train of thought.

"Still thirsty? Come have a beer at my place."

The wet cold was sapping my will to wait for the night bus to Ahuntsic, and I didn't want to blow another twenty on anything that wasn't a taxi to the casino.

"C'mon, make up your mind. I'm cold."

I followed Bébert to his house. He lived on Boyer between Mont-Royal and Saint-Joseph, a part of the Plateau where the streets all look the same.

We walked into a long narrow ground-floor apartment with low ceilings. The wood floor creaked. The mess all around clashed with the carved baseboards and solid wood doors. Bébert's roommate was sitting at a computer, working on a mixing program with DJ headphones on, his desk heaped with stained coffee cups, crushed cans of Milwaukee's Best, and an ashtray overflowing with roaches and butts.

All around the living room lay bits of plywood covered with high-contrast graffiti portraits. The facial proportions were clumsy, and graphically speaking it was uninspired; pretty bad, really. When he saw I was checking them out, Bébert told me they were his. I said they had attitude; he told me to fuck off. He crossed the living room to the kitchen. I sat there waiting. I heard him open the fridge.

"Hey Big, I thought you were at the Circus tonight," he bellowed.

His roommate took off his headphones.

"Huh?"

"I thought you were spinning at the Circus tonight," Bébert said again, as he reappeared with three cans of beer.

He tossed me one.

"Want a beer?"

His roommate shook his head and stretched.

"Forget that. Nate did it. I'm way too messed up. I haven't slept for like three days. Your buddy's shit is the bomb. Nothing like Landry's Doves and Blue Jays."

Bébert laughed as he cracked open his beer. I think he drained it in two sips, then started on the one he'd offered his roommate. I sprawled out on the couch, he took a chewed-up easy chair. MusiquePlus was playing on mute. Bébert rolled a joint, saying he'd be sous-chef by next week. Séverine was going to fire Christian, tomorrow at the latest, he thought. I listened, woozy from the alcohol and the apartments' dry heat. Before I could even drink half a beer I started fading fast. But I forced myself to stay awake. The roommate played Bébert the piece he was working on. On TV Claude Rajotte was eviscerating the first album by Ozzy Osbourne's daughter. I fell asleep, fully dressed, on the sofa, in clothes reeking of tobacco, detergent, seafood, and cooking oil.

CHAPTER 17

MY CEGEP was a fortress—the Tower of Orthanck, or the Citadel of the Autarch—and as I approached I felt like Severian the apprentice torturer before he was banished to the Matachin tower. I went out for some air in the walkway in front of the main entrance, In Flames in my headphones, Walkman cranked to ten. Under the concrete overhang, students were smoking between classes, chatting away in small groups about the impending end-of-semester parties, nights out at the Saint-Supplice or the Conneries, exams, and of course their past and future weekends. It all seemed to be unfolding in some faraway land. Their mirthful excitement irked me. My coffee burned the roof of my mouth. It was all I could keep down.

I felt old—no, not exactly old but spent, jetlagged like a traveller teleported in from another world.

I was killing time in the hope of regaining some composure or semblance of will to live, angling my face toward the cold early-winter sun as if it were a matter of photosynthesis, when two guys I knew saw me. I'd met Benoît and Éric in page layout class last winter. We had philosophy class together as well. I'd helped Benoît revise his final paper. Nice guy, basically illiterate.

They were smoking with two or three girls. One of them, who was kind of chubby with dreads, was telling a story with gestures that made everyone laugh. The two guys came up to me with a smile in the corner of their mouths, as if they'd stumbled upon a freak of nature or a revenant. I took out my earbuds.

"You look like death warmed over," said Éric.

They laughed, and asked if I'd be there for the end-of-term party tonight.

"Nah, I don't think so."

"Did you hand in your assignment to Pierre?"

I took a sip of coffee and answered.

"That's what I'm here for."

I had a frog in my throat. I looked at the group of girls they'd been with thirty seconds ago. Then I pictured Greg's friends. Then the students in classrooms, sitting in rows. Acetates on overhead projectors, the cafeteria, the notebooks. None of it seemed real.

"Anyway, it's been a while, man," Benoît said.

He was warming his hands in the sleeves of his snowboard jacket, his nose in a neck warmer.

"I've been busy. New job."

"You okay?"

I checked the time on my pager and got up.

"I'll see you guys at exams," I said, and put my headphones back in.

I cleared a path between them. My stomach was in a knot, the centre of my forehead a focal point of pain. I threw my coffee in a garbage can. Faces shone all around like phosphorescence. My eyes hurt. I joined the crowd of students swarming around the glass doors, inhabited by a focused energy that felt totally foreign to me. The semester was coming to an end. I ran through the previous night in my head, then the previous week. It was like glimpsing the memories of another person, a life completely removed from this sunlit, diurnal existence. It might have been the Cegep itself, with its series of assignments to be dutifully submitted. All of it felt decidedly like someone else's business. I seemed to be trapped in a single long hallucinatory night, a frenetic realm in which time was forever expanding and contracting.

I made my way through the overheated lobby. Crossed the crowded agora, with its stench of wet boots and burnt cheese emanating from the ducts. Members of the Student Association were working the crowd, exhorting students to donate to Christmas hampers. A big redheaded guy from the improv team yelled slogans in a nasal voice. I could hear it all over the In Flames and the pounding headache that seemed about to get worse. The guy was wearing boxer shorts and a Santa hat. I walked toward the escalators. My confidence was eroding. Usually I had a facility for self-delusion, and no compunction about lying to myself. Today I felt totally empty and exposed.

Pierre, who taught my illustration class, met me in the office he shared with his colleagues. He pulled up a chair and invited me to sit down. His hands were clasped, his forearms rested on his thighs. He looked disappointed. We were getting to know each other fairly well. He'd taught three of my classes, and in each one I'd been outstanding. At least that's what he'd told me. He looked at me a minute, as if he were sizing up the situation and endeavouring to choose his words with care. His usually warm smile was nowhere to be found. His face was expressionless. I didn't feel good at all.

"I wasn't expecting this from you," said Pierre.

I couldn't look him in the eye for more than a second or two.

"You're gonna have to start taking this more seriously. It's the end of the semester."

He turned around and fumbled with the things on his desk. There was a stack of student portfolios, with tracing paper sticking out the sides.

"It's not fair for the other students if I give you another extension."

"I know. That's not why I'm here."

I screwed up my courage. I was still burping up last night's vodka, mixed in with the bad coffee. He looked at me, waiting for more. I glanced at the pile of assignments, the metal desk drawer, the keyring, the cubicles and suspended ceiling.

"I came to tell you I won't be able to hand anything in."

He looked at me more searchingly, with a seriousness I'd never before seen in him. I remained silent. Apart from a sharp pain between my eyes, which was starting to throb in my forehead, I didn't feel a thing: not shame, not nervousness, nothing. I felt heavy and limp.

"You *can't* finish. Or you *don't want to*?"

Someone was hanging out in the hallway. I heard the loud laugh of a girl through the door, wishing someone Merry Christmas. I rubbed my forehead with a moist hand, without answering.

"You'll have to make some serious decisions. If you don't get it together, you'll be kicked out of the program."

Three months ago that possibility would have spurred me to action; now it left me impassive. All this would happen later. Right now I was trapped in a hermetically sealed racing car, speeding toward the ravine.

"I know."

"So you're not going to hand in anything at all."

The disappointment in his voice was hard to take. I felt like crying.

"No."

"And you don't have anything else to say to me."

"No, nothing."

He crossed his arms and watched me get up.

"Know what?"

I shrugged my shoulders and looked down.

He hesitated a moment before going on.

"I've taught lots of young people like you. I've seen people who were even better than you quit halfway through. Maybe you can tell me why so many of the most talented people are so happy to rest on their laurels?"

My hand was on the doorknob. I wasn't even trying to answer his question. I was looking somewhere between his office and my shoes, absorbed by the patterns in the polished granite.

"I hope you'll give it some thought over the holidays."

"I'll try," I said, lifting up my head.

I think it came out as a whisper. Pierre put his glasses back on. He got back to work. I left the room in silence. Though I was sad, something else had been unleashed in me. I felt lighter, almost liberated. But it didn't last. The stress and anxiety just came pouring right back. I thought about Malik, and then the guys from Deathgaze. I glanced at my pager, chased all these thoughts from my mind, and disappeared.

CHAPTER 18

MARIE-LOU worked slinging beer at a tavern on Rue
Ontario, close to my Cegep. She'd start in the afternoon
and stay on through the after-work rush when the place
filled up with broke students there for the beer specials. Obviously
I never played the machines when she was working.

Marie-Lou and I had lost touch during my first year of Cegep,
when she'd gone to work in Field, B.C. Then, last semester, we'd
started seeing each other again more often. After I quit my renova-
tion job at the end of the summer, I'd started spending a few nights
a week at her place. From that point on we were inseparable. When
I got into trouble and couldn't pay my share of the rent to Rémi
she'd offered to lend me money without a second thought. I took
her money. I promised to pay her back right away. Then I got right
back to gambling again.

A few weeks later, when she realized I was even deeper in debt
than before, I had to tell her where all my money was going. She
reamed me out worse than anyone ever had before. She told me
she couldn't trust me anymore. She told me I was weak. That if I
kept it up I'd end up all alone in the world. At the end, when she
saw the state she'd put me in, she just made me promise to never
gamble again. And I'd promised. I promised and I actually believed
myself at the time. I believed my battle was won, that she'd given
me an antidote to the poison in my head. Not even Malik had that

kind of power over me. Marie-Lou didn't kick me out that night. She told me I'd always be welcome at her place, but that I absolutely had to stop fucking up. It was the end of September, the days were still warm, and she invited me for a beer on a patio somewhere. We talked about other stuff, my comic projects, the social sciences program she wanted to start up again at Cegep, the Virginie Despentes book she was finishing. Then we went home drunk and watched *Donnie Darko* together and ate a bag of brownies. But the next day I could tell something was broken between us. Or maybe something was broken in me, maybe I was ashamed and just couldn't live with the fact that she knew. Four days later I was gambling again.

That was three months ago. Since then, Malik had also forced me to confront my actions. But I still owed Marie-Lou over four-hundred dollars. From time to time I'd slip her a twenty or two, which she accepted wordlessly.

I missed her. And I figured she'd be happy to see me. We hadn't spent much time together since I'd crashed at her place a couple days before moving in with Vincent.

You entered Chez Maurice through a big metal door with peanut machines next to it. The room smelled vaguely of detergent and flat beer. It had a terrazzo floor and limp ceiling fans churning the clouds of cigarette smoke. At that time of day the room was still lit by the sunlight filtering in through long tempered glass windows, on which you could read "AIR CONDITIONED" and "SPORTS FANS WELCOME." When I walked in Marie-Lou jumped into my arms. I didn't even have time to take off my headphones. She kissed me on the cheeks. It was heartwarming to see her so happy. I took a seat at the bar with my back to the row of machines that lined the street-side wall.

Afternoons at Chez Maurice weren't exactly action-packed. There was no one to serve except a few old guys who needed a fresh beer once an hour while they gambled away their cheque on *7s Wild*. The place was dead.

Marie-Lou brought me a beer.

"So, how's the new job?"

"My new job? Like working at the dump, under the trucks as they unload the garbage."

She looked at me with a mocking compassion.

"Poor *baby*..."

"Are you sure there aren't any jobs here?"

She shot me a look that made it clear my question irked her.

"Forget that," she said categorically. "Gee, do you really think this would be a good place for you to work?" She looked meaningfully at the VLTs that lined the wall behind me. "Sweet plan, dude."

She gave me a lingering look, and I felt myself turning scarlet.

"Yeah, thought so," she finally said.

Then she went to punch something in at the register. The system looked pretty rudimentary. Next to what we had at La Trattoria, it felt more like the till at a McDonald's.

"You going to see Iced Earth?" I asked.

"Nah, their last album is shit," she said. "It's weird that you're asking though. Jess really wanted to go with me."

She answered from the other end of the bar, scribbling on a pad next to a glass full of change. She hadn't dyed her hair since getting back from B.C. last year. Through her copper-coloured locks I could see the high cheekbones and snub nose that gave her the profile of a manga heroine. Her boss let her work with her piercing in. She played with it when she was deep in thought. At the mention of Jess, I tensed up all over my body.

"She got out of hospital last week, by the way."

"You mean detox..."

I averted my eyes from the reproachful look I knew she would have waiting. I couldn't refrain from adding:

"And I should care because..."

She acted as if I hadn't spoken, and went off to check on her tables. Three old-timers in work shirts had taken a seat. You could tell from their faces as they sat down that Marie-Lou was the best part of their day. The sleeves of her red and black-striped shirt hid the horned demon tattoos she had on each arm. Each time I saw her she looked even more beautiful. Seeing her here you couldn't tell she was a metal chick: she'd learned to transform her look at work so people who didn't know her would have no idea she was into Dimmu Borgir, Darkthrone, and Immortal. I guess we all did, to a point.

She was back behind the bar, clinking empty Molson Dry bottles together as she lined them up in the case.

"She talks about you a lot. She'd really like to see you again. Or at least hear from you."

I finished my beer.

"Not gonna happen," I said.

Jess was my girlfriend from fifteen through seventeen. She and Marie-Lou were childhood friends, two firecrackers who somehow ended up at our staid private high school. It wasn't long before Jess had got her hooks in me. And I was obsessed with her.

"She's changed, you know."

"Great. Speaking of change, let's change the subject," I said.

"Okay, okay, don't get mad," she said, before leaning over and looking me square in the eye with a worried expression, like a doctor examining a hematoma.

I laughed. Her face lit up, as if she'd just remembered a piece of good news.

"Hey, how's the album cover going?"

"Almost done," I said, trying to keep my smile. "I'm meeting the band next week, to show them the mock-ups."

"Are you gonna show me?"

"Hell yeah. It's the best thing I've ever done."

She took my hand, swept up with a sort of momentum, and then something made her stop, with a funny look. I didn't react. She looked uncomfortable for a minute, then gave me a sort of fake slow-motion right hook to the jaw. I didn't make a fool of myself. I didn't tell her I wanted us to try again, didn't offer to show her the drawing tonight. I just ordered another beer, happy to be there with her. Life wasn't coming to an end just yet. Her face took on a more serious look, the way it did every time she poured a beer.

Her lips grew a touch thinner and she scrunched up her eyebrows. Then she put a beer down in front of me.

"Finish late tonight?"

"No, not late. A little after dinner. Why?"

"Just wondering."

"I'm thinking of going to South America in the spring."

"Oh yeah?"

I shifted on my stool. She was making a rum and Coke, and talking into the glass.

"I thought you were going back to Cegep," I said.

"Nah, not yet."

"How long you going for?"

"A few months. At least."

That threw me for a loop. I took a sip of beer while I mulled it over. She stopped for a few seconds in front of me, before taking out the order.

"What's up with you?"

"Nothing, I'm just tired. It's the new job."

She gave me a sweet little smile and set off with her tray to the table where a guy with tribal tats sat reading the paper.

Once Jess and I finally broke up for good, after the suicide threats and the Tylenol overdoses and her drunk mum begging me to take her daughter back and Jess sobbing on the phone until two in the morning, after all that, I'd tried my luck with Marie-Lou. She still had a boyfriend at that point, though. Gilles. That guy freaked the shit out of me. He was twenty-four years old, and under investigation for selling weapons. Gilles hung out with a pack of lowlifes at the Longeuil Metro, people like Maureen the four-foot-tall Latina lesbian who had the whole King George family eating out of her hand. The first time Jess introduced me to her, she was packing a gun under her Lakers shirt.

The day was darkening. Some more washed-up old guys turned up at the bar. A few younger people too, barely older than me. I glanced at the machines out of the corner of my eye. Marie-Lou caught it.

"You're not starting up that shit again, are you?"

"No way. Don't worry," I said.

Her face hardened instantly. My cheeks were burning but I kept up my mask. I remembered the fiercest moments of our fighting, and tried to chase it from my mind.

"I'm gonna figure out a way to pay you back. Soon."

"I don't care about the money. I just don't want you going near those things anymore."

Her look cut right through me. I took a sip of beer.

"Did you finish the *Sandmans* I leant you?"

She was about to answer when Benjamin, Marie-Lou's boss, walked in. Benjamin was around twice my age. He moved with a laid-back confidence, as if he'd planned out each and every move well in advance, and it was working out just fine for him, and nothing could surprise him anymore. He said hi to a few tables of regulars as he walked by with a box of liquor, making predictions about the hockey game. In his long trench coat, with a smoke dangling from the corner of his mouth, he looked a touch like John Constantine.

Benjamin said hi to Marie-Lou and started rummaging around behind the bar. He asked her not to mix the empty imports with the Molsons. Benjamin always used a neutral tone, never raised his voice. He was a lanky, taciturn guy with red hair and a wide, bony forehead. The bags under his eyes gave him a somehow sleepy, detached look. At a first glance, he wasn't the friendliest guy around. If I didn't know Marie-Lou, he probably wouldn't have given me the time of day.

One night I was sitting at the bar waiting for Marie-Lou to finish her shift, and I'd brought a Stephen King to keep me company. Without even a hint of a segue, or so much as a hello, he told me I should really try Jack Ketchum next. I said I'd never heard of him. Suddenly this guy who never strung together more than two or three words was chatting my ear off, like a prophet in the throes of an epiphany. He talked to me about books for an hour. He recommended Dashiell Hammett, Elmore Leonard, and James Ellroy, who I pretended I'd heard of. Don't ever read them in translation, he stressed. I said I'd started *It* in English. He said reading translations was worse than watching the Sunday afternoon action movies dubbed with French actors on TV.

"What kind of sense does that make, having a hillbilly who talks like Vincent Cassel?"

"Not much, I guess."

I would have been hard pressed to tell you what a hillbilly was.

Two or three years later, when I started reading the French version of *Naked Lunch*, I remembered our discussion. The translation was so awful it was barely readable.

Back when Marie-Lou introduced me to Benjamin he had three pastimes: amateur boxing, tending bar, and reading a preposterous number of books. It was his fourth year in AA. Benjamin's years as a practising alcoholic had been unusually rocky. In those days he worked at Peel Pub, pouring pitchers for the Anglophone hordes who'd head downtown to drink until they forgot their mothers' names. Benjamin was the kind of guy who could finish his shift at midnight, go out and drink away four hundred dollars in tips before last call, then borrow a twenty from a friend for the cab home. He went on that way for years. His life was one long bender. At the end he was up to a twenty-sixer a day, with a twenty-four beer chaser. His drink of choice was vodka, room temperature, usually on an empty stomach. Then he quit cold turkey, the day after he fell off his balcony one night trying to unlock his front door.

Benjamin walked up to me and shook my hand. His grip was tough, his hand rough as sandpaper. He had a look at my copy of *Cthulhu*, sitting beside my beer.

"Still keeping busy with your fairy tales."

He smiled, a rare occurrence.

"Marie told me you're working at La Trattoria."

"Yeah, it's been a week."

"Greg still work there?"

Benjamin was still smiling, as he read the back cover.

"You know Greg?"

"Yeah. Surprised he's still alive."

"I guess he parties pretty hard."

"I guess you could put it that way."

"Where do you know him from? Did you work with him?"

"I knew Greg in my former life."

He put down my book without a word, and started emptying out the box of bottles he'd brought. He removed the pourer spouts from the empty bottles and screwed them onto the full ones. When he opened the forty of Jack a waft of floor polish tickled my nostrils. I'd always wondered how Benjamin could work in an environment so full of alcohol and never succumb to temptation. When I'd asked him, he said:

"It's not easy, but it's simple. You just tell yourself that you can make it through one more day without opening a beer. Don't think about tomorrow. You cross that bridge when you come to it."

I stole a glance at the machines. The fruits and the bells paraded by on their screens. That was when a tall man came into the bar. He seemed just a little older than Benjamin, maybe in his mid-forties, with a salt-and-pepper beard and wrinkles that lent his eyes a melancholy aspect. Benjamin stood up behind the bar.

"Ah, Mohammed."

I'd rarely seen Benjamin this happy. You could tell because he spoke just a touch louder, with a hint of surprise in his voice. When Mohammed smiled wide wrinkles formed around his baggy eyes and he took Benjamin's hand in his own giant fist and shook. Before he had a chance to order Benjamin had already placed a Perrier on the bar in front of him. He introduced me and Mohammed shook my hand as well, as if I were a man of his age.

"My friend, you aren't sleeping enough," he said to me. "Night is for sleeping as well."

Mohammed's voice was deep and velvety. I wasn't sure how to answer, couldn't tell if he was taking the piss or not. It seemed as if this man somehow knew my whole story. I cleared my throat before finally speaking:

"I'll keep that in mind."

Mohammed winked at me and clinked his Perrier against my beer.

"This here is the most dependable cab driver in town," Benjamin told me.

"Stop, please."

Mohammed said hi to Marie-Lou, and shook her hand as well. There was something comforting and ceremonial in his manner. They talked a little. He addressed her like a niece, or the cherished daughter of a close friend. Mohammed crushed the lemon slice in the bottom of his glass. Years later I'd learn that he was the one who had peeled Benjamin off the ground the night he fell from his second-storey balcony, and driven him to the hospital. That was the day they became friends. Now Mohammed stopped by the bar regularly to say hi.

Marie-Lou went off to check on her tables. Benjamin and Mohammed were talking sports, boxing mostly. Benjamin told him about a couple of bets he'd placed. Mohammed gently chided him. It felt a little like a script, and each man knew his part. Though Mohammed had a North African accent he peppered his speech with Quebec expressions, as if he'd been born in Joliette.

I'd never seen Benjamin interact with anyone like that. I knew he liked to gamble, place the odd bet. He was a regular at poker games that finished around dawn. He'd told me a few stories, about these games full of coked-up bartenders trying to double their tips by going all-in at nine in the morning. Benjamin claimed he'd never lost money, not even once. At the beginning of summer I'd asked him if I could go check out a game with him, and he said no. He didn't give a reason, didn't raise his voice, didn't lecture me. Just no.

I paid Benjamin for my beers, careful to conceal my wad of cash from Marie-Lou. When I got up to leave she gave me a kiss on each cheek and then a hug, holding me even tighter than when I'd got there. I held her close as well, would have held her against me all night, but our embrace came unlaced after a few seconds.

We weren't in that place anymore. Maybe it was better that way. She made me promise to do better at staying in touch. I put on my headphones and left with a wave for Benjamin.

Outside night had fallen. Tiny snowflakes floated through the air, like ground-up specks of glass sprinkled over the city. I turned my Walkman up to eight to block out the rumble of the traffic. "The other side of the platinum door/ Another day in quicksand/ Still feel close to nowhere/ I hope this is the right way." In Flames. I never got tired of *Clayman*. I headed down Ontario a while, to the stop on Saint-Denis for northbound buses. I walked by the Voyageur intercity bus terminal. Buses stood waiting in the parking lot. I felt like getting on one for Trois-Rivières. When the No. 30 finally arrived, I could still smell Marie-Lou's scent on myself.

I spent the whole trip dozing off, moving only to flip the tape in my Walkman. I looked around. A guy my age with shaved eyebrows in head-to-toe Karl Kani was talking to his girlfriend on his cell, offering fifteen different versions of the same excuse. An Asian woman buried under a pile of packages was letting her head bump into the window. Two private school girls in plaid skirts and aluminum-coloured puffy coats were sharing a pair of Discman headphones. A guy with a long but patchy beard was absorbed in a *Star Wars* novel. Just beside him, a black woman no older than me, her face a closed book, stared unblinkingly out the window. I turned up the volume.

When I got home Vincent was sitting in the living room La-Z-Boy, finishing off a frozen dinner with a two-litre of Sprite at his feet. The apartment was dark. He was watching the hockey game in an old pair of soccer shorts and the gym shirt from our old high school. Those t-shirts were so big they were practically robes, yet the fabric stretched tight over Vincent's pecs. I collapsed onto the couch that was also my bed. My clothes still smelled like last night's special blend of fried food and cigarette smoke. I didn't have the strength to change my clothes. I took a sip of Sprite.

"I still don't have any cash for... It's coming though."

"No worries, man. Just as long as you don't forget."

He dropped the box of his meal on the coffee table.

"Think I could steal a Michelina's?"

"Sure, just not the cheese. Take one of the tomato sauces."

His eyes never left the game. In the TV's glow his black skin looked almost blue. I went off to heat up a frozen meal.

"Have you finished your exams?"

I was talking over the hum of the microwave.

"Not yet. You?"

"I handed in my last assignment today."

"Nice."

I went over to sit down with my steaming-hot dinner. I asked Vincent to wake me when he got up the next morning.

"You sure?"

"Yeah, I've gotta be at work around eight or so."

I took a shower, came back out to the living room, and fell asleep in front of the hockey game.

CHAPTER 19

EVERY TIME Marie-Lou brought up Jess I ended up feeling guilty. So she was on my mind when I got up the day after my visit to Chez Maurice. Usually my thoughts about Jess were a muddle, but the one certainty was my sense of relief that we weren't together anymore. This time I felt something else as well, a strange nostalgia. It might be that my relationship with Marie-Lou had been stagnating for weeks, and though she appeared happy to see me she was clearly still struggling to trust me. She seemed to harbour a serious fear of gambling, or more precisely of what gambling was doing to me. Today I see she understood my addiction better than I did. Hanging out with me demanded a constant effort not to dwell on it, not to be constantly suspicious, not to challenge me or try to teach me a lesson. When she brought up Jess that afternoon, out of nowhere, it made me think about the first time I met Marie-Lou, three years earlier. Yeah, I met Marie-Lou through Jess. It was winter. Jess and I were in a rough patch, fighting all the time. Her mum was going through a relapse. It was a Friday. Jess and I had arranged to meet up at Longueuil Metro station, to do something with her friends. Basically she was doing whatever it took to avoid spending time at home.

I was at the station, leaning on the railing, slightly hidden by a bank of payphones. The crowd was coming off the platform, rushing toward the concrete stairs. People were on their way home from school or work, everyone rushing to catch their buses.

Groups of rap kids were waiting for their friends, gathered around the dépanneur right in the centre of the Metro station. Metallica's "One" played in my headphones. The station smelled like cement, cigarette butts, and fried chicken. With my Walkman turned up to nine, I was discreetly watching the group of sketchy kids in front of the glass doors of the McDonald's. I knew who they were. Jess knew them all. Maureen wasn't there yet. Maybe she was still sleeping. I hoped so: that chick scared the shit out of me. Even the baddest of the bad kids got nervous when she showed up. Maureen rolled with the real shit disturbers, the ones who lived on King-George, the ones you didn't want to look in the eye. When Jess introduced me to her—the one and only time she spoke to me—I'd barely managed to spit out a few meaningless sentences. I'd never experienced a more suspicious, truculent glare.

I'd been waiting around fifteen minutes. I checked out the gang one last time, to see if Jess was finally there. She'd figured out that she could keep me waiting. Luc was there, the dealer from Gérard-Filion high school, with a few of his jaded little sidekicks. Luc pretty much lived at the Metro station. His apartment was next door, in the Port-de-Mer tower. I recognized Théberge, who ran things in Fatima on the other side of Longueuil. He and the Hubert brothers always had some kind of beef. Frantz was there too, clowning around, talking shit and gesticulating with his fake Rolex spinning around on his wrist, twitching far too much for someone with such glassy eyes; they called him "Frantz the Queb" because he was the only Haitian around who didn't have an accent. Of course Goupil was there as well: he was a tall guy with an elephant's forehead who always wore his Tommy Hilfiger jacket unzipped and the collar of his polo shirt upturned. I knew who he was because he'd come to our school in the fall to beat up our kingpin. People said he was mixed up in a shooting behind a teen club in Brossard. The older Hubert brother had confirmed the rumour. Goupil had his eye on Jess, you could see it a mile away. As far as he was concerned, I was beneath consideration. I checked the time on one of the phones. Jess was twenty minutes late now. Heaven forfend that

I should ever show up even two minutes late, though; she'd tear a strip off me. The chorus of "Accident of Birth" was ringing in my ears. I chanted it under my breath, to boost my confidence.

I had another look over my shoulder, toward the McDonald's. People stood in line waiting to order. I saw a guy my age, maybe sixteen, no older. He wore a long wool coat and his hair in a pony-tail, with Coke-bottle glasses and blond peach fuzz. Engrossed in his Dungeons and Dragons Campaign Book. The big backpack at his feet was surely full of DM rulebooks, twenty-sided dice, bind-ers, and mechanical pencils. I knew exactly what he would get up to that night. No self-centred, temperamental girlfriend would be dragging his ass to some crowded party where a bunch of way older people were doing coco puffs. He wouldn't have to buy beer with a fake ID, wouldn't be the laughing stock of a gang of drop-outs stoned out of their skulls, wouldn't have to look after his girl-friend, who'd be all over Goupil after one beer, and ready to fight all comers after two, nor would he have to carry her home at the end of the night to her drunken-ass mum and a step-dad who was equally happy slapping or punching, depending on his mood; no, this guy wouldn't be stuck listening to her claiming for the twen-tieth time that she wanted to kill herself, wanted to be done with it all, or that he was too uptight, too young, too boring. For this guy there'd be no three a.m. emotional blackmail after his night went south. This guy was going to order his combo, gobble it down, and catch his bus. This guy would unhurriedly read over his DM notes, and then spend all night playing with his friends. And he'd have fun, more fun than I'd had in the last six months. On that day I would have given anything to trade places with this guy and live my life without a girlfriend who hung out with a bunch of skids, without the small recurring humiliations, without a thing to prove to anyone.

Jess finally showed up. She saw me from a distance, but acted like I wasn't there. My heart leaped up in my chest. It did that every time I saw her. She said hi to everyone, jumping into the guys' arms, standing there resplendent in front of Goupil, who hugged her and grinned like a degenerate. Every time she did that I wished I could disappear. It was like I didn't know this person, who was nothing like the Jess I knew. I wondered what she saw in them. As far as I could tell they didn't give a shit about her. They didn't care about the girl who was there to look after her mom every single time she clambered back on the wagon for a while. The girl who wouldn't let anyone tell her what she could and couldn't do, who was determined to make something of her life at any price—they had no idea who that girl was. The Jess who could draw a thousand times better than me, who'd plan our horror movie nights, who'd read more Stephen King than I had, who was hustling to finish high school so she could go to Cegep to study animation—that Jess pretty much vanished the moment she hooked up with this crew.

"Accident of Birth" was almost done and I still didn't feel up to facing them. Jess was wearing the coat I'd bought her for her birthday at Le Chatêau with the money I'd saved from the summer before, and jeans that hugged her ass so tight they may as well have been tights. She kept right on doing her royal rounds in the court of the skids, pretending she hadn't seen me. She wouldn't come to me. It was up to me to go to them. When I didn't, she'd eventually relent and come over to me, but she'd be mad, as if I'd insulted her, and then we'd fight in front of everyone, and Théberge, Goupil, and the rest of the crew would have a hearty laugh at our expense. At my expense.

The first chords of "Dead Skin Mask" made my headphones shake, and a shiver ran all the way down my spine. I felt prickly goosebumps popping up all over, as if my skin was turning into an armoured carapace. I turned the music up to ten. I sat there for a minute, listening to Tom Araya's dry, commanding vocals, holding myself back from headbanging, just letting the guitars and thumping drums work their way over the surface of my body. Then I raised my head. That's when I noticed that Jess had brought another girl along. She had short purple hair, cut around her ears except for two locks that hung down over her cheeks, and a pierced lower lip. She wore her jeans tucked into her Docs. Her boyfriend, a big guy in a white cap, with holes in his jeans who must have been around Goupil and Théberge's age, held her tight against him, tucked under his arms. They didn't really fit together. The final chord of "Dead Skin Mask" stretched out like the sound of an electrocardiogram failing to register a pulse, and the opening drum bit of "Rust in Peace... Polaris" came on. The guitars kicked in and a new wave of shivers came over me. I walked over to them, riding the swell of Megadeth riffs.

"Oh, you're here?" said Jess in an unfriendly tone, as if she were already tired of seeing me.

The skids barely looked at me. But her friend introduced herself.

"So you're Jess's boyfriend. I'm Marie-Lou. Jess talks about you all the time."

I shook her hand. My palm was moist, hers smooth and dry. Her grip was vigorous. I could feel the bones in her hand pressing against my own hand. Her boyfriend looked me up and down. He was wearing a three-quarter-length leather coat, stank of cigarettes, and looked even older than I'd first thought: probably twenty or so, based on his five o'clock shadow. Jess gave Marie-Lou a dirty look and pulled me toward her, to French kiss me in front of everyone. She stank of cigarettes too. I released myself from her grip, tangled up in the wires of my headphones, which had fallen when she put her hands around my neck.

Everyone was ready to get out of there. Marie-Lou's boyfriend kissed her and said he'd meet up with them later. He left us and ambled toward the parking lot. We went into the Port-de-Mer high-rise with Luc, who had to get some stuff at his place. Then we left the Terminus to buy Colt 45s at the dépanneur, and started walking. We went to Frantz's place. He lived in a tiny one-bedroom on Sainte-Hélène. We set up shop in the living room, on the busted-up sofa and kitchen chairs. The walls were yellow from nicotine and Frantz had sheets as curtains. The girls who were in Adult Ed with Jess showed up almost right after us. I didn't know any of them. One of them sat down in the living room, the others

stayed in the kitchen, leaning against the cupboards. Frantz had
already turned on the element and pulled out the knives. Luc was
handing out hash and bragging about it as if it could cure cancer.
People were talking loud over the music. Théberge put on *Wu-
Tang Forever*. You could hear the speakers' skins vibrating with the
bass.

I spent the evening in the background, sitting on the couch
nursing my 40 while everyone else laughed and yelled and did
coco puffs. Jess was dancing and rubbing up against Goupil. I did
my best to pretend it didn't bother me. Théberge was reefing joint
after joint, and hocking massive loogies out the open kitchen window. In between puffs he sipped on a mickey of Bacardi. The girl
he was talking to was doing lines of PCP. They were arguing over
how Biggie Smalls had died. She talked about it as if someone had
ripped out her own kidney. Fifteen minutes after Frantz's neighbour came by to complain about the noise, Marie-Lou's boyfriend
showed up with a two-four of beer.

Just when I thought everyone had forgotten I existed, Marie-
Lou came to sit next to me with a Smirnoff Ice. I had my Iron
Maiden shirt on, the one I wore over my school uniform, the one
that made the Haitian guys laugh because they thought it had
something to do with the Ghostface Killah album. Marie-Lou
pointed her finger at it and said that her brothers listened to it too,
and she did too sometimes.

"Really, you listen to metal?"

She quietly said yes as she took a sip. I cracked a big smile. It
almost didn't seem possible. Then I noticed her t-shirt, which she
wore under a black and red flannel shirt. I could see a band name
written in the spiky, illegible script that signified Black Metal.

"What bands?"

She started naming them off. She listened to a much wider
range than I did. I knew about half the bands she listed, and had at
least heard of the others: Opeth, Dark Tranquility, Death, Dimmu
Borgir, and some other stuff Malik wasn't into, Martyr and Quo
Vadis. Apparently one of her brothers was a founding member.

Being a metalhead between 1993 and 1999 was a bit like living alone on a deserted island. 1993 was the year Metallica changed its sound, Guns N' Roses broke up, and Bruce Dickinson quit Maiden. Grunge was at its apex, punk and indie were taking off, and hip-hop was beginning its long ascent to the top of the charts as classic album after classic album dropped. It wasn't until the 2000s, when the progressive European bands came onto the North American scene, that metal would finally find its legs again. But in early 1999 I was out there on my own, making my little discoveries. No one around me listened to metal. I would find one group, one album at a time. When I'd listened to everything I could find from a band and I knew all the songs on my mixtapes by heart, I'd call up Malik for some new suggestions. After *Live After Death* I'd bought all the other Maiden albums, starting with *Powerslave* and *Piece of Mind*. Then I'd gotten into their early stuff, with Paul Di'Anno screaming like a punk at the top of his lungs. I'd burned through every Megadeth disc, starting with *Countdown to Extinction*, then I got totally obsessed with *Rust in Peace*, with its cover showing a secret conclave in a hangar in Area 51. That prepped me for Slayer, which felt like Clive Barker stories translated into guitar riffs. The problem was that at that point all these bands had pretty much stopped putting out new music. All I could do was pray that Metallica would return to their *Master of Puppets* sound, or Bruce Dickinson might release a new solo disc. It was like crawling through a cave with nothing but a flashlight. With no one to advise me, I'd often buy albums blind, and when I found a treasure there was no one to share it with. From my first discovery of Maiden until that night at Frantz's apartment, I hadn't found a single person besides Alex and Malik who truly loved metal and knew a thing or two about it. The apartment receded. The Puff Daddy blasting on the stereo had become a barely audible crackling under Marie-Lou's voice. We talked for a long time—I don't know exactly how long, but I remember she got up a few times to get a fresh Smirnoff while my 40 grew warm between my knees. Every time she left I worried she'd head off somewhere else, to sit with her boyfriend or Jess's friends, and that would be the end of that, but each time she came back and sat next to me on the couch, clinking her light-blue bottle against my brown one, and we were back in the same place, outside of time and the world. Even when her boyfriend came by to let her know he had to make a delivery she stayed put and barely paused in the story she was telling me. As she talked she repeatedly tucked her hair behind her ears. Her incisors were set back a touch behind her canines, it gave her a mischievous look. From time to time she fidgeted with her lip piercing. As we talked she looked me in the eye, always with a smile in the corner of hers, and sat on her bent leg, angled toward me, with hands that never stopped moving.

Eventually she switched to Colt 45 too, there must have been no more Smirnoff Ices left. With her brothers she'd seen plenty of bands play live, and as she told me the stories I hung on her every word. I wasn't thinking about Jess anymore. She must have gone out on the balcony, or the dep. Two of her friends were dancing on the coffee table like they were in an LL Cool J video. I couldn't fathom what Marie-Lou was doing hanging out with these people. I didn't get where she'd come from. Since Alex had been kicked out, I was the only kid at my school who listened to metal. Close to 800 students and just one metalhead. At my school, I was the skid. Half the time I felt like Hellboy, taken prisoner on earth. I was living in a world where metal had suddenly disappeared and ceded its ground to Tupac, Snoop Dogg, and DMX on one side, Millencolin, NOFX, and Lagwagon on the other. But the unthinkable had occurred: I'd found a kindred spirit.

Our discussion broke off when peals of laughter erupted in the hallway that ran through the kitchen. I heard Jess's voice, yelling something inaudible over the music. Frantz was hollering and laughing. I heard a door slamming and a muffled banging on the wall. I heard Jess's voice again but couldn't understand what she was saying. I got up and made my way between the girls in the living room to see what was going on. Marie-Lou followed me. Jess was in the bathroom. She had her head in the toilet. Théberge was leaning against the doorframe.

"I told her not to do any," he said, in a weary tone. "I told her it was stronger than PCP. But she's stubborn as fuck."

Jess lifted her hand up to give him the finger. She was livid. Théberge turned toward Luc in the kitchen, who was heating knives on the stove.

"You the idiot who gave her K?"

"No way," he said, placing a chunk of hash down on a red-hot knife.

His expression reminded me of the guy on the Krispy Kernels package.

I heard Goupil's stupid laugh from the living room. He yelled.

"She wouldn't stop begging me for it."

"So you're the genius who gave it to her, then," Frantz said. He was mad too.

He shook his head with an exasperated look and bloodshot eyes. One of Jess's friend, a redhead in bell bottoms, came to look over Théberge's shoulders. Jess was throwing up now, catching her breath just long enough to tell everyone to fuck off, including me, in that furious voice I knew all too well. I put my half-drunk beer down and tried to help her up, help her walk, but she just pushed me away and insulted me and finally fell into me. She got up again and grabbed hold of my t-shirt, almost tearing it. Frantz came out of the bathroom, looking like none of this had anything to do with him. Marie-Lou had backed up to make room for us. No one was looking after Jess anymore. I held her up as we walked to the living room. Heads rose up over the clouds of pot smoke. Big Goupil and Théberge exchanged a knowing look. I put Jess on a chair in the kitchen and started gathering her stuff, which was spread all over the apartment. Marie-Lou helped Jess get dressed. She was fighting us, refusing to put on her coat, telling Marie-Lou to leave her alone, she was suffocating. The three of us left and Marie-Lou decided to come wait for the bus with us. Jess was out, sitting on a bench with her head rolled back. Marie-Lou was trying to hold her head up, rubbing one hand and whispering. We kept talking while Jess slowly regained consciousness. When the bus got there

Marie-Lou gave me her phone number and told me that when I called her she'd give me the names of other metal bands to check out. She helped me coax Jess onto the bus, as she gasped out that we should leave her alone, she could do it on her own. I watched Marie-Lou walk away through the dirty bus window. We sat on the front seats, where it was darker, and Jess started dozing against the window. She took my hand. Her face seemed at peace, her features relaxed, and you could hear her slow, deep breathing, as if her whole body were enjoying a welcome respite from the ecstasy and the rage, the jealousy and desires and loathing that increasingly gnawed at her from morning to night. At one point, without opening her eyes, she told me in a whisper to put my music on and give her a headphone, so she could listen too. I smiled. Maybe for the first time of the night, of the week, I recognized my Jess. The other one had slipped away. Just like every time, I told myself we were going to be okay, that we would be okay in the end, we were just going through a rough patch, we'd rent an apartment in Montreal and her toxic family would leave her alone. But things didn't play out that way. I was telling myself stories. I'd just met Marie-Lou. I was moving forward, with my hands over my eyes. It would become my signature move.

CHAPTER 20

WAKING UP that morning felt like emerging from a sarcophagus after two millennia in a coma. I hadn't gotten up that early since the beginning of the semester. Or really since the previous summer I'd spent driving around the South Shore in my boss's truck, fixing up old apartments that smelled like cat piss.

I'd drunk the last of Vincent's coffee a few days earlier, and hadn't replaced it. So I was half awake at best for the trip from the bus stop to the restaurant. I remembered the prep lists and wondered whether I'd manage to get through it all. I was so afraid of being late I had skipped breakfast.

It was strange leaving the apartment at the same time as the army of workers who usually finished their day as mine was beginning, not unlike revisiting a place that your memory has deformed over time. I got to work sleepy and starving. Bob was already there, bright-eyed and bushy-tailed. He was setting up the kitchen, singing a Meat Loaf tune with hilarious lyrics he made up as he went along.

"Rough morning? You look like you need coffee."

Bob showed me how to use the espresso machine. I watched the thin trickle of coffee filling the white cup, hypnotized, as he explained how to steam the milk.

In the dining room, the chairs were up on the tables. Daylight filtered in, casting yellow lines onto the brick walls. CHOM FM played quietly over the speakers.

"I heard you put that little shit in his place? Wish I'd been there to see it. I must've told Renaud to lose that guy a thousand times."

Bob was turning on hood vents and pre-heating the pizza oven. He rummaged through the line fridges to take inventory, then went downstairs to change. Séverine was already in the office. She said hi without looking up from her paperwork.

Bob unlocked his locker.

"Renaud said you're a fast learner. So I'm gonna leave you alone to do your prep most of the day."

Séverine pushed the door open a little wider.

"Bob, did Christian tell you Jason wasn't coming in at noon?"

Bob just laughed. He threw his t-shirt into his locker, and put on his chef's coat.

"No worries," he said, giving me a knowing look. "The dishwasher will give me a hand."

He put on a pair of old sauce-stained Vans. I put on my shirt and pants, still damp from two days earlier, which I'd left in Dave's old locker.

Bob asked me to follow him. We went into the walk-in together. He checked the backups on the shelves, threw out whatever had gone bad, and rotated everything, explaining how critical this last step was. As he shifted buckets around he made little cracks about Renaud or Christian. We went out and pushed the thick door shut. I stayed at his side while he made a list of everything we had to do on the prep board. He showed me where to start, and took the time to explain in detail how everything had to be done.

Then we went to the prep kitchen. He showed me how to activate the yeast in warm water to make pizza dough for the calzones and focaccias. You combined flour, eggs, salt, and oil in the big commercial mixer. It looked like a giant egg beater. Bob set the dial timer to fifteen minutes.

"When it's ready make sure the machine stops completely before you take the dough out," he warned me. "This bad boy can rip your arm off."

We had to make two big balls of dough, and leave them to rise on top of the fridges.

"Around three you have to make a double batch, for the night shift."

My exhaustion was lifting, but now I was starving. My hunger was so fierce it almost made me nauseous. I realized it was time to stop waiting around for Vincent to buy groceries. I was turning into the kind of guy who annoyed me, one of those dudes who comes back from visiting his parents every weekend with a week's worth of pre-cooked meals. I started in on my tasks, taking care to do a good job and looking over at Bob for approval now and then. He was relaxed as could be, as if he was hanging out in his own kitchen. Not rushing at all. Everything appeared to be perfectly organized in his head, and he never had to move more than a step or two to get it all done. Bob was portioning meat and swordfish, deboning salmon, making pestos and stirring the cream sauce. Though he barely glanced up at his work, he was always doing three things at once. It just never showed. He kept right on telling stories about other shifts or parties. He talked enough for the two of us, but it never got annoying. Bob just liked spinning yarns. He was a born storyteller, a stand-up comic with a sense of how to let his setup breathe a while before nailing his punch line. It broke up the monotony of the most repetitive tasks.

I'd been right: there was lots to do. By the time eleven rolled around I must have peeled four sacks of onions that weighed half as much as me, and then the shallots, and then chopped them all up in the robot-coupe. You had to peel every bulb with a paring knife, one at a time. My eyes were burning. I was crying acid tears, conjunctiva burning as if I'd swum thirty lengths with no goggles on.

After the shallots I had to slice zucchini lengthwise, cut eggplant into discs, and wash and chop bell peppers. Whenever he saw me getting bogged down Bob would come show me how to hold the knife, or the correct way to chop veg without losing a fingertip. He demonstrated the trick to economizing every movement, and how to always stand up straight at the prep tables so I wouldn't hurt my back.

"Don't hunch over like that," he said, giving me a little slap on the back to straighten me up. If you don't keep your back straight you won't be able to get up in the morning."

My next job was to marinate some of the veg and grill the rest. The smell of burnt peppers would cling to my nose for hours. I barely had time to mix up the eggplant marinade when the balls of dough were ready. I didn't have to prep as many focaccias and calzones as I did for the night shift, but it still ate up a precious half hour. Time was flying by. The idea of helping Bob with the lunch rush was making me nervous. There weren't enough seconds in a minute, or enough minutes in an hour.

I was squeezing the juice from an entire box of lemons when Bob showed up with three plates of scrambled eggs, sliced tomatoes, and bacon. He set mine down on the stainless prep counter and took one to Séverine in her office. I dropped everything to grab the plate, my hands dripping with lemon juice, and started shovelling it all in with my hands, almost without chewing.

"Man, that's good bacon!" I said.

"Not bacon, dude. Pancetta."

He was pecking at his late breakfast, with one eye on the cream sauce bubbling in the steam pot.

"Finish that box of lemons, then thaw out the shrimp. That way you can get them done after lunch."

It was getting close to eleven. Upstairs you could hear the sounds of the first customers trickling in: chairs and table legs being shuffled around, along with the clinking of glasses and cutlery. I gobbled up my breakfast in three minutes.

Bob took his time finishing his breakfast, then turned off the heat on the steam pot before disappearing upstairs with our dirty plates. I squeezed the rest of my lemons and went to meet him. I brought some kitchen dishes up in the hope of getting ahead, or at least a little less behind. I was throwing a few racks through the machine when Bob called me up.

He was placing order tickets on the hotside and coldside as he explained how things were going to work.

"The day menu's smaller."

He passed me a lunch menu. I was in charge of the station Jonathan worked at night.

"So go ahead and make five of each focaccia, ready to throw in the oven. That way you never get behind, and you can focus on your salads. Watch out for this one and this one"—he pointed at two salads on the menu—"you can't make them ahead, the dressing burns the lettuce. See how all the ingredients are marked underneath, in small type?"

He used the same system on his side. The shelves above the oven filled up with pans pre-loaded with the ingredients of the four lunch pastas. No matter what happened, Bob promised, we'd be ready for anything. He'd also put a bunch of osso buccos in to cook, even though only two had been ordered.

"The trick is to double up on all the tricky dishes," he said as he deglazed a pan. "You never get caught with your pants down. Worst case, you have an extra staff meal or two. Anyway you'll see how it goes. They always order whatever's trickiest."

I thought about the Bébert's emergency osso bucco the other night.

Day was nothing like night. Instead of multiple rushes interspersed with lulls, lunch was just one big rush. Everything came in at once. Once it started I felt like I'd been dropped from a plane with a broken parachute. But Bob was everywhere. He showed me how to read the tickets as efficiently as possible, and how to sequence my tasks in a way that never slowed me down.

"It's a hundred times more chill with me than with Renaud. You'll get used to it."

I was tearing lettuce leaves and throwing them in the mixing bowl. My hands were shaking a bit.

"It's not that bad, with him."

"You've never seen him when the shit hits the fan. Pray you never do."

All through the service, Bob guided me with clear instructions. It was almost telepathic. One of my jobs was to prepare the
portions of pasta. It wasn't that hard, there weren't fifteen different noodles to keep straight like at night. For lunch you got either
linguini or tortiglioni. Though the row of tickets on my rack was
growing wider, I kept my head above water. When I started lag-
ging Bob would give me a tip on how to work faster. Meanwhile
he was juggling multiple tables at the same time, frying slices of
prosciutto or calabrese, sautéing more onions and garlic, the first
step in every dish, sometimes using veg he'd toss onto the heat like
a magician sprinkling magic powder. He'd simultaneously deglaze
several pans with white wine. He'd add the sauces, then reduce
them by eye. Each movement smoothly and precisely succeeded
and completed the one before. He made it all look so easy, putting
up six or seven plates at a time. Instead of ringing the bell he called
out orders, joking around like they were specials in a fast food
joint. Number 4 with fries; Number 13, hold the onions. The plates
on the pass-through got picked up right away. Though Bob was
going full steam ahead, everything was smooth as butter, and he
always stayed one step ahead of the rush. It was a sight to behold.
And he stayed in a great mood as he worked, there was none of the
aggressive tension of the night shift.

When the first lull came he sent me back to wash some dirty
pans and bring up some clean ones. The thought of all the dishes
surely waiting for me in the pit sent me into a momentary panic.

But the buspans were mysteriously empty. I imagined the servers were as busy as we were and hadn't had time to clear any tables.

When I got to the dishpit Eaton was drying dishes, calm and
cool as can be. The pit was even cleaner than when I came in. He
flashed me a bright smile full of false teeth. I was even happier to
see him than he was to see me. I'd thought I'd be stuck taking care
of all the dishes on top of everything else.

We made it through the entire lunch without once slackening
the pace. I was starting to catch on. Bob made jokes with the wait
staff and sent the plates out in a seamless series of movements.

Not one second was wasted, but the man was having fun. Then everything slowed down, the orders dried up, and the clanking of cutlery on dishes and the chattering of customers tapered off.

By two p.m. the worst was behind us. Lunch more or less done. I left Bob in the service kitchen. I still had to deal with the prawns for the night shift. That meant shelling and marinating them. You took a single prawn, slid off the thin shell, then sliced its back to pull out the little black string of digestive tube. This job drove me fucking crazy. No matter how many times I wiped my hands they remained gummed up with the viscera I was spilling all over the place. Just when I was about to throw all the shells in the garbage, Bob came downstairs and stared at me like a madman poised to toss uncut diamonds in the trash.

"Don't throw that out dude! What do you think we use for the seafood caramel?"

Good question. I was slowly learning to keep nearly everything. The vegetable trimmings got boiled to make veg stock, the insides of peppers went into pesto or coulis.

After the second batch of focaccia and calzone dough, with the prawns finally soaking in their marinade, we took a break to eat. Eaton had made Indian pastries with the leftover calzone dough. Bob called them Samosas. They were really spicy, almost too much for me, but I was so hungry it felt like I'd never eaten anything so good.

We all sat down on milk crates in the dishpit. Bob had a smoke. His Red Sox cap was resting on his knee, and his apron was all bunched up on one of the shelves. He made us sit down and take fifteen minutes to eat, a luxury I'd never been privy to on the night shift.

I thanked him for being so patient during the service, and helping me through the rush. I asked him why he wasn't a chef.

"This here is like a vacation for me."

I chewed in silence, embarrassed to say that the job was exhausting for me. He told me he'd taken so much shit over the years that now he looked for jobs with no responsibility.

"Before I landed here I worked in a private club. Chef was a real dictator. If he wasn't satisfied with how something came out, he'd throw it in the dishpit in the middle of a rush. And dude was never fucking satisfied."

Before that he'd been in charge of garnishes and *entremets* at a restaurant whose prep list was so massive it kept him up at night.

"Insomnia?"

"Sort of, but worse. I had eczema breaking out all over my body, even my face! Me and the other guys were so stressed we were literally throwing up before every shift. I couldn't even eat anymore. All I could keep down were fucking apples. Everything else made me sick. I was going through five bags of Granny Smiths a week. Not that I had time to eat anyway, working sixteen hours straight without a break, no more than two minutes for half a smoke. There was always shit to do, make the stock, prep for the week. Then we'd get slammed, the place was packed every night. And no room for mistakes. The customers were paying fifty-five bucks for a steak, ordering four-hundred-dollar seafood platters. Fucking ridiculous."

He burst out laughing, as if he couldn't believe what he was hearing.

"What restaurant was that?"

"One of those big deal places. Red carpet and shit. Bono ate at the bar once."

"Seriously?" I said, laughing. "Bono?"

"Yeah, lots of others too. Céline Dion, Robert DeNiro."

"What made you stay, if it was so crazy?"

Eaton was washing dishes wordlessly. From time to time he'd look over and smile, though he couldn't understand a word we were saying.

"I was young. And back then it seemed like the best job I could ever find."

"You must have made good money, working that hard."

"Hell no," he said, breathing out smoke. "They didn't pay shit."

"So why didn't you get another job, when you saw how much they were paying?"

"When it's the same low pay wherever you apply, you choose the place with the most status. You get off on working at the hottest place in town. They don't take just anyone, you know. They've got people lined up around the block to work there. Man, even talking about it gives me the shivers. I'd show up at ten in the morning every day and barely have time to get through the prep list by six. Then it was one long rush, from the first table till the kitchen closed. And then, to blow off steam, we'd run to the bar and drink like fiends. Out till four, up at nine, sprinting to work. Crazy schedule, crazy life. But you know, man: *Bono ate at the bar once.* So you convince yourself you're somehow part of that glory. That's what they get you with, instead of a paycheque. It's the status."

As he told his story he gestured with his skinny arms.

"How'd it all end?"

He flicked his butt into the alley, pushing the door with his feet. I was washing down my samosa with big sips of Sprite.

"I got into blow. You're always hungover, so you just need a couple of lines to get ready for the rush. And then just a bump for energy, to keep drinking after the shift. I lost my girlfriend, thirty-two pounds, and a whole lot of friends. I hit a point where I just snapped. I gave it all up for two years. Now I set my own terms. I work with people I respect, and people who respect me. I've known Séverine for ten years. She's a friend. That's why I'm here."

"What about Christian. Does he treat you okay?" I asked, before taking another bite of samosa.

I dried my curry-yellowed fingers on my aprons.

"Christian . . . Man, that's a sad story. I met Christian years ago, when he was a sous-chef. Guy was a machine. Seriously, he could cook. But since his daughter died of leukemia he's been on downward spiral. Every time I see him I've got a little frog in my throat. 'Cause he lost his wife, too, last winter. Now he's kind of a ghost of himself. Lucky that Séverine is on top of shit, otherwise this whole mess would blow up. I've told her what I think plenty of times. But it's not my place. She wouldn't have to work so hard if her chef wasn't lost at sea. And Christian would be better off if he took a good long break. But sometimes your job is all you got."

Bob stretched, as if he was basking in the sun. Then he tapped himself on the thighs.

"All right, let's get back to it."

He tied his apron around his waist and addressed Eaton in English.

"Thanks for the food, Eaton."

Bob rinsed his own plate with the spray gun and set off with two stacks of clean pans, one cast-iron and one aluminum. He went back up to the kitchen. I heard him laughing with the servers drying cloths under the heat lamps.

The shift change was coming up. One at a time, the floor staff was leaving. I felt like a student struggling to finish a long exam while the rest of the class was already leaving the room. As the afternoon wore on, the prep list on the whiteboard just seemed to get longer. There was no time to breathe. And in addition to getting ready for the evening there was the prep room to clean. It looked like the day after an eighteen-year-old's housewarming party.

I realized it was four o'clock when Jonathan showed up. He looked bummed out again. He walked across the prep kitchen with his big headphones on, without saying hi to anyone. Bob came to meet me in the basement. He was still listening to CHOM FM, my dad's favourite station. Bob could talk about the former hosts, and knew all the nineties groups, even the one-hit-wonders. We'd list them off, laughing, trying to find the most obscure of all, the worst of the worst. Smash Mouth. Matchbox Twenty. Chum-bawumba. Bob always came up with the kicker, without slow-ing down as he filled up backups for the hotside. He was already getting ready for the night shift. He was doing a double as well. I was curious to see whether night would go as smoothly as the day had. Bob brought a different atmosphere to the kitchen. It wasn't as electrically charged as when Bébert was working. Eaton would stay to help me until nine. That was the deal until we found some-one to replace Carl.

Bonnie showed up next, looking much happier and healthier than the last time I'd seen her. She came up to see me while I was washing lettuces, before even changing for her shift. Her cheeks were still red from the cold. She took a mixtape out of her bag and held it out to me. "That's for you, man." She'd added an accordion-style booklet to the case, that she'd fashioned from a collage of fly-ers from shows. The song titles were written in her graffiti style.

"I put some good stuff on it. Hope you like it," she said in English. She must have seen just how surprised and happy I was. It made her smile as well. I tried to find a clean place to put down the tape, and thanked her in my rudimentary English. She seemed to understand. She set off to the staff room with an amused look, her purple hair a huge mess under her toque.

I spun the romaine. Though I longed to play the mixtape right away, I didn't want to look too keen.

While I was working away on the pasta roller, Jonathan was cutting up cherry tomatoes. He looked seriously down in the dumps. I had to ask how he was doing twice before I got an answer.

"Sorry, didn't hear you."

"You don't look so good. Everything okay?"

"Yeah, just tired. It's tough, working and going to school at the same time."

I was about to tell him I knew where he was coming from, but checked myself. What did I really know about Jonathan's life? I knew he was in cooking school Monday through Friday, and that he worked five nights a week here.

I finished my pasta and salads as fast as I could. After all I'd been through during the day, knocking off these two items on the list felt like a joke. And Eaton helped me clean the prep room. The guy was unstoppable. No matter how much work you threw at him, he just plowed right through it, smooth and steady.

I headed up to the next floor. Fatigue was starting to get the better of me. The service kitchen was quieter than usual. Bonnie and Bob were chatting as they worked, in English. They seemed to have friends in common. They were comparing their versions of a recent party. Lots of funny shit had gone down. A guy locked himself out on the roof. A girl fell down the stairs, spraying the walls with yellow puke on her way down. Bob told story after story from the party, he had a knack for putting his finger on the funniest bits. When it was Bonnie's turn she never quite reached the end of the story, she'd just start laughing halfway through a sentence. I couldn't resist watching her from my hiding spot behind the stacks of pans and clean dishes.

I stood around the order computer a while, to ask Maude for a fountain Coke. Jade wasn't there. The room was only about a third full. Through the restaurant windows I could see big snowflakes coming down. I was pushing into my tenth hour of work. My mind was starting to wander. I was slipping into an alternate dimension where everything moved in hazy slow motion, like being rocked by a gentle swell.

The night proceeded without event. Vague din in the dining room, routine clanging from the kitchen, businesslike chatter from the kitchen over Bob's rambling monologue, chatting away as he dispatched table after table without ever once raising his voice. Around nine a wave of crushing torpor washed over me. It felt like I'd been at the restaurant since the day before. The noises were muffled, my movements followed unconsciously one upon the other in a never-ending series. No longer conscious of what I was doing, I ran racks through the machine, sorted cutlery, and scrubbed the tile wall. My mind was numb. I started seeing improbable landscapes in the dishpit's sea of sauce and sodden food.

Nick would come back periodically, disturbing my sleepwalking with a request for cutlery or coffee cups, or just to have a smoke. We chatted a bit.

"Man, it's dead tonight. We aren't gonna make a cent."

I was loading clean saucers in a buspan while he finished his smoke.

"How much do you usually make?"

"I don't know. A hundred, one-twenty, one-fifty? On a good night. Why?"

I thought about Greg and the rounds of shots he'd bought the night we were drinking vodka. One-hundred-and-fifty wasn't bad for one night, but it wasn't enough to live like a rock star either.

"Just wondering."

"Another one wants work out on the floor? Your buddy Dave never stopped bugging Maude to see if he could train out front."

I imagined wearing fitted shirts, tight pants and pointy polished shoes, tiptoeing across the floor with my hand full of dishes, kowtowing to customers. Even making peanuts, the dishpit seemed the more attractive option.

"Nah, not for me."

"Yeah, didn't think so."

He gave me a cocky smile and went back out with his buspan of cups and saucers.

Eaton helped me until nine-thirty.

The only real rush came around ten. It wasn't enough to ruffle Bob though: just a group of thirty or so, going out after a play. All the orders came in at the same time, and pretty much all of them were for Jonathan. As the tickets piled up on the rack he grew increasingly nervous and swore quietly. Bob called out the plates like bingo numbers. Everyone wanted a different salad or focaccia, as if they were going out of their way to explore the entire menu. The little rush was pretty much exactly what you would order if your express aim was to torment Jonathan. A guy like Renaud would have left his garde-manger to deal with it on his own and gone out for a smoke, but Bob stayed close and helped him.

"Make the focs, and I'll do the salads. Then go grab a smoke."

Around eleven, the room started emptying out. Bob asked if I was hungry; I said I was starving. He invited me to come up and make my own meal, and used the opportunity to teach me the basics of pastas: how to deglaze the pan once the onions and garlic were starting to brown, how to properly cook prawns. He also showed me how to reduce the sauce so it coated to the pasta.

"Trust me, you don't want Renaud to show you. Unless you're into linguini soup. Or you like your prawns boiled, not seared."

As I ate I could scarcely believe I could have cooked such a meal myself. It tasted even better than the food at my parents'.

Not long after, Bob brought me the last of the kitchen dishes, so I wouldn't get stuck with everything at the very end of the night. There was nothing worse than facing the toughest part of the day running on empty

"All right. Tired of playing restaurant? I sure am. Enough for today. You coming out for beers?"

By now I'd figured out that it wasn't just Bébert: going out after the shift was an indispensable ritual everyone took part in. I managed to get my close done before the rest of the kitchen. Jonathan and Bob were doing a little prep for the next day down in the basement. Bonnie had snuck off, and was drinking her staff beer. I thought I might get a minute to talk to her alone. I drank my pint at the end of the bar, while Maude chatted with two customers.

Séverine was entering something in the computer with a look of such intense concentration I imagined the machine might explode under the pressure. Then she slowly looked up at the door. I heard a little "Fuck!" slip between her teeth.

I turned around to see what she was swearing about. There stood a massive bald man with a forehead that looked waxed to a shine, and a head and throat that seemed carved from a single slab, like a monolith. Giant hands stuck out of a black jacket. A jewel adorned his pinky. One of the waitresses kissed him on each acne-scarred cheek. Séverine put on a smile, like a mask, to welcome this man, though she hung back at the bar. Her heels weren't clacking as loudly as usual. The huge man spoke in a deep voice, rolling his r's.

"How are you, beautiful?"

It was mysterious: Séverine looked like a little girl in front of this man. Her voice became gentle. I'd never heard her speak like that.

"What can I get you, Piotr? Want a drink?"

"No, I don't have time."

He sat down, with half his ass on a stool. Unbuttoned his suit jacket, then looked Séverine squarely in the eye. She met his gaze. Her smile didn't waver.

"I was wondering, Séverine. Is Greg here tonight?"

"No, he's off. Why? Can I give him a message?"

"Ah, no. I just wanted to say hello."

The man's fleshy lips stretched into a grimace intended to look friendly. I remembered him now. He'd been sitting at the bar the night of my first shift. It was hard to forget a man so physically imposing, so immaculately dressed. Behind the bar, I could see Séverine sitting up straight, feet slightly apart as if readying to parry a surprise attack.

"Okay, sweetie. I'll see you soon."

He got up slowly and left the restaurant, saying goodbye to all the servers. But he'd wiped the smile from Séverine's face. She waited a moment, probably to make sure the guy was truly gone, then ran down the stairs toward the basement, slipping between Bob and Jonathan, who were on their way up, freshly changed, chatting about Renaud's uneven portions of osso bucco.

"All right," Bob said as he punched out. "Who's thirsty?"

CHAPTER 21

WE WALKED UP Avenue du Mont-Royal for a while. It was quieter than usual. We grabbed the first taxi that drove by. Bob and Jonathan took the back seat; I rode up front. As I did up my seatbelt, I noticed Bob reading the driver's name on his registration.

"Champlain and Ontario please, Mr. Jacques," he said.

Champlain and Ontario. Those two words echoed in my head, clearing a path right through the day's accumulated fatigue. I thought about the rows of VLTs in the bars along Rue Ontario. I suppressed a shiver, tried to reassure myself with an occasional glance over at Bob and Jonathan. I figured I'd be safe as long as I stuck with them.

"One of my roommates is at the bar. We're gonna meet up with him."

"Which one?"

"Desrosiers"

"Cool. Haven't seen him for a while."

The taxi drove all the way down Amherst, then turned left on the bottom of the hill, next to the market. At this time of night the buildings looked like eerie ruins, reminiscent of the cityscapes of a comic artist I loved named Druillet. Homeless people were sleeping between brick columns, sheltered from the wind by puffy sleeping bags. We drove by the Fun Spot. We passed the Desjardins credit union on the corner of Plessis. As we made our way

farther east, more and more "VIDEO LOTTERY" signs appeared in
the windows of bars. I closed my eyes and tried to concentrate on
the stories the guys were telling.

Both sides of the street were lined with closed-down stores,
windows covered with faded posters, entranceways piled with
dead leaves and stacks of flyers. In what was once a furniture store
pieces of cardstock on which you could still read "FINAL SALE" in
faded letters clung to the window by a single corner. There were
massage parlours with vaguely erotic monikers, abandoned-look-
ing hair salons, blue-and-yellow pawnshops with bars on their
windows and marquees proclaiming "WE BUY GOLD."

The driver stopped at the intersection Bob had given him. To
the west was an abandoned hardware store, its window display
messier than Zellers on Boxing Day. Bob paid the driver. We all got
out at the same time, and the taxi kept rolling down Ontario. We
could hear, fairly nearby, the sounds of cars driving down Papineau to take the bridge.

The bar was on the north side of the street. A skinny guy in a
sporty outfit, not much older than me, was picking through garbage cans, walking fast and talking loudly to himself. He looked
too preoccupied to catch cold. Two men in high heels and mini-
skirts chatted us up on our way to the bar. Bob said sorry, not
tonight, his girlfriend was waiting for him at home. Their hearty
laughs were raspy from smoking. Looking up De Champlain I saw
the imposing silhouette of Notre-Dame hospital.

We followed Bob into the bar. I was greeted by a row of
machines with flashing screens. My temples constricted; I felt my
ribcage tightening.

The place was bigger than it looked from outside. It had a
church basement speakeasy vibe, and somehow felt full though
there weren't many people: a few older guys with shaved heads
and carefully trimmed white beards, a crew of guys around my
age with abnormally thin faces that made them look like ghouls
who'd lost their way. At the back of the bar a couple of forty-year-
old muscle guys were shooting pool, wordlessly sharing a pitcher

of beer. Each hand was like a massive ham, each finger a fat sausage. They wore sweatpants and football jerseys.

A guy slightly smaller than Bob was sitting at the bar in a Thrasher toque. He had a seven-day beard, and looked twenty-seven or twenty-eight. He was watching the hockey game they were rerunning, with his arms crossed, in front of a big bottle of Laurentide and a pack of smokes. He turned around when Bob said his name. It was Desrosiers.

Bob said hi to his roommate and the bartender, then introduced me. The bartender's name was Martin. Broad shoulders, early thirties, flannel shirt with the sleeves rolled up over thick forearms: he looked like a roadie. We sat at the bar next to Desrosiers. Bob ordered for us.

"Nah, get me a pitcher, Bob. No school tomorrow."

Martin opened our beers with a flick of the wrist and poured Jonathan's pitcher, keeping a blasé eye on the screen. He served us our beers and asked Bob for matches, then lit a cigarillo.

The taste of the Laurentide reminded me of my first sips of my dad's beer, at family parties when I was a kid. I asked Bob:

"Is this your spot?"

"Yeah, I come here sometimes. It's chill. Close to home. I'm sick of places where you can't hear yourself talk."

Desrosiers was telling Martin about his next hunting trip. When Bob joined the conversation they changed the subject, started talking about a hockey pool Martin had organized instead. Bob was in the lead, by several points. I tried to focus on what they were saying and get the machines out of my mind. They were almost all free.

I'd hardly started my beer, and Jonathan had already drained his pitcher. He immediately ordered another. As he drank his tongue loosened, little by little. I was trying to get him to tell us why was in such a shitty mood.

"I'm fine, man," he said. "I'm just tired."

"Cough it up, dude."

"I told you. I'm fine."

He turned to Desrosiers and asked:

"Wanna have a game?"

Jonathan was pointing at the pool table that had just freed up. The end of his finger was still bandaged. Desrosiers got change from Martin and they went over to the table, drinks in hand.

"Is your roommate a cook too?" I asked.

"He used to be a chef at a Red Lobster. He just skates now."

"Skates? Like, for a living?"

"Pretty much."

I remembered the skaters from high school. The best of them used to hang around with a guy named Pierre-Luc Gagnon. I asked Bob if his roommate knew him.

"Yup. He's a buddy."

It's funny but this insignificant proof of the world's smallness made me feel as if Bob and I went way back. Or maybe it was his infectious calm, his unique way of setting everyone at ease.

Jonathan came back and ordered a third pitcher, with a goofy smile and a confused look. Then he stumbled back over to join Desrosiers. I turned around to scan the pool tables. They weren't playing anymore. I had a kind of cramp in my lungs, and felt a hot flash snake over me, all the way to my fingertips. Desrosiers and Jonathan were playing the VLT. Time stood still. I couldn't take my eyes off them. Finally Bob snapped his fingers in front of my face.

"Hey! Dude! You okay?"

"Uh, yeah, sorry. What were you saying?"

"I was asking if you wanted to try cooking. It beats washing pots."

I looked at him, surprised. He went on.

"You seem to have a good head on your shoulders. You know what you're doing."

I could hear the guys shouting out in joy. When I turned they were high-fiving. I imagined them hitting the jackpot, or swelling their credit count in a series of lucky plays. My mouth was getting dry. I tried to focus on the discussion with Bob.

"I don't know. Renaud told me it would take a while to find another dishwasher to replace Carl."

"Fuck Renaud, man. Dude can barely get his mayonnaise to thicken. It's no shocker that he can't find a dishwasher. Anyway, let me know if you're interested. I could always get you a job at my friend's restaurant."

Jonathan and Desrosiers came up to claim their winnings. One hundred twenty-seven dollars. I was dizzy. My heart started pounding, banging on my eardrums. It was all I could hear. A fog was rolling in, submerging everything.

Jonathan laughed as he counted out the bills. We'd have to do some shooters to celebrate their win. He was already slack-jawed and slurring his words. Martin poured us two rounds of Jack. I had to lean against the bar to keep the second one down. Desrosiers drank it down like apple juice. He lit a smoke. His little eyes sparkled over his freckled cheeks. Bob turned to him as he put his cap back on.

"I'm hungry. You?"

"Nah, man. Anyway, the smoked meat place is closed."

"Speaking of . . . Last call, boys," said Martin.

Jonathan handed him a twenty.

"No more pitchers for you. You can have one last beer, that's it."

Jonathan said something garbled. One eye was drooping. Martin poured a Blue Dry in a tiny glass, said it was on the house.

I asked Jonathan if he wanted to split a cab. It was a long ride to Ahuntsic.

"I'm not going . . . home!" he drawled.

"C'mon, dude. They're closing. We gotta go."

Bob gave Jonathan a pat on the back, to encourage him.

"No, man! I'm not . . . going."

Jonathan guzzled down half his beer in one swig. He was getting loud and testy. Bob spoke slowly and attempted to reason with him.

"I'm not going home," Jonathan said. "I'm not going anywhere."

"Cut it out, man. You're going to bed."

"I don't wanna! Fucking sleep. At fucking home..."

His gaze wandered and then he yelled it out, accenting each syllable by banging his glass on the bar.

"I'm. Not. Gonna. Sleep. At. Home. Till. She. Comes. Back!"

Beer was splashing over his hand and spilling onto the bar. Bob and Desrosiers exchanged a look, like bystanders watching someone about to spectacularly crash their bike. Jonathan knocked over the glass with the back of his hand. With catlike reflexes, Martin snatched it out of the air just in time. He eased it into the glasswasher. His face darkened. You could feel his patience wearing thin.

"And she can go... Wherever she fuck ... fucking wants!" he railed on. "I don't give a ... fuck."

Desrosiers took Jonathan by the shoulders, to calm him down.

"Let go, man!"

Jonathan was fighting all the way, windmilling his arms. He bumped into a table on his way to the door. Bob told Martin, quietly, "We've got this, man." They shook hands.

We all left. Desrosiers caught Jonathan just before he could get hit by a car. Jonathan gave passing drivers the finger, then started kicking a trash can. Eventually he lost his balance and fell onto the icy sidewalk. He lay there on his back, crying tears of rage. His sobs rang out, shaking like spasms. Bob and Desrosiers helped him up. He was sniffling loudly and shaking as if he was seriously hurt. His face was all puffed up and covered with slobber and snot.

Bob and Desrosiers lived a few hundred metres away, on De Champlain, across from the Notre-Dame Hospital morgue. It was a slow, arduous journey, trying to keep Jonathan on his feet. The light snow had stopped falling, and the cold had returned with a vengeance. We stopped a minute so Jonathan could throw up a little more.

"It's gonna be okay, buddy," Desrosiers told him, giving him a gentle pat on the back.

It took around twenty minutes just to make it to the corner. We finally got to their apartment, and then Jonathan threw up again, in the snow. Once he was done the four of us went inside. It was a railway-style apartment. Twenty pairs of sneakers, mostly skate shoes, were lined up in the entranceway. I asked if they were Desrosiers's.

"Ha ha, no, those are Bob's. He's got a bit of a fetish."

I took off my boots and laid them out with the shoe collection. The hallway opened onto one of the rooms, and at the end was the living room. That's where Bob and Desrosiers took Jonathan. They unlaced his big Sorrels and then took off his coat. He didn't interfere, just sobbed from time to time. They set him up on one of the living room sofas. Bob brought him a blanket and a bowl, just in case. I watched them do it, still wearing my thick flannel.

The living room looked like a teenager's bedroom, which was pretty funny given how old these guys were. One of the sofas was piled high with t-shirts still on hangers. I recognized the brands all the skaters in my school used to drool over. On his way over to hang up Jonathan's stuff in the hallway, Bob saw that I looked impressed.

"Don't worry, it's not stolen. Desrosiers gets free merch all the time. It can get a little ridiculous."

In the middle of the coffee table was a big popcorn bowl full of buds. Desrosiers sat down and picked up the remote in a single movement. He turned on the TV. The sports channel was on. He rummaged in the drawer for his grinder and rollies.

"Want some? That was this year's harvest."

"Uh, no thanks. Nice of you, but I don't smoke."

A single toke made me catatonic; two turned me into a raving conspiracy theorist.

"This shit's one hundred per cent natural. No chemicals. I grow it in my dad's fields up north."

The long narrow kitchen was separated from the living room by a linoleum counter. When he saw I was still sitting in the middle of the living room Bob called me over to sit on one of the stools at the counter while he cooked up a late-night snack.

"You'll see, we eat in style around here."

He searched through the fridge, and pulled out two legs of lamb in sous-vide, and half a litre of stock.

"You scoff that from work?" I asked.

He was still leaning over the fridge.

"Scoff? Hell no. It's my recipe Séverine uses. And I'm the one who cooks it. So I take my cut, that's just normal. Desrosiers, you drank all the beer? Bastard."

"Maybe. Don't know."

Desrosiers was crashed out on the sofa, playing *Grand Theft Auto III* and puffing on a joint. Jonathan was laid out on the other couch, his face finally at peace. He was snoring.

"If you're really desperate, I've got some of the vodka I brought back from China," Desrosiers said without taking his eyes off the game.

"Sweet. It's not like I need my eyesight or anything."

As he rummaged through the overflowing recycling bin, Bob told me how Desrosiers had spent six months in China with a bunch of other pro skaters the year before, as part of a promotion. There was a little factory across from the hotel where they stayed. Every morning a guy showed up with a box full of little flasks, and sold one to each worker. One day, out of curiosity, Desrosiers bought one. Bob showed me the green glass vial with ideograms written on it in black marker. It was almost full. It was the kind of liquor that would evaporate on your tongue, before you even had a chance to swallow. A single sip had been taken from the bottle, by Desrosiers. I was pretty sure the level wouldn't be going down any time soon.

Bob picked six or seven empty bottles of Johnny Walker out of the recycling. There were little mickies and bigger twenty-sixers.

"We might be able to scrounge a couple drinks out of these, hey?"

While we waited for water to boil for the noodles and the stock to thicken, Bob managed to extract almost two ounces of whisky. He poured it into two Montreal Expos glasses.

"Sorry, it's all I've got clean."

He was Marquis Grissom, I got Larry Walker. He put an ice cube in each one, noting that it was a no-no.

"But this time of night, it'll go down a little smoother."

It was true, the whisky went down way easier than I thought it would. Bob plated the food, almost as if we were at the restaurant. It was my first ever lamb shank, and it was incredible. Intensely flavourful meat melted away from the bone without coercion and the sauce clung to the fettucine, Bob had tossed it in a serving bowl with garlic, olive oil, lemon zest, and fresh parsley. He watched me digging in and said:

"Another trick for never getting in trouble in the rush: keep your dishwasher well fed."

He lifted his glass for a toast.

"Yo Desrosiers. Sure you're not hungry? There's lots."

Desrosiers said he was fine. He was reaching regularly into a big bag of Cheetos, absorbed in his game. Jonathan was sawing logs.

Bob asked if I was in school, and what I studied. I said I went to Cegep at Vieux-Montréal, doing graphic design.

"Cool. One of my exes did that. She makes a good living."

I talked about Deathgaze and the album cover. Bob told me about a guy he used to work with who had a band that was doing well. He said that in restaurants you met a lot of people with artistic sidelines. Bob knew a lot of people, and had a good story to tell about each one. As if every year of his life was really two, in kitchen years. He told me about the time all the cooks left in the middle of a rush, not an empty seat in the restaurant, because the owner hadn't paid anyone in a month. He told me about a place on Saint-Laurent that hired models instead of servers. They never said a word to the cooks, and were constantly screwing up and taking the wrong food to the wrong tables. Then there was the time the immigration agents showed up in the middle of a rush with rifles and bulletproof vests, to arrest anyone who didn't have work papers. Then he started listing off all the craziest chefs, starting with the one who burned his own neck with red hot tongs before the first service of the night, just to get fired up. Next it was time for the floor managers. He'd known some preposterous slave-drivers.

"The worst of the worst was at Galatée. Dude, you have no idea. He could load a room, pack it to the rafters, have people eating dinner standing up at the bar, whatever it took to squeeze three services into a night. He'd ride the servers until they had convulsions. The guy was a fucking machine. He was everywhere at once. But at the end of the night he'd turn into a monster. One time I saw him do two big rails, like this, right off the bar by the beer taps; just hoovered them up, then puked in the bar sink, right in front of the customers sipping their drinks. He rinsed his mouth out with Jack instead of Listerine, and went off with a cheque to a table, like it was nothing.

I asked Bob if he'd quit doing coke at some point.

"You never really quit doing coke, man. You may think you're done but you're never done, you're just taking a break. You go through phases."

At his lowest point Bob could spend whole nights going back and forth between his dealer's spot and his apartment, buying quarter-gram flaps because he was convinced every one was his last. He'd keep going till he got down to his last twenty dollars. I thought of the chorus of "Master of Puppets": "Come crawling faster. Obey your master. Your life burns faster."

Your life burns faster: it made me think of everything I was burning, one twenty-dollar bill at a time. It wasn't my life that was being burnt; it wasn't just my body that was subjected to the ravages of my own stupidity. I was burning everything I touched: money, friendships, girls, plans. Deep down I knew I wouldn't stop until everything was gone. But I kept right on gambling anyway. For a second I had an impulse to call Malik, but at this time of night it would just worry him. He was the kind of guy who just might set off from Trois-Rivières in the middle of the night to come get me.

We finished our food. Bob put the dishes in the sink and we went over to the couches. There was nothing left to drink. Bob rolled a joint and smoked it with Desrosiers, who was starting to nod off. I listened to the guys talking: Bob gesticulating, Desrosiers with his hands crossed on his stomach and his head laid back on the sofa. They were trading stories from Peace Park, some legendary place where skaters, junkies, and homeless people lived together in a strange harmony.

Bob and Desrosiers had known each other for ages, since they were kids. And it showed. I thought about my own friendships. The way things were going they weren't going to last. I told myself I absolutely had to pay Vincent rent, tomorrow.

It was almost five-thirty a.m. My drunkenness had lifted, giving way to irresistible fatigue. The day that had passed suddenly felt like a year. I glanced over at Jonathan, and figured it was time for me to go home and sleep too. I thanked Bob and Desrosiers for their hospitality, and left the apartment into the winter dawn. I went out looking for a Metro station. Outside the city was coming to life, as I walked down the streets, my own rhythms at odds with the new day dawning. I walked by warehousemen and cashiers and paperboys and labourers and the earliest of the office workers.

My eyes were scratchy from fatigue. After two blocks, I realized I'd put my headphones in but forgotten to press "play." I stopped at a bus stop and discreetly counted my remaining money. Made some calculations, estimated what I'd have once you added my paycheque. It was far from the two-thousand dollars Deathgaze had fronted me. I pressed play; there was Hetfield screaming. "Your life burns faster. Obey your master. Master! Master!"

I sighed and kept walking up Ontario in the glacial blue dawn.

CHAPTER 22

T HE SMOKE of cigarettes and joints rose in thick spirals above the mezzanine. The crowd grew denser as we moved forward, but Marie-Lou and I managed to squeeze up quite close to the stage. We were as excited as kids on Christmas morning. To the right I could see Alex's blond locks. He was by the merch table, with his friends. Good thing, too: Jess never would have let me come to the show alone with Marie-Lou. Since the middle of summer she'd been throwing little hissy fits because I was talking to Marie-Lou too often for her liking.

I surveyed the scene in the warm light emanating from the room's high ceilings. There were excited fourteen year-olds with peach fuzz moustaches and oversized tees, their hair not yet long enough to headbang properly, and people in their early twenties wearing wifebeaters under leather jackets, and girls with tattooed arms and black lipstick and bullet belts and lank dark hair, and couples around thirty, or some other age equally remote from my vantage point, in concert tees from tours that rolled through town when I was still in kindergarten. I had no idea what rock all these strange creatures had crawled out from. It seemed every metal-head in the province of Quebec was assembled here tonight.

A roar was cresting in waves. The Métropolis began to shake, I could feel it in every bone of my body and in my solar plexus. The crowd began chanting—"Megadeth! Megadeth! Megadeth!"—a refrain that grew more powerful with each iteration. I joined in.

An electrical current was flowing through a thousand upraised arms. The lights dimmed and we started yelling louder than ever. I shivered from head to toe. Marie-Lou lit a joint and then lifted her fist in the devil's horns. Telluric rumblings whipped the crowd into a state of excitement and then, in a beam of blue light, Static-X took the stage: four imprisoned demiurges, radiating pure energy. The two guitarists and the bassist were jumping on the spot. In a trance of sorts they spat out angular, dissonant riffs swept along by apocalyptic keyboards. At the back, the drummer was headbanging behind cymbals glimmering in the purple and cyan lighting. The musicians bounced around all four corners of the stage like rubber balls. The singer/guitarist, hair glued to stand straight up in the air, was standing on the monitors the better to light a fire under the audience. Though he generated a sizzling field of energy, it wasn't enough to win this crowd over. No one gave a fuck about the opening band. We were here to see Megadeth, and between each and every song we reminded them, yelling louder every time, so loud that by the time Dave Mustaine took the stage we all would have lost our voices from screaming it over and over again. Static-X was forced to cut their set short to make way for the headliners. The tour manager even came out to beg us to get behind them for their final two songs. But there was nothing to be done. When the intermission came, and the overhead lights came back on, I could no longer stand still. The crowd calmed down for a few minutes, then started changing again—"Megadeth! Megadeth! Megadeth! Megadeth!"—with the force of a revolutionary mob. It was deafening. When the room was plunged into darkness again Marie-Lou yelped and squeezed my arm in a show of enthusiasm. She turned to me. I could see her teeth gleaming in the half-light.

"Me-ga-deth, man!" I had to read it on her lips.

Onstage the roadies were finishing the equipment change. Above all the shaggy heads I could easily pick out Alex's. I yelled out his name. He saw me and gave me a thumbs up and a devil's horns.

One after another, the roadies left the stage. The overhead lights dimmed, leaving us in darkness. The crowd screamed as one, at a higher pitch than before. After an eternity the opening chords of "Holy Wars" poured forth from the amps, a thousand times louder than Static-X; it was an earthquake, a volcano erupting and spewing forth thousands of roaring lawnmowers. The drums kicked in. I could feel it in my chest, as if someone was pummelling me with their fist. Pyrotechnic explosions burned our eyes, and then the bass and second guitar came in. A shock wave rang through the already fully amped crowd and the mosh pit erupted like a sea of orks in Helm's Deep. Rabid fans were climbing all over us, body-surfing and jockeying for position and headbanging furiously. Dave Mustaine appeared in a white shirt, long armbands on his forearms; he was folded over his guitar, face lost in his red mane, which he gently rocked in time to the rhythm. When he came up to the mic all we could see was his grimacing mouth surrounded by copper-coloured hair. Ellefson and Friedman had taken up positions at the front of the stage, and were strafing the crowd with a hailstorm of notes sharp as saw blades. They followed up "Holy War" with "In my Darkest Hour"—a brief respite—only to come back swinging with "Reckoning Day," which was met with shrieking as the crowd cried out as one like a possessed tribe enthusiastically greeting the end of the world. I looked at Marie-Lou. She looked back at me. Her pupils shone in the darkness now zebra-striped with green and blue light. I smiled at her, possessed by a violent, irresistible joy. The crowd pressed her against me every time it surged forward. Sometimes her eyes were glued to the stage, sometimes she headbanged and yelled out lyrics. She knew every song by heart. We had to back up to keep from being sucked into the mosh pit. When "Hangar 18" came on, she really went crazy. She jumped into the melee, climbed over the swirl of bodies smashing into each other, then let herself be swept along by the crowd, tumbling over the human sea all the way to the foot of the stage. I followed behind her, flabbergasted. As the mosh pit grew bigger it sucked me up in its undertow and the craziness and I tapped into the mania swirling all around me. I was in a trance. There was no up, no down. I couldn't tell where my body ended;

I'd become part of this rocky, roaring wave of sound and sweating bodies. The entire Métropolis was shaking. As if by miracle, I found Marie-Lou again, right in the middle of "She-Wolf." She was wiping her bleeding nose on her sleeve, like a kid with a cold, and grinning so wide I could see her huge eye-teeth. Her forehead and cheeks were soaked with sweat, her army tank-top plastered to her body. When she saw me she screamed and pumped her fist. The veins on her neck popped out. She was dragging me deeper into the pit, into the eye of the hurricane where we would be immolated together by the same fire. The crowd was a shapeless mass of arms and legs, dangerously pressing us from every direction as we pushed back and together sang along with "Symphony of Destruction." The air was getting sucked out of the hall, the hammering riffs were getting under our skin and filling us up until bolts of cosmic energy shot from our fingers, mouths, and eyeballs. If this kept up we would soon be vaporized.

The cigarette smoke and dust clouds formed a thick fog through which we caught glimpses of Dave Mustaine's intense silhouette as he headbanged along with us, transporting us with solo after razor-sharp solo, raining down like a swarm of arrows. With a thundering roll, the bass and drums crashed over us in a wave. I was under sensory overload, ready to explode.

After the encore, calm gradually returned and the crowd broke into distinct groups of sated, sweaty fans. But the air was still thick with tension. A tiny spark would be enough to send this fire flaming up again, twice as strong. I couldn't hear anything over the ringing in my ears. Marie-Lou looked spent, her face and neck a purplish blue as if she'd just run ten kilometres. Her black eyes shone bright over her bright red cheeks. She held onto my arm while we went to get in line at the coat check. Outside, even in our coats, the November cold froze our sweat-drenched bodies. Twenty feet from the door Marie-Lou took me aside. She seemed to be looking for her smokes.

"Here, this is for you."

She handed me a tape.

"It'll get you into some heavier stuff."

She smiled. I took the tape and scrutinized it, as if staring intently enough would reveal its contents. I thanked her and she kept smiling. We looked each other in the eyes for a moment. She looked amused, or proud, I couldn't really tell which, as if she'd just discovered something secret about me.

"Hey lovebirds."

I heard Alex's loud voice over the fuzz of whistling and crackling in my ears. He came up and checked us out, looking somehow unsure, as if he'd caught us with our pants down.

"You coming out with us?"

He pointed at his crew.

"Nah. I have to go home."

"Come on, man. It's Friday."

"I promised Jess I'd go to her place after the show."

"Fuck, man, it's almost midnight. She's sleeping. She's got you wrapped around her little finger. We never get to hang out!"

He turned to Marie-Lou.

"What about you, feel like going out?"

I was sure she was going to say yes.

"No, I have to go home too. I'm working early tomorrow."

From his six-foot-two, Alex looked down at us with steel-grey eyes as if we were his clueless younger cousins. He shook my hand in silence, and leaned over to give Marie-Lou two shy kisses on the cheek before heading off to Foufounes Électriques with his long-haired friends. In his patched leather jacket, he looked like a biker. No doormen would ever card him.

We bought slices of 99-cent pizza and went up Sainte-Catherine to Berri Metro station. Marie-Lou was looking stronger, back to her old self. She said that no one but her brothers had ever wanted to go to shows like that with her. My eardrums were still scraped raw, but I could hear her every word loud and clear. Her voice cut through the ringing in my ears. We talked music the whole ride, from Berri to Longueuil. She kept saying that she couldn't wait to hear what I thought of her mixtape. Longueuil

Metro felt like an abandoned half-built cathedral, as the renovations just dragged on and on. Our voices rang out through hallways littered with drywall and sheet metal. We would have talked all night if we could.

When she got on the No. 16 bus, she said we'd have to go see another show one day.

"For sure."

As I waited for the No. 71 that would take me to Jess's the entire night replayed in my head. I flipped the tape case around in my hand like a talisman. Despite my ringing ears, and my exhaustion, I would have killed to listen to it right away. It felt like my whole life was just beginning, like time had been multiplied tenfold, like I was suddenly seeing in Technicolor.

When I think back to it now, almost fifteen years later, it takes my breath away. All that innocent happiness compressed into a single moment. But that was nothing compared to gambling. I'd make that discovery a little over a year later, killing time between classes at the Fun Spot. My very first video poker machine. That was all it took. That was my first taste of true euphoria. It was so intense, so intoxicating, that I wouldn't know what had hit me until I'd lost everything, even stuff that wasn't mine to begin with.

CHAPTER 23

I SLEPT IN, well into the next afternoon. Vincent had been careful not to make too much noise going back and forth between the kitchen and living room. I got out of bed with a burning desire to get my life back on track. Vincent was shut up in his room doing schoolwork. I went to the supermarket to stock up on frozen food and pop. I also bought eggs, bacon, and skim milk, since that's what Vincent drank, and on my way back I ordered us pizza.

I think it was Bob's coke stories that got to me. I'd never gone there myself but I'd seen firsthand what a crippling addiction it was watching Jess, who'd strayed down that road just like her father. If Bob had managed to quit, or at least take a break, as he put it, then surely I could stop gambling. If Bob and Benjamin could get a handle on their addictions, what was stopping me? I thought about Malik's advice. He kept saying I had to get back to doing what I loved, had to find my focus again. After putting back two slices of pizza I took out my sketchbooks. I made room on the coffee table, and spread them out in front of me, and began drawing faces, hands, and bodies. I started with pencil, 2B and then 6B, then shaded it in with charcoal. I wasn't as rusty as I thought I'd be. It was encouraging. I thought about Deathgaze. My Cegep semester might be a write-off, but there was still a chance I could finish the album cover in time. I thought about Alex and how he'd had kept his faith in me all these years. I didn't want to let him down. We'd be friends for life, like Bob and Desrosiers. I went into a drawing trance. I took out my felt pens. Countless sketchbook pages littered the floor, scribbled with unfinished illustrations. My hands were covered in charcoal and graphite. There were silhouettes of marine creatures in high contrast, underground temples infested with crustacean monsters, a nightmarish mythological world at least partly inspired by Lovecraft.

As the evening slipped away I made real progress on a few different drawings. I'd again found my way into that floating state where I could create without my mind drifting off perilously into dead ends of angst. It felt like being reunited with a long-lost earlier version of myself. The occasional burst of DMX told me that Vincent had emerged from his room to grab a slice of pizza. On each of his sorties he'd check out what I was doing, and ask me a question about grammar or verb conjugations. I kept going until the end of the night. Around ten he came into the living room after his shower, in basketball shorts and a spotless undershirt. He was clearly happy with his own day. We played a few games of *Twisted Metal* and then watched *Seinfeld* until we both fell asleep, he in his La-Z-Boy, me on my couch.

I slept well that night, despite an unsettling dream in which I was the only staff member in a packed restaurant, all on my own to cook the food, serve the customers, and of course wash the dishes after.

The next day when I opened my eyes Vincent was already hard at work. I also got up full of vim and vigour. I made us breakfast first, then washed the dishes. The window offered glimpses of blue sky. The trees that had shed their leaves and the fresh snow made everything more luminous. I felt joy welling up in me like just before Christmas holidays when I was a kid. After making coffee I got right back to drawing. I sorted my sketches from the day before, keeping only the ones that might work for my cover. Of the twelve or so I kept, my "octopus god" seemed most promising. The Deathgaze album would be called *Soul Claimer*. It struck me that I might be onto something really powerful, and perfectly attuned to Alex's ideas and tastes.

I spent the morning drawing up sketch after sketch for the band logo. I took out my scratch boards. I had just enough gouache left to cover them. Next I began scratching away with my burnisher, taking inspiration from the Black Metal groups Marie-Lou listened to make them a cryptic black-and-white-style logo. Their name was almost illegible. Each letter was reminiscent of a hairy spider leg, gnarled tree branch, or sinister knot. I tried a few other things as well. On backgrounds blackened with pastels or oil pencil I wrote "Deathgaze" in Liquid Paper, working in drips and splotches, like the Bloodbath or Darkthrone logos. I could go back to retouch and tweak it all in Photoshop later, once it was scanned.

I kept on like that into the afternoon, with barely five minutes' break to finish off yesterday's cold pizza. Then I worked some more, swept along by the same momentum, until I felt my pager vibrating. A voice message. I thought twice before checking it. I had a feeling it wouldn't be good news.

It was Renaud. They needed me to come in tomorrow. The new dishwasher wasn't working out. He asked me to come in early since I'd be on my own for the night. When I hung up I looked around the living room, which had morphed into a studio. Paper, felt pens, crayons, and Rembrandt pastels lay scattered all over the place. On the shelf was a sort of mood board made up of under-sea photos cut from *National Geographic* and photocopies of old engravings I'd been saving since I got the job.

I didn't feel like drawing anymore, so I just started picking everything up and sorting it, throwing out whatever was of no interest, gathering the images worth scanning. I jumped into the shower and then went to sit down in the living room, in boxers and wool socks, with my Isaac Asimov book. I wouldn't move for the rest of the night. As the cars drove up Henri-Bourassa, their sound muffled by the falling snow, I felt at peace. I read with a clear mind. If I could, I would have stopped time then and there.

CHAPTER 24

TWO DAYS off had seemed like an eternity. But the second I found myself back at the restaurant it felt like I'd already been there a week. The dishpit door was open a crack, I didn't even have to ring. Jonathan was sitting on an upturned plastic bucket having a smoke. When he saw me come in he leaped to his feet. He looked much better than last time I saw him, a few days ago.

"Man, sorry for the other night," he said. "I don't know what came over me."

"You're having a tough time. Happens to the best of us."

"I know, but that's no reason to lose it like that."

I was going to ask if he'd patched things up with his girlfriend but he beat me to the punch.

"Hey, did you hear?"

With his high-pitched voice, he reminded me of a kid about to brag about his latest prank.

"No, what?"

"Christian got fired. They had this long talk in the office, and ended up yelling at each other."

"Who's they?"

"Uh, him and Séverine," Jonathan said, as if I'd asked the stupidest question in the world.

"Renaud wasn't there?"

"Renaud. Pfft, nah man. That guy's never around when you need him. I didn't think Christian had it in him, to get that mad. You could hear them going at it through the door, all the way in the prep kitchen. Bébert was right, man. Christian was drunk at work. All the time."

Jonathan starting filling me in on all the details. I wondered if he wasn't embellishing a little. The way he told the story it was as if he'd been right there in the room watching Christian get fired. As he talked he was rubbing his chin, where a downy beard had sprung up in the two days since I'd seen him. It turned out the bisque was just a drop in a bucket, a final touch to make it look as if Renaud had pulled off his putsch. But the problems ran way deeper than that. What Bob had told me about Christian was on my mind as Jonathan told me his slightly disjointed story, hurrying along like he wanted to get everything out before someone caught him in the act. In the last six months Christian had been helping himself to the restaurant's liquor. He'd been showing up to work already drunk. He'd made mistakes on the payroll. At the end of their talk, Séverine offered to put him on leave for six months, so he could get help. If he got clean she'd hire him back. Christian said no.

"He came out of the office without a word. He looked way older. And just walked out, didn't say bye to anyone."

Jonathan paused. He looked at the pile of clean dishes, with his eyebrows scrunched up. Then he nodded suddenly.

"I've never seen Christian mad before," he finally said. "Not even a little. This time he was mad though. He'd stopped yelling, but he had a look on his face, like 'do not fucking get in my way.' He looked like he was going to shoot someone. Or maybe himself."

A cook I'd never seen before, a muscular bald guy in his midtwenties, came back looking for clean pans. Jonathan butted out in the ashtray and went back to the prep kitchen, tying his apron around his waist.

You would have thought Christian finally getting sacked would have put Bébert in a good mood. But when I saw him he was all alone in the basement, swearing away.

"Oh, you're here," Bébert said. "Welcome to Renaud's shit-show."

"What's going on?" I asked.

"Seen Renaud anywhere?"

"No."

"Well, that's what's going on. Since Séverine fired the chef we've barely seen Renaud out here once. I'm pulling thirty-two hours in two days, and a hundred bucks says he won't even show his face. And while I'm already stuck doing everything, shithead leaves me all alone to train his buddy."

"His buddy? Steven?"

"Nah man, new guy. You didn't see him? Looks like a neo-Nazi all puffed up on creatine."

As he talked he was pulling out a tray of crème brûlée.

"Check it: guy puts shit in the oven, doesn't set a timer, and takes off without telling anyone. Fucking retard."

Bébert threw the entire tray—water, ramekins and all—in the garbage. It was the second batch they'd screwed up. He slammed the oven door shut, then popped his head into the stairwell and yelled something at Jonathan, who you could hear working in the service kitchen.

"Fuck, I can't keep track of everything," he said, as if addressing an anonymous spectator.

The shards of porcelain glimmering on a mound of burnt brown custard and vegetable scraps at the bottom of the garbage bag gave me a pretty clear picture of the night ahead.

I changed as fast as I could. The staff room was a mess. Christian hadn't even cleared out his locker. His old cook's pants and work shoes were still there; it'd be days before they were cleared out and put away with the rest of the lost and found.

I went upstairs. It hadn't struck me when I arrived, but the dishpit was in a lamentable state. It looked as if no one had washed a dish since the night before. Everything had just been heaved in frustration and left to rest where it fell. As if it would magically clean itself. It exhausted me before I'd even started.

I went to punch in and stood in front of the computer a
minute, checking out the dining room. I envied the floor staff.
They didn't have to work up to the eyelids in food scraps, arms
immersed in ice-cold water or warm greasy dishpit soup. By the
front door, two couples were waiting to be seated. The men wore
silk scarves draped in the openings of their black coats, and their
immaculate white shirts were almost lustrous. The women looked
like older, more insouciant versions of Séverine. They wore fur
coats. I envied the customers like I envied the floor staff, imagined
they were equally fortunate. I told myself that once I got my life in
order, I should take Marie-Lou out for a nice dinner.

Jade was squatting behind the bar, stocking the last of the white
wine in the fridge. Her face appeared over the fridge door. Her
look of concentration melted into a big smile. She came toward
me, running almost, as if she had big news. Her hair was up in a
chignon, kind of Japanese-style.

"How are you doing?" she asked as she made me a long espresso
I hadn't asked for.

"Okay," I said. "Two days off in a row helps."

While Jade worked the espresso machine I peered into the service kitchen. I could see Steven filling the pass-through fridge with
backups he'd brought up from the basement. He had circles under
his eyes, and looked nervous. Renaud appeared from god knows
where, carrying clean pans from the dishpit. When he reached the
dessert side of the pass-through I asked him, jokingly, the name of
the hurricane that had ravaged the dishpit.

"Haven't found a dishwasher," he answered, without looking at
me.

He was shaking the sauce inserts in the steam table with an
annoyed look on his face. He hadn't shaved in a few days, and his
stubble stretched from his big Adam's apple to above his bony
cheekbones. Then he snapped back at me.

"If you hadn't gotten rid of Carl, we wouldn't be in this mess."

It made me sick that he had the nerve to say that to me.

"Don't listen to him," Jade whispered as she gave me a coffee. "He's stressed out because of all the changes." ·

I poured cream in my coffee. She stared at me, with an even bigger smile.

"What's up?" I asked.

"Do you want to go for a drink after work?" she asked.

"Uh ... okay. When?"

"Uh ... after work," she repeated, with a little laugh. "Like, later."

From the dessert side Nick was watching us, as he dried bread dishes. He pricked up an ear. I played with the saucer of my espresso dish. Jade's big eyes sucked me into their orbit. I took a sip of coffee and cleared my throat.

"Okay, sure. If we don't finish too late."

"Cool," she said, squeezing my arm. "It'll be fun."

She turned around, light on her feet, to take the drink orders. I watched her a minute, still smiling as she pulled pints and poured wine. Nick winked at me. I took off for the dishpit. I didn't know what to think. I really wanted to go, but was hesitant at the same time. I'd have to talk about me. I'd have to make up stories again. I set off to burn through my prep, convincing myself that Jade would change her mind by the end of the night. But if the invitation was still out there, I'd have to find a way to not stink of garbage too badly.

While I washed my lettuces Bébert beaked away as he finished off all the many jobs Renaud hadn't gotten to during the day. The guy could do the work of three cooks. Even though he was in a pissy mood he still found time to bring his prep dishes back to the pit. He even cleaned the steam pot.

"Tell your new chef he's got one cook who's not a lazy bastard."

Twenty minutes later I went back up with the focaccias. Renaud was on the hotside, coaching the new guy, whose name was Vlad. Steven was on the pass. It was the first time I'd seen him in that station. He was distributing tickets and calling out the plates with greater assurance than his hangdog look had led me to expect. It was like his mind was elsewhere. I gave Jonathan my focaccias. The kitchen was easing into a slow service, nothing like the rush from the previous nights. It gave me time to catch up on my dishes.

When I say Renaud was "coaching" the new guy it sounds like more than it was. Vlad knew exactly what he was doing, just needed to be filled in on a few details. The garde-manger was child's play for him. He moved with an agility none of the other cooks could match, his every motion a precise part of a larger sequence mapped out long beforehand. He wiped his knife after each use with a Samurai's martial grace, and kept his apron immaculate throughout the service. He never made an abrupt movement, didn't knock anything over. When he ran short on clean plates he came back himself to pick up a stack.

Vlad always showed up for work with face and head freshly shaved. He was as economical in his speech as in his movements, and never engaged in idle chit-chat. He would venture back to fetch things from the dishpit like a man on a journey to face his sworn enemy. Everything the guy did was of the utmost serious-ness; everything a matter of life and death. He was nothing like Jonathan or Bonnie, let alone Bob or Bébert. He knew the menu by heart before starting his first shift. One Sunday night when it was just me and him in the kitchen he brought me dinner in the pit.

"Here," he said.

"Is that for me?" I asked.

"You see customers here? Bon appétit."

Vlad had cooked me a tuna steak—there was one left over—using one of his own recipes, and garnished the plate as if I were a VIP client. In the middle of the dish, the tuna steak lay delicately balanced on a small yellow, red, and green pedestal of glazed veg. The fish was delicately sauced with some kind of salsa that looked almost like relish. He'd sprinkled a few drops here and there around the rim of the plate.

Usually I only ate fish that was overcooked, fried, in a pie, or doused in sauce, almost always salmon. But Vlad's tuna tasted like barbecued beef. It was so good that, ravenous though I was, I took my time and savoured every mouthful. All these years later I can still say without hesitation that this was one of the best meals of my life. I ate it on an upturned soap bucket, with my plate on my knees, in a dishpit redolent of bleach and used cooking oil.

The night was moving along nicely. Two consecutive days off had left me refreshed. I was getting through my work easily; it all seemed somehow much less arduous than my previous shifts. Maybe I was just learning to be more efficient with my trips back and forth between dishpit and kitchen. I had begun to anticipate what would need to be done, instead of being caught off guard by it. I wasn't getting in the juice, I was *swimming* in the juice, as Bonnie put it in her bizarre mixture of creaky French and Montreal English. This was a high compliment reserved for people who could stay calm even when there seemed to be a hundred orders on the rack.

The dining room never really filled up that night, so the floor staff had plenty of time to come back to the dishpit for a smoke. It didn't matter who came back for a five-minute break, they'd always have a chat while I scrubbed dirty plates or drained the soup of dirty food in the dishpit sink. Over several nights, these five-minute scraps added up to real conversations, laced with intimate confessions. A lot of people seemed to almost talk to themselves as they smoked. Part of washing dishes was being everyone's accidental confidant. Denver filled me in on his latest adventures with the bartender from the Diable Vert. Guillaume was worried as he waited for the results of his STI test. Sarah didn't know what to do about her boyfriend. And Nick never stopped letting on that every woman who came in to eat wanted a piece of him—except tonight, he was too busy teasing me about Jade.

"A barback going out with a dishwasher... Now I've seen it all, man."

Maude had a way of releasing the night's pent-up stress as she took a few drags of her smoke and told me little anecdotes. She'd been in the business ten years, and been smoking the same length of time. After one particularly ridiculous rush a chef had just handed her a smoke. "Just one dart, then we'll go back in." Maude didn't smoke at that point, but she'd accepted it out of fear that the alternative was to go right back in. For lots of restaurant workers smoking was the only way to get a break.

Around eight it was Bébert's turn to stop by.

"First time I've sat down today, fuck."

He was deeply relaxed, as if he had just taken a puff of Greg's hash. That was when he caught sight of the little sketchbook I'd brought along and left lying on one of the shelves between two stacks of clean dishes, next to my spare apron. I didn't notice him flipping through it until he shouted out in praise.

"Hey!" I said. "Leave that alone, man."

I went toward him to take it away. He pushed me with one hand and pulled the sketchbook away from me with the other.

"Whoah, chill. I'll be careful."

Carefully turning my sketchbook pages with one eye shut to keep the smoke out, Bébert looked like a monocled diamond merchant assaying the quality of a stone.

"You're good, man. I really like that one," he said, turning the book toward me.

He had flipped to the sketch of the massive Lovecraftian octopus god I was planning to rework for the album cover. It made me nervous. I was afraid he'd judge me, or think I was just a little art student. He went through, commenting on the different drawings, and looking more carefully at the goriest among them. He compared them to album covers of a band his cousin was into, Deicide. Eventually he put the sketchbook back where he'd found it.

"We going out for beers tonight?" I asked, filling up a rack of pans.

"Don't you have a date? With sweet Jade?" he said, holding in his smoke.

"Oh yeah," I said. "I . . . haven't decided if I'm going or not."

He squinted at me, incredulously.

"Yeah, I bet . . ."

He threw his butt out the open door.

"Anyway, not me, man. I'm done for the night. I'm going to meet my buddies. You can stay and close with these goofs. We'll go out another night, I'm stuck here all week. Ten days in a row."

"Are you finishing early because Steven's on the pass?"

The way he glared at me made him look more sinister than Greg on his worst days.

"What are you saying, dude?"

He really snapped it out. I turned toward him with my scrubber in one hand and a charred pan in the other.

"Uh, you know, aren't you usually on the pass?"

He looked me up and down. Then he calmed down.

"Renaud wants to get him trained up fast as he can. But he's not ready. No way I'm going to do the pass seven days a week I'll be back on the hotside in no time. I'm gonna be the night chef."

He unbuttoned his chef's coat and headed down to the basement to change.

The night went by without a trace of drama. After eight I was alone with Vlad and Steven. But with Vlad on the team everything went twice as fast. That much was apparent from the very first time we closed together. The second the orders stopped coming in, he got busy closing as if his life depended on it. When he got through with his station it was clean enough to perform surgery. He even scoured the prep room. Not to do me a favour: he cleaned it because it needed cleaning. I wondered where Renaud had managed to dig up a cook so unlike himself, and what common ground their friendship could possibly be based on.

When it was time to mop the kitchen I did it more carefully than usual. I wanted to at least approach Vlad's level of attention to detail. After closing I washed myself as best I could in the big prep room sinks. I soaped myself up to the underarms in degreaser and alien-green industrial hand soap. I rinsed my face off several times, to scrub off the greasy film that coating it from my forehead to my cheeks. Though my hair smelled like a combo of cooking oil, spices, and the grease trap, I drew the line at a shampoo.

I got changed and went upstairs. When I punched out, the clock read 23:23. I'd almost never finished that early.

Steven was finishing off his staff beer in silence; Vlad was already gone. He seemed like the kind of guy who would be eager to get a good night's sleep, the better to get right back to work the next day. A pint of beer was waiting for me at the bar. Jade had placed it across from her so we could talk while she finished her close. Maude was chatting with a few lingering customers. They must be regulars, since they thought nothing of camping out for hours with what was left of their bottle of wine. It must have been expensive. The glasses they drank from were taller than the others. I asked Maude what that was about.

"Shiraz glasses," she said, looking at them. "They let the wine breathe. You taste wine in your mouth, but it starts off in the nose."

I shrugged my shoulders. It all smelled the same to me, but I didn't say so. She turned around to see what her clients were up to. Her blond hair was cut in short, angular locks that fell over high cheekbones, and her face was somehow at once hard and beautiful. It was the first time I'd really taken a close look.

Like Séverine, she was a different person entirely with her customers. Or maybe that was her true self, and this her true element. She laughed often and smiled widely. The two customers competed for her attention while she surreptitiously filled their glasses, slowly emptying what was left of their bottomless bottle. Their teeth were stained blue from the wine and they were talking loudly. They were on their third bottle, it turned out. Maude kept the discussion going. She'd ask questions, stoke the fire a bit, and then slip off once it was up and running, and reappear at the perfect moment to sell them a digestif. In the meantime she worked her way through the bar cleanup, right in front of them, though it never looked like she was working. As I watched the way she maneuvered, I figured I could never do her job.

I talked to Jade while she polished the last of the glasses. When she wasn't speaking, she seemed to be singing to herself. It took around ten minutes to finish up. As she folded up her cloth, she asked if I wanted to go to the place across the street.

"It's chill, we can talk there."

Her shoulders were bare in her low-cut top. I took a sip of beer.

"Works for me."

Nick came out and threw his bag and coat on one of the stools. He sat down next to me with a half-empty pint and a big bratty smile on his face.

"Where are *you guys* off to?"

Jade turned to him and rolled her eyes.

"Oh, you're still here..."

"He better still be here," Maude said as she came up to where we were sitting. "He still hasn't put away the wine order."

The two stragglers were finally gone. They hadn't even taken two sips of their last drinks. She put their glasses in the glass-washer.

"Fuck that, Maude."

She was cleaning the bar where the two guys had been sitting. She answered in a mock-relaxed tone.

"Totally, fuck that. Greg'll be super happy to do it tomorrow."

She must have said the magic words. Nick tensed up. His face grew livid. He drained his pint and disappeared into the basement.

Jade took a last look around the bar to make sure she'd taken care of everything, then pointed at me as if I were the final item to cross off on her to-do list.

"Wait here. I'll be right back."

My cheeks were bright red from nerves and excitement. I finished my beer in the few minutes it took Jade to come back upstairs. Her shoulders had disappeared under the cowl neck of a beige sweater. She had punched out. We put our coats on and said bye to Maude, who'd started printing out the nightly reports, and set off into the night. Jade led the way; I followed behind.

She held me by the arm until we were safely across the taxi-filled street. The scent of her perfume blended with the car exhaust. I opened the door for her. She gave me a look.

"I think I know how they work, these 'door' things."

The place was full and the crowd was older than the Roy Bar or the Zinc. Polished mahogany lined the walls, the lighting was warm and dim. Behind the bar, dozens of whisky bottles shone like elongated amber jewels. The patrons were old enough that I didn't have to worry about running into anyone I knew. At the counter, fifty-year-olds with drawn faces nursed glasses of Scotch, taking dainty sips every fifteen minutes or so. I thought I recognized my Cegep French teacher sitting with a woman. At tables full of pitchers of dark beer thirty-somethings talked about politics and sports. I felt a little more in my element than at the lounge we'd ended up at that night with Greg. I didn't see any machines.

Jade led us to a table by the window. I took off my coat, hoping my "sponge-bath" had scrubbed off the worst of the stench of dish grease and cold sweat. She sat down across from me, relaxed, eyes shining with post-shift tiredness.

A server came to see us with a clinking of change. Jade asked what whites he had by the glass. He described two or three. She frowned, as if before someone who was about to drop a very fragile package, and ordered a pint of wheat beer. I had my usual amber ale. The beers arrived quickly and Jade paid the first round. I felt myself getting nervous again. I looked around. I rubbed my hands together. Some eczema had appeared around my knuckles, surely from soaking them in water all night. Jade touched my forearm.

"Relax," she said. "He won't bother us here."

I pretended to get what she meant. She added.

"Nick is banned here. Since the time with him and Bébert."

I remembered the story about shot glasses tossed across the bar.

She looked me in the eyes. I tried to calm down. I smiled. Had a sip of beer. It was hard for me to look her in the eye. She broke the ice.

"So do you think they'll move you up to the kitchen soon?"

"I have no idea."

I took another sip. She signalled that I should wipe my mouth, with a smile.

"I'd like to, anyway. It must be a little more ... rewarding than washing dishes. But you know, this is my first restaurant job. I guess you gotta start at the bottom."

"You never know. Some people climb the ladder faster than others."

She asked me what I was doing with my life, if I went to school. I said I was studying graphic design. She gave a look of approval.

"That's what my big sister is doing. She's at university."

She took the slice of lemon garnishing her beer and crushed it between her thumb and index. She sucked the juice from her fingers.

"So you like drawing."

"Yeah"

She beckoned with her hands, trying to get me to go on.

"I write stuff. And do illustrations too."

"Like comics?"

"Sort of."

"Cool. I do live modelling sometimes."

I rested my elbows on the table, bringing my chair closer.

"Do you draw too?"

"What? No, I'm terrible at drawing. I just pose."

I imagined Jade, naked, in the middle of a drawing class. My earlobes were getting warm. I was a bit taken aback, couldn't help it.

"It pays well," she went on, looking around the crowded room.

I didn't ask whether she was embarrassed to get naked in front of strangers, since the way she said it made clear she wasn't.

"What about you? What do you do besides working at the restaurant?"

"Uh, lots of things."

She started telling me all about it. She seemed to be sinking into her chair, with one hand between her crossed thighs. She was a little older than I'd thought—twenty-four—and was part of a Brazilian dance troupe. She also sang in a jazz group.

"That's what's cool about working on the floor: you can concentrate your hours, and still make decent money. It leaves me time for other stuff. Especially since the band is getting serious. We might go on tour this spring."

"On tour?"

"Yeah, a few shows in Quebec and Ontario. A couple of dates in the States, on the East Coast."

"Wow. How long?"

"Three or four weeks."

Her talk of touring reminded me of Deathgaze and the EP, which they'd need in time for their shows this winter. I chased the thought from my mind. My beer was going down fast. Jade was looking at me with a coy smile, like she was waiting for me to say something dumb.

"But . . . what'll your boyfriend think about you being away so long?"

She laughed.

"I don't have a boyfriend."

The place kept filling up. Despite the noise and swelling volume of the conversation we could understand each other perfectly. It must be getting close to twelve-thirty. She was eyeing the people coming in. One was a regular at the restaurant, but not with the woman he was with now. Another had once pulled a dine-and-dash. And there was a guy sitting near the back who Maude had once slapped because he pinched her ass.

I asked what it was like talking to people you didn't know all the time, being trapped behind the bar and always having to be nice.

"It gets automatic. It's really not as bad as you think. The bar is like a stage. It's your show. The customers just want your attention. They're there for you."

More beers showed up. She paid the second round too.

"Think you'd like working on the floor?"

The prospect seemed about as realistic as mastering telekinesis.

"At the restaurant?"

"Maybe not La Trattoria, but somewhere. It'd be even better than cooking."

"I've never done that, I don't have experience."

"You've gotta try it. You're all-right looking, you can handle yourself, and deal with unexpected shit. I'm sure you'd make a good busboy."

I listened as if she was talking about someone else. Working on the floor could be a good financial move, she said, especially while I was at school. I admitted I'd never even thought about it, especially since Marie-Lou made me think there was just no way without experience.

Jade asked me if I had a girlfriend. I seemed to hesitate a minute, then said no. It made me nervous again. My head was spinning. Jade seemed even more attractive away from the restaurant, just kicking back having a drink after work. Gone from my thoughts were Marie-Lou and Bonnie. Jade's cheeks were getting flushed from the alcohol. She took off her turtleneck, revealing a green tank top underneath, tight against her breasts. She was showing her shoulders again. A feeling of weakness shot through my whole body. I felt uncomfortable in my chair. I could feel my temperature rising. Jade was telling me about the places she'd worked before La Trattoria, and I was having trouble focusing. My beer was almost done. A long nervous shiver ran down my back; I tried to supress it. There were at least two good sips left in my pint, enough to keep her from ordering another round. Her beer was still half full.

"Sorry, I have to go to the bathroom."

I got up and slid between the tables, and took the pager out of my pocket: 1:11. There was still enough time. I emptied my bladder and then came back and sat down, with my pager. I pretended to check my messages. My eyes focused on the screen as I talked to Jade, as if an urgent message required my attention. Mainly I was trying to avoid making eye contact.

"I'm really sorry. I have to go. My roommate is locked out and his girlfriend is out of town."

"No way. That sucks. I can wait for you here if you want."

I rubbed my face.

"No, don't wait for me. I live far away. On Henri-Bourassa."

When I looked up from my pager, I could see that Jade was still smiling, as if the situation amused her. She put a hand under her arm.

"No worries. Next time."

She picked up her turtleneck and put in on in a smooth movement. The outline of her breasts disappeared under the thick wool. I was burning up inside, feeling something akin to muffled pain. There was only one thing on my mind.

To leave we had to fight our way through a disorganized group on their way in. I immediately hailed a cab, and purposely didn't offer to drop Jade off. She said bye with a long kiss on the cheek. I unleashed a flurry of excuses and promised we'd do it again soon. As I slid into the back seat I thought I heard her swear I wouldn't get away so easily next time.

I gave the intersection to the taxi driver. I spent the entire cab ride rubbing my knuckles, pulling off flakes of eczema-dried skin with my nails. In an attempt to calm myself down I closed my eyes, but it wasn't enough to chase the image obsessing me from my head.

I entered the establishment, repeating the ritual. The bouncer shot me a fluorescent smile and a "Long time, no see." I was wound up too tight to even answer. In the mirrors' reflection I could follow what was happening onstage. I floated along between the chrome chairs and the tables. The bartender recognized me and uncapped two Buds before I had time to order. I slid her a twenty, and left the change as a tip.

Without taking off my coat or even sitting down I positioned myself in front of the machine. I slid a twenty into the slot. I was burning up in my multiple layers of clothing. I selected my game: *Crazy Bells*.

For the first few rounds I bet big but won small. The electronic tic-tac sound of my rising and falling credits sent pins and needles shooting up my fingertips. It felt fantastic. My head was spinning. I was flying, five inches above the ground. In under twenty minutes I burned through almost $100. Still no win. But losing meant nothing to me. Playing was the only thing that mattered, the one thing I needed.

I bet the maximum and spun the spindle. Reds, yellows, oranges, yellows, greens, purples, and oranges blinked before my eyes. For a few hundred, or maybe a few thousand years, it spun. Something was crushing my chest. Finally the spinning slowed to a crawl. Sevens all over the shop, in eight of the nine boxes. A series of shivers made my eyelids shake and relaxed my every muscle, one at a time. The effect was amplified when, next round, six sevens turned up in the boxes. After my earlier losses I'd just won two-hundred-thirty dollars. It wasn't much. Next to nothing, really. But I'd had a winning sequence. I'd be leaving with more than I came with. I printed the ticket and headed to the bar to collect my winnings.

I was still kind of dazed when one of the girls came up to me. She said her name was Angélique. She had big thighs bulging under her miniskirt and heavy breasts stuffed into a neon-yellow bra. The smell of hairspray filled my nose. A few minutes later, we were in the booth. She was rubbing up on me lasciviously as my hands wandered clumsily over her ass and tits. I was still stunned by my lucky run. I wasn't thinking about Jade any more. I wasn't thinking at all anymore.

I got forty-bucks' worth of dances from Angélique, then went back to the machines.

Two-thirty a.m. I'd already burned through half of my winnings. I bet aggressively, in paroxysms of a nervous, electric euphoria. I was sure that sooner or later I'd hit the ultimate combo, bells in a cross formation. It never arrived. I got another run of sevens, five out of nine this time. My credits jumped up a notch. For a moment I was blind. I imagined myself a pitiful, haggard figure. I had to get out of there. I looked around. There was nothing but shadows dissected by phosphorescent rays and black lights. A group of customers in hockey jerseys were whistling at a black dancer who was kneeling on the stage with her ass thrust out toward them.

I had to get out of there.

The one truly terrifying prospect was the possibility of losing so much I could no longer play. I hesitated. I was riveted to the machine. I set the spindle in motion for one last round. The fruits started spinning on the screen. My eyes were dry and burning. I closed them. When I opened them again, nine gold ingots were blinking before me. The entire kitty won by the players before me would be added to my credits. I was thunderstruck. I drained my third Bud like a Gatorade, while the machine printed out my wins.

I counted and counted my tickets. I was too dazed to see them as money. It was pure potentiality, that precious substance that would enable me to keep playing. That was why I didn't want to use it for anything except gambling. Even with hundreds of dollars on me, a taxi to Vincent's felt like an unconscionable waste, worse than a sacrilege.

At Berri I took the night bus up Saint-Denis. I was slowly coming back down to earth. The fever that had taken hold of me when I was with Jade burned less searingly now. Gradually, calm was returning.

When I got off the bus, Henri-Bourassa had a sad nocturnal gleam, like a recently deserted outpost. I walked to Vincent's, the sound of my footsteps in my ears, impervious to the cold and the wind blowing on me from Ahuntsic park, an empty white expanse broken only by the occasional leafless black tree. Low clouds choking the yellow night. I was the only human being.

In front of the apartment door, I went through all my pockets twice. No keys. Suddenly I was stone sober. Luckily the lobby door wasn't properly locked. I went inside and rang Vincent's bell. No answer. He was probably at Janine's. I'd have to call him. There was a phone booth fifty feet from his place, but I couldn't bring myself to go outside. I might be cast out for good. Feeling lowdown, at the end of my tether, I slumped down in front of the heater and fell asleep, my head tucked into my knees and my earbuds in my ear.

CHAPTER 25

I DOZED off in ten-minute snatches troubled by a recurring dream where someone caught me sleeping in the hallway like a bum and kicked me out. Around five-thirty a.m. I fell into a deeper sleep, only to be rudely interrupted by the sound of the building's front door slamming shut. Whoever had entered the lobby crossed it in a hurry. The taste of Bud lingered in my mouth and I reeked of cigarette smoke and stripper's cheap perfume.

It was almost six-thirty. I got up, twisted in knots, limbs numb with fatigue. Though I was exhausted, more sleep was out of the question. And I was too hungry to wait for Vincent.

I went outside. It was still dark out. I spent a minute in the doorway. The cold easily located the chinks in my lumberjack shirt and creeped down into my bones. My Walkman batteries were dead. The wad of cash I'd shoved into my pocket had taken on monstrous proportions. I took it out and stared at it for a minute. I'd count it later. I put the money back into the pocket of my jeans and started walking again. Boulevard Henri-Bourassa was black and orange in the streetlights. Silhouettes paraded along the sidewalks, mummified in their winter parkas. Already crowds of cars and buses were making their way toward real life. There seemed to be no one driving them. The cottony opaque sky gave no hint of the coming dawn. The landscape was rendered illegible by my exhaustion, as if the habitual cycles of day and night had come permanently uncoupled.

I took a bus, I don't know which one, it was crowded with sleep-walkers reeking of aftershave, sweat, deodorant, and hair mousse. My eyelids closed of their own volition. I prayed for a free seat.

In the Metro, I slept from Henri-Bourassa all the way to Berri-UQAM, with its ambient odour of pizza and French Vanilla coffee. It reminded me of the beginning of the last semester, when I used to get up at the crack of dawn to make sure I didn't miss a class.

At a Dunkin' Donuts I had breakfast, staring off into space, taking a thousand chews on each bite of a greasy croissant stuffed with eggs, cheese, and ham. Then I wandered around the station, past people scarcely older than me with bruised faces and quaking voices begging for money and smokes.

I loitered a while in a Jean Coutu drugstore at Place Dupuis. Bought fresh batteries to coax my Walkman back to life, then dragged myself to my Cegep where I could lay down on one of the couches in the student union café.

Sprawled out on a battered old couch, unnoticed by the student hordes passing through the café, with my headphones in to drown out the conversations around me, I finally drifted into a deep sleep that erased everything I'd been through the night before, as if an evil spell had been lifted.

I spent the entire day hiding under my coat so I wouldn't bother anyone, sleeping an hour or two at a time, until late after-noon when I finally worked up the courage to call Vincent. I wanted to ask him to stop by the restaurant to drop off the keys to the apartment and clean clothes. After a few tries I finally reached him. He said he was sorry about what had happened, as if it was his fault, and asked what time he should come by.

My breath still smelled like stale cigarette and eau-de-stripper. It was disgusting. I went to wash my face in the bathroom. Two kids were talking about the strike that was on its way, surely in the spring. One wore a keffiyeh and hobo's hat that read "D E A T H   T O   T H E   E X P L O I T E R S." They went out again without noticing me.

The day crept by. It was time to go to work, a prospect as tempt-ing as jumping into the blades of a snowblower. I would rather disappear from the surface of the world, lay out on Vincent's sofa, and never get up again.

"Should have come in earlier. You've got a new guy to train," said Renaud, by way of greeting, as I walked into the dishpit.

He was smoking. I said he'd never said anything about training. He told me to fuck off. He was in foul mood and looked as exhausted as I was. His pale brown hair looked grey. There was something tense in his bony features.

Bébert was in the staff room, putting on Old Spice deodorant. He looked like he'd just woken up and the staff room was his bedroom. He swallowed a chalky white capsule.

"You doing wake-ups now?" I asked.

I went to get a clean shirt.

"Yeah, sort of."

"Working tonight?"

"Always working, man," he answered. "Three doubles in three days. Be like that until Steven and Vlad can run their own kitchen."

The guy I was supposed to train showed up while I finished getting dressed. His name was Lionel, and he was well over forty. Before we'd properly introduced ourselves he was already talking to me like we'd grown up playing street hockey together. Two missing teeth transformed his "sh's" into "s's." The guy followed me around like a puppy, laying his hands all over everything like a kid in a store.

"You guys make pizza here? Oh yah, I worked five years for a Greek guy made pizza, best pizza in town. I'm tellin' ya, we'd throw out six hundred pizzas on a Saturday night."

He told me he'd done a little time, the way you might mention taking a trip around the world. Now he was looking for a second job, he already worked days in a warehouse.

"Don't worry about me, I gots a degree in washing dishes. Should've seen the shit-ton of dishes I washed back when I was working for the Greek, eh."

Lionel reminded me of some of the guys I'd worked with as a construction labourer. His jokes were getting old fast, but his enthusiasm was enough to make you forgive pretty much anything.

I showed him around and explained the work we had to get through as efficiently as I could. He agreed with everything I said, with a smile of wonderment, as if I were a wizard with astonishing powers. I let him start on the lettuce, and went up to punch in.

In the service kitchen, Bébert was riding the two new guys hard. Vlad responded with mere nods as he organized his workstation. Steven was caught in the middle. Bébert didn't let up for a minute, just kept on laying into him, all, "Who showed you to do it that way?" and "That's not how we do it here!" I walked over to the order computer. Bonnie didn't seem to be there. Jade either. That was some relief.

In the dining room three tables were occupied. At one, two men in jackets and ties were chatting, papers spread all around their wineglasses. Apparently they'd been there since noon. As I punched in my employee number I asked Sarah if she could get me a coffee.

"Short or long?" she asked, placing the cup on the machine.

I could hear Nick's mocking voice.

"So, how about Jade? Good lay?"

Sarah stood there frozen with an espresso cup in hand, almond-shaped eyes wide open.

"What the hell, Nick?"

She looked at him like a three-year-old shouting out swear words.

Nick wasn't done.

"Did you at least get to suck a little tit?"

I turned to him, jaw clenched. His sentences were ringing in my head. I felt a mix of shame and rage. My hands were shaking. I kept everything inside and just stood there, unable to move. All I could do was glare at him, but that wasn't enough to wipe the bratty smile off his pretty-boy face.

"Well, that's none of your fucking business now, is it, Nick? So how about you shut your trap and polish your little spoons."

Bébert's voice rang out like a thunderclap from his perch leaning over the pass-through, next to the biscotti jars. I took a final look at Nick and, when Sarah handed me my coffee, went wordlessly back to the dishpit. Images from the previous night came flashing back: Jade walking down Mentana toward her place. Me slumping into a taxi. I knew replaying the scene in my head wouldn't change a thing.

My coffee grew cold on the rack of clean dishes before I could even take a sip. The night was unfolding without a snag. I left pretty much everything to Lionel, who peppered me with questions. The answers seemed pretty damn obvious most of the time, but his zeal and professional, concerned tone almost made it okay.

Nick didn't come back for a single smoke all night, and when it was time to pick up cutlery Denver or Sarah would appear, or I'd send Lionel up front. From the dishpit I heard Bébert riding Nick a few times, asking how it felt getting beat to the punch by the dishwasher. But all I felt, thinking back on the night before, was profound shame.

Around eight someone rang at the back door. I opened. Vincent was in the middle of the alley in his Nautica puffy coat. His face lighted up when he saw me, like when you see a familiar face at a show. I left Lionel alone for a few minutes. It felt like I hadn't seen Vincent in months.

"It wasn't too hard to find the place?"

"No, it wasn't hard. Where'd you sleep last night?"

"On Marie-Lou's couch."

He gave me my stuff: a t-shirt, a pair of boxers and a pair of socks, my keys. He'd stuffed it all into a plastic grocery bag, and passed it to me on the down-low as if it were an illicit substance.

"What're you doing after work? Want to come out with me. I'll be at the Saint-Sulpice with my friends from Business Admin."

He talked with his head held back a bit, and his neck tucked into his shoulders, to protect him from the cold.

"Cool. But I'm going out with the guys tonight."

I nodded toward the restaurant door, to show him which guys I meant. He was shifting his weight from foot to foot, staring at me intently.

"You sure?"

Deep down I knew that enduring his business-school pals long enough to share a pitcher, and then catching the last bus home would be the best possible outcome for the end of this night.

"I'll probably get off late anyway."

"Your call, man. Phone me if you change your mind. I've got minutes."

He took his ungloved hand out of his pocket. I shook it, and then we bumped fists the way we had since high school. And then he took off, shoulders tucked even deeper into his jacket. I watched him turn the corner in the alley, and felt bad that I hadn't paid him back then and there. I thought about calling him before he got too far away. I didn't.

I came back in to the humid dishpit. Lionel was filling a rack of dishes. He laid out pans and plates with an over-the-top precision. When he saw me, he wanted to reassure me, a big smile exaggerated the premature wrinkles that ran along his face; he said that he had "black friends" too, that they were "really cool." I didn't have it in me to come up with an answer so I just nodded and took a stack of clean pans out to the cooks.

I leaned against the door of the service kitchen. Through the shelves of the dessert pass-through I could see Greg sitting at the bar. He wasn't working tonight. He was having a smoke and chatting with Sarah. His friend Kasper was next to him, with a Bloody Caesar. When he took a sip, the band of his gold watch slid halfway up his forearm.

The dining room was two-thirds full. I scanned it for Nick but he wasn't there. Back in the kitchen Bébert was his old self again. His head was nodding to an imaginary beat. He was tending to the many pans covering his elements while singing Black Taboo lyrics right into Steven's ear. Poor guy was doing his best to ignore him.

His hands were shaking, and he was nervously wiping his fore-head every two minutes. Vlad paid zero attention to Steven and Bébert. There were no orders on his side, and he was using the lull to clean his station. His face bore its usual, almost military expres-sion of disciplined focus.

Greg saw me and beckoned me over. In his non-work clothes he was even more intimidating. I went up to the computer. He asked how I was doing. Kasper lifted his glass in my direction. He remembered me. He had glassy eyes and a ready smile. Bébert caught Greg's attention, with a voice like a foghorn.

"Blue cheese in your pasta?"

Greg gave him a thumbs up. I went up to the bar. Quietly enough so Bébert couldn't hear I asked Greg a question.

"Hey man. Do you know Benjamin Laurier?"

He turned to me, with a slight furrow in his brow. His smile was gone. Kasper cleared his throat and gave me a dubious look. Maybe I should have kept that one to myself.

"How about you. You know him?"

"Uh, yeah."

Kasper was listening, with his hands crossed over his empty glass.

"How do you know that dude?"

I could no longer hear Bébert clowning around or pans clang-ing on the elements or the customers chattering.

"He's a friend. My ex works for him."

Something had changed in Greg's face. As if he'd just recog-nized someone.

"Really... A friend."

He looked at me for a long time, looked me up and down from head to toe, shaking his head slightly. I wanted to retreat to my dishpit. Not because I was unreasonably extending the amount of time I could spend out front next to the dining room without a valid reason, but because Benjamin's name had made Greg react, and I couldn't tell if that was a good thing.

"A friend, hey. That's a good one."

Greg counted us with his fingers.

"Sarah. Shooters."

"Belvedere?" she asked.

"Yeah, five Belvedere. And one for that crazy mofo," he said, pointing at Bébert. And one for little fighter here."

Sara chilled the vodka in the shaker, then filled five shot glasses and handed them out. Greg picked up two, and put one in my hand.

"Here man. This one's for you."

"Uh, I don't think Séverine would..."

"I don't give a fuck what Séverine thinks. You're doing a shot with us."

Greg took me by the shoulder. His bony hand gripped mine like a bolt-cutter.

"So you know the Laurier brothers. Small fucking world."

I never found out exactly how Greg and Benjamin had known each other, and I never could say for sure if that worked in my favour or not. One thing was certain: the man's curiosity was piqued. Maybe in a good way.

From the other side of the pass-through Bébert yelled "Cheers, bitches." The people sitting at the end of the bar looked over at us like librarians eyeing a group of rowdy teens. The vodka went down without burning. I didn't even make a face. Sarah poured back her shot like water, then practically danced off with the empty glasses. She went around to see all her customers, smiling all the way, keeping it light. Kasper was checking her out. Greg answered his cell. He was done with me.

I went back to the dishpit with a light heart. Lionel was mumbling away, telling stories. Dude had no problem carrying on a conversation with his pots and pans. I would gladly have left him to close, if he knew how. I felt like I was running on empty. My muscles were still cramped from my horrible night.

My pager buzzed. A voice message. I hoped it wasn't Alex. I thought about the night before, and promised that, starting tomorrow, I'd get myself straightened out for good.

The night crawled by. The restaurant was dead. Lionel insisted on doing everything. I was bored.

Later, Bébert and Greg came back to the dishpit to smoke while I got on with on my close. They were speaking in code.

"That's not how it works, man," Greg was saying. "Just be patient. You'll see, it's worth the wait."

I pretended not to listen. Greg asked Bébert if he wanted to go to Stereo. He said maybe, depended who was DJing. Greg set off on a series of stories, without answering the question. It ended with a story that felt only half true, with Ziggy breaking some dealer's face against the washroom door.

It only took me forty minutes to close, and I was really dogging it. Maybe letting Lionel do everything all night was making me soft. When I came down to punch out, Greg and Kasper were still in the same spots at the end of the bar. Bébert had joined them. They were arguing with Sarah about the best after-hours clubs. If there was a place in town where fun could be had after three a.m., Greg seemed to know about it. Discreetly I took a seat next to them for my after-shift beer, observing the people around me and the room. Bébert was running on 220 volts now, and wouldn't shut up about how thirsty he was. Greg paid his bill with a wad around eight times as thick as my own, full of red bills with some brown ones as well. It now seemed pretty clear that he was more than just a busboy. I was naïve to have believed it. Sarah kissed him on the cheeks, and told him to be careful. They put on their coats. As they passed by, Bébert put me in a headlock.

"You coming?"

Half an hour later Greg parked his Monte Carlo on Ontario near Saint-Denis. The car reeked of hash.

We weren't far from the Saint-Sulpice. I crossed my fingers that I wouldn't run into Vincent.

We were meeting friends of Bébert's at a bar I'd never been to. Normally that kind of thing made me nervous, but nothing was intimidating when you were rolling with Greg and Bébert. Greg just kept going on about how he couldn't believe I knew the Laurier brothers. Each time I clarified that I only actually knew Benjamin, and each time Greg acted like he hadn't heard.

The bar was like a less punk version of Foufounes électriques: big, dark and smoky, with the smell of old beer clinging to the floor. It was packed with people in their early twenties. Years of partying had left their mark, from the walls to the furniture. We made our way through the crowd, advancing in Greg's wake. He must have been the oldest guy in the place. We found a table near the back where a big group was celebrating a birthday, or maybe the end of term. Whatever it was, it was loud. Greg asked what I wanted to drink, then headed off toward the bar. He shook hands with the bartender, kissed the women on the cheeks. The guy literally knew everyone. He came back with a round of vodka shots. The waitress brought our beers. He gave her a fifty, said it was cool. We threw back our shooters. The booze hit me hard and fast. My mouth was already starting to feel pasty when Bébert's friends showed up. One was Doug, who was built like a retired UFC fighter. There was another guy in a Yankees cap with a big diamond in his ear, a gold chain over a white t-shirt and Chinese characters tattooed all up his forearms. Bébert introduced everyone. The guy in cap was Mick or maybe Mitch, I didn't quite catch it. He and Greg immediately fell into a conversation I couldn't follow in my exhausted state, with the blaring music. It looked serious and not exactly above-board.

A Foo Fighters song was blaring, the only one Marie-Lou liked. I flashed back to weeks we'd spent together in her tiny apartment, eating Lipton soup and watching movies until we fell asleep together. The last night at her house I'd stayed up staring at her shoulders and white neck in the darkness. At that moment, stretched out beside her in the heart of a timeless night, I was happy. And when morning came I'd held her tight. It had been so long since we'd done anything together. The next morning Marie-Lou was especially happy, and relieved to hear that Vincent would let me stay with him until I got back on my feet again.

Greg was getting worked up now, drawing an imaginary map on the table as he explained something to Micky-Mick-Mitch. Every now and then Bébert joined in, leaning over toward them on his elbow, as if he were sharing secrets with one or the other. His voice carried over even the din, but I couldn't really pick out more than a word or two. Kasper stayed quiet and cool, hands crossed over his stomach, as if the die were cast and all that was left was to sit back and see where it would land. He was barely touching his beer. I was drinking mine too fast. The waitress came to see if we needed anything. The guys having their little meeting ignored her. I ordered another pint and went to piss while I waited for her to come back. The place was getting even more packed with suburban skate punks mixed in with people I saw around Cegep sometimes and a different crew who rocked polo shirts and white baseball caps and weren't above drinking straight from their pitchers.

When I came out of washroom someone gave me a shove.

"Good times, man? Partying away the money you owe me?"

I turned around, unsteady on my legs. I was drunker than I'd thought. It took me a moment to recognize Rémi's square face, and another to see he had a buddy with him.

"Fuck you, man," I said, trying to slip between them.

His friend, who was clearly of the football-playing persuasion, shoved me against the wall. I sized him up: tall, blond, body of a gorilla with the face of a Cabbage Patch Kid. The people around paid us no mind.

It sounded like Rémi had been practising his lines in anticipation of the day he's finally run into me. He started off with threats, which were as convincing as you'd expect from a guy who'd never fought in his life. He pointed at the ATM flashing away in the back of the room, behind the people and the cloud of smoke, and ordered me to take out as much as I could. I didn't have time to answer, or was too surprised to even think about answering; I just stuttered like a moron while Rémi got all up in my grill and stared me down. Then I heard Greg's high-pitched voice, tinged with just an extra hint of menace. Greg pushed in between me and my old roommate, and Rémi backed off. He and his blond gorilla weren't looking so tough now. A second later, Bébert thundered in.

"What's up?"

Bébert pushed me away from Rémi and stood next to Greg, who turned to me.

"What do these dipshits want? You know them?"

"No. Never met 'em in my life."

My scalp was tingling. I could read the expression on Greg's face well enough to know I'd better choose my words carefully.

"They said I stole their beer."

"What?" asked Greg, leaning into the guy. "You calling my buddy a thief?"

My former roommate's face grew less composed the closer Greg got. Greg repeated his question. The gorilla was now looking more like an oversized guinea pig. I had the feeling that in their shoes I'd be shitting my pants.

"Yo monkey, I asked you a question. You messing with my friend?"

When Greg referred to me as "my friend" I felt a cloak of invincibility enveloping me. It all seemed unreal, like a nightmare with a happy ending. Despite it all I felt ashamed, and afraid for Rémi, but that didn't stop me from actually enjoying the scene, at least for a few seconds. Rémi put up a hand to calm Greg down. Bébert chimed in.

"You stepping to our friend? Yes or no?"

I could see Rémi disappearing between Greg and Bébert's shoulders. He had the expression of a little tyke whose big sister had made him watch a horror movie. He tried to explain, but Greg thwarted his every attempt to squeeze a word out. The football player tried to pipe in; that just pissed Greg off worse. Bébert had to step in to calm things down. He repeated Greg's threats in calmer terms, adding that I wasn't the one who'd stolen their beer and the smart thing to do now was to get the hell out of there. Greg pushed the big blond guy against a wall. He'd lost control a little and was in the mood to rough someone up. His every muscle was taut, he was almost quaking. Kasper showed up, followed by Doug. My heart was beating in my temples. I was paralyzed. Rémi said:

"It's cool, man, it's cool. I don't want any trouble."

His words were about as effective as dousing a fire with gasoline. I prayed a bouncer would appear. Shoulders and heads were amassing in front of me. Doug surveyed the scene with a satisfied smile. Rémi and his friend were suddenly outside my field of vision. I lost track of what was happening. I didn't move, didn't see them take off. I guess I imagined them leaving; everything was fuzzy. Bébert brought me back to earth with a pat on the back.

"Dude, come get us next time."

I shakily walked over to our table to sit down. It was business as usual, as if nothing had happened. I was still all hopped up, just like after my fight with Carl. My nerves refused to settle and never would—not after a few more pints, not with a little fresh air, not even once we got to the next bar.

I followed Bébert and Greg to the Stereo. The doormen let me in because of the company I was keeping, but didn't seem especially taken with my outfit. I guess ripped jeans and lumberjack shirts hanging out of coats weren't part of their dress code.

The place was full and everyone was dancing away, as high as whirling dervishes. The crowd looked impenetrable. Behind a fortress of speakers a DJ was laying down techno with bone-shattering bass. They must have epoxied the wall to keep the paint from peeling off. Strobe lights momentarily revealed the individuals who made up this crowd, metrosexual guys in tight-fitting outfits, chicks covered in glitter. We worked our way through this jungle of undulating bodies, arms, and legs to the bar.

Greg had a quick chat with the barman. When he yelled in the guy's ear his jugular popped out. Bébert passed me a Red Bull.

"Drink this, it'll help," I read on his lips.

I surveyed the roomful of people dancing their hearts out on MDMA or other pills whose names I didn't even know. I imagined you had to be high to whip yourself up into that kind of frenzy.

Three girls appeared next to me, naked under short, light dresses. They were all three inches taller than me, with smiles sparkling as brightly as the jewels they wore. One of them asked me a question I couldn't understand over the pounding music. It must not have been kind: all three burst into laughter and then they slipped off into the shifting magma of silhouettes on the dance floor.

When I turned back around toward Bébert, Greg was gone. Bébert was taking in the room, sipping on a Red Bull. His cap was pulled down over his forehead, and his messed-up teeth gave him a sardonic grin. He sat back watching the people dancing. I was still struggling to parse what had just happened.

Before I had time to finish my drink, Greg was back. He looked furious. He yelled something in Bébert's ear. Bébert nodded in approval. Bébert tapped me on the shoulder and pointed at the door.

We went for a drive. Greg was barking at Bébert as if we were still at the club, going off on a tangent about some guy named Kovacs. He kept saying that shit didn't work that way, and he had a bullet in his .32 for that motherfucker.

"I hope he fucking does show up. I'll cap him before he hits my front porch."

Bébert tried to calm him down, but it was futile. That was when he used a first name: Piotr. It rang a bell. I remembered the guy who'd come in to see Séverine the other night. My ears were ringing. I was ensconced in the back seat, part of the furniture. No one cared that I was there. They just kept drawling on and on about someone I didn't know. As he drove Greg yelled at passing cars and pedestrians through his windshield.

I tagged along with them to a house party at a huge apartment on Saint-Denis and Sherbrooke. It was like nothing I'd ever seen outside the movies. The ceiling was hung with streamers and Christmas lights. Every room had a different DJ spinning, and every one was packed tight with party people hopped up on cocaine and pills who'd wandered in from the far reaches of the night. Revellers were dancing on tables, doing lines off any available surface, reaching into little baggies like kids hungry for more candy.

In the red light of the kitchen two of the residents had set up a bar, selling warm beer and hard liquor in Styrofoam cups with the flair of auctioneers. Two MCs were battling in what might have been the living room. My favourite looked around twenty-five, and was rocking a Proust moustache, a thin sweater, and a bowtie. Coke-bottle glasses framed his beady eyes. With one clever dig at a time, he was chipping away at the other MC, who was swimming in a pyjama-like velour tracksuit and had a deep raspy voice that almost made up for his weak rhymes. I was leaning against the arch between the living room and kitchen. A girl with fire-red hair emerged from the crowd and bumped into me as she weaved toward the bathroom. In her drunken stupor, she was reaming out one of her friends. Then she fell down and got back up, with no help from anyone, and continued her epic journey to the bathroom.

I came up closer to Bébert and Greg. We bought beers. Bébert knew one of the roommates. Greg was calmer now, even cracking jokes. His moods were hard to follow. He paid for our drinks with a fifty. I thought about my own funds. Even counting my next pay-cheque, I wouldn't have enough to print the album cover. I took a long sip of Molson Ex. What good would it do to get my shit together if I couldn't also get the album artwork done for the band? I needed more money, and I didn't have a lot of time. I could feel sharp peaks of stress mixed in with excitement. The Casino was open all night. I took another sip of beer and focused on what was going on around me. Bébert had located his buddies from the bar, Doug and Mr. Yankees cap. A girl with a shaved head, elaborately made up eyebrows, and an oversized tank top with a silkscreened Wu-Tang logo kept slipping in and out of the guys' conversation to do little dance moves. Her name was Nancy, and her arms were cut like a boxer's. When she talked everyone shut up and listened.

Other people were gathered around in the kitchen. We pushed up against the counters. They were all jam-packed with empties. Doug was telling a story that I was struggling to follow about the time Bébert pissed on a police car before they were able to get the handcuffs on. I screwed up my courage and went over to talk to Greg.

"Hey Greg. Uh, sorry..."

He turned to look at me.

"Say what?"

"Do you need anyone?"

He looked at me for a minute.

"Do I need anyone? What do you mean, man?"

"Uh, like for your jobs. Do you need anyone?"

Greg's face lit up with a mocking smile.

"For my jobs, huh?"

He took a sip of beer and wiped his upper lip.

"Why you asking? Looking for a little extra work?"

I was about to say yes when Bébert butted in. He hadn't missed a word.

"Yo kid. You already got a job, remember?"

Greg raised his hand.

"Don't interrupt, Burt. Kid's old enough to make up his own mind."

I mumbled something about washing dishes not paying shit, and needing a little extra cash. Greg was listening, clearly amused by my request. He said he was all about making a little extra cash here and there. Bébert looked me in the eye and repeated himself, in an even firmer tone:

"We'll have you cooking soon. That's a better job for you."

Even when he was breaking up the fight between me and Rémi earlier that night, Bébert's tone had been nowhere near that harsh. For a second or two no one said a thing. You could hear the beat, the rappers, the shouts of the party people surging into a roar in the big living room. Greg patted me on the shoulder. The circle regrouped around Mitch. I got the sense he'd known Bébert a long time, that they'd been roommates for a while. In the middle of some story involving moving hash in a sailboat and stolen cars in Chateauguay, he did a bump off a key and chased it with a sip of beer. Mitch could tell a story with the best of them, embroidering in outlandish details and jokes. Bébert was laughing. Doug just listened with eyelids grown heavy, probably sick of hearing the same story for the hundredth time. Nancy butted in from time to time, to correct a detail. Greg had disappeared. My beer was so warm it was starting to gross me out. I got in line to take a piss.

Five minutes went by, maybe ten. We hadn't moved an inch. After a long struggle I managed to finish my beer. I had no idea what to do with the empty bottle, so I just held onto it. Someone from the bathroom lineup went up and knocked on the door.

"You guys fucking in there or what?"

Bébert came up to me. After thirty seconds he was done with waiting.

"Fuck this, let's go piss outside."

I followed him out, feeling dumb for not thinking of it earlier. We had to traverse two tightly packed rooms. The bassline of Biggie's "Hypnotize" was loud enough to blow the speakers. I could see Greg dancing, with his hands on two girls' hips.

We left the apartment and went down the stairs to the front hallway. The street sounds hit us at the same time as the cold. We went into an alley. A guy in a parka was holding up his friend, who was yakking against a wall. It looked like he was crying.

"Tough night, guys?" Bébert said.

They ignored him.

I found a cement wall and Bébert leaned up against a dumpster. The urine sent little clouds of steam rising up.

"Dude, listen up," Bébert commanded. "Greg might seem like a nice guy, but he's not playing on the nice guy team. Don't ever— ever—put yourself in a position where you owe him. That shit's not for you."

"What do you know about it?"

He zipped up and spat on the ground.

"Forget about it, man. It's as clear as fuck."

I sniffled. He looked at me and pointed at me with his index finger.

"Don't get into that shit. You're smarter than that."

Bébert was deadly serious, more serious than earlier, more serious than I'd ever seen him before. This was no game to him. We left the alley.

The two guys we'd seen had turned toward the street and were staring at the flashing red and yellow lights. Two ambulances were parked in front of the party. We walked over. We could see someone pushing through the crowd that had gathered on the front stairway. It was Doug, Knight Templar of the Outer Reaches of Hochelaga, working his way toward the paramedics with a girl in his arms. The one who had bumped into me. Her head was rolled back, her face and throat covered in puke, her hair soaked and plastered to her forehead.

"Well, looks like the party's over."

"Should we wait for everyone else?"

"Nah, pigs'll be here any minute. I'm not in the mood."

Bébert dragged me to the Lafleur in Carré Saint-Louis for hot dogs. There were a dozen skinheads in line waiting to order. Bébert was as impatient as he'd been waiting for the bathroom twenty minutes earlier.

"Good thing Greg isn't with us. Dude can't help fighting when he sees skins. Once we were drinking at Yer'Mad and he made one of them take the laces out of his boots. You know the white laces?"

"His laces? Why?"

"To wrap around his fist and pound the guy's face to a pulp."

"Really?" I asked quietly.

"Don't go thinking that's cool. I'm trying to warn you, man."

The line was at a standstill. I thought about the machines. And then the idea of the casino popped back into my head, like an obsession.

"This is taking too long," Bébert said. "I've got some pizza and a few beers at home. You coming?"

"I think I'll get a taxi."

"C'mon, man. You can chill at my place till the Metro starts running. You never shut up about how you're not making enough.

Quit wasting your cash, fuck the taxi, and come over to my place."

He patted me on the back as we left the Lafleur. The cold was getting wetter. We were a good fifteen minutes from Bébert's. When we got there his roommate was exactly where he'd been last time: in front of his computer, behind the Great Wall of coffee cups, beer cans, and crumpled bags of chips.

Bébert grabbed the pizza box from the fridge and tossed it on the coffee table. His other hand held a stack of cans, Milwaukee's Best. He collapsed on the sofa, groaning with fatigue. He turned on the TV.

"Yo Pete, are the movies late?"

His roommate didn't answer. Bébert picked up the remote. The *Reservoir Dogs* menu appeared on the screen. He pointed at the sauce-stained pizza box.

"Eat."

I opened a can of beer and took a sip. Bébert ground up some bud.

"So you and Jade? Went out last night?"

He pulled out his Zig-Zags and started rolling, one-handed.

"Yeah, sort of."

"How'd that work out for you?"

I took another sip, and stared at the pizza box.

"Nothing ever works out for me."

It was exactly the type of answer that would have pissed off Malik. I missed my cousin.

"Oh that," said Bébert, sliding a filter into the end of the joint. "That's just life, man."

There was a moment of silence. My beer had an acidic taste.

"Are you serious about moving me up to the kitchen?"

"As soon as I'm sous-chef. Consider it done."

He lit the joint. The aroma of skunk suffused the room.

"When you're sous-chef, are you still gonna need Greg's help?"

"Greg's help?"

He took a puff. He was staring at me with half-closed eyes, through a cloud of smoke.

"Greg's not helping me. It's more what you'd call a quid pro fucking quo."

"Yeah, thought so."

I nodded slowly. He took a big toke and held the smoke in. Then he said:

"You know I've had plenty of chances. And fucked them all up. Sometimes I have to cheat a bit."

"You think I haven't fucked up my fair share of chances?" Bébert laughed.

"I'd be surprised, man. I can see it in your eyes. You didn't grow up under no rainclouds. That's cool, totally. No one goes out of their way looking for trouble. No one needs that."

I sat up on the couch. I was about to say something but he cut me off.

"When I was your age ... I was an addict, took more pills in a week than you'll do in your whole life. I ran with the biggest crew in Châteauguay, for chemical shit. Trust me. I've hung out with enough skids and fuckups to know that ain't you."

"I've done some shit too."

"Yeah, no doubt. Some heavy shit for sure!" he said, laughing and blowing out a cloud of smoke. "Let me guess, you put a potato in your math teacher's muffler? Man, you're smart. You need a break? Need a little extra cash? We'll get you cooking. But unless you really love it, unless food is your life, don't get stuck in the kitchen either. Focus on school, your drawing and shit."

Bébert snagged a piece of pizza from the box. His roommate looked like he was made of stone.

"What about you. You like cooking?"

"I love cooking."

"Is that what got you away from drugs?"

"Can't say cooking's gonna keep me away from drugs."

He laughed, ashing his joint in an empty can of beer on the table.

"My mum showed me how to cook. She made me want to do it. I've been into cooking since I was a kid. I swore to her I'd open my first restaurant by the time I was thirty."

"What'd your mum do? Was she a cook?"

"Nope. She had an art gallery."

"Had?"

"No idea what she's up to now. I haven't talked to her in five years."

Bébert threw his cold pizza crust on top of the greasy box. On the screen Steve Buscemi was losing his shit because they were making him be Mr. Pink.

I couldn't get the casino out of my head. I tried to imagine what kind of person Bébert's mother could be. I asked him for a toke.

"You sure? Shit's potent."

I hoped so.

CHAPTER 26

THE NEXT DAY was misty. A heavy blanket of fog had rolled in to smudge out the whole city and me along with it. I was sore all over. Two all-nighters in a row were taking their toll.

I took the No. 30 back to Ahuntsic, eating a twenty-pack of Chicken McNuggets to try to get my stomach right.

I couldn't face my voicemail until I got home to Vincent's. There was another message from the Deathgaze guys. Alex's tone made it clear he wasn't happy, though he seemed to be restraining his anger. I didn't have the guts to listen all the way to the end.

Marie-Lou had left a message too. She wanted to know how I was doing and whether I'd managed to keep my job, then asked me to come by the bar to say hi or watch movies some night. She had something to tell me. I listened to the message twice. Marie-Lou's voice always made me feel better.

Vincent wasn't at the apartment. I had no idea where he was. Probably off making something of his life. I piled up the sketchbooks I'd hidden under the couch, and told myself I'd put them back later. For the time being I couldn't even look at them.

I drifted in and out of sleep until evening came, troubled by dreams of searching for a girl, a hybrid of Jade and Marie-Lou. In my dream I wandered through nearly deserted bars linked by a labyrinthine network of hallways reminiscent of my primary school.

Every person I encountered was a stranger. No one remembered a thing, no one spat out a word. By the end I'd forgotten who I was looking for.

I woke up with no idea what time it was. It was snowing outside. Through the window you could see big flakes falling in the lamplight. I felt lonely, sad, and empty. I thought about everything that had happened these past few weeks. I thought about Trois-Rivières. I pulled the blanket over my head and went back to bed.

In the week ahead I was down for six shifts in five days, without a day off. I'd specifically asked Renaud to schedule it that way. The thing about work is it keeps your mind constantly occupied. Our arrangement worked for Renaud too, since Lionel hadn't shown up for his third shift. That meant I'd be training, training, and then training some more, as a revolving door of potential candidates made their way through my dishpit.

First up was Hervé: recovering alcoholic, thin as a reed, quiet as a mouse. He worked as fast as Eaton. The training went well. He promised to come back the next day. We never saw him again.

After Hervé, Renaud tried out a computer science student named Jeremy, a real chatterbox who saw fit to share every detail of his upcoming internship and the computer programs he'd written to crack RCMP databases. Clearly a natural-born hacker; totally incapable of scrubbing a pan. And the dude just wouldn't shut up. One minute he was giving me his full availabilities through March of the following year, converted to a precise number of hours, rounded to nearest minute; the next he wanted to know what operating system the bar computer was running. I sent him home after two hours. Renaud pretended to take down his contact info and promised he'd call back, just to shut him up.

Next up: Jean Charles. Age: fifty. Vocation: professional bullshitter. Now here was a guy who'd been everywhere and done everything. He'd lived in California, Venezuela, Sweden, and Siberia. Been a war correspondent in the Persian Gulf. Was in the barricades at Kahnawake during the Oka Crisis. Had he also found time to sail around the world single-handed, in the Vendée Globe race? Three times. Obviously he knew who was behind the September 11 attacks. He'd just gotten off the plane from Kabul.

"So why are you washing dishes?"

"You know, I was a chef in lots of different restaurants. In New York mostly, in the eighties. I felt like getting back to my roots."

Sadly, Jean-Charles was also a bit of a space cadet. Kind of guy who leaves a carton of milk in the cupboard, and his car keys in the meat drawer in his fridge. He accidentally threw a broken dish in the garbage bag, which of course split right as we were heaving it into the dumpster. Renaud had to spend twenty minutes explaining that he just wasn't right for the job. Jean-Charles threatened to sue the restaurant, for damage to his reputation. He knew several members of Parliament.

After this series of champs came an eighteen-year-old Brazilian guy, Eduardo. Salvation! Eduardo was fresh off the plane from São Paolo, living at his uncle's until he could find an apartment. Eduardo showed up ready to work, ready for anything, as if his future residency in Canada depended on landing this job. Bus-pans of dirty dishes emptied in a flash, and no matter how busy it got out front the dishpit was never less than spotless. He was joined by Basile who was sixteen, shy, and punctual as a digital watch. He'd unhurriedly work his way through piles of dishes with mechanical precision, and weather rushes with an astonishing calm. You'd turn around and find your work magically done. Basile was a private school kid like me: he went to Stanislas, where my dad and grandfather had gone, while I was on the South Shore. He reminded me of myself a little.

We hired both Eduardo and Basile. In Renaud's words, it was better to get two and have a spare just in case.

"A good dishwasher's hard to find."

As for me, I allowed myself to hope against hope that they'd hired two dishwashers to put Bébert's plan into action and move me up to the kitchen soon. Little did I know, Renaud had something else altogether in mind.

The nights before Christmas flew by. It was always just busy enough that by midnight we were tired but not exhausted. The main difference for me was that I was starting to know what I was doing. But our customers still never seemed in a hurry to leave. Séverine's friends especially enjoyed nothing better than showing up ten minutes before closing, ordering food that wasn't on the menu, then partying into the wee hours. I remember having to clean up the men's room the morning after one of those parties. Someone had thrown up undigested pasta in a urinal. I found a Moët & Chandon ice bucket full of brown bile. I guess the Holiday Spirit hit everyone differently.

Early in the week it was me, Vlad, Steven, and Bébert. Renaud was nowhere to be seen: he stuck to whatever day shifts Bob didn't take, and left the rest to Bébert, who still hadn't been officially promoted to sous-chef. I only ran into Bob once or twice. We promised to have a beer next time we closed together. The rest of the week varied, sometimes I'd be with the new guys, and sometimes the old guard: Bébert again, Jason (who'd given his two weeks to work at Latini), Jonathan (always sad and distracted), and Bonnie of the Perpetual Hangover. I never knew how to act around her. The friendlier I acted, the more her reactions were tainted by impatience tinged with malice. She was even nastier to Bébert, but it went right over his head: that kind of attitude just bounced right off him. At any rate, work had swallowed the man whole. He was tackling double after double, working full tilt and then getting right back on the horse after every shift. He was deep in some kind of alternative existence, like a touring rock star or a soldier at the front. Just watching him was exhausting. He was going out pretty much every night. I'd go with him, to save me from the machines, and from Jade, too, I guess, who knows. She hadn't asked me out again, but I had a bad feeling it was coming. At the same time, I was the only one who knew what had really happened the first time. I was avoiding her, staying in the pit and sending Basile out front when we wanted coffees or Cokes. Then I'd drink my staff beer while I closed, then slip out the back door with Bébert and Jonathan.

Bébert fought off constant fatigue with a battery of Greg's pills. As the night wore on he'd grow increasingly volatile, and liable to blow his top at any moment. I remember one night, his seventh or eighth shift in a row, fed up of the interminable closing, he just did a key of ketamine right there in the kitchen, before the waitresses' disapproving stares.

"What, I can't keep up with my friends? Just because we're serving goofs who can't eat at seven like normal people?"

Bébert was doing lots of ketamine, it was his favourite way to jump start his night. It helped the booze kick in and bring on the buzz he'd then maintain with an uninterrupted flow of beer and the occasional jolt of speed, to keep from crashing.

When we weren't out with Jonathan and his buddies at the Zinc we always ended up at Roy Bar. I would have followed Bébert anywhere. Being with someone who burned so hot helped me steer clear of my own temptations.

On the last night of a string of shifts I'd be working, I was sipping my staff beer at the bar after work. Bébert and Nick were going to the Stereo, and I didn't feel like going, that place wasn't my scene. That's when Jade pounced. Whenever she came within a six-foot radius of me it had the same effect on me: I grew feverish and nervous, just like when the need to gamble took hold. The same implacable fist in my chest. She was nothing like the metal and punk chicks I was usually into. Jade brought out another desire in me, one I didn't feel often. The deeply sensual energy she gave off was intimidating. She held me captive at the bar while she finished her close. Vlad and Steven had already taken off, and Sarah was chatting with a couple tourists.

"What are you doing tomorrow?"

"Renaud gave me a day off."

I was tearing a coaster into strips.

"We should do something."

"Like what?"

She took a sip of a glass of white that a customer had bought her.

"My friends are playing a show. You should come."

"What kind of show?"

"Jazz. Funky though. You'll see."

"Could be fun."

She poured me another beer, which Sarah didn't punch in, probably to save time. I watched Maude putting glasses away behind the bar. She opened the fridge doors and checked what was left. When her face took on a serious, concentrated look she was even more beautiful: her eyebrows scrunched up and her big eyes looked almost angry, as she counted bottles.

"Call me if something comes up."

We'd arranged to meet in two days at eight, at the bar where the band was playing.

I walked to Mont-Royal Metro station. In the dry cold every sound rang out sharply, in high definition. A crystal powder floated through the air. My head was spinning.

At that time of night the Metro only ran every twenty minutes. I pulled out *The Trail of Cthulhu* and reread the same page, reliving Abel Kean's walk toward Innsmouth five times. It was no use, I couldn't concentrate. I slid the book into my back pocket.

You could hear a distant rumbling of trains. The smell of dust and spilled soft drinks wafted through the station. Faint echoes resounded throughout the tunnel. It brought to mind the cavernous, forgotten chamber of a necropolis. Drifters of all stripes made their way through these passageways, spectres bobbing their heads under the flickering light of unaccommodated fluorescent tubes.

Beside me, two Asian guys were chatting in English, coming off night shifts just like me. They wore unfashionable clothing that looked like it came from the Salvation Army: parkas soiled at the elbows and cuffs, a faded Jazz Festival cap. One was trying to borrow money off the other. Nearby, an old woman was dozing in her parka with her hand on her shopping buggy. The Metro pulled up. The doors slid open. We got on. The woman remained in her seat, still sleeping. "Change Your Mind" played on my Walkman.

The following day I woke early. It was nine o'clock and I felt possessed with an unfamiliar strength, as if I were emerging from a prolonged catatonia. It might have been the day off, or the fact that Vincent was home with me. We cooked up a breakfast of scrambled eggs, enough bacon for a small army, toast, and peanut butter, and while we ate we caught up and listened to Dr. Dre. My renewed sense of energy spurred me to get my shit together. I made another coffee and went to set myself up in the living room.

I took out my sketchbooks, and spread out a few sketches I'd decided to keep. The most promising was a seascape with a giant octopus. I only had a couple of scratch boards left, but I also had two or three sheets of glossy cardstock. I carefully brushed them all with white oil pastel, then covered them with black gouache. Vincent came by to see what I was up to, sipping on a shake. Once the gouache was dry, I started working the surface with the back of my X-Acto blade, or the dry nib of a calligraphy pen I kept around for this type of job. As I scratched away the layer of gouache receded, revealing the white beneath. I worked on it all afternoon, until dusk fell, only stopping a couple times to make more coffee, eat a handful of chips, or take a piss.

Around five or six Vincent came in to see if I wanted to order St-Hubert chicken. He was still barefoot in an undershirt and Adidas track pants. When he saw the monstrous octopus in the centre of the page he let out an admiring whistle. The beast's tentacles were all spiralled up like boa constrictors around deformed human bodies.

"Sick, dude."

"It's not finished yet. I still have to fill in some volume in the tentacles, and add a sort of underwater temple in the background. And also a kind of vapoury aura, around all monster's head. That'll make it stand out more."

I wiped my hands, which were covered in dust and black gouache. I looked over what I had done. It was something. I was proud of how it looked. An entire day had passed and I hadn't thought about the machines, not even once.

Our chicken showed up. Vincent had ordered a thigh and a breast, and I had breaded filets. After dinner, while Vincent watched the hockey game, I looked through my sketches for the Deathgaze logo lettering. A few were really good. One in particular, with letters reminiscent of tarantula legs, would look perfect right above the monster's head.

The next day I got up early, still full of adrenaline. I was going to meet Jade that night, but that still left me some time to work on my illustration. I was on a roll. I picked up my octopus and my demonic-lettered "Deathgaze" logos and slid them delicately into my backpack. I'd left my leather portfolio at Rémi's. I searched through my stuff to find my zip drive and then, without even having breakfast, headed to school to use their equipment.

When I got to my Cegep I went straight to the computer labs reserved for the graphic design students. Walking in it hit me that I'd missed the smell of acetone and plastic, and the soft whirr of the computers. It felt like I hadn't set foot here for six months or more. There were five or six students spread around the room. All had the sickly pallor that comes at the end of the semester. Time seemed to pass at a different speed here. Someone asked where I'd been. Someone else, busy with their final project, wanted to borrow contact cement.

I logged in to one of the computers and went to scan my drawings and lettering tests. I set the resolution to 400 dpi, to give me some play. I had six or seven hours ahead of me: it wasn't enough to produce a final version, but it would give me something to keep the guys in the band at bay. I spent the day on Photoshop, fine-tuning the contrast on my octopus illustration, cleaning up my lettering tests, and sharpening and stretching out the edges. I tried out a few different logo positions. By three o'clock I had two preliminary covers ready. They were pretty badass. Definitely good enough to show Alex I was getting close. I took a deep breath, saved everything to my drive, then compressed the files so I could email them. I wrote Alex a long email, apologizing profusely. I blamed my own failings on my new job, said I was still doing my best to work out how to balance everything. I attached jpegs of the two versions, and hit send. I felt relieved. I checked the time on top of the screen. Four hours left till I had to meet Jade. I was proud of myself, and even thought about stopping by to see Marie-Lou, right then and there. She usually worked Wednesdays. I stopped at the Pita Pit for a sandwich to go and headed off. Big snowflakes were falling and sticking in the hair of the girls I passed on Rue Ontario. For the first time in weeks, I was actually looking forward to Christmas.

I'd just finished my sandwich when I walked into Chez Maurice. They'd strung Christmas lights along the walls. Diane was waiting tables. She was around forty, maybe a touch younger, with a laugh like a crow and jokes even dirtier than the filth you got accustomed to working in kitchens. Diane loved nothing better than making fun of me and Marie-Lou, as if we were an old married couple.

Benjamin was behind the bar. He was reading a book placed between a take-out coffee and a full ashtray, big forehead resting in his hand. He looked up at me.

"What can I do you for?"

He always asked me the exact same question, before getting down to business, never led with a "What's new?" or "How's it going?" He set a coaster down on the dented bar. I ordered a beer.

"You know when Marie-Lou's coming in?"

"Marie-Lou isn't working today. She got someone to take her shift."

"Oh, okay."

He looked kind of sleepy, looking around for his lighter with a smoke already in his mouth.

"Did you come to see her?"

"Yeah and no. I was in the neighbourhood, had some time."

He took a puff.

"Hey I just remembered," he said. "I have something for you."

He went down into the basement. I had a sip of beer. It was nice and cold. I relaxed, and had a look around. The room was full of regulars with beer bellies and two-day stubble. Diane was counting change at the end of the bar with a friend. They both favoured matching Pat Benatar hairdos. Her change purse lay on the stool looked like the carapace of some sea creature.

Benjamin came back up with a book.

"Here man, read this. It's good. And tell me what you think. The movie's coming out next week. Scorsese. But the book's actually old, from the twenties."

I read the title. *Gangs of New York: An Informal History of the Underworld*, by Herbert Asbury. I'd never heard of the author, but I sure loved *Cape Fear*, *Casino*, and *Goodfellas*.

"It's in English. I can't read that."

His coffee cup stopped moving halfway to his mouth.

"Remember what I told you about that. Just give it a try. It's not that hard. If you understand a little English you can read in English."

"Thanks, that's nice of you. But I haven't even started the last one you gave me."

"No worries, I've read them both twice. Keep them as long as you need."

We talked a bit. He served me a second beer. My tongue was loosening, and I ignored Bébert's warning. It's not like he was here to hear me anyway.

"Tell me about Greg."

"Who? Normandeau?"

"Yeah. How'd you meet him?"

He rubbed his hands together as he sized me up, as if trying to decide whether to tell me the story or not.

"Let's say he owes one of my brothers a favour."

"Which one? Simon?"

I'd seen Benjamin's brother Simon a few times. He was a real live wire, never stopped talking. He owned a bar on Saint-Laurent and another one in the Gay Village.

"No," he said, laughing. "François."

I'd never seen François, but I'd heard about him. Marie-Lou knew him a bit. He was like a stockier, even more laconic version of Benjamin. He'd been to prison.

In the end that was all I learned about Greg that day. A customer came up to the bar.

"Go tell your waitress there's no way I drank all that," the guy said.

The guy was in his late forties, with massive hands popping out of a winter-lined flannel shirt. He leaned over the bar next to me. He was holding up his bill. Benjamin took it from his hands.

"Let's have a look, Marcel."

The guy kept right on mumbling, something about how women couldn't count. Benjamin took a close look at the bill.

"Looks good to me. It's all there," he said, passing the bill back. "Don't forget the tip."

Marcel took the bill and crumpled it up. He turned red, as if he'd dropped a cinder block on his foot. Benjamin was stone-faced behind the bar.

"I'm. Not. Paying." Marcel said. "Your waitress can't count."

"How many beers did you drink, then?"

Marcel hesitated.

"See that's the thing. We count every beer you drink. Then we print them on the bill. If you want I can even tell you what time Diane took them over to you."

"I'm. Not. Paying."

Benjamin leaned over the bar, with open hands.

"Yeah you will. Just like every other time we let you run a tab. You drank those beers, now it's time to pay. That's how it works."

"Oh yeah. What if I don't?"

Marcel was getting cheeky. He started smiling with a mouthful of brown teeth. Benjamin was still leaning over the bar. He was calm: not in the least pissed off but not friendly either.

"You gonna ban me?"

Benjamin looked him in the eye.

"Believe it."

Marcel held Benjamin's stare for moment. He was a pretty intimidating guy. After a while his heavy eyelids blinked. Benjamin didn't give an inch, just kept right on staring him down.

"All right, fine," Marcel said, lowering his head.

The guy took three twenties from his back pocket and threw them down on the bar, in front of Benjamin. Then he crossed the room, limping slightly. He didn't say a word to anyone, just pushed open the big metal door and disappeared outside.

Benjamin brought me another beer.

"On the house."

He wasn't rattled in the least. On the other hand, who knew what was going on behind that impassive mask.

It was 5:45 on the big Molson Export clock. I checked my pager messages, in case Alex might have called back to talk about the sketches. I was on my fourth beer. I had a good sixty dollars left. It was more than enough for the night. I'd left the rest at Vincent's, just to be safe. It filled me with confidence, with a warm feeling that nothing could go wrong.

As usual I'd been careful to sit at the bar with my back to the machines. But I still had to walk by them to go to the bathroom. I'd gotten a little too sure of myself, and gone over to check out the jackpots. Almost all empty. One of them was sure to pay out soon. I went to piss and went back to the bar without a second look at the machines. But halfway through my beer, I started doing the math. What if I played just twenty, maybe forty bucks, I could come out with a hundred, one-twenty, even two-hundred. Especially if I picked the machine that was about to pay out. I imagined playing and my vision grew fuzzy. I bit my lips. I tried to catch Diane's eye. She was always ready to strike up a conversation, just jump right in without warning or niceties. With Diane conversation was a one-way street. You never had to utter a word. Usually it was annoying, but right now I would have killed to have her come up and tell me a few stories I'd already heard ten times, about her life as a "biker girl," her hard-partying teenage years at the Rouville campground, the legendary 1983 Plume Latraverse show, the time she and her boyfriend ordered hot dogs on acid, her friend who went out with a Hells Angels striker. But she was nowhere to be found. Even Benjamin had disappeared.

I could feel electric shocks running up and down my body, from my ankles to my neck. I looked at my hands. They were trembling. It was no use fighting it. Worst case I wouldn't lose that much. I picked up my beer and headed for the machine. I rationalized my decision, told myself I deserved it. I'd stop at twenty. After all, I'd been good for more than a week.

I climbed up on the stool and put a twenty in the blinking slot. Game on. For the first while I won small amounts, but whenever I bet a touch less cautiously I'd lose. I was riveted in place. It felt like I'd never breathed that deeply in my life. A second twenty found its way into the machine. All I had left in my pocket was one more twenty but, in this state of elated denial, twenty dollars seemed like a fortune, enough to live for two months. I patiently ran my wins up to seventy dollars. It was 7:30. I had nothing but time. I could definitely work my way up to a hundred dollars. It was doable. I'd done it before. If I could just bring it up to a hundred, it would be a perfect day.

But I was stuck at seventy. My wins and losses were balancing out, my lucky breaks fewer and farther between.

Eight-thirty. I'd just be a little late meeting Jade. A shadow loomed in my blind spot.

"What kind of idiot do you think I am? Jesus."

My dry eyes stayed glued to the screen. But I recognized the voice. It seemed I might melt then and there. She almost never used that cold, insulted tone of voice. My heart began beating at breakneck speed. My ears were buzzing. Everything slowed to a crawl: the fruits on the screen, the second hand on the clock, the rotation of the earth.

Marie-Lou was standing next to me with one of her friends. They were dressed up for a night out. She was wearing her bullet-belt and eighteen-hole Docs. Her friend had a pierced nose and eyebrows, and caked-on makeup. She looked like a porcelain doll in a khaki army coat.

"You've got some nerve. You're too busy to come see me. But you've got time to sit around gambling. At my work! With my money! No fucking shame whatsoever."

Her eyes were popping out of their sockets, her cheeks and forehead breaking out in red spots. With her upper lip curled up in a snarl, baring her teeth, she looked poised to bite. In the corner of my eye I could see the fruits, the 7s, and the bells scrolling by on the screen. I tried to mumble some sort of apology, or explanation, told her I'd come here to see her.

"Shut up!"

She stormed over to the bar to pick up something by the cash register. The soles of her boots battered the floor. Then she came back toward me. Her friend was staring at me like I was a piece of shit in a pool of puke, black-lipsticked mouth a grimace of disgust.

"You're just a fucking liar." Marie-Lou said.

"Marie…"

"Just leave me alone."

Her friend pushed the door open. Before leaving, Marie-Lou turned back to me.

"Keep my fucking money. But don't let me ever hear you call Jess a junkie again. You're way fucking worse. Pretending to be such a good guy. All hard done by. You make me sick."

They took off outside. Like a fighter struck by a knockout punch, I didn't move. I tried to pull myself together. I knew I should get up and run after her. But the money spinning around in the machine kept me anchored to the spot more firmly than the strongest chain.

Diane came by to make sure I was okay. I gave her a curt nod, without looking up. My shame had hardened into anger. I started playing aggressively. Maximum bet every time, as if I was doing my best to lose everything I had. Marie-Lou's words kept echoing through my head. My winnings would balloon, only to disappear again. I put what was left of my last twenty in the machine, then lost that too. The machine wouldn't take my last five, it was too crumpled. I got Diane to change it for two toonies and a loonie. Then I went back to my machine, the one I'd leaned a stool against to reserve. Benjamin had gone home, it was night, I was cold, I was hot, I felt like I was going to cry. I slid a toonie into the machine.

At 10:20 I left the bar, pockets empty, stunned by the violence of my shame.

CHAPTER 27

I SPENT the following day curled up on the couch watching movies Vincent had rented, *Reign of Fire* and *Men in Black II*. Last night's events had taken on the consistency of a nightmare come true. I was refusing to think about it. As Christian Bale and Matthew McConaughey vaporized dragons in some post-apocalyptic future, Marie-Lou's furious words haunted me, sounding in the echo chamber of my mind with a heightened brutality and ferocity. Then my thoughts turned to Jade. I pictured her waiting for me at the bar, looking at her watch, saving a stool next to her, pushing away anyone who attempted to cozy up to her, scanning the room for a sign of me, or doing whatever she'd be doing to keep busy once she saw I wasn't showing up.

I somehow summoned the strength to call Alex, who had paged me that morning, before leaving for work. We didn't talk long. He was at work, and his tone was a bit warmer than the last few messages.

"Man, I saw what you sent. It's rad. But do you listen to your messages all the way through?"

I was standing up in the living room, with my bag at my feet, staring at my still reflection in the window that looked over the now-dark Boulevard Henri-Bourassa.

"Yeah. Why?"

"So you understand we need it earlier? Are you gonna have our album cover done in time? We got three big gigs coming up in January. The EP has to be ready to go."

My eyes opened wide. I tried not to panic.

"Oh yeah, that. I got that. It'll be ready."

I tossed out a random date, without even thinking about it.

As I hung up I realized just what I'd done. It was one thing to finish the album cover, another to pay for printing. I knew what "cash on delivery" meant. I went straight over to count my money. Rechecked three times just to be certain. With my next paycheque coming in, I was short five, maybe six-hundred dollars. I thought back to the hundreds of dollars I'd squandered the night before. I started casting around for solutions, concocting all kinds of far-fetched schemes and ridiculous capers. This bitches' brew of bull-shit forced me to face an ugly truth. The Deathgaze gig was the break I needed, and I was proceeding to fuck it up. And once I did everyone would see me for what I was: a joke, a screw-up, a liar. That was the part that was hard to swallow.

When I went back to work after my day off I swore I was through with gambling. I was going to be disciplined. I'd come home every night straight after work, catch the last Orange Line Metro toward Henri-Bourassa.

I didn't see Jade until she got back from her days off. She ignored me. When work forced us into contact, we both acted like we were dealing with an ATM or a vending machine. I never tried to explain myself. Giving reasons for not showing up seemed worse than living with her indifference, and glacial indifference seemed like a fair reaction to getting stood up. I wasn't about to invent a second lie to justify what I'd done.

So I kept my head down. Meanwhile, Bébert was spiralling out of control. His funny side had gone on hiatus and his mean streak was on full display. He took the piss out of everyone, just for kicks. Fatigue was catching up. When he was working Bébert was still the most dependable cook on the line, except Vlad maybe. But he was slipping, harder and more often. He was talking as much shit about Renaud as he used to about Christian. Steven had become his bugbear, and Bébert peppered him with slander and digs, even though he was merely a stand-in for Renaud, the true target of his wrath.

"Hey, why don't you tell your buddy Renaud there's more to being a chef than watching porn in the office all day."

Vlad usually avoided confronting Bébert when he was on a tear, but one night he told him, coldly, to stop talking behind the chef's back. Bébert hit right back, saying Renaud could call himself a chef when he was clocking the sixty hours Bébert worked every goddamn week.

"And until then, I'll keep calling him 'wanker', if that's okay with you. Or 'Head Wanker' if you want."

And he didn't stop there. He was cursing out everyone all the time now, even to Séverine.

"I don't pay you to talk shit about my staff," she answered with an otherworldly calm. "I pay you to put out food. If you've got something to say to Renaud put on your big-boy pants and say it to his face."

"He'd have to come out of his cave for that," Bébert shot back.

It was a fact: Renaud had up and vanished. You'd only ever see him with his clipboard doing the ordering. He'd spend an hour or two in the office, then head out at the end of the lunch service, leaving everything unfinished and Bébert holding the bag, while he waited to be officially named sous-chef.

I was the only one Bébert spared. He'd still come back to the dishpit to smoke and vent. There was a new theme now, about how everyone was out to get him. But he wasn't going out like that. He had big plans. Different ones each time. One night he swore he was going to punch Renaud out, truss him with ten feet of nautical rope, toss him in a hockey bag and thrown him off the Champlain Bridge. When he finally cooled down, he said he would have to negotiate his promotion directly with Séverine. I was Bébert's confidant, his witness and secret ally. This sudden trust was incredibly important to me. Here at least was one person I had to make sure to never, ever disappoint.

CHAPTER 28

I'D ARRANGED with Renaud to work December 31 and January 1. That gave me a valid excuse not to go see my family for New Year's. But there was no getting around Christmas. Even if he was going to Cuba, if I skipped Christmas Malik would catch wind of it and hold it against me for a long time.

On Christmas Eve I set off from Vincent's in the early afternoon.

When I cleared the top of the stairs at the Longueuil Metro station, I joined the sea of people immersed in the final preparations for celebrations. The McDonald's was full. Since they'd finished the renovations, the skids that usually hung out around the pay phones had abandoned their old turf. At the taxi stand old friends were jumping into each others' arms, weighed down with bags of every shape and size. I made my way through this joyful commotion and let it rub off on me, and for a moment I was almost lighthearted. I realized I was looking forward to seeing my parents.

I took Bus No. 20 along Highway 132 home, along the still-unfrozen St. Lawrence River. The water glimmered under a low-hanging sun and on the banks the year's first snows hadn't melted. The neighbourhood I grew up in was snowy as well. I got off a few stops early, by the overpass where we'd smoked our first joints and drunk our first beers. I wanted to walk the streets a bit. Elaborate Christmas decorations lit up the fronts of houses and poked their heads through the haphazard snow in flowerbeds.

My parents welcomed me like an intrepid traveller back from a trip around the world. My mum jumped into my arms, and held me tight, and I held her too, happy to hear her voice and smell her familiar scent again. My dad shook my hand, with a wide smile under his long beard. They were both dressed up. Then I went to say hi to the rest of the family. Everyone was gathering in the big kitchen. Malik's dad Claude had driven up from Sherbrooke. Standing there like a giant in his turtleneck and jacket, he shook my hand vigorously. Jacques, my mother's youngest brother, was there too, with his daughters and new girlfriend. I was both relieved and disappointed Malik wouldn't be there. He was the only one who knew the truth about my life across the river.

Once I'd said my hellos and given everyone a hug, my dad handed me a beer.

He clinked his bottle against mine. I looked at my mum. She was laughing with my uncles. My dad and I leaned against the counter, next to the oven. It smelled like cloves and browning pie crust.

"I've got something for you to listen to. An oldie but a goodie, I think you'll like it. Mountain."

My mum was serving veggies and dip, pickles, and marinated olives. My uncle Jacques was teasing her gently, with a whisky and water in one hand and a butane lighter in the other. My dad gave me a little pat on the shoulder.

"That reminds me. Malik told us you had a little contract? For an album cover? That's cool."

I was about to take a sip of beer, but stopped short.

"When did he tell you that?"

"At Jacques's place, when we were over for dinner. You never tell us anything, so we get our news wherever we can..."

"Oh, yeah. Sorry, I'm super busy."

"Still, you could have told us that. Your mum is really proud. Is it coming along?"

"Yeah, it's almost done. I'll show you once it's finished."

He clinked his beer against mine again. The adults were chatting as they sipped their drinks, and my cousins were bickering about something. Jacques cut in and happily asked them to sing us the theme song of their play. The oldest one rolled her eyes up to the ceiling.

My mum had made tourtière, and pork hock stew as she did every year. I helped her serve. I now saw the thoughtfulness that went into her every gesture, and from the way she talked to me I could tell she was happy to see me. She told me she'd set aside a bunch of books that were waiting to be catalogued at the library where she worked. She'd been doing that since I was a little kid, whenever a new title came in that she thought I'd like. That was how I'd read all the *Thorgal* series, and a bunch of Druillet comics. At the table she and her brothers were swapping family stories. At one point Claude went and got the sparkling wine that they'd put outside to chill by the patio door.

"So, big guy, how's life in Montreal?" he asked as he poured me a glass. "Where are you living?"

"I'm not too far from Ahuntsic park. On Henri-Bourassa."

"Really? You moved?" my mum asked.

"Well, yeah," I said, taking a bite of tourtière. "Vincent's room-mate moved out, and I wasn't getting along with Rémi, really. It's way better with Vincent. We're on the same page more. I should have moved out with him from the beginning."

"It's true, Vincent's a good boy," she said, picking up Jacques's empty plate.

She headed to the stove to give him a second helping. Claude said you couldn't make him live in Montreal again, not in a thousand years. In Sherbrooke he had peace and quiet. My dad and Jacques talked about the cottage. He said it would be a good idea to spend Christmas there next year. Then he got up to change the music, put on a Charlie Parker disc, and went downstairs for more wine.

Jacques hadn't touched his sparkling wine. He kept going back for more whisky with water. He'd loosened his tie and rolled up his sleeves. His girlfriend was picking at her food and following the talk, her gaze travelling from one person to the next.

"What about school? How's that going?" Jacques asked, turning toward me.

"Yeah, this semester was great. My illustration teacher is amazing. He thinks I have what it takes to be a graphic designer."

"It'll be Julie's turn soon enough."

He made a face at his oldest daughter sitting across the table. She sighed.

"C'mon, dad, Cegep isn't for like a million years."

"Are you going to have such a heavy course load next semester?" my mum asked.

"Yeah, it should be just as busy. The teachers are already warning us about next fall. The projects are going to be much more challenging. I'm looking forward to it."

"You should try to find a little time to come see us once in a while. Montreal's not that far, it's not like you're in Sherbrooke."

She gave Claude a mocking smile, and he shrugged his shoulders, with an apologetic look. Then she went on.

"Your dad stays home Sundays now. You could come for dinner."

"Okay, I'll try. And I could cook for you. I'm working in a restaurant now. I'm learning tons."

"In a restaurant?" my dad asked.

He stopped in the middle of opening a bottle of red wine, genuinely surprised.

"Yeah, I work a couple of nights a week."

"That's not too much for you, on top of school?" asked Claude.

He was looking at me, with his fork in one hand and his knife in the other. When he chewed he looked serious. It gave me a glimpse of Malik twenty-five years from now.

"No, it's just right," I said. "It gives me a little extra for expenses. I'm not using up all my savings from last summer, it's one less thing to worry about."

"Really. That doesn't sound like you, planning ahead and all. Eh, Jacques?" my mum said.

"But you aren't actually cooking are you?" my dad asked. "The fanciest thing I've ever seen you make is a tomato sandwich. Tell me the name of the restaurant so I can make sure to never eat there!"

He gave me a pat on the back and a glass of wine.

"Actually I'm washing dishes."

"That's more like it."

Sitting there talking, it was as if the zombie plunging ever deeper into debt in front of the video poker machines was a figment of the nether regions of my imagination. My anxiety had dissipated. My appetite was back. I was having seconds of everything, and laughing at the childhood stories my mum was telling her brother's new girlfriend. He was looking at my mother with a smile, proud of his youngest-kid shenanigans, holding an unlit Players between his fingers.

After we gave out presents, my dad took me aside and led me down to the music room, the way he always did when he wanted me to hear a new disc he'd just bought. Upstairs everyone was having fun, you could hear their conversation and bursts of laughter over the sounds of dishes being rinsed. Next to the bookshelf was a big present wrapped in brown paper. Clearly my dad's wrapping job. My mum would never use that much tape, or be caught dead wrapping a Christmas gift in kraft paper. He leaned over to pick it up and give it to me.

"Here, this is for you. A special present."

The box contained a bunch of novels from the Robert Laffont science fiction series *Ailleurs et demain*.

"When I bought the first volume, I was younger than you are now!"

He pulled a few books out, and held one out to me. It was *Dune*.

"You know Iron Maiden wrote a song based on this one," he said. "But Herbert wouldn't let them use the book title for the song."

I started laughing.

"Don't act like you read an article about it or something. I know you're listening to all my CDs, now that I'm not here. I bet you caught Dickinson's rant on the live version of 'To Tame a Land.'"

"You crazy?"

The other six volumes of the *Dune* cycle were there as well. It brought a lump to my throat, and took me back to when I was twelve. We were watching David Lynch's film version of *Dune* after my dad picked up the first volumes of Jodorowsky's Metabarons series on my bookshelf. He told me that Jodorowsky tried to make a movie of *Dune* before David Lynch had even heard of the book. That was when he showed me the first titles I ever saw from the *Ailleurs et Demain* series. I was impressed by the row of silver spines on the bookshelf. These books looked like holy scriptures from outer space.

One after another, I took the books out of the box to look over and flip through them. There was *The Lazarus Effect*, which Frank Herbert wrote with Bill Ransom. I never knew why but the title had always given me the shivers. My dad told me not to read that one yet.

"There are two other volumes before it, but I can't find them. Maybe at the cottage somewhere."

At the bottom of the box was *Ubik*, by Philip K. Dick. The moment I picked it up, my dad could tell that one had hit home.

"That's my only copy. It's yours now. Take good care of it."

The cover was still shiny. It looked brand new.

"Happy?"

"Yeah," I managed to get out. "Really happy."

He was proud of himself. I carried the books under my arm as we went back upstairs. I locked myself into the second-floor bathroom. Looked at myself in the mirror and washed my hands. I was sick to my stomach, and about to cry at the same time. I threw some water on my face. There were black circles under my eyes and my skin was grey. I looked seriously burnt out. My parents hadn't said a thing.

CHAPTER 29

BETWEEN Christmas and New Year's I barely saw daylight. I'd get up around three in the afternoon, then get ready for work. Eduardo or Basile started at four, and I came in at six. It was the kind of schedule that put me at risk of relapsing, but being there with Bébert and company was safer than finding myself alone on the street at ten at night, surrounded by hundreds of bars where I could put my feet up on a stool and lose my head.

Those shifts are a blur of choppy nights whose rushes helped us work through the previous night's hangover, memories lit in the heat lamp's yellow gleam or the dim hues of the smoky bars where Bébert and I washed up and put back round after round, battered by the ever-spinning wheel of work and booze. Those nights were really more like one long night, devoid of content, buttressed by the hope that Marie-Lou might once again deign to talk to me. In the meantime I promised myself I wouldn't gamble again, as if to prove I wasn't really the person she took me for.

Bébert was still showing me the ins and outs of the garde-manger, behind Renaud's back, whenever he had a spare minute. He'd rather have me in the kitchen than deal with Steven, who turned into a clumsy spineless lump around Bébert.

"You'll see, man. Together we'll rock this kitchen."

New Year's Eve was nothing like a normal shift. I alternated between making salads up front and washing dishes in the pit,

smoothly moving from station to station like at an activity day at
school. It was me and Basile, who was laid-back and unflappable
as ever. The cooks tried to get him drunk before we even closed.

I remember the surreal countdown to midnight while the
kitchen was still putting out its final plates, everyone shaky from
the shooters of Godfather Séverine kept sending back. The room
was twice as full as it should have been. Séverine's friends mostly.
Everyone was out of their heads, dazed from the dope and the
music, staining their ridiculously expensive clothes with wine or
worse. One of Séverine's friends danced on the bar until she fell off
and almost broke her neck, taking down a series of cocktails and
pints on her way down. No one even bothered hiding the rails they
were chopping up right on the dessert counter.

Basile took care of the close and the mop. All the booze he'd put
back didn't seem to have affected him at all. I was getting pretty
tanked. At one point Bébert pulled me outside, and we guzzled
Champagne straight from the bottle, against the wall outside
the dishpit. The night was mild. Bébert was calm. He was looking toward the end of the alley, which was yellow in the night. In
the distance you could hear shouts of joy, horns honking, people
laughing.

"You're a good guy, man. You're smart. Have a good year. The
best."

He spoke slowly, without looking at me, then passed me the
bottle.

"You're not so bad yourself."

High drifts of snow had piled up against the fences along the
alley. I lifted up my head to look at the sky. The stars were spinning
a little.

"It's good to have you as a friend, man."

Bébert chuckled. It sounded like an engine turning over.

"Friends. You're gonna make a lot of friends in the kitchen,
man. Thing is, you never keep them long. You know how shit goes.
Take it as it comes. Turnover's high."

There was something sad in what he'd said. The din from the dining room reached us even outside. I wondered if I'd still be working here six months from now.

"You too, man. It's good to have you as a friend."

He gave me a pat on the back and flashed me a broad smile full of broken teeth.

"Giddyup. Let's finish this night and get fucked up!"

CHAPTER 30

STILL no word from Marie-Lou. If I had a calendar I would have started marking each day of radio silence with an X. Those rare times when I did work up the nerve to call her, I got the machine. I never left a message.

I also hadn't gambled since the time she walked in on me at Chez Maurice.

Abstinence had strange effects. I now lived my life in an ominous, undisturbed serenity. It was like lounging next to a pristine swimming pool. The day is sunny but the horizon is troubled by dark clouds shot through with lightning, and there's thunder too, even if you can't hear it yet.

I'd deposited eight hundred dollars in my bank account, as protection against relapsing, and to convince myself I'd won back my losses for good. I figured that when my next paycheque came around I'd have three-quarters of the money from Deathgaze. I'd tell Malik the whole story, and ask him to help me out just one last time, to make up the difference and pay the printer. I'd work doubles all through February, March too if that's what it took. Everything would work itself out. At least that was the story I'd been repeating like a mantra since a grim New Year's Day spent alone in Vincent's dark apartment waiting to go to work, running back and forth between the sofa and the bathroom to heave, my stomach twisted into knots by the vast quantities of champagne, whisky, and amaretto I'd put back the night before.

On January third, or maybe the fourth, I was late for work. Basile didn't seem to mind. I came running into the restaurant, dishevelled. He was sitting on the pile of plastic dishracks in a tranquil dishpit, waiting for something to happen.

Bébert had the night off. I remember it clearly because Bonnie was on the pass, which was unusual. Her stress and impatience were palpable in her every move: the way she threw pans over to the hotside, the way she slammed the oven door too hard, the way she swore and spit between her teeth.

I got changed in the staff room. The office door was closed. Inside I could hear voices, in animated conversation. Eventually Vlad emerged, stone-faced as always. Séverine was behind him, already opening her flip phone. Renaud came out last. When he saw me a strange expression came over his face, somewhere between surprise and distrust. He came over and asked if the two new guys were still working out. He seemed to be casting around for something to talk about. But at the same time he was friendlier than usual, and full of questions he'd asked me before and must already know the answers to. He asked if I was happy washing dishes.

"It's okay. I'm getting the hang of it."

"How'd you like to move up to the kitchen? We could train you if you want."

"Oh yeah? When? I'm ready."

Before he had time to answer Nick came rushing down the stairs, yelling. They needed me upstairs.

"Move it, something's wrong with the glass washer."

"The glass washer?"

Since when was the glass washer my problem? I walked up the steps as I finished buttoning up my shirt. I walked alongside the kitchen. Vlad, Bonnie, and Steven were getting started on the service, like three hostages lashed to the mast together, hoping against hope to make it out alive. I caught up with Nick by the espresso machine. He nodded toward the other end of the bar, with a snotty grin.

"See, over there? The glass machine."

Jade was sitting with a guy at the bar. They were sharing a tomato-bocconcini appy.

"Never mind. Looks like someone got there first."

Nick clapped me on the back. I pushed him away, unable to contain my anger. He stood there with his cocky grin. I left him to it and got back to my dishpit.

In a rage, I started working. I was throwing pans and dishes into the racks, knocking everything against everything else, more or less doing my best to break dishes. I'd become as irascible as Bonnie.

"Dude, you okay?" Basile asked me.

He was watching me banging around.

"How about I wash?"

"Uh, okay. Give me five minutes."

I went out into the alley for a breath of fresh air. I was about to boil over. My throat was tight. Through the window of the restaurant next door I could see people sharing stories with animated, amused expressions on their faces. I stayed outside a good long while, until my breathing grew less frantic and I started shivering from the cold. When I got back in I took over in the dishpit and Basile went back and forth bringing the dirty dishes and keeping the cooks stocked. Nick didn't come back for a smoke all night.

I let Basile go around ten-thirty, once he finished scrubbing the prep room. There was nothing left to do but sit around and wait for the close. We got it done in record time, just like every time Vlad was working. Between trips bringing back inserts from the steam table and empty pots of sauce Bonnie took a quick smoke break. She seemed to have calmed down.

"So. Do you like the mixtape?"

I kept fiddling with my dishes. I wasn't in the mood. I took a few seconds to think over my answer.

"I like it, actually. Bunch of stuff I'd never heard before. Like Suicidal Tendencies. It's cool that you put that on."

"Glad you liked it. I'll make you some more."

I put away the piles of dishes while Bonnie took her time finishing her smoke. She had her own particular way of holding her cigarette, tucked deep between her index and middle fingers. She looked exhausted. When she took off her cook's hat her wild hair came cascading down in big purple locks over her face.

"So, what are you doing after work?"

She looked surprised that I'd asked.

"Why? Wanna hang out?"

"Sure."

"I'm supposed to meet up with B-Bert at Roy Bar."

"Cool."

I was surprised. Last time I saw her and Bébert together they'd looked ready to throttle each other.

Bonnie waited for me out front at the bar while I got changed. We walked toward the Roy Bar through a city blanketed by yet another snowfall. The night sky was clear. Bonnie was her old self again, mocking, almost chipper. On the corner of Rivard and Marie-Anne she pushed me into a snowbank and broke into a maniacal laugh in her unique voice that was capable of cutting through the din of even the most packed bar. I pushed her back, and we wrestled for a while.

The backstreets were like tunnels of cotton. Bonnie said she wanted to go snowboarding on her next days off. She told me a little about the year she'd spent at Banff. It sounded like one long party. The story made her smile, and that brought out the scars on her face. She was pretty, but it was her attitude I loved most: when she was in one of these moods I never wanted the time we spent together to end. I would gladly have kept walking with her in the snow until we reached the city's edge at the St. Lawrence River.

Roy Bar was off the beaten path, which made it feel almost like a speakeasy. But two out of three nights it descended into mayhem, and tonight was one of them. You had to fight your way to the bar if you wanted to order. People were spilling beer all over themselves as they drunkenly bumped into each other, telling stories at the top of their lungs. I saw Bébert. He was more than warmed up.

When he saw me he roared like a walrus, and gave me an enthusiastic, almost violent hug. I was surprised. He wasn't usually the cuddly type.

"Motherfucker, how you doing?" he yelled.

Doug was there too, parked at the bar in front of a 40-pounder of St-Leger whisky. He was talking to Nancy, the girl from the house party, and constantly licking his lips between words. His pupils were dilated to the size of dimes. Bébert was carrying on three conversations at once, and finding time to yell special requests at the DJ cowering under his headphones ten feet away. Across the bar the pierced and tattooed bartenders looked like Suicide Girls. Bébert slid a little baggie of pills into the hand of a friend, a skinny dude with an emaciated face, bleached-blond hair like Eminem, and a tattoo of the Eye of Providence over his Adam's Apple. I tried to pull Bébert aside. Instead of following me, he shoved a shooter into my hand. It smelled like shoe polish.

"Renaud said he'd train me for the kitchen."

Bébert was too drunk or high to listen.

"Fuck Renaud, man."

He clinked shot glasses with me, knocked it back without wincing and chucked it on the varnished wood counter. The little glass bounced a couple times, then dropped to the ground on the barside.

I leaned over toward him, almost yelling to make myself heard.

"Did you talk to Renaud to get them to move me up?"

"No, man," he said, only half listening. "Not yet."

"You didn't say anything?"

"Hey. I'll take care of it. Leave it to me."

He put his hands on my shoulders, as if to reassure me. He was shit-faced.

I managed to order a pint through the forest of arms jockeying for the bartenders' attention, and tried to find Bonnie. She hadn't even come over to say hi to Bébert. I'd lost her in the crowd, a mix of Peace Park regulars and pill kids waiting for Aria to open so they could dance until eleven in the morning. I saw Desrosiers,

Bob's roommate, up against the bar chatting with a much younger girl. Her platinum hair was sticking out of the hood of a sweatshirt unzipped low enough to show off pert breasts in a leopard-print bra. She was talking with a hand in front of her mouth like a little megaphone, revealing tattoos on her wrist.

The place just kept getting more packed. Fan blades lazily churned the clouds of cigarette smoke gathered a foot below the ceiling.

I finally saw Bonnie in the arms of her bartender Sam. He was the one she'd come here to meet. They were making out. I remembered Bébert trying to school me at the lounge. Even I could read the writing on the wall now. I would never be her type; there would always be a Sam around.

Someone grabbed me by the shoulder. A beer crashed into my still-full pint.

It was Desrosiers, who'd just recognized me too.

"Sup, dude?" he shouted in my ear.

I shook his hand.

"Who you here with?"

"Work people," I said.

I pointed at Bébert, who was now leaning over the bar trying to steal lime slices to huck at the DJ. The Beastie Boys were playing.

"Bob with you?"

"Nah, man, haven't seen him for a week."

He took a slow drink of beer.

"How come?"

I couldn't tear my eyes away from Bonnie. She was doing shots with Sam and the bar staff.

"Spent the weekend in jail."

Above the sea of heads Desrosiers waved to the bartender for another beer. She gave him a thumbs up and served him before the thirty-odd people clamouring for her attention. They seemed to know each other.

Bébert was arm wrestling with Doug, who easily took him down. Then Bébert drained a third of Doug's bottle of whisky.

"In jail?"

Desrosiers took a long sip of beer.

"You know, too many unpaid skateboarding tickets."

Bonnie and her man were still making out. I grabbed Desrosiers by the shoulder.

"I'll be back in a few seconds."

"No worries, dude."

I worked my way into the crowd. I took a swig of beer, and it
foamed up all over my nose. I set my barely touched pint on a table.
Sam whispered something in Bonnie's ear. She burst out laughing.
I opened the bar door and set out into the cold, humid air.

CHAPTER 31

A THOUSAND orange flames flickered on the surface of the immense black St. Lawrence below. The Christmas decorations affixed to the De La Concorde overpass swayed lugubriously in the wind. I was calm. I kept glancing up at the rear-view mirror, as if to make sure the person in the back seat was really me. The taxi had the road to itself. The faint gleam of its headlamps lit the road ahead. The silhouette of Notre Dame Island stood before us. After the bridge we took a wide road next to a body of water. To my left the South Shore lights danced in the fog clinging to the river. A limousine languidly slipped by, stealthy as a spaceship. In the distance ahead a spiky ivory apparition gleamed in the night. A comforting warmth enveloped me and slowly resolved into the languorous relaxation that precedes a surge of adrenaline. The intensity of this sensation never dulled.

The taxi dropped me off in front of the casino. It was lit so brightly it might as well have been noon. Next to another limousine, a group of tourists were chatting away in an unfamiliar language. The women wore fur coats. White-gloved doormen opened doors. I went in and felt immediately at home, like entering a place you'd been a thousand times before. I was already a bit high.

I crossed the lobby. Ponds and fountains dissected banks of slot machines. I walked toward the row of cashier's booths. They looked like the counters of a venerable bank. Behind golden bars, tuxedoed attendants converted bills into chips. I changed all the cash in my pockets, close to three-hundred dollars, and was given little plastic coins in return. In this new form, the money felt stripped of half its value.

I took in my surroundings. Chandeliers overhung a sprawling atrium ringed by mezzanines and upper floors. The railings and balustrades were plated in gold, the ground covered in plush burgundy carpeting. Everything around me sparkled with the ersatz shine of fake antiques. The burble of fountains blended in with the faraway babble of gamblers. Even the stairs were covered in burgundy carpet. I climbed them. I peered over the railing onto the sprawling labyrinth of the lobby below. The slot machine sounds reminded me of video games. The machines themselves were nothing like the ones in bars: they were much bigger and looked straight out of another era.

I passed two large, grand dining rooms full of white-clothed tables whose cutlery gleamed even in the dim light. Tables were arranged in a loose circle around a small, untended bar. There wasn't a soul in the room. I went exploring. Each dining room led to yet another, like in a hall of mirrors. Each room seemed to silently await guests who would never arrive.

I continued my journey, traversing a massive room of deserted blackjack tables.

On a raised platform, five or six old men who looked like the ones who whiled away their days in front of the video poker machines on Rue Ontario had gathered around a racing game. They leaned on the rails of their Lilliputian hippodrome, cheering on miniature metal horses.

The next floor was cut into three sections. Each was full of gamblers. Every inch of flooring was carpeted with a red, purple, and brown hexagonal motif. You could see the downtown lights through a row of high windows. On one side were blackjack tables. Almost all were occupied. Gamblers waiting for a spot to free up watched the action play out on the baize. Some took notes. A woman in her early fifties with a porcine face and fat fingers, shoved into a sequin dress several sizes too small, was boasting loudly behind her stacks of chips. She had a laugh that squeaked like an unoiled hinge. When she won, two or three spectators clapped, perhaps hoping for a piece of her good luck.

Farther off in the distance lay poker tables peopled by a clutch of laconic, bored-looking players. The ante was too high for me. I wandered on. New sections and rooms kept opening up, each one begetting another, as in a dream.

On the other side were roulette tables. Again the ante was too rich for my blood. A gambler was swearing at the croupiers. He'd probably just lost more than every one of my Trattoria paycheques combined.

Now I reached the baccarat tables. Here the ante was much lower. I took a seat, and placed my tokens on the felt in front of me. The croupier welcomed me politely. He was in his sixties and as immaculately uniformed as any Tsar or Kaiser's valet. I was surrounded by chubby Asians with sad looks in their eyes. A waitress in a white shirt and bowtie appeared to offer me a drink. The taste of red ale from the Roy Bar still clung to my mouth. I thought it over, then ordered a vodka rocks.

Baccarat isn't hard to wrap your head around. It's kind of like War. The croupier deals two hands from the shoe, one for the "banker" and one for the "player." You can bet on the player, on the banker, or on a tie. And since you can go double or nothing, it's possible to start out with a little and win a lot.

An LCD panel behind the croupier displayed the results. My vodka arrived, buried in ice. I took a sip. My temples were burning. I loved savouring the moment before laying my very first bet.

I checked the last results before joining the game. The house had won five hands in a row. I took another sip and bet three twenty-dollar chips on the "player." The croupier dealt a five for us, then a jack for the bank, followed by a three for us and a four for the house.

I won the hand, and learned that face cards counted as zero. The croupier distributed each player's winnings. He slid three twenty-dollar chips toward me. The hair on the back of my neck stood on end.

I doubled my initial bet: six chips, player.

Queen for us: nothing.

I took a deep breath. My fingertips were on fire. I kept my eye on the baize.

Eight for the bank. Eight.

Seven for the bank. Seven.

Six for us. Six.

Eight for the bank. Fifteen.

No: five. Multiples of ten didn't count.

I thought that was it, but we got a third card.

A five. Which made ten, so our total was zero.

Six for us; zero for the bank.

I'd won again. Just barely this time.

I was given another six chips, plus the ante. I stacked them on top of my others, in little columns. Then I picked up ten chips and placed them in the centre of the table, betting on a tie. I didn't realize that the chances of a tie were microscopic.

One of the Asian guys, with a toothpick between his lips, was fiddling nervously with his tokens and staring at the centre of the table. Two others crossed their arms after placing their bets. I felt like all eyes were on me.

King for us. Zero.

Six for the bank. Six.

Ace for us. One.

Four for the bank. Zero.

Nine for us. Zero.

Tie.

The table cried out in astonishment. Toothpick man congratulated me in English. So did the croupier, a model of restrained politeness.

The croupier placed eight hundred-dollar chips on the baize and pushed them toward me. My bet had quadrupled. My hands were shaking. My eyes were dim. The scoreboard formed a halo around the croupier, a pointillist red and yellow aura.

I tried to calm down, and assessed the results. I bet two chips on the bank. Adrenaline was coursing through my every limb.

Two for us. Two.

Ace for the bank. One.

Five for us. Seven.

Eight for the bank. Nine.

The round was over. No third card. Player won. I was having trouble grasping what was happening.

I felt my heart pounding, crashing like thunder in my head. The croupier gathered up my two chips. I put down two more, right away, in the exact same spot. The bank won. The croupier raked up my bet, plus the two chips I'd lost on the previous hand. I took it as a warning.

So feverish I could scarcely concentrate, I did some calculations. I had fourteen-hundred dollars in tokens. I counted again, short of breath. The idiot grin refused to leave my face. It seemed impossible. If I added my winnings to what was left in my account, I had more than enough for the print job. I'd almost won back everything I'd stolen from the band. I counted again, just to be sure. With my paycheque, I'd even have a little extra left over. I could pay back Marie-Lou when she finally calmed down.

I looked around for a booth to cash in my chips. There weren't any on this floor. They were all downstairs, in the lobby. I went down toward the stairway, through the roulette section. I walked up to one of the tables. A handful of fifty-year-olds were leaning over the rectangular table. There was something enthralling about roulette, like watching a campfire. I felt like I was in a movie. A hazy montage from all the James Bonds and Scorsese flicks and the rest of the forgettable Hollywood gambling scenes flashed before my eyes. One of the gamblers gave off an acrid, peppery cigar stench. A gold watch hung from his wrist. He chewed gum as he stared at the red, green, and black squares.

The croupier welcomed me. She was every bit as polite and elegant as her colleague at the baccarat table. The minimum bet was a hundred dollars. I decided I could afford it. The second the ball started spinning and dancing, with its little dry rapping sound, the euphoria I had felt earlier returned. It was invigorating, delicious. The little ball came to rest on twenty red. The croupier announced the result. I didn't understand a thing. It didn't matter. The man in the gold watch doubled the bet he'd placed on the second twelve. He'd also won eight-to-one on his other bet straddling seventeen, eighteen, twenty, and twenty-one. The croupier collected the other players' losses with a golden rake.

I bet on black again. Same amount as before. The croupier spun the wheel and dropped the ball. Thirty-five black up. I won back what I'd lost the round before. The euphoria was still with me.

I bet again, copying my neighbour's tactic: two hundred-dollar chips on ten-eleven-twelve-thirteen, and three more chips covering one through twelve. My legs were strafed with pins and needles, my knees numb and liable to buckle beneath me. Two centuries came and went as the wheel spun around and around and around. Finally the ball came to rest on twenty-one red. My five chips were raked up. After that I started betting randomly: twenty on the twenty-one, sixty on black, a hundred on odds, two hundred straddling sixteen and nineteen. The ball danced. Zero. The croupier raked up the chips.

I placed my two remaining hundred-dollar chips on the baize, and bet on ten, eleven, twelve, thirteen, fourteen, and fifteen. The croupier let me know that I'd win five times my bet if any of those numbers came up. The euphoria crystallized in every limb. I stood perfectly still. I watched the ball dancing among the lacquered numbers of the roulette wheel. I clenched the table edge hand so hard my knuckles turned white. The ball finally dropped into its little hollow. The croupier announced the winning number. I didn't hear her. I was overtaken by vertigo. She raked up the last of my tokens. The faces around me clouded over. Everyone, including the croupier, retreated behind indistinct, pale masks.

A minute later I was standing in front of one of the twenty Desjardins ATMs scattered throughout that floor, draining my account. I went back to the baccarat table I'd played earlier. The same players were still there, their expressions unreadable. The impeccable old croupier greeted me again. I sat down and bet, my head empty, my eyes glued to the green baize. The bank won. I bet another hundred-dollar chip on the player.

Three for us. Three.

Queen for the bank. Nothing.

Jack for us. Three.

Four for the bank. Four.

Ace for us. Four. Tie.

The croupier raked up my chips along with those of the other losers. I sniffed. Put a new token on the table, betting on a tie. The cards fell, one after another.

Seven for the player. Ten for the bank. My token was raked up. I felt like I was drowning in the buzzing in my ears. I was cut off from the rest of the world, sucked by a powerful orbit into the far reaches of the night. If my mother lay dying fifty feet away, I wouldn't have gotten up from that table to help her. Almost all my faculties were numbed, anaesthetized. No matter how badly I wanted to stop I kept right on betting, fastened to my chair by the tingling of thousands of pins and needles up and down my spinal cord. There were the bets, and my hand, and the baize. There was the slow, silent music of the spheres, nebulae of chance and time collapsing endlessly in upon itself. All around me the other players sat behind stacks of chips that just kept growing. Though I didn't move a millimetre from my chair, my own stacks were dwindling, my chips disappearing as if I were tossing them into a black hole. I bet my very last chip, on a tie. The perverse logic in my delirious brain was telling me I could win it all back in a single hand that way. The player side won. The croupier swept up my chip. I vacated my seat for another player and wandered aimlessly on unsteady legs through the games rooms where I watched other people winning, stacking up piles of chips. I was incapable of formulating a single thought. I couldn't have told you my name. I penetrated deeper into the casino, devastated. I was moving but within me the void was total. There was no feeling, no language, just an abyss of night and emptiness.

Around six-thirty in the morning I walked out of the casino. The cold rose up off the river on the wings of a biting, implacable wind. Finding an exit took eons. With my hands in my pockets I walked until I reached the bus stop, to wait for the shuttle to Jean-Drapeau Metro station. I got in line behind a group of ten other dispossessed persons with glassy eyes and downcast faces. Dawn was slow to come. The downtown lights sparkled from across the river. I closed my eyes.

CHAPTER 32

I'D FALLEN ASLEEP fully clothed on the couch. An entire day went by as I oscillated between dream and reality in the dark, silent apartment. Vincent had left the venetian blinds drawn. Time and again I awoke with a start and the reflex to rifle through my hiding spot next to the couch legs, to make sure my wad of bills was still there. But there was nothing left. Not even five dollars.

"Come, we'll play in the fire," was a line Peter Steele had added in at the end of his version of "Black Sabbath." The song played in a loop on my Walkman as I lay inert on the couch.

I got up around 2:30. An issue of *Hellblazer* lay on top of my art materials on the coffee table. Vincent must have started reading it while I was gone. On the cover John Constantine was smoking a cigarette in front of a giant bingo card. The irony wasn't lost on me. The box with the *Dune* series was where I'd left it by the front door of the apartment. I was calm, or maybe dead, like a lake in winter. Eventually I forced myself to get up and rinse off the cobwebs in the shower.

Greg was sitting at the staff table with a big Ziploc bag of white pills stamped with happy faces. Two by two, he was transferring them into little baggies he was putting in a fanny pack that looked like a bartender's belt. He was acting exactly as if he was filling salt shakers or tea boxes. He said hi without interrupting his work.

Renaud was in his office. I got dressed, then went to see him. Our intrepid Chef was playing Minesweeper. He turned toward me. I shut the door.

"Uh, Renaud? I wanted to ask... Do you think I could get a raise?"

My voice felt snuffed out, far away. It was the first time I'd spoken since the casino.

"A raise? You haven't even been here a month."

His voice sounded ill at ease and a little put out.

"Well, it kind of seems ... like I'm doing a lot. For a guy who hasn't even been here a month."

He smiled as he looked at me.

"You think you're hot shit, that's for sure."

Years of smoking had yellowed his teeth. I realized I didn't like his smile, or his bony cadaverous face. He went on.

"You're a hard worker though. You look tired."

Renaud never seemed to open up completely, always seemed to be keeping a card up his sleeve. He opened Maitre'D on the computer to check my hours for the last two weeks.

"It's true, you've been working a lot."

He scrolled through the file.

"Wait a sec. Christian already gave you a good raise. You even make more than Eaton. The only way we could give you another raise would be to make you a cook."

He closed the window with a click of the mouse. I fiddled with the loose board in the doorframe. I was tempted to tell him I really needed that raise, but didn't want to come off as desperate.

"You still want to move up to the kitchen, right?"

"Yeah, for sure."

"Give me a few days and I'll make it happen. Now get to work!"

When I left the office Greg was gone. The ice machine was spitting out new cubes, the hum from the electrical room seemed louder. I felt sluggish, with tingling eyes. I had no clear sense of whether I'd slept or not. A memory from years earlier welled up: me and Marie-Lou, together in the mosh pit at the Megadeth show.

The smell of her sweat, her toothy grin and fiery eyes. I rubbed my face and headed off to wash my lettuce.

After finishing my prep I dragged my dejected ass up the stairs. Bonnie was in the kitchen yelling at Steven. There was no reasoning with her when she was that hungover. Steven couldn't get a word in edgewise. Bonnie was hurling her salad bowls onto Steven's workstation and yelling to wait for the ticket before going on the mains. At the end of the bar, next to the order computer, Maude was talking with Greg, trying to convince him to go pick someone up. Renaud appeared behind me, in his coat. Maude stepped away from Greg, who bounded off to set tables with a dozen wineglasses in a single hand. She came over to Renaud, who was punching something in on the computer.

"Do you think you could stay? Just until he gets here. Just to be sure..."

"It's not the first time he's been late. He'll get here. And the book's almost empty."

"C'mon Renaud, you know that doesn't mean anything. If Bébert doesn't show up we've got no one for the hotside."

"Whatever, Steven can handle it."

"Steven?" Maude asked, unconcerned that the man in question was ten feet away. "Are you fucking with me?"

"It's my day off, Maude."

Renaud pulled a smoke from his pack.

"When you do as much as me around here, then we'll talk. Until then, have a good night. You kids'll be fine."

Maude's face clouded over. I thought she was going to slap him. Renaud gave her a little wink on his way out and then slipped between a party of five on their way in. Maude watched him go, wide-eyed. Greg came back toward the bar.

"No stress, honey. I'll handle Bébert."

I heard the backstory a few days later. It all started the previous night after I left the Roy Bar for the casino. Their night took a turn for the worse, too. After putting back three forty-pounders of St-Leger whisky, Bébert and his crew started popping speeds to keep the party going. Then Nelly, one of Bébert's exes, showed up and started playing mind games with him. She figured it was a good time to introduce her new boyfriend, and also make out with Bébert a little whenever the guy went to the bathroom for a piss or a bump. Doug wasn't amused. He ended up pulling them both out by the scruffs of their necks, with Nelly kicking and screaming like an elf yanked from her den. They popped a few more pills, and closed the Roy Bar. The saga continued at Aria, followed by a friend's house, where Nelly came back for more. This time not even Doug could handle the situation. When the dep opened first thing in the morning the crew came back with a couple of two-fours of cold beer. Bébert had disappeared with Nelly sometime between noon and one. No one had heard from them since. His shift started at 3:30. It was almost 5:00.

Greg put on his coat and headed off. The moment he walked out the door customers started pouring in, as if every fridge in the neighbourhood had simultaneously emptied and everyone had decided that dinner at La Trattoria was the perfect remedy.

The first orders caught Steven and Bonnie off guard. They just couldn't nail their timing down. Steven was as shaky on the hot-side as Maude had predicted. He was going table-by-table, instead of grouping his orders by menu item. And Bonnie was more iras-cible than ever, with dark circles that seemed to have spread down to her cheeks. She was trying to steer Steven in the right direction, but he categorically rejected any instructions that came from her. Because Bonnie was incapable of explaining anything calmly, Ste-ven's pride kept him stubbornly heading in the wrong direction. In need of an outlet for her rage, Bonnie was slapping down the pans she'd prepped for Steven and winging them toward him, while handling the coldside, cursing up a storm, and solemnly swearing to ditch this job the second she had the chance.

Everyone was freaking out all around me, but I was immune. Their panic bounced right off my back. I thought back to one of the first things Christian told me: it's just a restaurant.

Maude was trying to establish a semblance of authority by giving Bonnie and Steven directions over the pass-through. To no avail.

The tables themselves weren't helping. There weren't only a lot, they were also unusually demanding. And new customers kept pouring in. There was practically a line-up. Denver was everywhere at once, laden with dishes and breadbaskets. Every time he came back to pick up an order he'd fix his hair. Then, with furrowed eyebrows and a clenched jaw, he'd try to parse the orders Bonnie was carelessly tossing out onto the pass-through, almost as if she was going out of her way to make the worst possible mess the better to blow this night up as quickly as possible.

Eventually Greg got back. He rolled his coat into a ball and tossed it behind the bar, then jumped back into the fray, as if he hadn't missed a beat and he had the whole restaurant under control.

Bébert sauntered in ten minutes later.

He came in through the front door. Maude's eyes never left him as he limped through the dining room. Later he explained that he'd gotten glass in his foot, though he couldn't say how. The hood of his winter coat was up, shadowing his eyes. In his hands he held a brown paper bag with the neck of a bottle poking out. He took a pull, right there in front of all the customers. Foam from the beer gathered on his hand. Maude glared at him.

"He's here, y'all can chill," Greg said, as he watered new tables.

Bébert punched in, then limped back to the dishpit to find me. He laboriously extracted a smoke from his rumpled pack of Export As. His every movement seemed to be in slow motion, as if his brain had to double-check the route before approving it. He wasted half a dozen matches lighting his smoke. Peering at me through bleary, half-closed eyes, he beckoned me over. I was less than a foot away. He dug through his pockets and liberated at least twenty bucks in loonies and toonies, dropping his keys in the process. The corner of a torn-up baggy was in with the coins. He held out the handful of change.

"Go to the store and get me a twelve-pack of Heineken. Or Blue if they don't have it," he said slowly and deliberately.

He dumped the coins in my palm. And dug into his jacket pocket and pulled out a pill, which he washed down with a sip of beer.

"Don't forget. If they don't have Heineken . . . Blue."

He set off to the kitchen. I threw a rack through the machine before jogging over to the dep on Mentana, between Mont-Royal and Villeneuve.

I had enough for a twelve of Heineken, but bought the Blue instead. It was five bucks cheaper. I spent the difference on scratch-and-wins, idiotically convinced I would win back my fortune. I set my case of beer down between my work boots and scratched the tickets right there. Nothing. Not even two dollars for another ticket.

When I got back the cold dishpit was exactly as I'd left it. The buspans were overflowing with floor dishes, but I knew I could burn through them. In the kitchen, Steven had crawled back into the garde-manger that was his hole and was mechanically working away in silence. He looked like a wounded animal. Bonnie was on the pass, seething away and carelessly tossing up orders that were never quite complete. Bébert was back in the land of the living, mysteriously possessed of an otherworldly vigour. He was handling the pans with a firm hand, perhaps to offset the clumsiness of his movements. When he saw me he gave out a victory yelp. Steven turned toward me. He saw the case of beer, and cradled his face in his hand. Bébert opened a bottle before setting the case under the steam table.

Greg came by the kitchen.

"So Burt, my Tylenols working?"

Bébert replied with an ursine growl. He was stumbling through the rush with the efficiency of a quadriplegic. It was like watching a tragedy unfold while the unwitting protagonist just keeps cracking jokes, cockier than ever. Every ten minutes Steven's face turned a new shade of pale. Bonnie was rapping her fist on the counters, swearing in English as sobs of rage took form in her throat. She looked like a maniac. I was almost scared she might grab her knife and stab someone.

Bébert was dropping full pans as he cooked them, and knocking over the ones Bonnie prepped for him. He was sending out the wrong pastas with the wrong sauces, and blithely rolling dirty pans under the oven as if the kitchen were a bowling alley. He never stopped hounding Steven, asking whether he knew how to flip a pan or if Renaud moved him up because he gave good head. He dropped the bottles of white wine and oil, knocked Bonnie's water pitcher into the insert of tomato sauce, dropped his beer in the cream sauce. On the other side of the pass-through the room kept getting fuller. Bébert was fixing his mistakes with a childish, defiant laugh. When Bonnie got fed up with his drunken shenanigans and told him to fuck off he just laughed louder. He was cracking barely passable jokes about Sam, asking if he knew she got it on with coworkers when he didn't call her back. Bonnie just kept saying the same thing over and over, "Fuck you! Fuck you! Fuck you!" She had tears in her eyes. And she too was knocking over everything in her path. Maude was literally tearing her hair out. The customers kept flooding in. At no point did she regain composure. She was yelling at Bébert, who responded with a finger and a bratty smile on his droopy face. The servers hustled around the room, trying to keep everyone happy as they waited for orders Bébert was having to start over twice and even three times, when he didn't forget them outright.

I stuck to the background. I wanted no part in this gong show—as far as I could tell, it wouldn't affect the stacks of dishes I'd have to wash or the messes I'd be left to clean up. It felt like I was floating above the melee, flying high above it all. I'd already met my Waterloo. There was little that could phase me now.

Bonnie stormed into the dishpit. She was angry as ever, her eyes full of tears and her face a deep red.

"Yo Steven, where the f—"

She turned to me.

"You seen Steven?"

I answered nonchalantly that I hadn't, as if she'd inquired into my opinion on the colour blue. I threw a rack of pans through the machine and asked why she wanted to know. Without answering, she ran back to the kitchen, where the cacophony was growing louder by the minute as pizza sheets rained down on the oven and the pans jockeyed for position on the elements and the microwave door slammed shut.

I went down to the basement to pick up the prep room dishes. Steven was pouring white pepper on a cut, dressing his wound as he repeated over and over that he'd fucking had fucking enough of fucking working with that fucking madman. When he saw me he said, in a serious tone, that there was no way we'd make it out alive tonight.

"He's off the fucking rails. Crazy bastard. I'm not going back up there. No way!"

It was more than just an impression: Steven's voice was trembling. He was choking back a sob. Bébert bellowed at him from the top of the stairs.

"Get up here, faggot, we've got orders. Want me to cut you up for real?"

Something kicked in then, an instinct to make it through this shift and out of this madhouse alive. I took Steven by the shoulder.

"I'll do garde-manger. Take care of the prep kitchen and dishes, okay?"

I didn't wait for an answer. I ran up with my baking sheets piled high with inserts of sharp-smelling vinegars and marinades.

I strode into the kitchen like a boxer entering the ring. Bonnie looked at me, almost with disdain.

"Fuck you doing here, man?"

I got right to the point.

"Simmer down. I'm here to help."

I was getting a handle on Bonnie's expressions, enough to throw them back at her once in a while.

That seemed to calm her down. At any rate, she stopped fighting me over everything I said. She was drying her tears on her sleeve and sorting order tickets as they spat out of the printer. I read the tickets on the garde-manger rack and, remembering Bob's advice, began by getting everything straight in my head.

I started by clearing out all the appies together, then moved on to the salads ordered as second courses. I was so focused that Bébert's bullshit and increasingly spectacular accidents didn't even register. Bonnie also seemed to be getting a hold on herself. She was working through her orders more steadily than I'd seen in weeks, and even finding some energy to manage Bébert, who was driving straight off the cliff with his foot on the gas. He was spitting out snatches of Eazy-E, "Mothafuck Dre, mothafuck Snoop, mothafuck Death Row . . . and mothafuck this Osso!" He was tossing burned pans under the pizza oven. Once in a while he'd snag a pan prepped for the hotside on the shelf over the range, which knocked over the rest of them in a cascade of broccoli bits and prosciutto slices and cherry tomatoes and bell peppers. By this point some customers were giving up and leaving before their food showed up. It made no difference; new ones were standing by to take their places. The racks overflowed with orders. At one point Bébert lost his shit. He threw all the order tickets in the garbage and made an executive decision: Fuck it, everyone was going to have linguini carbonara. Everyone froze. Denver, Maude, me. Bonnie slunk off to the dish-pit. I heard her hammering something and screaming in rage. Just above the dessert pass-through, I saw Maude's face wrinkle up like a dehydrated mushroom. Her eyes were wide as snooker balls. I gave up. I ignored Bébert's decree and kept making appies and salads, orders I remembered and knew how to make. There was no other way to make it through this nightmare.

By ten Bébert had killed his case of beer, and Greg had discreetly brought him back a pitcher to keep him from crashing. That was when Maude had the bright idea to close the kitchen. She had aged ten years and sweated out what looked like ten litres of fluid.

End of the night. The service kitchen looked like it had been ransacked by the Huns. Bébert disappeared after dumping all his dirty dishes into the pit in a random heap of pans, ladles, and tongs. Bonnie cleaned the service kitchen as best she could. Steven helped me finish the dishes. Just when we thought it was over, we saw that Bébert had fallen on his way down the stairs with the buspan full of sauces. The bottom steps were soaked in rosé sauce. He'd left everything where it fell and disappeared into the night. We never found out where.

Maude poured me my staff beer. She thanked me for helping her out in the kitchen, and promised to tell Séverine how I'd stepped up. Her features were softer now, she had regained her usual "heroine of the future" look. I could tell I'd been promoted to the category of people she held in high esteem.

The catastrophic rush we'd survived gave me a new perspective on my night in the casino. I thought about Alex, and Marie-Lou. Malik and Vincent. It wasn't too late to dig myself out of this hole. But I had to act fast. I needed money. I took a long sip of beer. There must be a solution, a way to convert ten cents into two bucks. The date I'd given Alex was fast approaching. I could still get my hands on the money. All I had to do was push my luck a little further. I heard Greg's high-pitched voice.

"Wassup, fighter. Not too tired?"

He laid his smoke in the ashtray next to my pint.

I turned to him, startled, like when your teacher catches you daydreaming. I always felt the same particular combination of nerves and curiosity around Greg.

"I heard you talking to Renaud earlier," he said. "What, they're not paying you enough?"

I took another sip of beer.

"No, it's not that. I'm in a bit of trouble."

His hand was resting on the bar. He had a gold pinkie-ring.

"Were you serious, the other night?"

"Yeah," I said. "Serious."

He wasn't smiling. I squirmed on my stool.

"Okay," he said, taking his smoke. "I may have a little something for you."

"Yeah?"

"Maybe. How much do you make every two weeks?"

I gave him the figure from my last cheque. He smiled. If his smile had revealed fangs in place of eye teeth, it wouldn't have surprised me at all.

"With me you could make that much in one night."

My face lit up. His smile didn't last long.

"But it's not just a quick buck. I don't need a guy who'll leave me hanging after a week. I need someone I can count on."

I said I could handle whatever he had.

"Good. I'll just have to make sure I can trust you first."

"No problem, Greg."

Maude came in and asked Greg for a drag of his smoke. He turned to her.

"I told you it was a bad idea to bring him in."

"What else was I supposed to do?" she said, exhaling a puff of smoke.

"Get Séverine to make the rat bastard stay."

"Renaud didn't care. He didn't want to stay."

"Séverine would have twisted his arm. That's for sure."

"Anyway," she said, leaning in toward me, "good thing you were there. I was sure Bonnie was gonna bolt halfway through the shift."

I didn't know what to answer. I shrugged my shoulders. Greg checked the time on his flip phone.

"C'mon, man, finish your beer. We've got stuff to talk about."

CHAPTER 33

PEOPLE like Grégoire Normandeau don't go around doing people favours. Nothing comes free. But back then I was too green to know better.

I got in the passenger side of his black Monte Carlo. If there was one car I'd like to own in my life, that was it. Public Enemy was blasting. Greg broke the ice by asking if I'd heard their songs with Anthrax. A metalhead like myself should know that shit, right? The two beers I'd had at work loosened my tongue. We got to talking about the "Big Four" thrash metal bands, Anthrax, the Metallica–Megadeth rivalry. He kept saying he couldn't believe a kid my age knew all the music he'd been into as a teenager. He told me about the Slayer show at the Verdun auditorium. I just couldn't picture Greg at fifteen or sixteen. I wiped the steam off my window and shivered. The car interior was humid, the Monte Carlo hadn't had time to warm up.

We drove down Rachel, then parked next to the lounge we'd been at a few weeks earlier. The bar was smoky and hopping, every booth packed tight with well-dressed, perfumed yuppies in their early thirties. I followed Greg around like a lapdog. Young women were clustered at the bar drinking martinis, lips shiny in the dim blue lighting. They saw me without seeing me, like a mailbox or a fire hydrant. When people saw Greg, though, they greeted him with unabashed joy. The guy seemed to be *loved*. But he played his cards close to his chest. The sharper edges of his personality, his quick temper and authoritarian side, lay dormant beneath a veneer of friendliness. He always looked cool and laid back, always had something smooth to say in French or English, always made you laugh. I watched him interact with people like a star with inside knowledge of the way the world worked. It was hard to credit the stories Bébert had told me. The violence that coursed through him at the restaurant seemed to have dissipated. I tried to understand what he did to keep all eyes on him and inspire such extravagant admiration. Everyone felt blessed to be in Greg's company. He was like some kind of modern-day nobleman. No one noticed the scars on his scalp. Bébert had told me a guy from the Bo Gars gang broke a bottle of champagne over his head at some club, maybe the Orchid. It ended in a knife fight. I never heard how the other guy made out.

Women Greg's age would come up in pairs and kiss him on the cheeks, yelling over the music that they missed him, that it had been too long, that he should stay in touch. He introduced me to a several of these sublime creatures. After Greg's rounds we took a seat at the bar and he ordered a vodka rocks. I had the same, without a second thought. He introduced the barman, we shook hands. I was starting to feel like his protégé.

"So your girlfriend works for François Laurier."

"François Laurier?"

I furrowed my brow, stumped.

"You said you knew François Laurier, through your girlfriend."

"No, I know Benjamin. François's brother, Benjamin Laurier. And it's my ex"—how sad and strange it sounded to say it—"she works for Benjamin."

"Oh...Oh, okay."

He took a sip of vodka and smacked his lips together. I saw a gold tooth. He turned toward me and sized me up a bit.

"Doesn't matter. Same difference."

He paused, and looked at me distractedly for a few seconds. He was drumming his finger on the edge of his glass in time to the song. Missy Elliot sang, "And think you can handle this gadong-a-dong-dong."

"Wednesday night," he said. "I've got a guy out on an errand. I need someone to back him up."

I was scheduled to work Wednesday, but decided not to mention it. I'd handle it. Worst case I'd call in sick.

"What kind of errand?"

I must have looked pretty stupid with my in-the-know, scared-of-nothing act.

"An errand errand."

He took a sip of vodka.

"No big deal, nothing to worry about. Shouldn't be anyone packing."

"Ha ha, cool," I said.

Only when Greg's last sentence finally registered did the magnitude of the shit I was getting into finally sink in. This wasn't a movie. There would be no slow-motion, no slick stills. Things weren't going to play out that way. Not at all. All of a sudden I felt like an idiot. Not just a fuckup, but a complete idiot. I glanced at the door. Two guys and two girls were coming in. Out front people were chatting. Little clouds of steam rose from their mouths. The air current snuck in, snapping the backs of our necks like an ice-cold washcloth. The guys wore long dark coats, and moved in a leisurely manner. The girls talked quietly, in light-coloured belted coats and tall leather boots. Of course guys like Greg didn't do business with slingshots in their pockets. The promise of a quick fix to my problems was preventing me from seeing just what a janky plan this really was. Yet here I was sitting with Greg at the bar. Objectively, there was no backing down now. I couldn't just get up and walk away. The idea of coming off as a coward in front of Greg scared me more, it seemed, than the prospect of a gun in the face. I told myself people didn't actually shoot guns very often. Surely way less often that we imagined. This was Montreal, not Bogotá or Compton. One of my friends had told me that his dad, a Montreal Police

Detective-Sergeant, only discharged his service weapon once in his entire career. You never thought about that. I convinced myself that knowing everyone else was walking around with a little something in their pockets must make people think twice before they acted. It'd be fine, I thought. Greg knew what he was doing.

"You're gonna ride with Will."

"Who?"

"Will. All you've gotta do is go along with him while he runs the errand. Kind of like going into a public washroom when your friend has to take a shit. All you gotta do is be there while he does his thing. Know what I'm saying?"

He laughed.

"So this 'errand'—is in a washroom?"

Greg's laughter stopped abruptly.

"Fuck no, dude."

He checked something on his flip-phone. He looked calm, well-rested. Not worried in the slightest. He had laugh-lines around his eyes. You wouldn't have guessed he'd just finished a crazy shift at work.

"They'll meet you at Pie-IX Metro, next to the ..."

"They? More than one?"

"My guy and his driver. They'll be parked behind the taxi stand. In a blue Civic. You're meeting at nine at night. Don't keep them waiting."

I took a mental note of everything. The ice-cold vodka made the inside of my mouth numb. It went down like water. Greg ordered us two more.

"You don't take your eyes off him. Got it?"

He was pointing at me as he said it.

"Got it."

"If this goes well, we'll talk about another thing."

I lifted my glass. He clinked his against mine. I figured this Will couldn't be worse than the skids Jess hung out with when we were together. I imagined him with the face of Gilles, the crazy dealer Marie-Lou went out with back in the day. It was going to be fine. I'd just follow Greg's instructions to the letter, and everything would work out fine.

Some girls came over to sit with us. I was starting to get a healthy buzz on. The conversation I'd been having and the alcohol spreading through my bloodstream made me feel like another person. The Lauryn Hill lookalike from the other night came up and sat with us. Her braided hair was all over the place. She pushed up next to me, with a malicious gleam in her eye.

"Hey," she said. "You a friend of Greg's?"

I nodded, with a smile.

She was wearing a loose-fitting tank top with nothing underneath, and I could see half a dark aureole. With a slight French accent, she told me she was a graphic designer. She'd studied at the same Cegep as me. She worked on Web stuff now, but liked print better. I was having a hard time focussing on what she was saying. She said Pierre, my illustration teacher, was the best she'd ever had. I said I thought so too. I flashed back to our chat in his office, his disappointed face. I drained my vodka. Greg had ordered a twenty-sixer of Belvedere, on ice. We drank glass after glass, with the women, with Lauryn Hill who was sure to realize, sooner or later, that I was just a kid.

One thing was certain: the more we drank, the less interested she was in me. Now she was chatting with Greg and the other girls. I sat on my stool, feeling increasingly sullen. A lot of the talk was going over my head. I was off somewhere, floating drunkenly, sweetly drifting over the dub beats, excited and drunk and thoroughly exhausted. I was a thousand miles away, in a distant land untroubled by my thoughts. When I heard Greg say they were going to the Stereo, I still had enough of my wits about me to realize he didn't need me tagging along. I stayed there glued to my stool, like a guy finishing up his last drink on his own. Like a boss.

"Good rest of the night, man," Greg said. "Don't forget about Wednesday. I'm counting on you."

He set off with his three graces. I mumbled something indistinct. I wasn't used to straight liquor, it had gotten the best of me.

I contemplated ordering another drink, but remembered that I didn't have a cent. I looked around. In my hazy state, I could see faces with broad smiles, beautiful people clearly living out their lives under a lucky star. And I was once again myself, a broke-ass kid who washed dishes for a living. I checked my pager. No messages. I pictured Marie-Lou's angry face. She'd have to forgive me sooner or later. One more drink would have given me the courage to knock on her door. Instead I left the lounge and ambled to the bus stop to catch the last No. 30 back to Ahuntsic. I stumbled into snowbanks, grunting. The smell of the wet cold reminded me of my elementary schoolyard at the end of the day. I saw my reflection in the black window of a closed restaurant. I could see my breath turning to steam. My face was limp, my features sagged. It took me a minute to recognize the reflection as my own. I flashed myself a peace sign and continued on my way to the bus stop.

CHAPTER 34

I'D GOTTEN Eaton to cover my Wednesday night shift by trading for one of his mornings.

I showed up at Pie-IX an hour early and so nervous I felt like I might explode. The wait was interminable. It was like showing up for a blind internet date, back when that was a big deal, only a thousand times more stressful. When Greg had offered me this job, sitting back swirling my vodka around in its glass, it sounded like a piece of cake. Now that I was here I would have given anything to be elsewhere. The surroundings were bleak. Small clusters of people in winter coats and scarves emerged periodically from the Metro station, then disappeared into the cold night.

The blue Civic came rolling down Pierre-De-Coubertin with a sound like a death rattle, as if it might shed a hunk of engine at any moment. It parked where Greg had said it would. I walked over.

As per the plan, there were two people inside. The driver—a chubby little dude with an early onset double chin and finger full of rings—pointed, indicating I should get in the other side. I walked around the car. The guy in the passenger seat rolled down his window and pushed his head out a little, as if to spit on the ground. The one who must have been Will was four or five years older than me. He shot me a truculent, condescending look. They were listening to old Snoop Dogg. Will had an eyebrow shave, hollow cheeks, and chapped lips struggling to contain his buck teeth, and was rocking a visor toque, gold chains over his warm-up suit, and a fake Rolex. He gruffly asked my name. The driver scoped me out without a word. He looked like a big baby with peach fuzz. I answered in an equally unfriendly tone, to stand my ground.

"Get in, dude. We got shit to do."

I got in. I went to buckle up, but caught myself just in time. These weren't the kind of guys who followed safety procedures. The driver hit the gas. The car hurtled forward, almost running a red light. We were doing a good twenty kilometres over the posted limit. I was sure we'd get stopped by the cops.

"I don't know what Greg told you, but listen up, yo. Follow my lead. And if you see him before me, tell him I don't need a fucking babysitter. I can handle my shit."

To the left, the massive, luminous scoop of the Olympic Stadium rose from a blanket of low-hanging clouds. Over Will's shoulder I could see a big sports bag shoved under the glove compartment. Probably full of Uzis or rolls of cash. I slumped down in my seat, like a kid frustrated to have chosen the wrong ride at the amusement park.

We kept on to the end of Pierre-De-Coubertin, then turned onto Viau. The car's suspension felt ready to give out at any moment. We took Hochelaga. If it weren't for the street signs I would have had no idea where we were. We turned onto another street, then slowed down. Will gave directions in the snarky tone he summoned every time he opened his mouth. We parked next to a city park. Soft melting snow fell gently on the deserted playground and dilapidated swing set. The driver lowered the volume. Will turned to me.

"All right, man, do exactly what I say now. Try not to fuck it up."

He turned to the driver.

"And call me if anything's up, y'hear."

"No worries, chief," said the driver said, staring at the end of the road ahead.

Will got out first, then me. I was so nervous I was dizzy. It didn't help matters when I saw something that looked like a pistol butt sticking out of Will's team jacket. I had to steel myself just to put one foot in front of another. Will slung the sports bag over his shoulder.

"All right, let's go."

We went up the street. Will was looking around every ten seconds. We skirted the edge of the park. In the stands in front of a snow-covered soccer field a group of kids was checking us out. My one desire was to get this over quickly. On the other side of the street, three shapes bundled up in puffy coats were looking in our direction. One was leaning against a car. Will told me to get a move on.

To the right was a complex of brown brick apartments with windows like arrow slits. The grounds were littered with twisted scraps of bicycle and torn-up garbage bags. A tattered couch lay upended in a snowbank. No one was looking through these windows.

We went onto the grounds of the social housing complex. I was having a hard time keeping up with Will. We crossed an interior courtyard covered in cracked cement blocks. The place was deserted. I mindlessly followed Will. I had no idea why we were here. We entered a narrow, overheated lobby. Dented mailboxes lined one wall. The other held a panel, with units and names written in Bic pen next to doorbells. Will pressed one. It coughed out a nasty buzz. The main door eventually unlocked. We walked into a labyrinth of hallways. The walls were a despondent beige, the apartment doors unconvincing turquoise. The commercial carpeting was greyish and spotted with stains and burns. I followed Will into a stairwell that smelled like the top floor of my primary school, the decommissioned one we took anyway sometimes when we were in a rush to get to class after recess. Will pushed open a big door with a small square of tempered glass. We finally reached the apartment we were looking for. He knocked once, hard. He rubbed his nose. Muffled sounds from the apartment. I must have been white as a ghost; my body felt as insubstantial as a radio transmission. Sweat was running down my sides. I was dying to take off my coat, but figured it was too late to unzip it.

Someone opened the door and checked us both out. He closed it again, surely to unlock the night latch. There were metallic sounds, then the door opened again. We went in, Will first.

A tiny two-bedroom apartment. Sparse black melamine furniture, all of it on its last legs. An aura of hash so thick you could have scraped the walls for resin. Two girls stared at the TV. The volume was turned up to deafening, their unfocused eyes barely open. They couldn't have been much older than me. Cloudy glass pipes lay on the coffee table next to open bottles of Bacardi and crumpled bags of chips. A guy with big cheeks in a hoodie and a toque pulled down over his eyebrows scoped us from his La-Z-Boy, with minimal interest. He looked like Raekwon in the "c.r.e.a.m." video, and was using the remote to tap out an imaginary beat on the arm of his chair. Someone called out to us from the kitchen, beyond the living room. Wholly absorbed by the TV, the girls didn't bother looking up at us. Jerry Springer was trying to calm down his guests, who were deep in a battle royal.

Nothing in this kitchen suggested the preparation of food; nothing made you feel like eating. Naked lightbulbs gave off clinical light. The stovetop was covered in junk. On the table I counted ten Ziploc bags stacked like little greenish pillows. A thin, muscular black guy with a shaved head gave Will an exasperated nod. I accidentally caught his eye. I was sure he'd take it as a dis. He wore an immaculate wife-beater and oversized dark jeans. One of his friends sat on a counter, chewing a McDonald's straw. Staring us down, testing us. I could see my reflection in the window. I looked out of my depth. Will dropped the bag on the table. He took out two bags full of pills, the same ones I'd seen Greg with in the staff room. He placed them one on top of the other, next to the Ziplocs of weed. The guy in the wife-beater picked one up and turned to me:

"Wait in the living room, man."

I did as I was told. The two girls had woken up a bit, but didn't register my presence. Raekwon watched me like a hawk. One of the girls packed the pipe. From the smell and the effect it had, I could tell it wasn't pot or hash. From the corner of my eye I watched Will and the other guy. I could see them in profile. He held out stacks of bills strapped in elastic bands. Will took them, put them in the sports bag, and zipped it up. I looked away.

Will walked back in with the bag on his shoulder.

"We out."

Worked for me. I was in no mood to linger. The girls had slipped back into comatose bliss. One had the pipe in her hand again. Her head was angled back and she had the vacant eyes of a dead doe.

A minute later we were back in the courtyard. I already felt lighter. I could feel the pressure dropping.

Then everything happened, all at once and out of nowhere. The shit came raining down on us. I heard the scraping of sneaker soles on wet cement, then menacing yells from every direction. We were surrounded. There could have been five of them, or fifteen, for all I knew. Will lifted up his hands to appease the crazed mob, then raised his arms to ward off the blows. I had the same reflex. They jumped us and started beating. The blows came from every direction. They hit me in the ribs, the side, the head. Something was burning my eyes. I tried to get back up and cover my eyes. They were spraying liquid in my face. It burned my eyes. I couldn't tell where it was coming from. I felt my right eyebrow swelling up and hardening. I teared up and my nose filled with snot, like when you get campfire smoke in your eyes, only a thousand times worse. The pain was leeching in behind my eye sockets. Everything was hazy. My eye hurt so bad everything else seemed secondary. I was thrown down to the ground and hailed in kicks—on the stomach, on the jaw. All I could feel was the burning in my eyes and on my face. I played dead. I saw Will out of my good eye. He was shielding his eyes with his hands and yelling that they were all dead, those motherfuckers. I was sure he'd pull his gun. I figured he'd start shooting any moment. I was all balled up like a prawn in a frying pan, with a pain in the stomach and sides, while a voice kept yelling at me not to move. From my position I could only see the top of his face. The rest was hidden by his neckwarmer. He had an Anglo accent.

Finally the gang took off. Will came to see me, leaned over, and asked if I was okay. For the first time his voice had lost its abrasive edge.

"It's okay, I'll make it."

"C'mon, man, get up, let's go."

I couldn't really see where I was going through my tears. I followed Will as best I could. We ran to the Civic. It felt like my face was imprisoned in a white-hot cake pan. The only noise that got through to me was the sound of our footsteps over a sidewalk covered in greyish snow and slush. When Will opened the door the driver asked:

"Fuck, man, what happened?"

"We got jumped. Right when we were leaving. Fucking niggers got the money."

I didn't say anything. But the guys who attacked us weren't black. At least not the one who'd held me down. The driver stared, confused and open-mouthed. He started the car.

"But what happened?"

"Motherfuckers *maced* us!"

Will was rubbing his face to ease the burning. He sniffled loudly.

"What, we get set up?"

"Fucked if I know."

"Wait a minute, bro," said the driver, reaching for the glove compartment. "Let's go back and get 'em."

Will pounded on the dash.

"Fuck no, we're outa here."

"C'mon, we can't let them get away with that."

"Yo boy, I said we're leaving. Get us out of here. I need to wash my face. Now!"

CHAPTER 35

I SPENT a good hour at the Second Cup across from La Trattoria, licking my wounds, terrified by the prospect of going in to work and facing Greg. The Americano I'd bought with a handful of change wasn't going down right. I'd been nauseous from the moment I opened my eyes that morning. How I'd managed to sleep at all was a mystery. I got up and crossed the street, shivering as I went. Night had fallen. You could just barely make out the fluffy snowflakes in the halo of lamplight and the headlights of cars shooshing by. I went back up the alley and into the restaurant as discreetly as possible. My right eye was bloodshot, my eyebrow was still swollen, and a big bruise coloured the left side of my jaw. My ribs still hurt. It was a struggle just to put my work shirt on.

When I punched in, Jade noticed my face and asked if I was okay. Gone was the icy tone of the last few shifts. Without looking at her, I said I was fine. I walked along the wall of the service kitchen and back down to the basement, dodging Jonathan and Bonnie's questions. I got started on my prep, dreading the moment Greg would appear.

While I kneaded my focaccia dough, I heard someone running down the stairs. Bébert. He crossed the prep room slowly with big headphones on. He looked fresh and rested, fully recovered from his epic bender. He didn't see me. I heard him throwing stuff around: a keychain landing on the table. The rustling of a winter coat. The thud of boots tossed into a locker.

He came back to say hi to me. When he saw my face he started.

"Woah, man. You get herpes or something? Your eye's swollen up like a balloon."

"It was like that when I woke up. Must be an allergic reaction."

He came in for a closer look, with his clean rags in one hand. I instinctively backed away. It was still burning.

"What the hell kind of allergy is that?"

"I don't know. A spider, maybe?"

I answered without looking up as I ran my dough through the rolling machine.

"Does it hurt?"

"No, I'm fine."

"What about your jaw? You allergic to doorknobs too?"

I felt myself turning red. I didn't answer, and pretended to be engrossed in my job. Bébert sighed and went upstairs without another word.

Eduardo was rinsing pans and I was sorting clean dishes when Greg appeared in the dishpit. I hadn't seen him come in, had almost convinced myself he wouldn't show up.

"Let's go for a smoke, man."

I told Eduardo I'd be gone a couple minutes. He gave me a thumbs up. The knot in my stomach stubbornly refused to loosen. My legs felt weak.

Greg went out first and didn't hold the door for me. He leaned against the wall under the lightbulb that lit the back door. Despite the cold he had his sleeves rolled up. I was freezing; not him. He looked me up and down.

"You look rough, man."

The way he said it was almost cheery. He lit up, took a few puffs, and let the silence unfurl. Then he pulled out a wad of fifties and hundreds. He snapped off two hundreds.

"Here. That's for you."

He held out the money. It felt like he was testing me. In the end I took the bills. He leaned in close.

"They really worked you over, hey?"

Two tons of lead had been lifted from my shoulders. I started breathing easier, but still felt an underlying tension. I kept waiting for Greg to turn violent.

"Aren't you gonna ask me what happened?"

My voice came out quiet as a whisper.

"Why would I ask you that?"

I didn't understand. I was watching him, trying to find my words. He was freshly shaved, and I could smell the aftershave mixed in with tobacco smoke. He didn't seem angry, not even mildly annoyed.

"Uh...because..." I stumbled.

"Did you do what I asked?"

I said I had.

"That's all that matters."

He took a puff of his cigarette. It was barely half-smoked. He threw it in the snow and exhaled. He seemed a little too calm for my liking. I didn't like his attitude.

"But...Did Will tell you what happened?"

"What, I look like a guy who doesn't keep track of my business?"

I didn't answer.

"Stop talking about it," he said. "You did what you had to. You showed me I can count on you. Give me a couple days and I'll have something else for you."

He opened the door.

"Good job, fighter."

Greg bounded into the dishpit and grabbed a load of clean cutlery without slowing down. I was left all alone in the alley. I no longer felt cold. I had no idea what had just happened.

Eduardo waited until halfway through the night to finally ask, in his surprisingly good English, what had happened to my eye. I said I'd gotten in a fight. He said nothing for a few seconds, and looked surprised, as if he was chewing over what I'd just said, and then his face lit up. He said he used to get in a lot of fights too, back in Brazil. At least one every week. Then he explained how he got the little cross-shaped scar on his left cheek. From a knife. Then, getting a little more worked up, he undid his belt and dropped his pants. He wanted to show me his thigh. There were two little circles of burnt skin the size of quarters, next to his boxers. Bullet holes. He was fourteen when it happened, he said laughing. My eyes widened.

"How old are you now again?"

"Eighteen."

Every time he said his age Eduardo's voice filled with pride. A lot of his friends hadn't made it past sixteen.

He told me that's how it was in the *favela*. I figured "favela" must be the name of a town in Brazil. The more Eduardo told me about his past life, the more I thought about what I'd done the night before. And the dumber I felt for taking this shit so lightly.

That night, after closing, Bébert took me to Roy Bar. He seemed unusually calm, which came as a relief.

We didn't talk on the way to the bar. He only stopped once, to tag a wall in the alley. It was warm. The sprinkling of snow had stopped falling. Low-hanging clouds were illuminated by the city lights.

The Roy Bar was practically empty, nothing like last time we were there. The hammerhead shark hanging from the ceiling was a funny colour in the TV's glow. We sat at the bar.

I ordered a pint of red. Bébert had a big bottle of Tremblay. He bought the round, insisted on it. He started talking, eyes never leaving the skateboarding videos.

"Sorry about that fucked-up shift on Sunday. I totally lost it."

"No worries. It happens."

"It's not supposed to happen."

He was cradling his beer between his massive hands, while following the skaters' acrobatics. Somewhere in that face I caught a glimpse of the little boy he'd once been. Accident-prone, hyper-active, ready to talk your ear off.

"Now it's your turn to say sorry."

He was still looking at the screen. I played dumb, even though I knew exactly what he wanted to talk about.

"Greg told me the whole story," he went on, in the same even tone. "I told you, man. You do *not* want to be Greg's errand boy."

He turned to face me and pointed his bottle at my face.

"Dude, it almost cost you an eye."

"Chill," I said. "It was just a little cayenne pepper. I'm fine."

I could still feel a burning behind my ear. A little earlier, getting changed for work, I'd noticed a big purple and yellow bruise that had appeared on my left hip. Bébert sighed and shook his head at me.

"Poor kid. You really don't get it, eh?"

"What?"

"Wanna play gangsta? That's not you. You're a nice guy. They'll eat you for breakfast. Trust me, you're not cut out for that shit."

"That's my business, Bébert," I said. "There's no problem. Greg said everything was fine. I did what I had to do. It's all good. His guy told him the full story."

Bébert broke out in a gruff laugh, like an evil spirit. He took a sip of beer.

"Yeah, I bet. Know where his guy is now?"

I was about to mumble something.

"Saint-Luc Hospital. Emergency room."

"C'mon, bullshit. He got hurt less bad than I did. We just got pepper-sprayed and beat up a little."

"Listen to yourself, man," Bébert said. "'*We just got pepper-sprayed and beat up a little.*' Shit, you got it all figured out for sure. You're on top of it, man! You're on it!"

He straightened up and looked me in the eye, with one elbow on the bar and the other on the back of his chair. He wasn't laughing. This wasn't remotely funny to him. Deep down I knew Bébert was right, but didn't see quite where he was going with all this.

Mostly I was trying to figure out what Will was doing in the emergency room.

"All right, wise guy. Let me draw you a picture. You're walking around with four large in your bag. A bunch of guys jump you. With *mace*. A couple of sprays, a few kicks and off you go. Man, I know dudes been stabbed over fifty bucks. And they got away with your shit, no guns, no drama..."

I cast around for something to tell him. It was true that it didn't quite add up. Since yesterday I'd been wondering why Will hadn't pulled his gun. That might at least have made them think twice.

"They weren't that organized. Maybe they just took a chance. We must not be the only guys who come by there..."

I could see in Bébert's eyes that he was starting to think I was seriously retarded. He rubbed his temples, as if trying to chase away a headache.

"You have no idea how this shit works, eh? The guy you went to see yesterday is Kasper's cousin. *No one* in that 'hood would even think about stealing Greg's shit—ever. No one would be dumb enough to steal from Greg. Except maybe one of his own guys."

A few seconds went by before the light went on. Just a tiny detail: the guy leaning over me while they were kicking me. His accent. His blue eyes, the colour of his skin. He was white as cocaine. And then Will's words: "Fucking niggers got the money." Maybe I was the only one who got pepper sprayed, maybe Will was just pretending.

"So you're saying we got jumped by a bunch of Will's friends? That's what you're saying?"

Bébert lifted his two hands, palms in the air, making a face.

"That's right, genius. Will set the whole thing up. Greg's had his eye on him for a long time. It just so happened that you were there when Will made his move. They're gonna roll him out of hospital in a body cast."

Bébert ordered another Tremblay. My beer wasn't sitting right.

"You know that whole thing could've gone sideways. Bad. You're a lucky bastard. So do me a favour. Stay away from Greg and his business."

I didn't answer, just stared at my flat beer with my arms crossed.

"I needed money. I *need* money."

"Want more money? We'll move you up to the kitchen, you can count on me. But Jesus Christ, man, don't go around playing gangsta. Go see Greg and tell him you're out."

"I don't want him to think I can't hack it."

He dug around in his hoodie for his smokes. Pulled one out of the pack with his mouth. I thought about telling him Renaud had already promised to move me up to the kitchen, but Bébert hated the man so fiercely I decided to hold my tongue.

"Okay," he said, hatching a bright idea. "I'll talk to Greg myself. Forget it. As long as I'm around he'll leave you out of his dumbass schemes. Now promise me you'll stay out of that shit."

I nodded, sheepishly. He raised his beer for a cheers.

We stayed at the bar until closing, and it stayed dead. We had the place to ourselves. We shot a little pool, and talked about all kinds of stuff. He told me about growing up in Châteauguay. His first acid trips. How he got his start in the kitchen, cooking school at Calixa-Lavallée, his first jobs. I was eating it up, those were the kind of stories I'd happily listen to for hours. At the end of the night he said that three years from now he'd have his own restaurant. Partying was all well and good but it was time for something different.

"Me and some friends'll open a Southern BBQ joint: brisket, jambalaya, cornbread, mac and cheese 'n' shit. We'll even have a smoke pit, somewhere out of town. Not some yuppie spot for fancy pants with something to prove. Fuck that. Just a casual place with good food."

Bébert and I parted ways at Saint-Denis and Rachel, not really drunk.

"See you tomorrow, man."

"Don't forget your promise. And I won't forget mine."

We bumped fists and he took off, shoulders flexing in his snowboard jacket.

The cloudy sky was a gloomy ochre. I just stood there on the sidewalk for a good long while. I was spent. I didn't check my pager, what was the use, I knew there'd be no word from Marie-Lou. The snow on the sidewalk was heaped into little dunes covered in what looked like golden ash. I went up Saint-Denis to Laurier, then caught the night bus. I sat near the front in the dark.

CHAPTER 36

I WOKE UP feeling like I'd narrowly averted a fatal accident. I got out of the shower and brushed my teeth. When the mirror unfogged I noticed that the swelling around my left eye had gone down a bit. It wasn't nearly as bad as the day before.

Before leaving for work, I went into Vincent's room and left a hundred-dollar bill on his desk, clearly visible against the black melamine.

I got to the restaurant in time for my six-o'clock shift. The smell of chicken stock was again wafting through the alley, taking me back to my very first shift. I rang. Basile opened almost right away. The dishpit was gleaming. He was leaning against a shelf of clean dishes eating a plate of pasta.

I walked by the kitchen. Bonnie and Jonathan both looked bummed out. I thought about making a crack, to cheer them up. Bébert had half disappeared under the steam table, all you could see were his legs sticking out, like a mechanic under a car. I went to punch in right away. Séverine didn't seem to be around. At the end of the bar, next to the computer, Sarah and Denver were talking about someone in the past tense, as if they had just passed away. I went back to the kitchen, and said hi to Bébert who had emerged from under the steam table. But it wasn't Bébert, it was Vlad. I turned toward Jonathan, and then Bonnie.

"Bébert take a day off?"

They looked at me wide-eyed, as if I'd told a racist joke. I shrugged my shoulders.

I went off to change. In the staff room I was greeted by the familiar mess: shoes lying everywhere, torn-up copies of the free weekly, dirty cook shirts. The table was littered with tobacco leaves. A spent lighter, a rolled up used phone-card. Bébert's locker door was wide open. No coat, no spare clothes, no clogs. Renaud's face appeared in the open office door. He told me to come see him.

"We're moving you up to the kitchen this week. Jonathan's gonna train you."

"This week."

"Yeah, this week. Why?"

He was clicking on an Excel spreadsheet as he talked to me. He went on.

"Bonnie's on the pass, with Steven. He'll be taking hotside shifts too. So I need a new garde-manger. Vlad's full-time hotside now. He's the new night-chef."

I wasn't sure I'd fully understood. I looked at Renaud, but he was scrolling through pages of numbers.

"Vlad?"

"Yeah, Vlad."

"Is Bébert taking a vacation?"

"Bébert isn't with us anymore," he said. His tone was robotic, inhuman.

The news hit me in the gut. He enunciated each word like he was reading from a textbook, eyes never leaving the screen. On the desk, not far from the keyboard, I saw an open chequebook. A cheque had just been written. I could read the details on the stub. Alexandre Brière. I didn't recognize the name. Renaud looked up at me, almost surprised to find me still there. Goddamn hypocrite. Then I remembered where I'd seen that name: on the list of staff phone numbers. Alexandre Brière was Bébert's real name. It sent shivers down my whole body. I saw stars, like when you get up out of your chair too fast.

"Bébert isn't with us anymore?" I asked, my voice quaking. I didn't even realize I was playing back gutless sentence, syllable by syllable.

"No," Renaud said without looking at me.

He was still cycling through his Excel sheets, and from time to time he'd write a number down on a piece of paper next to the mouse.

"So you start next week. Okay?"

I said it was fine. I was still reeling from the news. All that remained in Bébert's locker was a half-drunk bottle of Bawls and a few cans of MTN 94 spray paint splattered with yellow, black, silver and magenta.

The first service went by with an eerie smoothness. In the kitchen no one said a word. No one opened their mouth unless it was strictly necessary. Bonnie and Jonathan looked bereaved. Something was missing. I was heartsick, and outraged, but wasn't able to give it more than a few seconds of thought at a time. My own problems had me in a stranglehold. I was suffocating in the dishpit, wallowing in my anxiety, saddened and angered by the underhanded way Bébert had been fired. But all these feelings gave way to panic when my thoughts returned to my own predicament. I couldn't concentrate or focus on anything at all. I wondered what I would tell the Deathgaze guys if I couldn't come up with a solution, and fast. What would I tell Malik? My mind was spinning like a hamster on a wheel, staring at the back door, enthralled by the idea of an escape. I imagined vanishing out the door, like a quivering ghost. It was all I could do not to cry out in rage. I breathed in deeply. I had to calm down.

Between two rushes Jonathan came back to the dishpit for a smoke. He was gloomy, and his jaw never unclenched. He seemed to be elsewhere.

"Was it that bad, the other night?" he asked between drags.

"It was hell," I said. "I hope I never have to go through that ever again. As long as I live. Still though, Renaud had no business..."

I couldn't go on: I was trembling, distraught. I got back to work. Everything was all mixed up in my head. On the outside my body was fulfilling its orders. I put away clean dishes with precise gestures, barely slower than usual. I breathed through my mouth. Basile loaded the racks for the machine, methodically and silently as ever. From time to time he flashed me a look, not daring to ask any questions. Jonathan was on a milk crate, with a rounded back and slumped shoulders.

"It's definitely won't be as much fun. With Vlad," he said.

I didn't answer. He tossed his smoke out the door and got up. He put his chef's hat back on over his dishevelled light-brown hair, and got up with a sigh to head back to the kitchen. I thought about Greg. Now that would be one more situation I'd have to handle on my own. I was already dreading the moment he'd come back with another errand for me. Even if Bébert was gone, it seemed important not to break my promise to him. Bébert was right, the whole thing was a sham. That was no life for me.

Toward the end of the shift, as I mopped the dishpit, I thought I heard Bébert's loud laugh ringing out in the dining room. But when I went out with a big grin to see for myself, I realized my mistake. It was a customer sitting at the bar, a massive fifty-year old guy with a bushy grey beard. I stood there clutching my mop. Bébert's words on New Year's came back to me. I would make a lot of friends in the kitchen. "Thing is, you never keep them long. Take it as it comes. Turnover's high." It happens so fast, every time. You blink and they're gone. Bébert had been my guardian angel, my friend from the other side, from the night. Now he was gone. All I had left was my messed-up life, my debts, my lies, and a shrinking group of people I could turn to for help.

CHAPTER 37

AFTER my shift I stopped by an ATM to deposit my cheque and get some cash. My mind was blank. It wasn't one a.m. yet. I walked down Ontario, and stopped by Chez Maurice to see if Marie-Lou was working. Her silence had become too much to bear. I needed to see her again.

The place was practically deserted. Benjamin was chatting with a regular, a big salt-and-pepper bear of a man in coveralls. The walls were still decked with Christmas lights that cast cheerless light on empty tables. I took a seat at the bar. Benjamin interrupted his discussion and came over. He had a faded black eye.

"Unruly customer?" I said, with a forced laugh.

I pointed at my eye. It took him a minute to catch on.

"Not here. In the ring. At the gym. We got carried away a bit. Yours isn't too shabby either. You take up boxing too?"

My face was a little swollen, and visibly bruised.

"Not really. It's nothing."

Now it was his turn to let out a forced laugh.

"You just get off work?"

"Yup."

"What can I do you for?"

"I'll have a beer."

He placed a glass on the cardboard coaster in front of me, then went over to punch in the beer and came back with a bag from the Archambault bookstore.

"Here. Marie-Lou left these for you."

I looked in the bag. My *Sandmans* were all there. I felt a pang in my chest. I put the bag down next to my beer.

"I was wondering when she's working? I thought she'd be here tonight."

Benjamin looked a bit surprised. It was a strange look on a guy who was usually so stone-faced.

"Marie-Lou doesn't work here anymore. She went travelling."

The ground shifted beneath my feet. I must have made a face, because he immediately asked the obvious question.

"She didn't tell you?"

I looked at my beer and didn't answer.

"Are you okay?"

"Just tired. Rough shift."

Benjamin lighted a smoke. He asked if I'd ever thought about moving to the floor, and told me about some of his first jobs in the restaurant business, bussing in the clubs on Prince-Arthur. He was in an unusually talkative mood and full of stories from his former life. But my heart wasn't in it. I wanted to ask him about Greg again, but the news about Marie-Lou had thrown me for a loop. I made up an excuse to take off after my second beer. It was two a.m. on the big Molson Export clock. I had my full paycheque, in cash, in my pocket.

Maybe it was the certitude that I was on my way to losing everything I had, or the realization that winning and losing had lost all significance, but something broke my momentum. I could easily have bet everything I had. I wouldn't have felt a thing. But I didn't. Not out of any strength of will, but sheer fatigue. I walked away from the machine and went to sit at the bar.

"Another Bud, dear?"

I nodded.

On the stage, a blond girl with a boob job was sliding up and down the pole, head down, curly hair undulating like seaweed, her legs flexed and spread out like the branches of a compass tracing the parabola of a nonsensical calculation.

I looked all around. Torn carpet. Tables sticky with beer. The stubborn smell of mothballs. The holes in the wall. The streaked, dusty mirrors. The black lights weren't enough to mask every sordid detail, but they helped. Though she was probably white as milk in the daylight, in here the dancer's skin had the copperish hue of good crema.

Everything about this place was fake, hollow, and meretricious, contrived to transfer money from one set of hands to another as efficiently as possible.

The bouncer was chatting with the DJ. Isolated men of indeterminate age, each alone at his table with a beer in front of him, stared at the stage with hollow eyes. Two strippers were chatting away at the end of the bar.

I counted what I had left on me. I checked out the machines. A foul taste filled my mouth. I got up without finishing my beer. I marched toward the door, dizzied by the paralyzing shakes the thought of gambling gave me. I started an awkward shuffle, like someone running to the bathroom to throw up. I ended up on the sidewalk with my coat in my hands.

Saint-Denis was practically deserted. I hailed a cab. A Taxi Coop car pulled up in front of me. Not a single speck of slush sullied the car's gleaming doors. The car looked like it had come straight from the car wash. I slid inside. It smelled like fresh mint. In the large rear-view mirror, two gentle eyes stared at me from under bushy eyebrows.

"Hello, my friend. How are you?"

The driver's deep voice rang a bell. The car interior was comfortable and scrupulously clean. I relaxed. The dashboard lights gave off a warm, amber glow. The compartment under the radio held a stainless-steel Thermos and a little well-thumbed Koran that looked like the one Malik's mother had.

"Where to?"

I gave him an intersection near Vincent's house.

"Off we go, my friend."

The driver headed down Berri, then turned onto Cherrier to take Saint-Denis northbound. I could barely hear the dispatcher on the radio. The interior was padded against outside intrusion. When we got to the Métropolitain Autoroute the driver winked at me in the rear-view mirror.

"You look tired, my friend. I've told you before: night is for sleeping. You have to take care of yourself."

That was when I recognized Benjamin's friend Mohammed. The cab driver who'd picked him up after he fell off the balcony.

"I just had a bad day," I said. "Nothing's working out."

I couldn't see the lower part of his face, but his eyes tensed up and wrinkles appeared. He was smiling. There was a deep wisdom in his face, an abiding compassion.

"Things have a way of working out, my friend. Don't worry."

Under other circumstances, this commonplace would have irritated me. But at that precise moment it was just what I needed to believe. We didn't exchange another word for the rest of the ride. Through the windows I saw rows of buildings unfurl, each alike with darkened windows, cornices, snowy staircases and Christmas wreathes still nailed to the doors.

Mohammed dropped me off in front of Vincent's building.

"Goodnight, my friend. Go sleep now."

I thanked him in Arabic, the way Malik had taught me.

Vincent was still at Janine's. I went to bed the moment I came in the door. But I wasn't able to go to sleep until I'd gone and taken back the hundred-dollar bill I'd left on Vincent's desk.

Shokran.

CHAPTER 38

THE ALBUM COVER was supposed to be finished and printed the next day. I hadn't worked on it since the night Marie-Lou caught me gambling at Chez Maurice. And it wasn't like I had the money for the printer. If I'd once entertained the notion of sending in the files for printing anyway, to buy a little time, I'd long since gotten discouraged and given up. The images weren't done anyway. I was caught in my own trap.

I got to work, scared to death. I knew it was only a matter of time before I ran into Greg. And I also knew when I did he'd send me off on a job that I couldn't refuse.

I changed slowly. I was struggling to get motivated. Renaud showed up with a bag of clean laundry. He was separating the kitchen rags from the service cloths, leaning over the jute bag.

"Hey Renaud, think I could take a couple of days off next week?"

He looked up at me. A big vein traversed his pink forehead.

"Next week? We're training you for the kitchen next week, remember?"

He leaned back over his linen.

"Yeah, I know, but…"

The way his body stiffened made it clear I was pissing him off. He was about to say something when Séverine came out of the office. Her face had clouded over with a strange weariness I'd never seen on her before.

"Renaud, I need to talk to you" she said.

Her voice was muffled. She looked like she might have a cold.

Renaud made a gesture indicating that he was tabling our conversation for later, and they shut themselves in the office. I didn't go out of my way to listen at the door, but for a second I thought I heard Séverine crying.

I went up to find Basile. He had put on some French rap, IAM's *L'École du Micro d'Argent*. I listlessly started giving him a hand. It was pretty dead. He'd been doing just fine without me. We wouldn't start feeling the rush for an hour or so.

Nick came back for cutlery. I was a little surprised to see him.

"Wasn't Greg working tonight?"

"Nah, man. Greg's not coming in."

Nick was standing in the middle of the dishpit with the clean cutlery in his hand.

"Is he sick?"

I didn't have Greg pegged as the kind of guy to miss work for a sore throat or the after-effects of a good party.

"I heard he got taken to the hospital last night. Séverine says he's in intensive care."

I stared at Nick. Even Basile came out of his bubble to listen.

"A bullet in the lung. And two more in his chest, not far from his heart. He lost a lot of blood. Apparently it's in the paper."

Then Nick set off into the dining room, as if he'd just told us the score in the hockey game.

My first reaction was panic. I couldn't move an inch. I figured it had something to do with the setup in the housing project. I sat down on a milk crate, and wondered whether I was hallucinating, or had maybe missed something.

"Are you okay, man?" Basile asked me.

I gave him a wave that was halfway between, "Yeah, I'm fine," and "Leave me alone." Everything was mixed up in my mind. I had a flash of the big bald guy who'd come in looking for Greg at work the other night. I saw Séverine standing in front of him. Snatches of the story came back to me. A name, Kovacs. Greg making threats in his Monte Carlo on the way back from the Stereo.

It finally sunk in just how deathly serious Bébert's warnings had been. Greg was literally dangerous. I sent Basile to get us Cokes. I felt suddenly drained, devoid of willpower. From where I was standing I could see the bar. Sarah was smiling and chatting with customers. Jade, more beautiful than ever, was drying glasses, hips gently gyrating as if she were swaying to a beat. The din of the room reached me. Unconsciously, I sought out Bébert's voice rising above the ambient hum. I was sick of it all. Basile came back with our drinks. I asked if he'd mind closing for me.

CHAPTER 39

I LEFT as soon as Basile gave me the okay. Several hours later Vincent came and met me. He'd gotten the dozen messages I'd left. The last five were slurred, but he got the gist. After work I'd headed straight to Café Chaos to get blind drunk. Vincent showed up just before the bartender threw me out. I'd emptied four pitchers. Though I could no longer stand up, I was irately demanding a fifth.

I remember the blurry figure of Vincent coming into the bar. In baggy pants and an oversized Nautica jacket he stood out among the studded vests, torn-up jeans, and bullet belts of the crowd here. As soon as I saw him I threw my arms wide open.

"Finally. You're here!" I managed. "Do you have money . . . one more pitcher?"

I slid off my barstool. Vincent leaned over and grabbed me, to try to stand me up. He looked at the bartender.

"I've got this."

He put his hand around my shoulders and dragged me outside. I vaguely remember throwing up in front of the bar, and slipping on the icy sidewalk.

I woke up the next day unable to move, disoriented and raw as if I'd woken from a cryogenic coma. Vincent was there. He didn't ask a single question about how I'd gotten so wasted the night before. I wouldn't have known where to start. Everything was a jumble in my mind. He went to rent some movies, old favourites that never let us down: *Menace II Society, Fight Club, Payback, The Blair Witch Project, The Abyss.* We just watched one after another until night fell. Vincent made us Lipton soup and went to get me Gatorade from the corner store. My pager informed me that I had new voice messages. Two. The first was Alex. In a strained voice he was telling me off, until a psychopathic-sounding Mike broke in mid-message to let me know in no uncertain terms that he planned to break every bone in my hand, so I wouldn't waste anyone else's time with my scribbling. I could hear the two of them arguing in the background, followed by a crashing that sounded like a phone coming into contact with a hard surface. Then the line went dead. I listened to the message with a grey face and a throbbing skull, then erased it. The second message was Malik. He wanted to catch up. He was sorry he hadn't called when he got back from Cuba, he'd been swamped. He said we should get together, he'd be in town in a few days.

I called him around eleven at night. He was happy, almost excited. We set a meeting for the next day, after my shift. This time I was scheduled to get off before the other dishwasher.

Malik was waiting for me at the bar. He was the one who'd wanted to meet me inside, to see where I worked, what kind of place La Trattoria was. He stood up when he saw me coming out the back. Maude was surprised to see he was my cousin. She had good things to say about me. Malik was smiling, taking it all in, visibly out of his element in such a high-end restaurant.

We drove around for a while, while he told me a little about his trip. He asked how I was doing but didn't push for details the way he usually did. Good thing, too; I was in no mood for a lecture. He took me to a pool hall on the South Shore, where we'd hung out a lot my first summer before Cegep.

After a few games of pool we took a seat at a table. Malik went to get us a second pitcher and bowl of peanuts. The beer wasn't going down right. He asked how the Deathgaze job was going. I wasn't sure how to answer, so I told him that the drawings were basically done, and there were just a few technical details to iron out. Then I told him some restaurant stories. Mostly about Bébert, and how he'd gotten fired.

"Sounds like a real piece of work, that guy."

Malik couldn't see what was so compelling about Bébert. A couple of women were playing nine-ball at the table we'd left. Malik watched them for a minute. He was in a good mood. The trip to Cuba and the time off had relaxed him. I sniffled.

"Do you think maybe you could lend me two hundred bucks?"

Malik snapped back around and stared at me. His expression had grown troubled. He didn't say anything right away, just stared at me. I could see he was thinking hard, and trying to keep a hold of himself.

"My paycheque isn't coming for a week, and I'd like to help Vincent with the rent."

Malik set his glass down on the table and pulled his chair in closer. He looked me in the eye.

"Are you asking me for money to go gambling again?"

"I just want to pay Vincent my share of the rent."

I'd put on a half-outraged, half disappointed look. When I saw his reaction I immediately regretted it.

"You're really sitting here asking me for money to go gambling again."

His tone was harsh, his judgment final and without appeal. He slowly shook his head. A muscle tensed up in his jaw. He took a sip of beer, then put his glass down and sighed, running his hand over his face.

"You know I had a talk with your buddy Vincent."

"When?"

"Doesn't matter. He told me you still haven't paid him a cent of what you owe."

"That's not true."

"Cut the shit, right now," he snapped. "You're lucky you still have a friend like that left. He's not even mad at you."

I took a deep breath. Malik pulled his glass of beer away. He put his hands down in the middle of the table. I looked at the girls a while.

"Please," I said. "Just one hundred bucks. That's all I need. I'm in trouble...And Alex..."

I hesitated. Malik gave me a cold look. His face was set in a hard expression.

"Alex what?"

He asked me again, more slowly, as if to make sure I'd understood. I spit it out in a single breath.

"I owe the guys from Deathgaze two-thousand dollars. I need money fast. I've gotta get their album covers printed fucking now. I'm already late."

"Come again?"

Now a change came over Malik. His elbows were propped on the table, as if ready to pounce. His face darkened over. I'd never seen him on edge like that.

"Didn't you say they were paying you once the job was done?"

I was about to answer something, but then he said in harrowing voice:

"So you...when you came to see us in November, you'd already lost all the money. While we were all trying to figure out ways to get you out of trouble, all you were thinking about was when you could come back to Montreal and start gambling again? All the promises you made me, that didn't mean shit? And then what? All the money I lent you? Your paycheques from the restaurant? You gambled all that away too?"

I was nervously picking at the eczema flakes on the back of my hands. Malik threw himself backward into his chair, crossed his arms, and stared at me. I looked away.

"So you've just been lying to me the whole time. Lies, lies, lies. You never stopped lying to me, from the beginning...Yo! I'm talking to you!"

I rubbed my face. I couldn't look him in the eye.

"You're not the only one who's disappointed," I said.

He slapped the table so hard that our glasses of beer almost tipped over.

"Shut the fuck up! Stop that shit right now!"

He was breaking up the syllables as he talked, his voice trembling with a contained rage.

"I've got no more time for your whining, man. You got me once. It's not gonna happen again."

I lowered my head. When I lifted it up again, my face was twisted in a pathetic grimace, and a stifled moan emerged from my throat. The girls playing pool next to us abandoned their game, picked up their coats and purses, and moved to another section of the bar, far from us. I couldn't hold in my sobs any longer. A headache was pounding my temples. I wiped my mouth and nose, which were dripping with snot. Malik was staring at me, holding his forehead in his two palms. He looked totally overcome and disgusted. He slowly exhaled.

"It's true, I lied to you. I lied to everyone. Marie-Lou won't even look at me anymore. I can't stop gambling. I can't control myself. I can't do it."

I was struggling to squeeze out these last few sentences through the tears and the snot. Malik stared over my shoulder, gesturing to someone, as if to say that we were fine, and to leave us alone. He poured the rest of the pitcher into his glass.

"You need help, Stéphane."

I wiped my face with the sleeve of my shirt.

"No," I said, sniffling. "I'll handle it."

Malik was still leaning back in his chair, staring at me.

"You just said you couldn't do it."

"I don't need anyone's help."

Malik pounded the tabletop again. He looked like he was about to scream. He waited a few seconds, without saying a word, and then looked at me, deep in thought.

"Okay, enough. Don't talk. Just listen to me. And listen good. We're going to do exactly what I say. First of all you're going to quit your job. Tomorrow."

"No way. I can't quit now. They're moving me up to the kitchen."

"I don't care if they're making you chef or CEO. You're going to quit that shit right now. Then, you're going to go see your friend Alex and tell him the whole story."

I turned pale. The colour drained from my face.

"I can't."

"Oh yes, you can, and you will. I'll give you two days. Then you're going to shove all your shit in a bag and you're coming to Trois-Rivières with me."

"What'll I tell my boss? I can't leave with no notice. I can't say no to a promotion. And I need the money. To pay back the band."

"Jesus Christ. Are you hearing a word I'm saying? This is what's gonna happen: you're gonna quit your job, and go see Alex and tell him the whole story. Or else I'll call your parents and tell them the whole story."

He leaned backed in his chair and stared at me, waiting for me to react. I was trying hard to maintain my composure. I didn't need long to weigh my options. There was no way I was going to let anyone breathe a word of this to my mum or dad.

"You're blackmailing me. That's not fair."

His eyebrows raised up to the middle of his forehead, as if he'd suddenly turned into a mime. He acted like he'd just been privy to the most revolting, inappropriate sentence uttered in the history of humankind. I immediately regretted my words. He looked all around the pool hall, with the expression of someone searching for backup, or trying to find a witness for an extraordinary phenomenon unfolding in front of him.

"I don't think you have any idea what deep shit you're in. It's not a money problem, what you have."

He never once stopped looking at me. I could no longer form coherent thoughts. I was exhausted, running around eternally in a labyrinth with neither beginning nor end.

"You're sick. Do you understand that? I mean, you have a disease. Tonight you're coming home with me. You're gonna stay at my mum's. We'll sort out your shit tomorrow."

CHAPTER 40

ALEX had been gone a good half hour and I hadn't left Chez Maurice. I'd been back here once or twice in recent weeks, perhaps in the hope that Marie-Lou might magically appear, though I knew all too well she didn't work here anymore. I pictured her scaling some Mayan ruin with a backpack on her shoulders, her tattooed white skin grown dark in the sun.

The bar's heating wasn't up to the challenge of the cold creeping in. Through the windows the gloomy grey sky of each and every identical winter afternoon was hardly distinct from the faded facades. Grainy light filtered into the room.

Alex had listened to my story. He heard me out to the end, although I'd led with the punch line. He just sat there listening, serious and silent, without even touching his beer. Telling my story proved easier than expected. Once I was done a feeling of calm took hold. I felt free. I breathed easier. I could look him in the eye again.

"Do you have any idea . . . how much I stood up for you? How much I had to argue and fight with Mike because of you? How long have we known each other, man? This is total bullshit."

Alex didn't lose his temper. He just kept repeating himself. You didn't do that, you didn't do that to a friend. I started saying something. He made an unambiguous gesture telling me to shut up. I hadn't used Malik's words, hadn't said it was a disease, or anything like that. I didn't want to provoke him. I just wanted to get this over with as quickly as possible, before the conversation went sideways.

"Don't, man. Don't say a word. Forget about the whole thing."

He got up. He looked even bigger than before. His straw-coloured mane fell over his shoulders. He put on his patched-over leather jacket. He looked like a biker. He drank his beer in two sips, then banged the empty glass down on the table with a clack.

"I never want to see your face again."

The next day I told Renaud I was quitting. I said I had a personal emergency and couldn't give my two weeks' notice.

"Man, you can't just leave us hanging like that. I need you in the kitchen."

"I know," I said. "But I can't stay in Montreal."

"Why not?"

I stuck to the script Malik had devised and told him the same thing I'd told everyone else.

"It's a long story. I'm changing schools. I'm going to live in Trois-Rivières."

That pissed him off. Almost disdainfully, he wrote a cheque for my vacation pay. I had the night off. As if a switch had been flicked, Renaud began treating me like a worthless object. I knew quitting without notice would leave them in the lurch. He'd even planned to move me up to the kitchen as part of the shakeup after he got rid of Bébert.

And I was disappointed to leave. Sure, I'd miss the money, but it was more about the people.

Adding to Renaud's problems didn't bother me a bit. Not after what he'd done to Bébert. The scattered parts of Renaud's Machiavellian schemes resolved into a clear picture in hindsight. He'd started setting little traps long before I got hired. He'd dangled the sous-chef job in front of Bébert's nose because he needed help to get rid of Christian. He'd made him work double after double, seventy hours a week through the transition from Christian's reign to his own. He'd brought in his allies, Steven and Vlad. Getting rid of Christian had never been the whole plan: he'd had Bébert in his sights all along as well. Bébert was standing in his way, preventing him from establishing his authority. Bébert's disastrous shift was no more than a pretext. Renaud knew enough to understand that if he packed in enough hours in a short enough period Bébert would eventually blow. He was counting on it, to fire him. It was one more devious move, like the bisque he'd "discovered" in front of Séverine the night of the forty-five. These manoeuvres hadn't been figments of my imagination. Years later, one of the last times I saw Renaud alive, as it happened, one night after my shift, he'd admitted everything, without a trace of regret. It was abhorrent. As far as Renaud was concerned, that was simply the way of the world.

I silently emptied my locker, throwing everything in my backpack.

I ran into Bob in the prep kitchen. He was making gnocchi, cheerful as ever.

"Dude, when are we working together again? Renaud told me you're gonna be a cook now."

"Actually I don't think we'll be working together again."

Bob looked disappointed. He took off his Red Sox cap and scratched his forehead, getting a little flour in his hair.

"What's up? I don't get it."

"I'm leaving."

He gave me a surprised look.

"That sucks."

"I'm going to study in Trois-Rivières."

"Trois-Rivières?" he said, almost perking up. "Well, good luck with that. If you need work I've got a friend who has a café there. I'll talk to him if you want. Give me a call once you get there."

He scribbled his cell number in marker on parchment paper. He had the handwriting of a child. I thanked him and we did a low-five.

I went upstairs and walked along the kitchen, without anyone noticing. Twenty minutes after punching in, I punched out. I took a lingering look into the dining room. Sarah was entering an order on the computer, Nick and Denver were talking about someone

I didn't know. I was invisible. The restaurant was as resplendent as ever, but it all looked somehow different now. The bottles all lit up behind the bar. The well-stocked wine cellar. The chandeliers that had so impressed me the first time I came in the room. It was all somehow lacklustre now. I looked over to the kitchen, where Bonnie and Jonathan were busy arguing like two kids at daycare. It made me smile. Vlad was doing his mise with military precision. Jade was taking liquor inventory, leaning over bar fridges. The wheels kept right on turning as if nothing had happened. I didn't even feel like saying bye to anyone. I slipped off to the dish-pit. I pushed open the back door one final time and headed into the alley. My heart was light. It wasn't overly cold.

Basile was smoking by the door.

"You smoke now?"

He gave me a shy nod. I shook his hand and told him I was leaving.

"Oh, that's too bad," he said. "Are we ever going to see each other again?"

I said I didn't know. He looked disappointed, but smiled. He must have been happy for me, imagining that I was moving on to greener pastures. As it happened we would see each other again. Years later, when he owned a restaurant. The sky was full of pink and grey clouds in the distance above the buildings. I put on my headphones and walked out into the alley. I didn't look back.

CHAPTER 41

MALIK made me stay with him from late January through mid-June. He put me up in the little room that had been his office, and helped find me a job at a warehouse. It felt strange to wake up early in the morning and live a daytime schedule again.

From the very first week at Malik's I started drawing again. He lent me his university library card so I could take out books. At first he deposited my paycheques into his own account, so he could manage my money for me. Then, around March, without a word, he started letting me do it myself. The snow was melting, the days were getting longer, and my bank balance was growing. Malik wouldn't accept any rent from me, but I'd often come home from work with groceries for both of us. I understood I was getting a second chance, and that not many people had someone in their lives capable of bailing them out and looking after them like this.

We went out for beers once in a while, and one night Malik even took me to a bar with a row of machines against the back wall. Again, we didn't need to talk about it. He was happy to have me staying with him, and he took an interest in the progress of my drawing. When he had some free time we'd order pizza and watch movies, in boxers and wool socks. It was as if developing some structure for my life, and spending more time alone, had chased away the need to gamble. I wasn't cured. But I could tell things were going to work out. That was something. I was starting to do what it took for things to work out, one day at a time. Today I know that if it hadn't been for Malik's help I never could have done it.

I moved back to Montreal in late June, just as the heat grew stifling. It felt like I'd been gone for years.

It was June 27. I came out of the Papineau Metro station and walked down Dorion all the way to René-Lévesque. The streets were bathed in the thrumming golden light of long, slow summer nights. I still felt fragile, but was happy to be back in this city, where I had to start everything from scratch again. School, work, friends. It seemed strange to be walking these same streets again, so close to the bars I'd spent hours gambling at not long ago.

In the distance the Molson brewery towered, iridescent in the sunlight. I crossed the viaduct and went up the steps of Cité 2000. The yeasty smell of beer was pungent as ever. In the lobby, two warehousemen pushed boxes on dollies. The door of the service elevator looked like the open maw of a mechanical monster. Behind the front desk sat a chubby security guard with white hair and red cheeks. I leaned over the counter to talk to him. He was doing a Sudoku puzzle.

"I want to see the guys from Deathgaze."

"Room number?" he said, without looking up.

"322."

He looked it up in his register. Then he called them.

"They'll be down, shouldn't be long."

I was pacing around the lobby when Mike came out of the stairwell. The neon light gleamed off his bald head. He was wearing unlaced work boots and a beat-up Cannibal Corpse t-shirt. When he recognized me, a look of scornful contempt crept over his face.

"The fuck you doing here?"

I lifted up my hands to tell him I came in peace.

"Is Alex here?"

"Alex isn't in the band anymore."

He was about to turn around and leave.

"Wait," I said.

I held out an envelope.

"What's that?"

"Your money."

He snatched the envelope from my hand, had a look inside, and lifted his head back up.

"All right, you got no more business here. Get lost."

Benjamin hadn't heard from Marie-Lou in months. I wanted to leave her an envelope anyway, with all the money I owed her. Benjamin wouldn't take it.

"I don't even know if she'll ever work here again. I think you've got a better chance of seeing her again than I do. She's your friend, right?"

CHAPTER 42

A LITTLE before Canada Day I finally decided to pay a visit
to La Trattoria. I got off at Mont-Royal Metro station. The
last time I'd walked down Mont-Royal the sidewalks had
been covered in snow, the lampposts hung with Christmas decorations. Today it was thronged with shoppers in shorts, sandals, and
sunglasses.

I went in through the front door, and was greeted by the
immediately familiar hum of the dining room and the underlying rumble of the service kitchen. They were finishing the lunch
rush. I instantly recognized the smells of familiar dishes floating
through the entrance. There were only two servers on the floor,
setting tables. I didn't know either of them. One of them strode
decisively toward me, as if she were waiting for me.

"You the new dishwasher?" she asked. "Next time come in
through..."

"Uh, no. I just came in to say hi to someone."

That's when I saw Bob behind the dessert pass-through. Right
as I tried to wave at him he disappeared into the back.

"Who did you want to see?"

"No, it's okay. I'll come back another time."

I turned around and went out on the sidewalk. It was true. I
should have known better than to go through the front door. Better to try my luck at the back door. My chances of catching Bob
were better there. For some unfathomable reason I felt nervous.

It was weird walking through the alley in the bright summer sun-light. Someone was smoking outside, next to the wide-open door. It couldn't be Bob, the person was too small. When I recognized Bonnie I felt a pang in my chest. She had shaved her head. Her face was deeply tanned, and her hands even darker. When she saw me she hesitated a minute, as if she wasn't sure she recognized me. Then suddenly she leaped up and gave me a big smile.

"Hey, man. What are you doing here?"

She flicked her butt and gave me a hug. It was the first time we'd ever done that.

"Man, it's been like forever."

She seemed genuinely happy to see me.

"I came to see if you were still here. I just got back in town. I was away for a few months."

"Bob told me you were in Trois-Rivières."

I was about to tell her the story about changing schools, but I stopped myself. I didn't want to lie to her.

"I needed a break," I said. "What are you doing here so early?"

"Oh, I don't work nights anymore. Keeps me away from the booze. Haven't had a beer in two months, man."

She filled me in on everything that had happened since I left. Séverine had ended up firing Renaud. Vlad was the chef now. I asked if she had heard from Bébert. She looked sad.

"No, not really."

Her shaved head really brought out the ochre and turquoise highlights in her beautiful big green eyes. Her scars traced dis-coloured lines on her weather-beaten skin.

"Actually, I was here to see Bob. I didn't think you'd be here during the day. I wanted to give him this, to give to you."

I pulled a mixtape from my jeans pocket. She burst out laugh-ing, then put her hand over her mouth. She was serious again, and a shy look stole over her face.

"For me?" she said, grabbing the tape from my hands. "Good ol' mixtape, man."

She checked the case. I'd listed all the tracks. She read out a few song titles.

"Whoah, lots of stuff," she said. "But I know all these tracks and most of them suck."

She passed me back the tape, with an expressionless look. I stood dumbstruck and open-mouthed. She broke out laughing.

"Man, you should see your face!"

She was really cracking up now, almost bent over double.

"I'm kidding," she said. "That's sweet of you. I'm gonna listen to this right after work. Merci, Stéphane."

She gave me a kiss on each cheek.

"Hey I don't go to Café Chaos anymore but maybe we can grab a coffee sometime?"

Just when I was about to answer Bob showed up at the door.

"Dude!" he said happily. "What are you doing here?"

He was waving his arms around, with his cap in one hand and his tongs in the other.

I told him I'd just got back to Montreal.

"Yo, want to come out for a beer with us this weekend? It's Jonathan's last shift. He's going to live with his girlfriend in Rimouski."

"Uh, I don't know. Maybe," I answered.

"Anyway, let me know."

From the service kitchen I could hear the order printer. Tickets rolling out. Customers still coming in after the lunch rush. Bob made a "call me" gesture and went back to the kitchen, putting his cap back on as he went. As if she were echoing him, Bonnie put her cook's hat back on as well.

"Don't be a stranger, man."

She followed Bob back into the kitchen.

I stayed out in the alley for a minute, listening to the sounds of the kitchen.

One night in the middle of July I was having a beer with Vincent and Janine on the balcony of their new apartment on the corner of

Châteaubriand and Chabanel when I got a voice message. Janine gave me a teasing look. She had heard a series of long beeps. I hadn't put my pager on vibration mode, in case a potential employer called. I'd spent the day dropping off resumes all over town.

"Must be your girlfriend in Trois-Rivières? I bet she misses you!"

"That'd surprise me," I answered.

Vincent came back on the balcony with a bowl of Doritos and three cold Coronas. He had no shirt on. Janine wore a white floral cotton dress. A hot dry wind was blowing through the leaves of the trees. It felt like we were at sea.

"Do you need the phone?" Janine asked.

Every time I got a page I hoped it would be Marie-Lou. At nine at night, it definitely wasn't an employer.

"Yeah," I said as I got up. "Where is it?"

"In the living room, next to the TV."

I went in. I dialled the number on my voice mail. It took a few seconds to recognize the voice. When I did I burst out laughing. I was so happy I listened again, and again, five or six times in total.

"Hey motherfucker. Hope you're doing well. Been a while. I went to La Trattoria the other day and they told me you quit last winter? Anyway, give me a call if you're looking for a job, we need a prep cook. Get a pen: 514-749-9445. That's my new cell number. Anyway, call me back even if you don't want the job. We'll go for a beer. Later."

EPILOGUE

TIMBERLAND pushes open the door, then walks out as well. You can hear him say, "Same address as last time?" to his buddy who's lighting a smoke. Then they're outside my field of vision. I push aside my book and my beer and lean over the table, toward Bébert. I say quietly:

"Who are those dudes?"

Bébert recovers his crooked-toothed smile and answers:

"Man, it's so cool running into you."

"What's going on?"

"Forget about it. Listen, it's nothing, just a couple of goofs playing tough guys. Cheers man!"

He leans in toward his big bottle. I bring my glass forward. I'm trying to size up his expression, but his poker face is impenetrable. We clink glasses and drink. He wipes his mouth and grabs my book. He flips it over.

"You and your books."

The bartender starts watching his game again. I feel like I'm staring at an illustration, a photo, everyone is jumping back into their places.

"I'll lend it to you. Take it."

"It's good?"

"You're gonna love it. Take it!"

"What's the story?"

"It's about an English guy, in the twenties. He ends up washing dishes in a hotel in Paris. And after than he goes to live with the tramps in London."

"Fuck, sounds pretty boring man."

"It's the same guy who wrote *Nineteen Eighty-Four*."

"Yeah, I think I read that one. It was good."

"Shut up."

"I'd like to, but I don't really have time to read, know what I'm saying? I'm always working, always tired."

"You know the expression 'Big Brother is watching you'? That's from *Nineteen Eighty-Four*."

"Cool."

"I'm telling you man, you'll love it. You can give it back in a few weeks."

"Yeah, I'd rather not. I don't know when I'll be able to give it back to you."

"You live right across the street."

"No, I don't want to take your book. I mean, what would you do without a book to read?"

He drops the book on the table.

"What ever happened with your drawing? Your comics?"

I pour myself another beer.

"I quit."

Bébert makes a long face.

"I'm working on something else."

"What is it?"

"I'm writing books."

"Seriously?"

"I've got something getting published. It's coming out in the fall."

"Good job, buddy. So the publisher, that's like a record label. Or more like the producer?"

"Bit of both."

"So does writing books pay?"

"Depends on the sales. So you better buy a copy!"

Bébert's face lights up. He raises his bottle.

"Fuck yeah I'll buy a copy. Why didn't you tell me before?"

I smile in my beer.

"I always knew things were gonna work out for you. A good guy like you always gets what he deserves in the end."

I feel a pang in my chest, and remember the promise I made Bébert, back in the day. I guess I kept it, in a way. Maybe because I'd made the same promise to myself.

We keep on catching up like this for a while. Outside, Rue Ontario is covered in snow. It looks peaceful in the soft halo of lamplight. How many times had I walked down this street, farther west, with a wad of bills burning a hole in my pocket and my stomach in knots whenever I passed a bar with video poker machines?

We hear the familiar police sirens somewhere out in Hochelaga. I think back to Greg, and La Trattoria. Bonnie, Séverine, Bob. I think of Marie-Lou and Vincent. I lost touch with all of them long time ago. I think of Malik, the one who stood by me all these years, through the many disappointments, and was always the same guy, and who never gave up on me.

"So tell me about your book."

"I'll tell you the story some other time. It's sci-fi."

"Fuck sci-fi, man. Not like it's any of my business, but you should write a book about me instead."

"Yeah, I bet you'd read that one!"

"Hellz yeah, I'd read that. I'd want to know how it's all going to end, all my stories."

Bébert's face falls. I turn toward the bar's front door. A fat dude approaches the counter. He half sits, one ass-cheek on his stool. Brush cut, big brown circles under his eyes, broken nose, oily skin ravaged by rosacea. He's got a cell phone in a hand full of rings, a flashy touch that clashes with his mouse-grey sweat pants. He gives Bébert a tired look. My hands are moist again. Now it's Timberland and Puma's turn to come in. Puma stomps his sneakers on the floor to shake off the snow. This time there's no break in the pool game, the guys keep on talking, exchanging wisecracks, egging each other on. But I don't hear any of it. I don't even hear the music. Bébert takes a long swig and slaps his empty bottle back down on the table.

"It was great seeing you again, buddy. Really great!"

He gets up slowly. The chair legs scrape on the floor.

"Now I really have to get going," he says.

I get up as well. The big dude at the bar, Timberland, and Puma all act like we don't exist. Bébert gives me a bear hug and enthusiastically slaps my shoulder blades.

"Take care, buddy!"

It all happens so fast I don't know how to answer. He picks up his coat and steals a glance at my beer.

"Take your time, finish your beer" he says.

His tone is dispassionate, his gaze insistent. Then he goes to the bar. I hadn't noticed but Puma has taken up a position in front of the bar's back door. The fat guy is by the machines, between the bar and the front door. The bartender watches all four people as he rearranges his clean glasses.

"Where we off to, ladies?" asks Bébert as he puts on his coat.

Timberland pushes him to the back of the room.

"Shut your trap and move."

Bébert slows down even more, like a man who has all the time in the world. He's purposely stalling, checking the slot in the payphone by the pool tables for change. The pool players gathered silently around the table don't move an inch.

"C'mon, get fucking going," says Timberland, giving Bébert another shove.

Bébert breaks out into a cocky laugh. Puma walks out, followed by fat guy. Bébert and Timberland raise their voices, cursing each other out. Bébert is in front, getting pushed out the door. The snippets of their voices are soon drowned out by the door banging shut.

For a few seconds nothing happens. Then one of the players leans over the pool table and takes aim, and a "clack" echoes through the bar, right into my eardrums. The game goes on. The bartender is looking at me now. I'm still standing next to the table with my glass of beer. It's not going down right, but I force myself to take another sip. I pick up my Orwell and slide it in the back pocket of my jeans. The bartender's attention is back on the hockey game. I take another sip, thinking, still kind of upset by what has just happened. Seeing that I haven't moved, the bartender looks at me again, completely expressionless. I look toward the back door, then back at him. He nods his head slightly toward the front door. It's clear as day.

A few long minutes go by, while I shift my weight from foot to foot. The bartender seems to have already forgotten all about me. I take a final sip of beer and put the glass down on the table. I look around the shitty bar. The video poker machines are lined up on the back wall like boxy multicoloured robots from a bygone era.

I zip up my leather jacket. For a second I picture Bébert's cocky grin the way it first appeared to me all those years ago.

I smile and walk out the front door, squinting against the crystalline snowflakes.

TRANSLATOR'S ACKNOWLEDGEMENTS

The translator would like to thank veteran chef Geordy Mullin, who generously read the manuscript and provided valuable feedback. Thanks also to Éric de Larochellière of Le Quartanier, and to author Stéphane Larue and Biblioasis editors Stephen Henighan and Dan Wells for their contributions to this translation.

ABOUT THE AUTHOR

Stéphane Larue was born in Longueuil, Quebec, in 1983. He holds a Master's degree in comparative literature from the Université de Montréal. He has worked in the Montreal restaurant business for more than fifteen years.

The Dishwasher, Larue's first novel, in addition to being a finalist for Quebec's Junior College Students' Prize and the Governor General of Canada's Literary Award, won both the Quebec Booksellers' Prize and the international Senghor Prize for the best first novel by a French-language writer. A feature film of this novel, directed by Francis Leclerc, is in production.

ABOUT THE TRANSLATOR

Pablo Strauss has translated seven books of fiction from Quebec and washed dishes in nine restaurants. He grew up in Victoria, British Columbia, and lives in Quebec City.

Mount Laurel Library
100 Walt Whitman Avenue
Mount Laurel, NJ 08054-9539
856-234-7319
www.mountlaurellibrary.org